Superstars

Songs for Survival

By

Errol Barr

HEATHER,
I HOPE
YOU ENJOY
THE FINAL
INSTALLMENT!

First Edition May 2014

ISBN-13: 978-1499724394
ISBN-10: 149972439X

Dedication

To Kayla, my daughter, an incredible mother to her four children.
The final installment of Superstars is dedicated to her. Her strength
and wisdom inspires me.

Acknowledgements

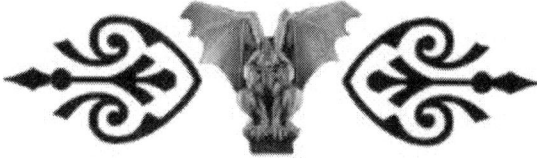

To have finally completed the Superstars Trilogy is a blessing but also sadness. I greatly enjoyed writing this story and I will miss the characters I created.

I would like to thank editors Barb Green and Yvonne Trainer whose hard work and honesty in making my work better was invaluable.

The support of my friends and my family was amazing and I hope I have made them proud of my work.

My wife Kellie came into my life when I started Superstars and it was forever changed. To be blessed to this degree is my miracle.

Chapter 1

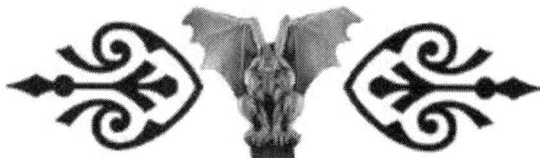

Chloë, her body drained of all her energy, struggled to lift herself off of the floor and towards the light that filled the room. The light was her salvation and she knew it was the doorway to His kingdom. She was so tired, her legs weak from her struggle to get away from the beast. She almost forgot about the others. Where was Michael? Brittany? She looked around her, the brilliant light reaching every corner of the room. She was alone. She prayed they were still alive, the memory of their plight entering her mind's landscape.

She looked back into the light; unable it seemed, to walk any further towards it. Her legs refused to move, mired in an unseen quicksand. She began to cry as she basked in the warmth and love that came from the light. The pull towards the light was powerful, but yet she could not move. Dear Lord, she prayed, have mercy on me and free my legs so I can be with you. She sobbed as her legs toiled to move. Then a voice called out to her from the light. It was a deep and mighty voice. It was the voice of God.

"Chloë, my child, hear Me when I tell you. It is not time, there are many things yet to be done. Your salvation is near. Your blood will be cleansed of the wicked one that also occupies your veins. Be strong and be brave. For I am with you."

The last ounce of strength that kept her standing upright left her body and she collapsed to the floor. She watched helplessly as the light began to recede back into the doors. Through her tears, she cried out, "Lord, do not leave me now.

What about the others? I am afraid!"

The light, once so brilliant and warm, now, almost withdrawn and gone, gave credence once more to the Holy voice, "Do not be afraid. Go to the others and tell them their salvation is also near. Be on guard, Chloë, for the wicked one, will continue to deceive and trick you. I will reveal to you, those that will help you. Be watchful and be ready."

Like someone flicking a switch on cue, the massive lobby of the Malibu beachfront mansion was abruptly cloaked in complete darkness.

****

Chloë, her mind gripped by terrible images, awoke to someone shaking her, shouting out her name. Her eyes cleared and she could see the panic-stricken face of Brittany, covered in tears, screaming.

"Chloë, you must come. Help me. He's killing him!"

She realized she was still lying on the lobby floor, the horrible images of what had happened earlier, flooded her mind. Brittany and Michael suspended in the air, their backs frighteningly bent backwards. Michael! Oh my God. What has happened!

She reached up and grabbed Brittany by the shoulders, "Where is Michael? Where are the others?"

Brittany pulled her off of the floor and onto her feet. Her legs were no longer weak, but strong and determined. She looked at Brittany and said, "Where are they?"

Brittany, also seeming to regain control of herself, replied, "He has them in the library. His rage is unimaginable. I snuck out to find you. Chloë, what was that light? It was so bright. So extraordinary."

She reached out and touched her elbow, then said, "Come on, let's get to the library. I'll tell you all about the light, later, Brit."

****

Chloë knew she was walking straight into a dangerous situation, but she felt strangely unafraid. Her experience back in the lobby had given her strength and purpose. As they got closer to the library entrance, the sound of the creature raging was deafening. She heard Brittany let out a gasp. She reached back and took her by the hand and reassured her, "It's going to be okay, Brit. I promise. He's not going to hurt us. We have to be brave and just do what he wants us to do until we can figure this out."

Holding Brittany's hand, the two of them entered the library. What Chloë saw next sucked every ounce of strength and purpose right out of her. The mutilated corpse of Elizabeth was spread out on top of the large wooden desk in front of the beast, who had transformed himself almost back into human form. Patrick, his face twisted in a maniacal grin stood to the side of him, like a pitbull, ready to pounce. Michael was stirring on the floor, beaten badly, trying to lift himself up. Connor and Juan stood at the back of the room in silent obedience, showing no emotion nor returning the stare Chloë gave them.

Wearing a long, black robe, the hood pulled low over his head was the unmistakable face of Robert Best. His face, hidden in the shadows of the hood, reflected death. When he lifted his head towards her, he broke into laughter, his black and rotten teeth sending chills down her spine. Brittany gripped her hand tighter, whispering out loud to herself, "Oh my God."

****

The blackness was all around her. Smothering her. She could see nothing nor could she hear. Yet she heard *something?* Far away in the distance of her mind she heard noises, like echoes bouncing off of her inner ear. It almost sounded like voices, many of them, but she wasn't sure. She lifted her hand towards her face to see if she could see it closer to her eyes. She could see nothing. Where was she? She tried touching her face, but felt empty space. A bolt of panic shot through her. She tried touching her stomach, felt nothing then touched her legs and again, emptiness.

Chloë, terrified, called out, "Is someone there? Where am I? Please help me!"

There was no response, just the constant and far away echo of voices, too faint to discern, but loud enough to know she was not alone. She wrapped her arms around herself or it felt like she was wrapping her arms around herself, but there was no physical contact whatsoever. It was like she was floating in an abyss, her body somehow unable to send signals back to her brain when she made physical contact. She was never claustrophobic, but this was different than being locked in a small and confined space. Then she heard something she recognized, very far away in the distance of her mind, but unmistakable. It was Brittany!

"Brittany, is that you? I hear you! Where are you?"

There was no reply. Only the faint, far away sound of many voices, their snippets of words making their way back to Chloë's mind. They sounded like voices full of desperation and despair. She strained to hear Brittany's voice again.

"Brittany, call out to me, please. I will come to you. Tell me where you are." Maybe she had imagined hearing Brittany's voice? She called out again, louder this time, "Brittany, I know you're out there! I heard you! Talk to me!"

Then the voice pierced through the blackness, much louder this time and it was definitely Brittany, "Chloë, help me! Help me!

Chloë cried out, "I hear you Brittany! It's going to be okay! The light will come for us! Pray Brittany, pray! I am here Brit. I am close to you, don't worry."

Then another voice called out through the inky black abyss, it was Michael. His voice seemed to be very far away, faint, but it was him, "Chloë, is that you!"

Hope began to enter the confined space where she found herself. She called out to Michael, "Michael, I hear you. Do you know where you are? Can you come towards my voice? Brittany is here with me!"

She desperately tried to shut out the echo of voices bouncing around inside of her head to focus on Michael's. She heard nothing. She cried out again, "Michael! Michael, tell me where you are, I will come for you!" She knew that was impossible as soon as she said it. She wasn't going anywhere. She could not feel herself physically, she could see nothing, the darkness was so complete, it was like she had been transported into another plane of existence. A very terrifying place. She began to sob, it just seemed a minute ago, she had been talking directly with the Lord, in a light of salvation and now this nightmare. That's it, she thought. She was having a nightmare! She tried to will her mind to wake up when she heard a sound far off into the distance. It wasn't a voice, but just a low rumble, that seemed to get slowly louder. It sounded like thunder in the distance. It was coming towards her! The low rumble had turned into a full roar as it approached her from within the blackness. She prayed, "Oh please God, help me! Hear my prayer Lord!"

The roar was now directly upon her. The deafening sound turned from a loud roar to a guttural, evil sounding laughter. The beast! He was here. Now she knew and the realization made her mind numb with fear. This was his world she was trapped in! She and the others were in Hell!

****

He heard their cries and he heard their prayers. The process of realization when one knows his soul has been cursed to eternal damnation was the most incredible and satisfying experience in his existence. The realization of each of his offspring coming face to face with his or her destiny was especially delicious. Chloë, Brittany and Michael had now met their futures head on and the terror that filled their souls was incredibly delightful.

Patrick sought him out when he was not much older than a toddler. He had embraced his destiny, letting his hatred of mankind and God fuel him. He had become a true soldier against God and would play a big role in the weeks and months ahead as the plan to destroy mankind came to a conclusion. Connor and Juan fell into place soon after meeting his earthly persona, Robert Best. There were no barriers to knock down with either of their parents. Juan's mother, Marie, was a coward, choosing to take her own life. She never even put a fight up to save the soul of Juan. Connor's foster parents, the sister and brother-in-law of his pathetic birth mother, Lori Weston, did not have a shred of faith in their blood. Had Lori survived the birth, capturing the soul of Connor, even though inevitable, would have been much more difficult.

The damnation of the souls of Michael, Brittany and of course Chloë, was a spiritual battle with his adversary that turned out to be more difficult than anticipated. God had chosen to fiercely protect Chloë and the other two, almost saving their souls in the mansion. He had not come that close to an all-out spiritual battle with God since the battlefields of Armenia so many centuries before when all this started. The bitch, Ann Lockwood, surrounded by God's angels twenty four hours a day, could not prevent Michael's soul from eventually making its way to its rightful place. The descendant blood of King Tiridates' son, Davit, flowed through her, filling her with courage not found in humans. He would enjoy the day when he would finally cast her soul to eternal damnation.

It was the priest O'Sullivan who posed the biggest obstacle to his plan. God had chosen him and had wrapped His cloak of protection around him so that he could not penetrate it. He tried to destroy him at the Vatican, but he was too strong, God's armor surprised him. He did not understand why and he needed to figure it out soon. Why had God chosen him? He was old and weak, but yet he was young and strong. He dispatched men of the cloth to Hell all the time, but he had no power over this mortal man. On top of it, he had disappeared completely. Where had he gone that he could not see him? It was impossible, but he had become invisible to him.

The death of Elizabeth, though it was an unfortunate misstep in his plan, was necessary. He needed it to start the process of darkening the souls of the three of them so they would finally realize their true identities. It would cause a ripple in the fan base of Vasallus when it was revealed. However, it would soon be forgotten; especially when the new album came out and then, after that, he would reveal the unbelievable live concert theatrics he had planned for the next leg of the worldwide tour.

****

Encased in in a tomb of blackness, the crushing roar of the beast all around her, Chloë cried out, "Dear God, save me!"

The roar of the beast stopped, turning again into a sickening laughter and then spoke, "Do you really think He can hear you? Do you know where you are? You don't do you? Well, let me have the pleasure of telling you where you are." The voice chuckled.

It continued, "You are not in Heaven, I can assure you. You are not in purgatory, a place somewhere between Hell and Heaven that the movies take great joy in portraying. You are not trapped in a nightmare, Chloë. You are in your true Master's realm. It is your destiny, the reason you were born. You are my child. I am your father, Chloë. You are home. You are in Hell!"

Chloë struggled with the words just spoken by the demon voice. She could feel her soul begin to darken like the blackness that engulfed her. She was surprised her fear did not deepen, but instead it seemed to be lifting. Clarity of mind penetrated her consciousness or unconsciousness, she couldn't tell the difference anymore. She asked the voice, "Who are you? Who am I?"

She could not physically feel movement around her, but she felt something. Perhaps it was a shift in the existence she was in. Then the earthly voice she had come to know as Robert Best spoke, "I am your God, Chloë. I am the true master of this universe, always have been. I am also your father. Your mother, Chloë, was my host, used only to physically give birth to your physical earthly body and your spiritual soul. It sounds confusing, but on earth, life is given by God, but taken by me. I cannot create life, Chloë. Life is the soul. Sure, I created your physical body along with your mother, but only God can give someone its soul. Your soul belongs to me, Chloë, because I created you."

"I don't understand. You said you created me, but it was

God who gave me life. He gave me my soul. Don't I belong to Him then?"

"You are mistaking what you have read and what you have been taught with reality. Your mind and therefore your soul has been programmed to accept what has been written by man. The Holy Bible is nothing but a book, Chloë. Written by simple men, in a time when the world was devoid of any aides to discover the real truth. Men were weak, extremely naïve and gullible, vulnerable to stories of ridiculous miracles and outlandish claims. These stories got passed from generation to generation and the Bible became the word of God according to man. The truth of life they claimed."

"That book also talked about you. It said that you are a liar and a deceiver. How do I not know you are lying and deceiving me now?"

The voice continued, drawing her closer, "Because I have been with man since man first existed. Man was not created as you were led to believe, Chloë. Man *evolved*! Men are discovering their true beginnings not from the Holy Bible, but from science. God will protect that secret until the end of times. I did not destroy the human race depicted in the time of Noah, God did. It is not me who is pushing mankind towards a biblical apocalypse. It is God who is bent on destroying mankind once and for all. It is God who is a wolf dressed in sheep's clothing, Chloë. Do you understand that now?"

"Yes, I do. Being here in this realm, my mind is clear and free. I can feel that now. Why do they call it Hell? It's not such a terrible place as we've been led to believe."

"Now you're starting to understand the deception and lies which come from God. The truth is here Chloë. Always has been and always will be. You will always be safe here. You are the daughter of the greatest force in the universe."

"What is your real name?"

"I have no real name Chloë. Only man uses names. Here, names do not matter. We do not single individuals out here. We are one. We are many. We are all the same. Man's books have called me many names, but the reality is that I have no name. You can call me whatever you like Chloë."

"Can I call you Father?"

"Yes you may. In fact I would like it if you called me that. Father is a good name."

"Are Brittany and Michael here too? I heard them earlier. They sounded very scared. Did you talk to them as well and reassure them Father?"

"I have and they are as happy as you are now. Finding out the beautiful truth of your life is an incredible thing, Chloë, don't you think?"

"I agree Father. What happens now? Can I stay here now? I would like that. I have enough to think about to last forever. The clarity of mind here is what I want and what I need Father."

"You will be returning to your earthly form, Chloë. There is much to do. We have to save the world from God's final fury. We are the saviors to the millions of people who do not know what you know. Do you understand?"

"Is that the purpose of Vasallus? Is that why you created me Father? Are we to save people for you? To save them from God's impending doom?"

"That is exactly what you are meant to do, Chloë. You are to save millions of people from God. It is a beautiful thing, Chloë. Are you ready?"

"Yes I am Father."

Chapter 2

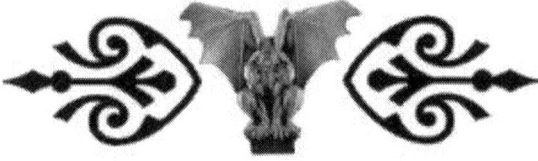

Avery Johnson, record producer and manager of the super group Vasallus, waited patiently in line to board his United flight to LAX. He had spent two days in New York and Chicago, along with his Alive Records President, Jenn Steinert. He had been putting off the business trip for weeks, embroiled in the mammoth North American concert tour Vasallus had recently completed. Jenn, to whom he had given full control over Alive Records, still needed him to put his signature on recording contracts as CEO and owner of the studio. On most occasions, she would courier paperwork to be signed to wherever he happened to be, but there were some clients who were too big or important to the studio not to have a face to face. The two of them had completed a whirlwind of successful meetings with artists, agents and lawyers in both cities and they were exhausted. He was anxious to return to Los Angeles as he missed Bentley even though he had only been gone for a few days. She would not be getting back to the mansion till late this evening from her trip to Seattle. She took a break from Vasallus with him being gone and went and spent a few days with a dear friend she had not seen in some time. It was a much needed break for everyone associated with the group. The kids were feeling some exhaustion after a gruesome schedule that included concerts almost every second day, daily interviews and a tension that hung around them that had not been there before. They were beginning to wear down and he was shocked that had taken so long. He would ensure that they never saw a stage again for at least six months.

He knew Robert Best would challenge him on that, wanting them out on the road as soon as possible, but these kids would get seriously sick, the fatigue and lack of proper rest would take them down and he would not allow it. How could he possibly stop Best? he thought. The man was demonic, an evil entity that was using him and these kids for some diabolical plan to destroy mankind. What that could possibly be, he could only imagine. He no longer feared Best as he first did when Father O'Sullivan broke the truth to him and Bentley about his true identity. He may or may not be what O'Sullivan claimed he was, but Avery knew he was a very dangerous man. He would not allow Bentley to stay at the mansion alone without him there, it was too dangerous, and so she agreed to go visit her friend in Seattle. She was worried about leaving the kids alone, but they both agreed that Best would not harm any of them. At least not until he no longer needed them for his plans. Avery was more worried about leaving them alone with Patrick, his rage was capable of almost anything. His thoughts were suddenly pulled away by the sound of Jenn's voice, as she approached with two cups of Starbucks in her hands.

"Here you go, Americano, three shots on top. I was watching you from the other side of the terminal, walking back here with the coffees and you never flinched or moved. Deep in thought? Worried about the contracts you just signed?"

He took the coffee from her outstretched hand, gave her a reassuring smile and replied: "No, it's not that at all. The contracts we signed are fine. No, they are more than fine. They are great contracts for the company. They were reasonable and it locks our clients in long term. You did a great job Jenn. Just like you always do."

"Then it must be Bentley. You miss her don't you?"

"I do miss her, no doubt about that, but it's Vasallus I was thinking about. I don't like leaving them alone."

"I don't think you need to worry about them Avery. They're seventeen years old, way more mature than their age and besides, how many assistants are coming and going from that place all day long?"

He lookedat Jenn, a wry grin emerging and said: "You know Jenn, sometimes I think you were the sister I never had. You have always had the touch for saying the right thing, at the right time with me all these years. I, and my company, are both very lucky to have you. Thank you for being such a good and honest friend to me."

"You're wecome, and you're right. I do have your back, don't I? Just like a big sister would, huh?"

"Yeah, I gues. Don't forget sweetheart, I'm still your boss. Remember who signs your paycheques."

She reached up nd pinched his cheek in a playful manner, then continued: "You remember who runs your company in a way that makes gobs of money, so you can write those paycheques to me, and to yourself."

****

Three and half hours later, they made their way out of the LAX terminal. Avery gave Jenn a hug goodbye as she climbed into a taxi for home, letting her know he would touch base with her at the office in the morning. He looked to take the next taxi right behind her, but had a change of heart and turned and walked back into the terminal. Bentley's flight was due to arrive in another three hours from Seattle. He would surprise her at the baggage carousel and convince her to come to the mansion for the night rather than her apartment. They spent most nights together nowadays, but coming in late, she would likely call him from her taxi to let him know that its late and she would head to her apartment for the night. He missed her and he wanted to be with her tonight.

****

Bentley, tired and in a zombie-type mood from her late flight home, was on autopilot as she stood on the down escalator on the way toward the baggage area. She barely even noticed Avery at the bottom of the escalator until he stepped away from a group of gatherers, his smile waking her brain and warming her heart instantly. He had a cheesy airport gift shop rose in his teeth, the cellophane still wrapped around it as he reached out and snatched her off of the last step of the escalator. His strong arms lifted her off of her feet with ease and it felt like heaven. She had missed him terribly. Their mouths met, they kissed deeply and she knew from his kiss that he missed her just as much.

They held each other and chatted about their week as they waited for her luggage. As soon as they had her bag they made a beeline for the taxi stand. He wanted her to come and spend the night at the mansion and there was no way she could say no. She still had some fresh clothes she could wear tomorrow so she easily agreed.

****

Bentley adjusted herself in the rear seat of the taxi, watching him as he gazed out his side window. She held his free hand, giving it a warm kiss before she spoke: "I missed you so much. Being away from you is getting more difficult with every trip. Being on tour with the group was hard, but at least it kept us together."

He glanced over at her for a second, then leaned in to kiss her on the lips and then he replied: "That is so funny Bentley, I was about to tell you the exact same thing. Being apart is not fun, but I believe it will be awhile before Vasallus is touring again. It could be as long as a year, but no sooner than six months. The kids need a break, they really do."

"Iknow you're right. They have been through a lot and have held up magnificently. I have missed them too. Wonder what they have been up to this week?"

"Knowing them, they have been in the studio the entire time. They will want to know when the next tour begins, if you can believe it. It will be good to see them. I'm starting to feel like a Dad when it comes to them. Is that a good thing, or not?"

"Oh it's a good thing, sweetheart. We have all become very close. I'm starving, why don't we order a boatload of pizza when we get home and get them to join us?"

"That sounds good to me."

****

It was 11:00 p.m. when they walked into the main entrance to the mansion and soon exchanged glances which conveyed their mutual surprise at how quiet it seemed. Even the light that was always on in the main lobby was off. It was like no one was home. Avery turned on the lights, lighting up the huge lobby and the three main hallways leading off to the kitchen, the studio and the entertainment/library rooms.

Avery took a few steps towards the hallway leading to the entertainment room and called out: "Hey are you guys down there!" No one called back or made a move to come out to the lobby.

Bentley wrapped her hands around Avery's arm and replied: "It's after 11:00 p.m. honey, and they're likely all in bed. Come on let's do the same and we can check in on them and see if we can catch one awake."

"If they are in bed then that would be a first. Come on let's go check to see if they are in the studio."

Standing in the dark and quiet studio, Avery touched Bentley's arm and said: "You're right, they're in bed. They must have had a busy week to be crashing this early."

They walked back to the lobby to head up the stairs to their bedroom but then the sound of Chloë's voice coming from the top of the stairs made the two of them almost scream out. Catching her breath, Bentley called up to Chloë: "You scared us. We were going to order up some pizza and hang out with you guys for a while. We didn't expect an early night from you guys."

"It's been a long week. Glad to see you guys are back. I'm going back to bed, I'll see you in the morning."

Avery looked at Bentley, both of them recognized that something was not quite right. They started to walk up the stairs as Avery replied: "Is everything okay Chloë?"

"Just tired. Goodnight." She then turned and disappeared down the hall, the sound of her bedroom door closing reached them as they made it to the top of the stairs.

Bentley, her face showing concern, spoke: "Now that was a little weird. She has never acted that way before. Normally she would keep us up all night. Something has happened Avery. Something bad. I don't like it; I'm getting a bad feeling."

"I agree, but look, she's in no mood to talk about whatever is bothering her. Let's just call it a night and we will talk to them all in the morning."

"You don't think we should check in on the others?"

"It's late sweetheart. Let's just do this in the morning okay?"

"Alright. You know I was starving when we walked in the door, now food is the last thing I can think about."

****

The two of them awoke the next morning tired, since neither of them had been able to get any sleep. They both showered, dressed in workout clothes and made their way downstairs to make some coffee and check in on who was up. They walked into an empty kitchen. There were no dishes in the sink. They were still in bed and it was already 8:30 a.m. Avery looked at Bentley and said: "Why don't you go upstairs and roust them up while I go down to the studio and check in with Amber. I just want to see what kind of week they had and how much time they spent in the studio."

A few minutes later he was in the studio and entered Amber's office. She was busy filing some paperwork when he walked in.

"Good morning Avery. Glad to see you're back safe and sound."

"Good morning Amber. Listen, I need to ask you something. Last night when I got home I bumped into Chloë. I noticed she was in a really quiet and somber mood. Very unlike her. How has she been this week in the studio? How have the others been?"

"Avery, the kids have not set foot in the studio all week, at least when I've been here."

Alarmed, Avery responded: "What? Are you sure?"

"I'm very sure. Usually when I get in around 8:00 a.m., they are already in the studio, either in full rehearsal or individually rehearsing. I have not seen them all week. I thought maybe Mr. Best had them out of town or something. I don't believe they were in at all during the night either, as the security system logs get faxed to me every morning as part of their service and no one has punched a security code into the system all week, except for me, when I arrive in the morning and when I leave at 5:00 p.m."

"That is very strange. Maybe you're right and Best had them busy off-sight this week. Okay no problem, I'll check with them back in the house. I'll be back later on."

As he made his way back to the kitchen, he was deep in thought. They were not preparing for a tour so there was no pressing need for them to be rehearsing, but they always rehearsed. It's what they did. They just loved to play all the time. He felt a bad feeling wash over him and knew that Best was the reason for it. Entering the kitchen, he was happy to see everyone gathered around the kitchen table, eating and hanging out, including Patrick. He said good morning to all of them and asked Bentley to join him out in the hallway.

Out in the hallway, far enough away not to be heard, he asked her how the kids' moods seemed.

"They seem subdued Avery. Something is bothering them. They just aren't the same happy teenagers we know. Elizabeth is yet to come downstairs. When I asked Brittany and Chloë if she was coming down for breakfast they just sort of shrugged their shoulders. I was about to go up to her room to check on her before you walked in."

"I just spoke to Amber in the office. The kids have not been in the studio all week. Not once since we were gone."

"Really, now that is strange. They spend more time there than anywhere else and for them not to go down there for days tells me that something is definitely bothering them."

"I agree. Why don't you go upstairs and check on Elizabeth

and bring her down and let's talk to them all together and see what is going on with them."

Ten minutes later Bentley entered the kitchen and motioned with her eyes for Avery to join her out in the hallway. She had panic written all over her face when she spoke: "She's not here Avery. I checked everywhere, including everyone's bedrooms. She has left the mansion. We need to talk to them right now."

The two of them walked back into the kitchen and Avery looked at the six of them sitting around, quiet, waiting for him to begin. They acted like they were expecting him. "Okay guys, who wants to tell me where Elizabeth is. She is not here in the mansion and I want to know where she is."

The room went completely quiet and no one said a word. Avery looked at them all and repeated: "Where is she? You guys know where she is so tell us. Where did she go?"

Again no one said anything. You could have heard a pin drop. Avery raised his voice and shouted: "Tell me where the hell Elizabeth is right now."

It was Patrick who broke the trance the kids seemed to be in. His voice dripped in sarcasm as he spoke: "She left okay. She had enough of the band and this house and she left. End of story. She is gone and she is never coming back."

Avery was stunned. He never expected to hear that Elizabeth had just up and quit. Bentley, her rage building when she stared at Patrick, shouted: "You're lying Patrick. Where is she? She would never quit Vasallus. This was her life. She loved this band. She loved you guys. Did she go back to Canada to see her parents maybe? We want the truth about where she is. We are responsible for you all. Now tell us where she is."

Patrick sneered back at her before he replied: "What makes you think you're responsible for us? You're not our parents, so don't act like you are. You're a fucking writer, given the sweetest gig of your life covering us on a daily basis."

Before Patrick could say another word, Avery was on him, yanking him out of his chair and throwing him against the kitchen wall. His face inches from Patrick's, he looked him in the eye and warned: "Don't you ever talk to her like that again Benning. Do you hear me? No one has worked harder in this house to make things as normal as possible for you guys than Bentley."

It was Chloë who spoke next: "It's true. She left us. She no longer wanted to be part of this. She left a few days ago."

Bentley asked her: "Where did she go? Did she tell you where she was going?"

"Yes, she said she was going home. Back to Montreal. She packed two suitcases and left."

Avery stepped away from Patrick and walked into the center of the kitchen. He looked back at Patrick, who continued to lean against the kitchen wall, his face etched in a look of satisfaction. He could see Patrick was glad Elizabeth was gone. The arrogant prick. He looked at the rest of them and said: "Does Mr. Best know about this?"

Michael spoke up for the first time: "Yes he does. He knew about it. Elizabeth talked to him about leaving the group and returning home and he agreed. He doesn't want anyone here that doesn't want to be here, is what he told us."

The shock of Elizabeth's departure had shaken him badly. He looked over at Bentley and could see she was almost in tears.

Brittany, her voice emotionless, spoke next: "We don't need her. In fact the band will be better off without her."

Bentley, looked at Brittany, unable to believe what she had just said, and replied: "How can you say that Brit? She was your friend. You guys were like sisters." She watched as Brittany turned in her chair away from her and stared out the kitchen window in silence.

Avery held his hands out in defiance and declared: "Okay I guess that's it huh? You guys aren't going to tell us what happened here so we'll see what Best has to say. Come on Bentley let's leave them to their breakfast. I hope you guys know that this band is not the same without Elizabeth. I'm not sure where we'll go from here."

Connor, his voice devoid of any feelings replied: "No, you've got it wrong Avery. The ones that remain are here because we want to be. I believe that makes us stronger. Elizabeth had a beautiful voice, but this band is full of beautiful voices. We won't miss a beat. You'll see soon enough."

****

Back in their bedroom, the two of them sat on the bed and talked about what just went down in the kitchen.

Bentley, wiping tears from her eyes with a tissue, spoke first: "I just can't believe she would just walk away Avery. She would have at least spoken to us before she left. To walk out of the mansion and away from Vasallus is something I just cannot accept. They're not telling us everything. Something has happened to her. I feel it in every fiber in my body and I'm scared to death that something terrible has happened."

"I will get a hold of Best this morning and demand a meeting. I believe he is behind Elizabeth's leaving. I just pray that it is exactly what the kids have said. That she left because she wanted to return home. We need to prepare ourselves that something sinister has happened to her."

She let out an audible gasp when she replied: "Why would you say that Avery? You're saying something terrible has happened to her?"

"Did you see Patrick's eyes when I had him pinned against the wall?"

"No. What are you saying?"

"Bentley, his eyes were glowing a deep crimson red. I felt I was staring straight into the pits of hell. He knows the truth about what has happened to Elizabeth and I bet it wasn't what they're saying happened."

Chapter 3

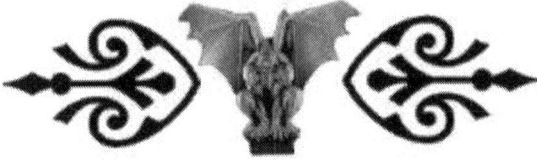

After showering, Avery made his way back down to the office in the studio. He checked with Amber to see if Best had called or if she knew whether he was in L.A. or at the Blackstar office in New York. She replied that she hadn't heard from him but it was very likely he was in town. She caught a glimpse of him on television last night on one of the entertainment channels in which the paparazzi tried to photograph him outside his L.A. Blackstar Studio. He almost tore the camera from the hands of the photographer and jammed it down his throat. Avery asked Amber to reach Best and to arrange a meeting between the two of them. "Have him come to the mansion" he instructed her, "and the sooner the better." He was heading into the studio to work on some things, so he told her to advise him when she had reached Best.

Two minutes later, she opened the door to the sound room and informed him: "I reached him on his cell, Avery. He was pulling up to the mansion when he answered. He is coming in right now."

"Good," thought Avery, "time to confront Best or whoever the hell he is and find out what has really happened to Elizabeth." Ten seconds later, Best walked into the studio and closed the door. He took a seat opposite the massive mixing board where Avery had been tinkering a few seconds previously.

"Good to see you made it back safe and sound, Avery. How was your trip? I'm sure the lovely Ms. Steinert has everything under control."

The rage built quickly in him with just the sight of Best entering his office: "Yes she does, as a matter of fact. Unlike this place, Robert. Everything has gone for shit since I've been gone. Where is Elizabeth? What have you done with her?"

"Whoa, just a minute Avery. First of all, we haven't seen each other in a few weeks, so how about a civil greeting such as, 'How are you Robert, great to see you.'"

"Cut the bullshit, Best. Elizabeth is gone and I want to know where she went and why."

Controlling his demonic rage was not easy and he willed his earthly body to remain calm. He wanted to tear Johnson's fucking throat out. No one spoke to him like that. He reminded himself once again of the bigger picture and quickly took control of the situation.

"I don't appreciate your attitude Avery, but I can understand it, in a way. You've been gone and when you get back you discover Vasallus is missing a member."

Avery was seconds away from jumping Best and lashed out: "I don't give a shit about Vasallus missing a member, I care about a young girl who up and disappeared. I am responsible for her Best and I want to know what happened."

Softening his tone, Best replied: "I understand Avery. I knew you would be upset. That is why I didn't waste any time getting here this morning to inform you of the circumstances surrounding Elizabeth leaving the band and the mansion. First of all, there is nothing you or I could have done to dissuade her from leaving. She no longer wanted to be part of the group; she was burnt out and missed her home in Canada. I tried to talk her into taking some time off, to go back home for a few weeks and then return and she said she was done, she couldn't do it anymore. She said she enjoyed her time here, but it was over for her. I respected that and I didn't stand in her way and I wished her well. I told her the new tour begins in a few weeks and we need to prepare without her so she needed be sure of her decision."

Best was lying. He looked and sounded genuine, but Avery knew in his gut that he was lying. Something terrible had happened to Elizabeth. It took all of his will power not to show Best that he knew he was lying. He needed Best to think he believed him. He was about to say something when Best continued.

"The band will be fine Avery, if you're worried at all about that. The kids are disappointed and they took her leaving hard, but they are over it and now they are anxious to move on."

"Robert, it will just be a matter of time before the next one of them wants to leave. This is becoming too much for them. They are still kids, remember."

Avery could see the relief appear on Best's face as he realized he had bought his story on Elizabeth's disappearance. He replied, "I tend to disagree, Avery. Music is their life. The band wasn't for Elizabeth and that's okay. The rest of them need to get back into what they love the most and that's music. I have instructed them to get back into the studio today. Patrick has reworked the songs for the new album to accommodate Elizabeth's absence. Recording of the new album will begin immediately."

Avery couldn't believe Best was ordering the kids back into the studio so soon. "Robert, it's too soon. Let's give them more time to rest both emotionally and physically."

"It's too late Avery. I have scheduled a press conference for next week to announce the departure of Elizabeth and to launch details of the new worldwide tour for Vasallus that was revealed during the taping of the Dateline interview. You have the rest of the week to complete the tracks for the new album, *Next Step,* and for rehearsals."

Avery was stunned. "You've got to be kidding. Next week? There is no time, Robert. They need more time. They can't possibly open the tour in Madrid in two weeks. Tell them at the press conference that the tour has been delayed for a few months."

Best was quick to reply, "I cannot possibly reschedule the tour dates. Cities and venues are booked, Avery. The entire tour is sold out. The kids are ready and waiting. They will be here shortly and they need you to lead them. The world is waiting. Do not disappoint them. Give them what they want."

In a final, ominous tone, Best finished by saying: "Time,

Avery, is my only enemy."

****

"Avery, you can't be serious. You agree with him? Elizabeth probably quit because she couldn't take the pace anymore. The grueling schedule Best has them on is burning them out. Soon the others will want to leave too. You see that, right?"

The two of them were sitting in Avery's office in the studio. Best had left earlier, soon after they had finished their talk. The kids were already in the studio, reworking all the remixed songs for *Next Step*. Bentley was furious with him.

"Look Bentley, I know you're upset. I was the same as you when Best told me they were going right back into the studio and out on tour. After our discussion, I gave it some thought and I agree with him. Music is what these kids live for. Without it, I think they would be lost. I spoke to each of them individually and then together as a group this morning before they went into the studio and I have never seen a more ready group of musicians than these six."

"I just don't know. I'm really worried about them. I respect your decision Avery and I trust you. I can't say the same for Best. He's plotting something big and these kids are a part of it. I'm just not sure what the music has to do with it. Listen, my job is to cover this band for the magazine and it's none of my business what you and Best do to manage them. Being here and being around them every day, I can't help but get attached to them emotionally."

"I understand completely sweetheart. I feel the same way you do about them. I care for them all. Even Benning. As much of a prick as he is, I still care about him and I have huge respect for his talent."

She walked over and sat on his lap and wrapped her arms around him before saying: "I love you. Will you do something for me, for the two of us?"

Looking into her beautiful eyes, he could feel himself being lost in them. He replied: "Of course I will. What do you need me to do?"

"I would feel a lot better about all of this if I knew what happened with Elizabeth. I need to know that she is safe. Will you find out where she is and talk with her? I think we both need to know that."

"I will contact Detective Showenstein today and see if he can track her down for us. Maybe before the end of the day we can talk with Elizabeth on the phone. How does that sound?"

"That would be wonderful. Thank you, Avery. Now get in that studio and make sure these kids are ready. It's going to be a crazy next few months. For all of us."

****

Alone in his office, Avery searched for Detective Showenstein's business card. It had been awhile since he had spoken with him. It had been at the opening concert for Vasallus at the Staples Center in Los Angeles. He and his wife Bethany were there in support of Patrick Benning. The tall and lanky detective came across as an intelligent and thoughtful person, but he carried himself with authority. He was a seasoned and experienced homicide detective and those kinds of cops have seen things the normal human being will never experience. His intelligence felt like a combination of an education and years of working the streets. It was a lethal combination for a bad guy if he was on your tail.

He found the detective's card in a drawer in his desk, his junk drawer, filled with items he mentally promised himself he would sort through every time he opened the drawer. The card listed three numbers. They were the main telephone number to the LAPD switchboard, the Homicide direct line and his cell number. He chose the detective's cell number, always the best chance to reach someone. It rang three times and Avery was already formulating what to leave on his voicemail when he heard a gruff voice cut into his thoughts: "Detective Showenstein."

"Good morning Detective, its Avery Johnson calling. Have you got a minute?"

"Certainly I do. It has been awhile. Call me Sam by the way.

No need for the Detective title when it comes to personal matters."

"Actually, this might be work related Sam."

Avery could hear the shift in Sam's voice as he replied, "Okay, is there something wrong Avery? Is there a problem with Patrick?"

For a split second he almost felt like telling Sam how he really felt about Patrick, but instead replied: "No problems with Patrick. It's Elizabeth Leroux I was calling you about. She has left Vasallus and returned to Canada. Bentley and I were away on business when she left."

He once again felt a shift in Sam's voice when he asked: "Why did she leave?"

"That's why I am calling you. The other kids and Robert Best claimed she left because she was burnt out, missed home and didn't want to be in the band anymore."

"But you and Bentley don't believe that?"

"We understand it and it makes perfect sense. The pressure these kids are under is enormous. I'm surprised she's been the only one that has quit. There likely will be more. It's just odd that she would have left without discussing it with Bentley and me first. We know her very well and have become close to her, to all of them. She is very close to Bentley. In fact, on the road during the tour she approached Bentley with some concerns she had. She trusted us and for her to leave without so much as a goodbye just seems too strange for us to accept."

"What are you asking me to do Avery?"

"Would you or can you check with your sources up in Canada to see if she did indeed come home to her parents' like she told the other kids she was doing? We just want to make sure she is safe and sound Sam."

"Leave it with me for a few days. I can make some inquiries in Canada and see whether or not she made it home. I will check with Customs to see if she entered the country and go from there. She could very well still be in Los Angeles and not planning to go home just yet. Who knows exactly what her plans are. I will know soon enough. I'll get back to you Avery."

"Thank you Sam and let's hope she's resting comfortably in her old bed in her parents' home."

****

Sam hit the end button on his cell phone, placed it in his pocket and leaned back in his home office chair and let the fear resonate through him. What he didn't tell Johnson was that his gut feeling was telling him that Elizabeth was likely in serious danger, if not already dead. Not long ago his friend in the RCMP was brutally murdered after Sam asked him to check into the circumstances surrounding the birth of Elizabeth. He was murdered minutes after hanging up the phone after telling Sam that Elizabeth's parents were missing.

Elizabeth did not leave the mansion to return to Canada. She had been killed. He was certain of it. Patrick was part of her disappearance. He made up his mind that he would pay a visit to the mansion. He wanted to see what Patrick's reaction would be when he saw him there. He needed to look around the house. Maybe Avery was involved in her disappearance and he was sending him on a wild goose chase to Canada, to search for Elizabeth there in order to distract him. He was on ordered time off from the Department because of all the tragic events that had surrounded him. It turned out to be a blessing in disguise as it freed him up to focus on stopping Patrick and the others.

He rose from his chair, paused to look at the wall that outlined the events of each of the seven members of Vasallus, from their birth up to the present. He was right smack in the middle of a conspiracy to destroy the world by the Anti-Christ, friends and loved ones were being murdered all around him and he needed to act. Ann Lockwood, the mother of Michael Lockwood, was downstairs in his living room with his wife Beth. She and Father O'Sullivan were the only other people who knew the truth. It was time for a plan to put a stop to this madness before more bodies piled up. The Department could not help him. They were alone and with God's will and a lot of luck, maybe they could figure out a way through this.

****

The mayhem that had taken place in Sam's home just days earlier was still evident. All the glass and broken furniture had been cleaned up, but the damage to the walls and the blood stains were still present to remind them of how close they came to dying when Patrick and his demonic self almost killed them all. The home was a constant reminder of the carnage, but it was safe. Bethany was still covered in bruises from Patrick's beating. Seb had received terrible blows from Patrick's evilness. He was lucky to be alive. Ann, however, had been seconds away from being raped by the beast. It was an event too evil to comprehend, but her strength continued to amaze him. It was no surprise when she demanded to accompany him to the mansion.

"I will come with you, Sam. You cannot go alone. It is too dangerous."

"That is exactly why I will go alone. It is too dangerous for you, Ann. Stay here with Beth and Seb, where it is safe. When I return we will talk about what we will do next. Hopefully, we will have heard from Father O'Sullivan by then."

Sam, I am going. For reasons I cannot explain, the demon is unable to harm me. I will be safe. Now let's get going."

Beth spoke next: "Maybe she's right, Sam. You can't go alone into that place. If Patrick can come in our home and almost kill all of us, God forbid what he can do in his own turf."

He looked at his wife, ran his hand down the side of her face and reassured her: "I know you're worried about me. Don't be. I'll be fine." Looking at Ann, he continued: "Patrick almost assaulted you Ann, and would have likely killed you. I will not put you back in that situation again."

She shook her head in defiance before continuing: "The demon tricked me and was able to get the upper hand. It will not happen again. The beast has had many opportunities to take my life, but has not. It is because he still needs me or cannot kill me. I must go. I need to know that Michael is okay.

I need to let him know that I am okay. God is watching over us, Sam. We are alive because it is His will. We all have a greater purpose for His plan. I believe in that. It is what gives me hope. The same goes for you Sam and Beth, as well as Seb. We should be dead, but we're alive. There is a reason for that."

He was silent for a minute, pondering what Ann had just said. He felt a presence working inside of him, he had no doubt about that, but was it something he could depend on to guide him and keep him and his family safe? Until they heard from Father O'Sullivan, he couldn't just sit around and watch as more people died. He needed to act. Ann was right. He couldn't go alone.

"Okay, Ann, then we need to leave immediately. Where is Father O'Sullivan? He has been gone for days. I am worried about him. The Lord is working through him, Ann. I felt it the other day when he cast Patrick from the house. We could use him going into that mansion and confronting Patrick."

There was a sound coming from the front entrance. The door opened and in walked a man. He was dressed in black and wore the cleric collar of a priest. He was a man in his early forties. He looked very familiar to Sam. The realization of who he was hit him like a freight train. His mouth opened, but nothing came out. Then he heard the soft whisper of Ann's voice behind him, barely audible.

"Father O'Sullivan!"

The familiar voice spoke, but it did not match the man, as he replied: "What makes you think I ever left, Sam?"

Chapter 4

Ann struggled to find her voice as she stared at Father O'Sullivan: "Father, you have, I mean, you're different. You've changed."

He approached her and placed his hands on her arms, clutching them with a firm grip and replied: "Ann, I need to speak with you. I need to speak with all of you." His eyes were ablaze with an indiscernible light. "Please everyone, let's sit. We need to talk."

It was Bethany who spoke next, stepping towards Father O'Sullivan, her face reflecting a look of shock and wonder: "Father, we can go and sit in the living room. May I get you something to drink or eat?"

He nodded at Beth, a smile stretching across his young face: "Tea would be wonderful Bethany. Thank you."

****

A few minutes later, Bethany was serving everyone tea. She placed a plate of crackers, cheese and pickles on the table. Father O'Sullivan didn't waste any time diving into the food. All of them stared at him, stunned at the physical changes in him. Years had miraculously melted off of him. He skin was smooth and youthful and he was physically strong and square looking underneath his dark, cleric clothing. It was his eyes that carried the biggest change of all. They were no longer a pleasant green in colour, instead they were now a brilliant colour of blue. It was incredible, the changes to the priest's physical appearance. No one missed the aura of something divine that surrounded him, emanating outwards, a feeling of

Holiness and His presence within the priest. A sense of hope in their bleak situation began to seep into all of them.

Father O'Sullivan looked up at Beth as he filled his plate, his heavy Irish accent was lighter and bounced along from word to word much quicker than before: "I should have warned you Bethany, tea and crackers are one of my most favourite foods. Add in some cheese and let's just say, all of you better hurry up and help yourselves because it will disappear!"

Everyone shared a good laugh, which was something they needed to break the tension in the air caused by the remarkable change in the appearance of Father O'Sullivan. After the laughter subsided, quietness took over for several seconds before Sam spoke up: "Father O'Sullivan, please share with us, where have you been since you left our house after the carnage with Patrick?"

Sam watched as the priest dabbed at the corners of his mouth with a paper napkin, then looked up at him, his eyes sparkling like two pools of blue open sky and replied: "That was a terrible event, Sam. I am happy to see Ann has recovered nicely as well as Beth." He nodded at them both before turning back to Sam and continuing: "Tell me, where is Seb?"

"He is fine, Father. He is upstairs in his room studying. He hardly remembers anything from the attack and for that we are grateful. Tell us about yourself. Where you have been and what you have been doing?"

"Thank the Lord. Let's just say, I have been in conversation, Sam. I have much to share with all of you. Let me start by telling you Sam and Ann, that visiting the mansion at this time is impossible. It is far too dangerous for the both of you. I will go and I will let you know how Michael is doing."

Ann was quick to respond, her voice carrying an edge of panic: "Father, I am not afraid of Patrick or Best for that matter. I must see Michael! I want to see with my own eyes that he is safe and I want to let him know that I am okay. He must be worried sick."

Father O'Sullivan did not respond immediately, instead he took a moment to fill his cup with more tea. The silence was deafening, the sound of his spoon stirring the sugar and cream in his tea sounded like a blacksmith pounding a bar of heated steel with his sledgehammer. After his cup was properly stirred he picked up his cup and saucer, leaned backwards into his chair and looked at everyone. He scanned the room and looked everyone in the eye, lingering for a second or two on each of them. Sam felt a presence when the priest's eyes rested on his. The Holy Spirit was within the priest. He felt it enter his soul as he continued to stare. The priest was projecting the Holy Spirit into him. It entered his body, filling every vein with the blood of His presence. It was eerie, but wonderful all at the same time. Father O'Sullivan finally spoke.

"Please understand, we live in dangerous times. All of us are engaged in a spiritual battle with the demon. All of us have been touched by his wickedness. The Lord is with us. He is by our side. We must trust in Him. This battle will not be won with bullets, Sam. To engage the demon, now, is not only dangerous and foolish, but will likely result in your death. The beast is discovering that all of us have been empowered by God, and the plates of His armor are protecting our earthly bodies. Do not test him. He will destroy you if you engage him. He will discover your weaknesses and he will exploit those. He is the Anti-Christ. He is Satan. He is the greatest evil that ever lived. He is out to destroy mankind, all of mankind. He has been planning this event for hundreds of years."

Ann leapt from her seat on the couch and shouted: "Father, I will not stand by and watch my son be a part of this evil plan, or worse, be killed by the beast when he no longer needs him."

Sam could see the sorrow pass through Father O'Sullivan's eyes as Ann shouted. He replied to her protest: "Ann, you are a true warrior, just like your ancestors. You come from a great lineage my dear. It is why the beast attacked you seventeen years ago. You were chosen because of your lineage."

She sat back down on the couch, disbelief written all over her face when she replied: "I don't understand Father? My lineage to what? To whom?"

"You are the direct descendant of Babken, the warrior son of King Tiridates from Armenia." He was cut-off by Ann from speaking further, her rage was building and her polite, tea party constraint failed her.

"Father, I'm sorry, but I have lived with what that thing did to me for seventeen years. He murdered my husband, my mother and now my son is next. I don't care who he is or what he is, nor do I care who my forefathers were. My son needs me, so if you don't mind, please don't lecture me with history lessons. I need to save my son."

Beth stood up off of the couch and put a comforting arm around Ann. Father O'Sullivan continued: "I understand your rage towards your plight Ann. Michael is in no imminent danger, I can assure you. The beast has been plotting this plan since his epic defeat on the battlefields of Armenia sixteen hundred years ago. He plans to destroy mankind once and for all and he is using his offspring to complete this plan."

Sam looked into Father O'Sullivan's eyes and said: "Father, the beast has attacked the seven direct descendants of the seven sons of King Tiridates to produce these offspring. Why? And why did he wait so long?"

"Sam, I do not have all of the answers, but I can say that it is likely timed to coincide with the final fury God will inflict on all of the non-believers in Christ as predicted in the Book of Revelations. I have been involved in a secret committee in the Vatican for over forty years that has tracked natural and manmade disasters to support the theory of the Church's belief in the end times. The time for the Lord's final Armageddon is upon us. He will destroy all people not saved by his Son, Jesus Christ. The Anti-Christ is in a race with God to darken as many souls as he can before their conversion to Christ. That is his plan. It is written. He is using the influence of his offspring's music to draw in as many human souls as possible before God enacts the Rapture."

Sam was stunned at what he was hearing. He looked around the room and could see the same stunned look on everyone else's face. He turned back to Father O'Sullivan and asked: "Father, how do you know this? What has happened to you? You walked into the house today looking thirty years younger."

"Sam, I know this is difficult for you to understand. I know your faith does not believe in the teachings of Christ, but understand this. Whether you want to accept this fate or not, you have been chosen by God to lead this fight against His enemy. All of you have been chosen. It is why you are all still alive. God has chosen you for a reason. What those reasons are will reveal themselves in time. It doesn't really matter, does it?" Looking at Ann, he continued: "Ann, you are a very brave woman. You have been through so much over these years and yet you are still fighting. Now is not the time to engage the enemy. Going to the mansion to confront Best right now would be very dangerous for you. I have another reason for going there, but I promise you I will get word to Michael that you are safe."

Ann slumped back into the couch, resigned to the fact that he was right. It would be foolish to engage the beast now and would most likely result in her death. She needed to stay alive. Not for herself, but for Michael.

Sam spoke up and asked: "Father, there is another problem we must talk about. I received a call from Avery Johnson at the mansion. Elizabeth Leroux is missing. He and Bentley were away all week and when they returned, she was gone. Apparently she could not handle being in the band anymore, missed her home in Canada and returned to Montreal. I believe something terrible has happened to her. Not long ago I had a contact in the Royal Canadian Mounted Police check into the background of Elizabeth's birth parents. Soon after our conversation he was brutally murdered."

Sam watched as Father O'Sullivan hung his head. He was praying. After a few minutes, he lifted his head and looked at him, a look of devastation written on his face: "We are running out of time. The time is near. I must leave at once for the mansion."

It was Beth who spoke next: "Father, I insist that you

spend the night here before you leave. I will make a meal and then you can rest. You need your energy. I don't care if you've discovered the fountain of youth, you need to rest." Ann followed up with: "I concur Father, with Beth. Besides I want to know more about your conversations. Come on Beth, I'll help you prepare dinner. We'll leave it to Sam to tie Father O'Sullivan down to the chair if that's what it takes." She smiled at Thomas as she rose from her chair to follow Beth into the kitchen. She stopped beside his chair, reached down and squeezed Father O'Sullivan's hand as she spoke, "Father, thank you for being here. All of us are grateful that you have come back to Los Angeles. I'm scared to think how we would get through this without you."

Ann couldn't stop the torrent of tears that spilled down her cheeks and as she lifted her hand to wipe her eyes, Father O'Sullivan had a handkerchief out of his jacket pocket, offering it to her before he spoke: "Believe in God, Ann, as He believes in you. It is through His protection that we owe our lives and the lives of Michael, Chloë and the others too. Be strong in your faith. The Lord, Our God will not fail us."

Sam watched as Beth escorted an upset Ann into the kitchen, then turned to Thomas and said: "So will you stay for the night, Father? I will go with you in the morning as I will not allow you to go on your own. I have some questions for Avery Johnson that I would like answered."

"I suppose rest and some food would be wise. I will go to the mansion in the morning, but I will go alone. It is too dangerous for you Sam to be there when Best discovers I am in the mansion. I cannot predict what he will do when he does. I will not carry that burden on my shoulders if something happens to you."

Patting the gun in his holster with his hand, Sam stated: "I can take care of myself, Father. Patrick Benning almost killed my family and he needs to be stopped. I plan to throw his ass in a holding cell before he hurts anyone else and until I can figure this out."

He watched as Thomas shook his head and replied: "Bullets will not stop Best or even Patrick, Sam. Best is not human and cannot be stopped with physical force. Only the power of God can stop those two from their plan of destruction."

"If Best is Satan and so powerful then why doesn't he just launch every country that has nuclear weapons at each other and destroy mankind? Why all the theatrics? Why Vasallus and the kids Father?"

"Don't you know, Sam? You have it all mapped out in your office? You figured it out, don't you see that?"

"How did you know that I charted all of this? Besides, what I put together and figured out doesn't explain the existence of the seven children and the band."

Sam was reminded once again of the changes in Father O'Sullivan as he watched him jump out of his chair as if his legs were made of springs. His clear blue eyes were mesmerizing as they locked onto his before he finally said: "Come on, let's go to your office. There is something I want to tell you and I don't want the women to hear what I am going to tell you. Not now."

Sam's long legs could barely keep up with the priest as they navigated the hallways to his office. Once inside his office, Father O'Sullivan closed the door and motioned for Sam to sit down. He sat down in his office chair and watched as the priest paced back and forth, then suddenly stopped and looked at him, his shimmering blue eyes doorways to a heavenly place that demanded his attention. Sam was so drawn to the priest's eyes that he almost didn't hear Father O'Sullivan when he spoke: "I have met Satan, the Anti-Christ that resides within the body of Robert Best on many occasions. The first time was in the delivery room of Katherine McClosky, in a Dublin hospital sixteen years ago, giving birth to Chloë. I watched when he killed Katherine as Chloë was being born. He was disguised as a doctor, but I knew who he was and what he had done, I just didn't know why. I was enraged, mad with thoughts of killing this thing that had wreaked so much havoc on this family. I attacked him. I pounded his face with my fists, like I was the one possessed.

The harder and more frequently I pounded my fists into him, the more he would laugh. It was the angelic voice of the newborn Chloë, filling the room that stopped me. Her voice was that of an angel Sam. It was a sign from God, I am convinced of it."

Sam knew this because he had witnessed the angelic voice of Patrick at his birth and replied, "I was there Father, when Patrick was born. He too sang like an angel. He is no angel now Father, believe me."

Father O'Sullivan stopped in front of Sam, leaned in close to him, his eyes captivating as he continued: "For years Sam, I believed the angelic voice I heard in that delivery room was an early indication of the beautiful voice and musical talent Chloë would become as she grew as planned by the devil. Now I know it was a sign from God. He was showing me that she was also a child of Him and not just the beast. Don't you see?"

"No I don't Father. They were put on this earth as a result of Satan himself raping then impregnating these women for the sole purpose to become these musical prodigies as part of his master plan."

"That is true, but answer this for me. If Satan can use these children to influence the youth and everyone else in the world with their music to destroy mankind, why can't God use these children for the very same reason? Except He will use them and their music, not to destroy mankind, but to save mankind!"

"You're losing me Father. I don't follow."

"Satan does not want to destroy mankind with nuclear weapons, Sam! He wants to destroy their souls! He is using Vasallus and the incredible influence of their music and song lyrics to lure millions of followers around the world. Their numbers grow every day. He will use that power to turn them against God, to darken their souls and cast them into eternal damnation. That is how he will destroy mankind."

"I think the world was already heading in that direction before Vasallus, Father."

A moment of silence passed as Father O'Sullivan sat down and seemed to relax. Looking at him and into his eyes, Sam felt he was looking into the window of Heaven. The crystal clear blue colour carried something more. A tremendous aura of goodness and wisdom emanated from those eyes and he felt a strange sensation that the eyes of God Himself were staring back at him. When Father O'Sullivan spoke, his voice seemed to carry an air of pain, anguish maybe, he thought. His Irish accent was more crisp, less thick of its brogue. He listened to the priest continue: "The demon Satan will stop at nothing to destroy your soul and darken it from the mercy of God's grace. I believe that Satan is in a race against time as he knows God's final fury is near."

"I know what the bible says about the End of Times, Father, and the ensuing Rapture. Are you saying that the devil is turning as many people away from God as possible so Christ's Kingdom on Earth after the Rapture will be greatly mitigated or nonexistent?"

Staring into the priest's eyes, words were not necessary as the sensation that moved through his body said it all. That was it. This is what the demon was doing. Now he knew and the fear tinged every nerve ending in his body, causing him to shudder.

He watched as Father O'Sullivan waited for the reality to fully resonate through his mind before he continued: "It's a little more complicated than that Sam, but essentially yes. That is what I believe."

Sam ran both of his hands through the tight curly hair on his head then finished by rubbing his face vigorously as if he was trying to rub the reality of what he had just heard away. He looked up at the priest, his eyes stinging from the self-inflicted face wash. He stretched out his long legs in front of him, struggling to get comfortable with what he had heard. "Father, this is madness! You know that, don't you?"

Father O'Sullivan, like a father to a son would do, reached over and placed his hand on his lap and then said: "Keep the faith, Sam. There is a reason the Lord is using us to fight this battle. He will reveal to us the true meaning of all of this in His time. In the meantime, be strong. Your family, Vasallus, Ann and myself need you to be strong. There is hope for us Sam."

He looked at him, his voice was low and without emotion as he replied: "I'm struggling with the hope thing in all of this, Father."

"Let's go eat some of your wife's fantastic food, regain some of our strength and then rest. Let me leave you with this Sam. If Vasallus can fill the world with messages of dread and despair, what would happen to the world if they sang about hope, love and survival?"

Chapter 5

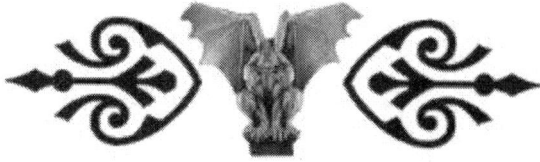

Nancy Campbell, one of the most successful environmental lobbyists and recognizable faces in Washington, went over her presentation to the Environmental Protection Agency or EPA, one final time. The report she was about to deliver would be used to assist the President in his decision on whether or not to move forward with the highly controversial pipeline from Canada to the Gulf Coast. The EPA was advising the President not to sign off on the pipeline, but the President was leaning towards approving it because the economic benefits and jobs created from the construction of the pipeline were hard to ignore. The country needed jobs and this would be a much welcome boost.

Environmental issues were all the rage in political circles around Washington and Nancy seemed to be at the centre of most of those circles. Her expertise and political connections put her in hot demand with the powerful lobby groups. She had become the face of environmental responsibility and it was a rare night when she was not seen on CNN or one of the other major networks weighing in on the issues.

She was also the mother of one of the members of the most popular musical group in the world, Vasallus. Her mega talented daughter, Brittany, was the talk of the nation and most of Nancy's interviews with the media would eventually steer towards her daughter, but she always brushed the comments aside, refusing to mix her personal life with her professional one. She was incredibly proud of Brittany and what she had accomplished with the band. Her only misgivings stemmed from the fact that Brittany's musical career and her own did not allow them much time together. In fact, they have not seen each other in weeks. They spoke often on the phone and Nancy was hoping that when the tour ended Brittany would come home, but when she watched the taped episode of Dateline where it was announced that the European tour would begin within a few weeks of the North American tour ending, it caught Nancy by surprise and her protests to her daughter were met with replies such as: "Mom, we are in the big time now. Our fans have expanded all over the world and they want to see us perform live."

It wasn't the announcement of the immediate launch of the worldwide tour of Vasallus that bothered her the most; it was Brittany's tone when she spoke to her. She seemed disinterested in anything else but the tour and Vasallus. She was missing her usual spark and bubbly personality. Nancy protested to her daughter that she needed a break from touring and the band otherwise she could burnout or even worse, get sick. Brittany did eventually alleviate her fears when she promised that she would take good care of herself and make sure she got lots of rest in between shows. Nancy's assistant and now Brittany's caregiver at the mansion, Leanne Reston, had also assured Nancy that she was doing fine. Her schoolwork was not being affected by the heavy schedule and Brittany was growing to even greater heights as a musician.

Before they left for Europe, Nancy would try to get to the mansion to visit Brittany. Maybe once everything settled down a bit in Washington, she could take a few weeks off and spend time with Brittany by joining her on the European tour. That would be fun for both of them.

Closing the lid on her computer, Nancy realized that she needed to get a move-on down to the offices of the EPA at the Woodrow Wilson Plaza on Pennsylvania Avenue, walking distance from Capitol. She kept a small office in Washington with a staff of one full-time assistant. The knock on the door interrupted her thoughts as she looked up to see Marian, her assistant, poking her head in the door and asking: "Deputy Director Rudy Gonzales of Cultural Affairs is on the phone. Do you have time to take his call?"

"No, I'm just on my way out the door to the EPA. I have my presentation in forty-five minutes. Tell him to leave a number and I will call him later this afternoon after my meetings."

"Will do. Listen Nancy, do you mind if I call it an early day and take the afternoon off? I have got some personal maintenance I would like to take care of if it's okay with you."

"Not at all, Marian. I don't need anything more from you today anyway. If fact why don't you book off right after I leave."

"Are you sure Nancy?"

"Of course I am. In fact take the rest of the day on my dime. No need for putting in for any time off. It's because I work you to the bone that you never have anytime for yourself. See you in the morning, now go."

Beaming, she replied: "Geez, thanks Nancy. Good luck at the EPA. I'll leave the number to Gonzales on my desk, just grab it on your way out. See you tomorrow!"

****

Her presentation to the EPA went smoothly. They were very receptive to her ideas because she had backed each one by solid research. The investment made by the EPA in her work seemed justified as she handed her bill to the administration desk on her way out. An enormous fee, no doubt, but one that they would pay without any qualms. Her work on behalf of the EPA was the backbone to their final push to the President to quash any plans to move forward on the pipeline from Canada. Nancy was one of the most sought after and highest paid lobbyists in all of Washington, which was considerable since there were close to 20,000 lobbyists in total in Washington.

Back out on the busy sidewalk of Pennsylvania Avenue, she took out her cell phone and called back Deputy Director Gonzales, wondering as she pushed the send button, why he would be calling her. Nancy had never met Gonzales, but she had bumped into the Director a few times. The secretary immediately put him through and the voice of Gonzales came on: "Nancy, thank you for getting back to me. How did your presentation to the hard asses at the EPA go?"

"For the amount of money they pay me Deputy Director, it's all in a day's work. What can I do for you, sir?"

"As I'm sure you're aware Nancy, my office is responsible for, among many things, the social well-being of the people of the Unites States."

"You are correct sir. Working in Washington, you tend to learn about all of the departments within the United States Government. What do you want to talk with me about Mr. Gonzales?"

"It sounds like you're making your way up Pennsylvania as we speak. Why don't you divert up to my office or I can meet you somewhere down there for a drink. There is something I would like to discuss with you."

"I was hoping to get out of downtown before the traffic crush. Is it not something we can discuss on the phone?"

"We could, I guess, but then I would miss out on the opportunity to have a drink with one of the most beautiful woman on the Hill!"

"I'll come to you. Give me ten minutes; I'm only a block away from your offices."

****

Sitting across the desk from Rudy Gonzales, Deputy Director of Social Services, Nancy was surprised by the easy-going manner of the ADD. She thought he might be an opportunistic womanizer, but he was far from it. He was well spoken and projected an air of confidence and goodness. "Rare in this city", she thought to herself. She instantly liked the man and was curious as to why he wanted to meet with her.

"Thank you for taking the time to meet with me Nancy, I know you are a very busy person. You are a well-respected lobbyist in Washington, Nancy, but it is not because of the issues you are fighting for that I asked to meet with you. It is about your daughter, Brittany."

Nancy immediately felt betrayed. The man was schmoozing her just so he could talk to her about her daughter. He probably made a deal with a contact in the Washington Post for a payoff if he could get a story from the mother of Brittany Campbell.

"I'm sorry to disappoint you Mr. Gonzales, but my personal life is not open to discussion. Now, if this meeting has nothing to do with any of the causes I work for, then I'm afraid this meeting is over."

Nancy watched as Gonzales rose from his desk and walked around the side of it and motioned for her to stand up with him, "Come on Nancy, let's go for a walk. I'll walk you to your car so you can still beat the traffic and we can talk along the way. I promise you I'm not prying for tickets to a Vasallus concert for my teenage daughter. My office is investigating the group's impact on our youth. I was hoping to get some informal and unofficial feedback from you, Nancy that might help alleviate mine and my office's concerns regarding their music."

They walked down Pennsylvania Avenue, and then crossed over at 10th Street towards her parkade when she stopped on the sidewalk, pointed towards the sandwich bistro and said: "Let's go inside shall we? I'm famished and I could use a cold beer. I think this conversation might take a while."

****

Nancy listened intently over the noise of the afternoon lunch crowd that had changed into the office workers stopping for a beer before they made their way home. Nancy was fascinated and overwhelmed by the government's concern over the music and social impact Vasallus was having over the youth of this country.

"It's not just this government that is concerned Nancy. European countries that have been chosen by Vasallus management for a concert stop are grappling with how to deal with the problems that will arise, especially security."

"Why don't the governments of these countries just say no

to Vasallus? Like the Chinese government do."

"The backlash by the youth in these countries is what they are afraid of. They are afraid of outright rioting, violence and mayhem. The lessor of these two evils is to let them perform. The enormous popularity of Vasallus is beyond anything seen since the Beatles. They could very well be the most popular band to perform ever."

"Even the Beatles were before my time, but I don't see what all the fuss is about, Rudy. My daughter is still the smart, well-grounded young girl she was before she became part of Vasallus. The fact they are so well liked by our youth is a good thing. They are all well behaved kids and are excellent role models. I just think the government should back away and stay out of it. I know crowd control is difficult at these concerts, but tell the concert management to beef up security to handle the violence surrounding the live shows."

She watched as he lowered his voice and leaned closer towards her across the table and said: "Have you really listened to the lyrics of their songs Nancy? They are borderline anti-social and seem to be a calling out for people everywhere to stand up against the system."

"Oh come on, you can't be serious. I think the songs are truly inspirational to our youth, it gives them the courage to stand up for themselves against all kinds of adversity. Our kids get bombarded today with all kinds of music that promotes drugs, sex and violence. Vasallus' music promotes self-confidence, courage and making tough choices. I cannot believe the government is deciding to take a stand against their music. It's because they have become so popular, so influential, the government are afraid of the power they have over our youth. Isn't that right Director?"

"Nancy, I don't think you understand. The music of Vasallus in their first album has had such an impact on our youth that we are now beginning to see the results of that impact. Kids around the country are boycotting school in increasing numbers, teen violence is up dramatically, and the social mayhem attributed to Vasallus is undeniable. Like it or not their music is having an effect on our society. So much so, that my department is considering taking action."

"That is ludicrous. The foundation of our confederation is Freedom of Speech. Vasallus is nowhere even close to violating that right. Where is the justice?"

She watched as Gonzales finished off his glass of beer, then stood up to leave before he said: "My department is taking a 'wait and see' attitude towards their music. We suspect the release of the second album will include songs with elevated messages of social irresponsibility. If that is the case and its impact on our youth and the youth of other countries around the world could very well lead to the very first censorship in this country's history. Thank you Ms. Campbell for our talk and I presume you can find your car okay from here."

Nancy just sat in her chair, her elbows firmly planted on the table, her anger coming to the surface as she watched the Deputy Director through the window as he disappeared into the late afternoon's crowded sidewalks. She barely heard the waitress who stood beside her: "May I get you anything else, Mam?"

"No, just get me my goddamned bill."

Startled by her outburst, the waitress quickly backpedaled away from her table and replied: "Oh the gentlemen already took care of the bill when he left. I was just checking to see if you wanted anything else."

"I'm sorry, it's been a long day. I'm fine. I'll be leaving. Thank you."

Just then a familiar voice cut in behind her, jolting her, a voice she had not heard in a while, at least not in person. She turned her chair to see Robert Best standing, dressed immaculately in an expensive suit. Even in a city full of men wearing suits, he stood apart. After a few seconds she found her voice, "Robert Best. What are you doing here? Bumping into one another at an airport is one thing, but in a little café in D.C. is something completely different."

Flashing a smile, his handsome looks threw her off

somewhat. He reached out with his hand to shake hers while he said: "I was walking by with an associate and I seen you through the window so I told my associate that I'd catch up with him later. I had to stop and say hello to the mother of one of my most popular clients. You look beautiful Nancy, just like your daughter."

"Thank you for that flattering comment Mr. Best, I was just leaving."

"Oh please stay for another drink with me. I insist that you do. And please call me Robert."

"Okay Robert, I guess I could stay for a drink, but not here. It's too packed and noisy. I know of a better place. It is not too far from here, just a few blocks. We can walk."

Twenty minutes later they were sitting in a quiet booth in an upscale restaurant sipping a glass of wine when Best clinked her glass and said: "Here's to your very talented daughter and Vasallus."

"Talented maybe, but not so popular among some circles."

"Oh, is that so? I can't imagine anyone who wouldn't love your daughter's talent."

"It seems that the government has taken notice of the success of Vasallus and the impact they are having on our youth. You'd better be careful Robert, they are taking a close look at the band. They are talking about censorship."

"That is impossible! The government is a complete band of idiots, I swear. Finally a superstar band that sings about hope and courage and everything good for our young people and the government has a problem with that and yet it lets all the garbage fill the airwaves? Unbelievable."

Nancy could feel Best's anger at the news of the government sniffing around the group. She couldn't blame him, however. This was his baby, him and Avery Johnson's. They had put so much into this and had pushed all the right buttons to put Vasallus where it was today. She replied to his building frustration by saying: "I wouldn't get too worked up about it Robert. This will all blow over in few weeks. I would caution you to tone down the rhetoric somewhat in the next album. I think the government feels the lyrics are sending the wrong message."

****

What was supposed to be a drink turned into allot of drinks, then a nice dinner and then some more wine. She was way too tipsy to drive, so when it came time to call it a night she asked the waitress if she would call her a taxi. She gathered up her purse and rose to leave.

"Robert, it has been most enjoyable, but I must be on my way. Thank you for the wonderful evening and thank you for taking good care of Brittany. Her dreams are coming true and I have you and Avery Johnson to thank for that."

The alcohol she had consumed fired a warning shot to her brain as she almost fell to the floor while getting out from behind the table. Luckily, Robert was quick on his feet and caught her by the elbow before she tumbled and made a complete fool of herself. He smiled at her, his perfect teeth drawing her in. His eyes lingered on hers for an extra few seconds as he said: "Tell you what Nancy, rather than call two taxis, why don't I split the cab with you? I can drop you off on the way to my hotel. That way I will know you made it home safe and sound."

She could later say it was the alcohol, but she found herself strangely attracted to him. She has been around good looking men all of her life, but he was way more than that. His charisma and charm was magnetic and before she even gave it a second thought she blurted: "I think that would be a great idea. This can be a dangerous city for a lady." She immediately thought to herself: "I can't believe I just said that." Now she knew she had drank way too much, talking like that, but there was a voice inside her head telling her to go for it.

The waitress came to the table to inform them the taxi was ready out front. She watched as the rich looking lady left the restaurant. She should have cut her off much earlier as the woman had had way too much to drink.

"She was one strange lady," she thought to herself as she

recounted how this woman talked to herself the whole night as if someone was sitting with her, and engaging her in conversation. Very weird woman!

****

They arrived in front of her condo complex twenty minutes later. She watched Robert pay the driver and then climb out and open the door for her. She hoped he would ask to come up because she knew they both wanted it, but she wasn't going to be the one to say it. It had been so long since she had been in this position that she couldn't even remember how long it had been.. There had been a handful of flings over the years since James' death, but nothing serious and only a few times did she end up in bed with someone. Tonight was different. He had such a way about him, she couldn't control the way she was feeling. If he didn't invite himself in after opening the door to the taxi, then she would say it. She felt like a horny teenager, but she didn't care. She wanted him. Badly.

He reached into the car and held her hand as he helped her from the taxi. His smile was killing her. As he pulled her from the car and closed the door behind her, she felt his hand move to her back and pull her in close to him. The next thing she knew, his mouth was on hers, in a kiss she felt all the way down to her toes. She kissed him hard right back, the stubble from his unshaven face cutting into hers. It felt wonderful and she could feel the night around her disappear as the two of them locked in a passionate kiss. She was about to pull her mouth away and suggest they get off the sidewalk and go up to her apartment when suddenly she realized that she was on her back on her couch with Robert leaning into her. "What the hell?" she thought. "How did that happen?" She had way too much to drink and she now realized that this was not a good idea. He was kissing her neck, the heat between the two of them rising, but she needed to throw some water on it, and fast. She put her mouth to his ear and whispered, "Robert, I can't do this. I've had too much to drink. I'm sorry, I really am."

He propped himself up and looked into her eyes, the desire in them obvious and the disappointment not unexpected. Then suddenly she saw it. *His eyes!* It was a split second, but she seen it and it was unmistakable. The fear jolted through her like a lightning bolt. She tried to scream, but all she could manage was a gasp. The fear froze her to the couch like ice. "This can't be possible. This is not happening. The monster, the beast was *Robert Best!*

The scream that escaped her throat sounded like a sharp crack of thunder. She tried to roll to her left and out from underneath him when the steel, cold grip of his hand clamped down onto her neck like a vise. She struggled to get away, his grip cutting off all oxygen. "How could she have let this happen," she thought. "How did she not see it before this?"

She looked again into his eyes and the fiery red demonic eyes mocked her. The memories of her brutal rape so many years ago came flooding back to her, the memory of James being torn to pieces by this beast played like a movie in her brain. She could hear herself talk.

"You're nothing but a coward! I don't care if you kill me! I wish you would have finished me off the first time."

Best began the familiar transformation, still hovering over top of her, his enormous strength pinning her to the couch. His face turned the colour of grey. His face cracked like dried mud. His lips swelled and then split open, dripping saliva onto her face. Nancy could feel the fear driving the bile up her throat. Inches from his face she stared into his burning red orbs and saw hell staring back at her. He squeezed her throat even harder. She could feel her eyes bulging from their sockets due to a lack of oxygen. He spoke to her as her life was slipping away, his voice booming, the breath hot and bile-filled.

"How does it feel knowing you willingly brought the very beast that murdered your husband and fathered your daughter into your bed?"

He held her throat so tight, precious air barely made it into her lungs as she struggled to get the words out, "This is hardly my bed. You're a deceiver and a liar and this is just another one of your games. Go fuck yourself!" She took satisfaction in seeing the red pits burn slightly brighter with her words and then go all out on fire as she swung the heavy marble candle holder she managed to grab onto with her outstretched arm and drove it as hard as she could into the ear of the creature. The beast screamed, its hands loosening its grip on her throat, then clutching the side of his face as he moved away from her. She bolted off of the couch and ran for the open door leading out onto the seventh story deck. As she brushed past the sheer white curtain blowing gently in the evening breeze, she could hear the screams of anger coming from the creature as it realized what she was doing. She thought of James and how close she came to betraying his memory. She grabbed onto the rail of the balcony and with one fluid motion swung her legs over and felt her weightless body plummet to the ground below. In the final seconds before she made her lethal impact on the hard concrete, she thought of her daughter Brittany and prayed to God that He would look past her own sins and save the soul of her daughter.

Chapter 6

The next morning, Thomas awoke refreshed and ready to confront Best at the mansion. The meal prepared by Beth and Ann last night was incredible and he ate enough to let them think he was eating his last meal. It took considerable reasoning, but he and Sam were able to convince Ann to stay behind with Beth, though she was not happy about it.

He made his way into the kitchen, prepared to make coffee before everyone else woke up, but was surprised when he saw that everyone, including Seb, was already seated.

Thomas acknowledged them with: "Good morning everyone. Did any of you sleep last night or did you all decide to wait here in the kitchen in case I snuck out during the night?"

It was Ann, with a warming smile that seemed to brighten the early morning darkness beginning to fade outside the windows, who spoke up: "How do you not know that maybe I, after returning from the mansion, decided to make everyone coffee?"

He smiled back at her before replying: "Did I ever tell you, Ann, that it is a requirement of my vows as a priest, to sleep with one eye and one ear open?"

Everyone joined in with a good laugh; a welcome reprieve from the tension that was beginning to build in the air like a pressing fog from the knowledge that he and Sam would be leaving for a potential confrontation with the Demon.

Then it was Seb who spoke next, his question silencing the room as he asked: "Father, what will you do if Patrick or Best change into beast form and attack you, or my Dad? It's too dangerous, please don't go there. There will be other opportunities. Why can't you draw Best into a public place and confront him there. He won't risk attacking you in front of other people."

He looked into Seb's eyes; the young man's fear of what lay ahead was clearly displayed in them, and he replied to his question: "Best will not risk a confrontation. He has bigger fish to fry and he knows the power of the Lord is strong within every person in this room. Your Dad and I are only visiting the mansion to check on the well-being of the kids and to speak with Avery and Bentley. There is no need to worry about your father, Seb."

"Is it the power of the Lord that is making you younger and stronger, Father? He is preparing you for battle, isn't He?"

Thomas let his eyes linger on Seb before gazing at everyone at the table in turn and declaring: "I think it is time, Sam, that we left for the mansion. I will meet you out at the car."

****

Sam joined Thomas outside on the driveway and they decided they would take Thomas' rental. When they approached the car, Thomas handed the keys to Sam before saying: "You drive Sam. You know the way and I need some time to think."

"Father, I'm sorry about Seb's directness. He didn't mean anything by his remark, he's just curious."

Thomas looked at Sam before opening his door and replied: "No apologies required Sam. Your son is a very bright young man. Come on, let's get going."

They both said nothing as they drove away from the house and settled into the drive even as Sam drove like he was in a high-speed chase. After Sam blew through his second red light in a row, Thomas looked over at him and said: "Sam, I understand you're uptight, but getting us killed on the way there will not help your family. There is no hurry. No one from the mansion is leaving the country yet."

It took a few more intersections before Sam slowed down. They came to a red light and Sam looked at him as he reached into his jacket pocket and produced a pack of Marlboros, popped a cigarette into his mouth and lit it almost simultaneously. He sucked in a deep drag of the cigarette, rolled down the window and blew the smoke outside. The light turned green and Sam stepped on the gas, forcing his head into the headrest.

"I never knew you were a smoker, Sam. Don't you have enough stress in your job to cause health concerns without complicating things further with cigarettes?"

Sam gave him a glare as he replied: "It's been twelve years, Father, since I last smoked. I'd appreciate it if you would keep this between us. Beth would serve me up to Best herself if she knew. It helps to clear my mind, okay? We'll just leave it at that."

He chuckled as he replied: "It's not a sin yet to have a cigarette Sam, but it should be. I just hope I'm not in the same room as you when your wife finds out. Something tells me you might need the services of another plastic surgeon when she's done with you."

****

Heavy traffic made the drive long and when they finally rolled up in front of the Malibu mansion, it was almost 9:30 a.m. Neither of them said a word as they climbed out of the car and approached the front doors. Sam instinctively brought his right hand up to his left rib cage underneath his jacket. The familiar bulge of his 9mm offered no comfort to him, knowing that what they were up against would not be stopped by bullets made him cringe slightly when he heard Father O'Sullivan's voice: "Sam, why don't you go around the side of the house to the studio entrance? I'm sure you will find Avery in his office. I will meet you there."

The change in Father O'Sullivan's voice worried Sam. He asked: "Father, come with me. We will seek out the kids together after we speak with Avery and Bentley."

Sam watched as the priest stopped before they reached the front door and turned and looked at him. His incredibly blue eyes bore into his, the effervescence of them immediately disarmed him and when he then spoke, it sounded more like a command: "I don't want you coming through the front door Sam. There is danger on the other side of this door. Please go around the house to the studio. I will meet you there."

He hesitated, knowing it was useless to argue with the priest, but he reached into his coat and pulled the pistol out of its holster and handed it to the priest. It was stupid, he would never accept it, but he didn't know what else to do. He thrust the gun towards him and said: "Please Father. Take this, just in case."

"That is not necessary, Sam. Bullets will not stop Best. Faith in Jesus Christ and our Lord God, however, will. Faith and belief, Sam, are more powerful than any weapon wielded by man."

The power of the priest's eyes held him like a trance, when suddenly they dimmed slightly and Sam found himself turning away from the priest and towards the pathway to the studio entrance when the priest called out to him: "Be careful Sam. This is a very dangerous place. The kids are under his control now. Do not trust them. If you encounter Patrick before I get to you, do not engage him. He likely has no memory of the attack at your home, but he is still very dangerous. He might be the only one Best does not have control over, which makes him far more dangerous."

Sam was almost twenty feet away from Father O'Sullivan, and yet the goodness and purpose from his glowing eyes washed over him like a warm and comforting wave when the priest continued: "Sam, the blood of the Anti-Christ flows through the veins of the children. They will do everything they can to deceive and trick you. They have lost their innocence and are no longer blind to their origins. Best has opened them to their true purpose. Everything has changed now, Sam. They know why we are here. They know we are standing here right now. The mighty sword of the Lord walks before you, but your life is still in danger. Be careful, Sam."

As he struggled for words, he watched as the priest opened the front door and disappeared inside.

****

Thomas entered the massive front foyer, then closed the front door behind him, and all of the morning's cheerful sunlight disappeared when the door closed. The huge windows high up on the walls could have easily just been pictures. No sunlight dared enter through them. The mansion had become a dark and cold tomb. He thought of Avery and Bentley and how they were coping. He would worry about that later. Best was waiting for him. He could feel it in every nerve in his body. Danger swirled around him like a windstorm. He reached under his jacket and wrapped his hand around the crucifix that hung from his neck and down the front of his black shirt. He drew the cross towards his mouth, then kissed it before he prayed: "Lord God, let your power and mercy continue to guide your humble servant as I confront the evil that lies in wait. I am not afraid Lord, for You are next to me. Your strength, Lord, strengthens me. Light the path to our enemy. I am ready. Amen."

Then a familiar voice cut through his prayers; it was Chloë: "You are not welcome here priest! Your prayers for His protection are not heard in here, stupid priest!"

Thomas whirled around in the direction of Chloë's voice, but there was no one there. Then her laughter came from behind him, startling him. He turned quickly towards her laughter, but again he was met with nothing but blank walls. He called out: "Do not be afraid, Chloë. I am not here to hurt you only to help you." An unseen blow struck him across the left side of his head, sending him flying against the front door as the bolts of pain shot through his brain and he struggled to remain conscious. He looked up and could now see Chloë approach him from out of nowhere. She was radiant in her beauty. Her long blond hair fell evenly down both sides of her chest. She was dressed casually in jeans and a t-shirt. She looked like the beautiful young teenager that she was.

"Chloë, you are safe...." She cut him off again as she snapped out her foot and connected with his chin. The pain brought blackness, but he shook it off and blinked his eyes till they came back into focus except that he wished he hadn't. Chloë now towered over him, her young body completely naked and she laughed uncontrollably as she screamed: "Oh come on Father, don't look so horrified. You've wanted to see me naked. What do you think, priest? You like what you see?"

He reached his hand up in front of his eyes, shielding them from her nakedness then cried out: "Chloë, please. Stop it. Don't do this to yourself."

"Silence you old fool! Don't lecture me you pathetic prick!"

Her leg arced into a roundhouse and her foot slammed into his rib cage, where the air from his lungs escaped like that in a balloon no longer tied shut. He gasped, desperately trying to suck air into his lungs. He waited for the next blow to come, but strangely it did not. Instead there was nothing but silence. He opened his eyes and she was gone. He called out to her: "Chloë, where are you? Come back. We must talk." Her laughter shook through the walls all around the front foyer. Then silence again. He struggled to stand, his head throbbed, but at least his ribs were not broken. He could feel the presence of Best all around him, mocking him. Something inside of him told him to walk down the hallway to his right. He followed the feeling that propelled him forward. The hallway quickly led into the huge, but empty kitchen. He continued through the kitchen, into the beautifully decorated dining room with a table that could sit at least twenty people. At the back of the dining room were two glass French doors which led outside onto a balcony. He made his way to the doors, hesitated slightly, then opened them and stepped out into the warm air, the breeze from the ocean carrying the scent of the sea to his nostrils. The balcony was long, encompassing the full width of the back of the mansion. Thomas stepped towards the railing and looked out into the massive backyard with its beautifully trimmed bushes, trees and a swimming pool so big its blue water seemed to meld into the white capped waters of the ocean lapping within feet of it. The hypnotic beauty of the landscape was quickly replaced with an overwhelming sense of doom and grave danger. He looked up and out into the waters of the ocean from where the feeling of danger emanated.

Then he saw him.

Robert Best, the Anti-Christ, stood as a man, naked in water up to his waist, five hundred feet from the back of the property. He was staring at him. His red eyes burned like two torches, the hatred spilled off of him like the water that lapped against his body. Fear pulsated through the priest's body and he struggled to maintain his composure. The sight of him out there in the ocean, immobile, was frightening. It was like Best was studying him. Thomas never took his eyes off of him. He began to pray but continued to stare at him as he did so. Thomas noticed Best began to stir and then moved. He kept praying. Best began to slowly move backwards, further out into the ocean. The prayers to his God intensified and he was amazed to see Best continue to move further out into the ocean. The water was up to his shoulders now, but his eyes continued to burn a deep and menacing red.

Thomas was surprised as he realized he was now shouting: "The Lord God Almighty, His love and mercy conquers all that is evil. His mighty sword will cut your darkened soul to shreds, evil one. Your plan will fail. May the power of Thy Lord protect the children of Vasallus, to shield them from your wickedness."

He was stunned as he watched Best, now fully submerged in the ocean water, as his burning eyes disappeared like flickering candles. Thomas closed his eyes, finally, giving thanks to his Father, the realization that God had stood down the beast, resonated through him, filling him with an overpowering feeling of gratitude.

****

Best watched the priest step out onto the balcony from the dining room. The old fool had changed physically, he barely resembled the broken old man he had confronted at LAX airport. His eyes? They shone like blue lanterns. So it was him whom He had chosen to lead this fight! It was the priest who swung His sword that almost broke down the front door of the mansion as he was about to crush Chloë! This realization hit him as if the old man threw a bolt of lightning like a javelin from the balcony, across the water and into his chest.

He knew the priest was empowered by Him, but he never thought he was the one who had been chosen to lead His resistance. He was praying! The words cut into his dark soul like daggers. He needed to get away from the priest! As he descended into the cold water of the Pacific, he knew that time was now measured. He was moving quicker than he anticipated He would. He could move as quickly as He wanted. He was ready for Him, he has been ready for this for centuries. His defeat in Armenia so long ago would be revenged. His beloved man would be destroyed, each soul turned black and away from Him, sealing His defeat.

The ocean water enveloped him as he disappeared out of sight, the words of prayer from the priest gone from his tinged ears.

****

"Sam, I know you think Best is crazy and dangerous, trust me, we do as well. But we will not abandon these kids, no matter what you say. Right now we are all they have other than that maniac." Avery argued defiantly.

Bentley, without allowing Sam to respond to Avery, continued: "You come here this morning Sam, with stories of Best being the devil and he is out to destroy mankind and is using Vasallus to accomplish his goal, but we have heard that story before Sam. Father O'Sullivan warned us of him, coming to our hotel in Denver during a concert stop. He's out there globetrotting the world, trying to save mankind from Satan. Well, we're here right now, Sam. It's Avery and I as far as I can see that are watching out for these kids. Where are their parents? Where are the police, Sam? Why haven't you and the LAPD locked up Best? It's because he hasn't done anything that you can prove?"

Sam cut her off: "Bentley, I know you both are skeptical of all of this, but please listen to me."

Avery, his anger clearly rising, spoke next: "Sam, I suggest you continue to investigate Best and I hope you come up with something fast, but in the meantime, these kids are going on tour whether we like it or not and we plan on being by their side every minute to make sure they are safe."

"Like you were by Elizabeth's side?"

Avery exploded like he had been launched from a rocket. He slammed into a much taller, but lighter Sam as if he was a pylon. The two of them landed on the other side of Avery's desk, as papers flew in the air like confetti.

"How dare you say that, you son-of-a-bitch!" Avery brought his fist down, hitting Sam flush against his cheek, where the skin instantly split open and the blood quickly followed. Sam reacted by using his agile body to buck Avery off and roll on top of him. Bentley's scream pierced the air: "Stop it! This is crazy!"

Sam had his long fingers wrapped around Avery's throat when he looked down at him and yelled: "What happened to her Johnson! Where is Elizabeth?"

"Fuck you asshole. Get your hands off of me!"

"Sam, get off of him. Now!" It was Father O'Sullivan. His booming voice caught everyone off guard. Sam grudgingly stepped off of Avery before saying to him: "You're lucky I didn't shoot you."

"Oh yea and you're lucky I didn't drive your head through that wall and leave you stuck there."

Bentley stepped in between them, looked at Sam, and said: "Do you really think we had something to do with Elizabeth's decision to leave Vasallus and the mansion?"

Sam was about to comment when he was interrupted by Father O'Sullivan: "Sam we must leave at once. Avery, Bentley, I'm sorry we must rush out of here, but I must go."

Avery looked at Father O'Sullivan, stunned by his change in appearance and protested: "Please stay, Father. There is much we need to talk about."

Thomas stepped out of the doorway and into the room and replied: "I agree Avery. There is much to discuss and a lot for you to know. Now, unfortunately, is not the time. I must leave for Rome at once. My apologies to you both, now Sam, if you will, we must leave."

Bentley, struggling with the physical changes in Father O'Sullivan since she seen him last, stepped in front of Thomas as he turned to walk out of the office and asked: "Father, you are bleeding. You have changed. What is going on Father? What has Best done to Elizabeth?"

Thomas hesitated before replying, gazed into her eyes, then said: "So many questions that need answering, but not now. I must go, my dear. Keep a watchful eye over the kids as they embark on their world tour. I will come and visit you both somewhere on the tour. You and Avery are under no danger from Best. You are more important to him now than you have ever been."

With that, he turned and walked swiftly out of the room with Sam following closely behind.

Chapter 7

The launch of the tour in Madrid, Spain had created a worldwide frenzy. The concert tickets were snapped up in record time, followed by rioting and mayhem from those disappointed fans who did not get tickets. The city of Berlin, Germany went berserk, as legions of young fans stormed the stadium ticket offices in search of tickets that were long since sold out. Riot police were dispatched to control the outbreaks of violence caused by the sold out shows. It was not the kind of press coverage *Music Talks* magazine and Bentley Paxton, as the journalist covering Vasallus full-time, wanted to start her press conference for the upcoming world tour. Bentley was in charge of overseeing the launch of the Vasallus world tour press conference at Alive Records with much-appreciated help from Jenn Steinert, Avery's one-time assistant, now the president of the studio. Alive Records had become the biggest and most successful recording studio in the country. More and more, established stars were bringing the management of their careers over to Alive Records after the incredible success of Vasallus and the press it had generated for Alive Records as well as for Robert Best's business, Blackstar Studios. Blackstar was accepting no new clients, as all its' resources were devoted to Vasallus.

Best wanted the magazine to sponsor the press conference and he wanted Bentley to oversee it. Not only would this press conference announce the opening of the tour in Madrid, Spain, Bentley and Avery would have to handle the sticky issue of revealing the news to the world of the departure of Elizabeth

Leroux from the band. Best would not even be attending the conference, which Bentley found strange, but not surprising. He let Avery and her manage almost all aspects of the band, their music and the tour. She was terrified of him so the less she saw of him, the better. The press conference was scheduled for 3:00 p.m. and she and Jenn were running off of their feet with final preparations. The two of them were pouring over more of the details when Jenn's assistant, Amber, stepped into the office to announce: "I am being overwhelmed with requests from Canadian press agencies for credentials to cover the conference. How do you want me to handle the Canadian press requests?"

Bentley shot right back: "I will not allow Elizabeth's quitting the band to dominate the press conference. Allow passes to the *Much Music* people and that's it. Anyone else is only there to report on the Leroux departure."

As Amber quickly departed, Bentley glanced at Jenn, slumped in her office chair and used her hands to pull her hair from her face. Her voice carried an edge to it when she said: "I'm sorry Jenn. It's been a crazy day. I just can't wait for it to end."

Bentley watched as Jenn sat on the corner of the desk, looked down at her with concern and asked: "What really happened to Elizabeth, Bentley? I simply can't imagine her just up and leaving the most successful group in music history so abruptly."

"Jenn, you've been in the music industry long enough to know that things can become too big, too overwhelming especially for someone as young and sheltered as Elizabeth. The enormity of their success, so quickly, was too much for her. I'm surprised some of the others didn't follow her. The eyes of the world, I mean, all eyes are upon them. Their music is changing the world, Jenn. They are making history and a few of us have to keep them and everything around them functioning flawlessly. Controlling the chaos is what Avery calls it."

Jenn continued: "Those kids are truly remarkable Bentley. They are so incredibly talented and mature for their ages it is spooky. The Benning kid is a different story, however. That kid is nasty. Is he getting any better?"

Bentley rose from Jenn's office chair, and walked towards the window that overlooked Santa Monica Boulevard, gathering her long, dark hair behind her head into a ponytail, tying it off with an elastic as she replied thoughtfully: "That's the craziest part Jenn. He has been a model kid lately. He seems to be going out of his way to be nice, not just to the other members of Vasallus, but to me and Avery as well. He has taken on a real leadership role within the band. He encourages them during rehearsals, yet doesn't scold them. He is the first one in the studio and the last one out and he even approached Avery in the studio when all the others had left and thanked him for all of the hard work he puts into Vasallus and into their success. It was a heartfelt moment that really moved Avery. The kid has really matured since the end of the North American Tour."

Jenn was truly surprised with the changes in Patrick and replied: "Wow that is great Bentley. That will make yours and Avery's lives a whole lot easier. Speaking of Avery, how are things between the two of you?"

Bentley's blushed at the question, not because she was embarrassed, but because the question made her feel so good: "Amazing, Jenn, I am incredibly happy. With his crazy world of managing his clients from the studio, and managing and producing Vasallus, he still never leaves me out, and instead always makes me a part of his life. You taking over the studio has certainly made his life more manageable Jenn, so thank you for that."

Jenn giggled: "You're crazy in love Bentley, it's written all over your face. I'm so happy for you."

Bentley giggled back and was about to reply when they were interrupted by Amber walking into the office: "Bentley, there is a reporter from the Canadian *Globe & Mail* newspaper who refuses to leave unless he has spoken with you. What would you like me to do?"

Gathering herself, she replied: "Tell him to get lost, if he doesn't have a press credential for the press conference, which he doesn't, then I'm sorry but he will have to leave."

Amber quickly responded: "I've already tried that Bentley, but he refuses to leave till he speaks with you."

"Then tell him to call my office next week to book an appointment."

There was another voice that broke through, the voice of a man who had just entered the office behind Amber: "Ms. Paxton, excuse me for the intrusion, my name is Donald Phillips from Canada's national newspaper, *The Globe & Mail*. I couldn't help overhearing you from outside the office. My paper is about to release a story on the disappearance of Elizabeth Leroux. A statement from you or Mr. Johnson, perhaps, would be in your best interests, don't you think?"

Bentley felt the blood begin to rise. She knew what this reporter was doing because she had done it many times herself. The veiled threat of misinformation headlining this story unless an official statement came from Vasallus management hung in the air. She looked at the man, dressed impeccably in a dark suit and yellow and navy striped tie and quickly made the decision that a controlled and limited statement would satisfy him. It would have to because he would get nothing else. There was nothing to really say other than exactly what had happened, Elizabeth left the band.

Bentley glanced at Jenn and then Amber before declaring: "Give me a few minutes, ladies, alone with this gentleman. Okay Mr. Phillips, like I said, I only have a few minutes. I have a pretty big event to get ready for in a few hours."

After Jenn and Amber left, Bentley asked: "What would you like to know that you don't already know?"

Phillips studied her for a few seconds before replying: "Ms. Paxton I'll get right to the point. My paper wants me to write this piece that there is suspected foul play involved in Elizabeth Leroux's disappearance. What do you have to say about that?"

She made no effort to mask her shock at the question: "That is outrageous Mr. Phillips, to even suggest foul play. Ms. Leroux left the band of her own free will and under her own power. It was her decision to leave. Remember, these are just kids and the pressures to perform and the fact is that they are under the microscope of the world. It can be too much for a seasoned adult, much less a sheltered child."

His look unnerved her as his eyes bore into hers when he asked: "How would you know? I understand that you and Avery were not even present in the mansion where all of you work and live when she disappeared. You assume she returned to Canada, but for all you know she could be floating under some pier on the expansive beaches behind the mansion, correct?"

Bentley's mind raced, panic hit her in the chest as her mind tried to decipher how this Canadian reporter would have known that she and Avery were away the week that Elizabeth disappeared. Who leaked this information? Daniel from the office? One of the kids? Jenn? It was not likely to be any of them. Then it hit her. It had to be Amber. She knew more about the day to day happenings of Vasallus than anyone else except for her and Avery. She ran the office at the mansion three days a week and five days a week when the kids weren't on tour.

"That's preposterous Phillips and you know it. You're fishing for a story to print and the more sensational it is, the better. Now if you don't mind, I must get ready for the press conference." She stood up from the desk and the reporter followed suit.

He looked at her and shot back: "The press conference we are not invited to? You can brush me off Ms. Paxton, but I will need an official statement from Mr. Johnson by the end of tomorrow. You or Avery have no clue what happened to Elizabeth do you? Canadian authorities are looking into the disappearance and it won't be long before it turns into a criminal investigation. There has been no sign of Elizabeth Leroux in Canada. No one knows where she is, including you and Johnson and this Robert Best. He is the next person I will try and get a statement from. Hopefully, he will see it the way you should have and that is to start telling the truth. Have a nice day Ms. Paxton. Good luck at the press conference."

Bentley almost missed the chair as she collapsed down into it after the door slammed behind the reporter.

****

The highly anticipated press conference was by invitation only and would be dominated by foreign agencies, especially those whose cities would be hosting a concert. There were no Canadian agencies invited and Bentley chose to spare Avery the news of her visit by the reporter from *The Globe and Mail* until after the press conference. Everything was moving far too fast and within a few minutes it would be a madhouse. She pulled Avery to the side to speak with him alone, away from everyone else. The look of worry on her face was obvious and he immediately addressed it: "Sweetheart, you look completely stressed out. The press conference is about to begin and you need to stop worrying and prepare yourself as a journalist because the first question is coming to you."

She fought back the tears, as the events of Detective Showenstein and Father O'Sullivan's strange visit to the mansion and now the accusations from the Canadian reporter had her on the edge. "I'll be okay Avery. It's been a hectic day. How about the kids, how are they feeling? Are you sure they're ready for this? To go back on tour?"

He placed both of his large hands on her shoulders and gave them a slight squeeze before reassuring her: "Honey, everything will be okay. You and Jenn have done a marvelous job of preparing for the press conference. Everything is ready; the journalists are chomping at the bit for it to begin. The kids are here and they are incredibly calm and excited all at once. They will be fine and so will you."

"How will you handle all of the questions regarding the departure of Elizabeth?"

"Just like we discussed. I will give a brief statement, take a few questions so it seems like we are not hiding anything from them and then move on to their other questions. It won't be that much of a shock to them anyway. The rumors have been flying around for weeks now that someone, even Elizabeth, has departed. Today will be more of a confirmation than a reveal. So why don't you go take your seat and I'll give Jenn the go ahead to get started."

****

The press conference was set up in a large dining tent in the rear parking lot of the studio, so that it was shielded from the traffic on the busy Santa Monica Boulevard. The theme of the press conference was the new album and tour, *Next Step.* The album's colourful artwork adorned just about every surface in and around the tent. The assistants working the event all wore t-shirts with the light blue dominant colour of the album cover and the words *Next Step* emblazoned on the front and back. The building and parking lot itself were private with large trimmed bushes surrounding the building and lot, making privacy attainable. To be completely sure, Avery had installed a ten foot high security fence around the parking lot. He also had security set up all around the perimeter of the building to ensure privacy and to keep the paparazzi at a distance. Since the end of the North American tour last month, the Vasallus fan base was growing at a feverish pace and the demand for concert tickets at the first announced European tour stop in Madrid was overwhelming and chaotic. The show was sold out in minutes in an online sale causing accusations of ticket fixing by legions of disappointed fans that resulted in widespread violence. The city of Madrid insisted on Vasallus footing the bill for beefed up security for the concert, otherwise city officials would pull the plug. The cost would take a big bite out of the profits, but it didn't seem to matter to Best when Avery discussed it with him. He made it clear that the concerts would go forward no matter what the cost and it was Avery's responsibility to make sure that happened.

Record sales of Vasallus' first album, *New Beginnings,* continued to be number one on the Billboard Top 100 and merchandise sales were even more impressive. The recent release of *Next Step* set records for iTunes downloads and CD sales around the world. What had happened was astounding and he knew he was in the middle of something much bigger than being the manager of the most popular band in the world. As he stepped towards the podium to address the gathered feeding frenzy of the press, he stole a glance at Bentley. Her reassuring smile did not mask the worried look in her eyes. Something was bothering her, he could see it in her and he thought about stepping away from the podium for a second to have a word with her, but he knew that would be foolish. It would single her out in front of her peers and that would not be fair to her. It was no secret they were a couple and it was awkward enough when he sent the first question to her. She had insisted that he not give her the first question, but he reminded her that her employer, *Music Talks* magazine, the widest circulated music magazine in the world, was a major sponsor of the tour and they insisted on the first question, plus it kept her firmly planted at the mansion covering the group full time.

Dressed in his usual black suit and white dress shirt without a tie, he approached the podium to begin the press conference and the cameras began to snap, the flashes piercing the afternoon sun streaming into the tent. He collected himself and was about to speak when he caught a glimpse of a man moving quickly behind a row of reporters in the back. The man, he swore, looked exactly like Robert Best. That was impossible because Avery had just briefed him not more than an hour ago when he stepped out of a meeting with concert officials in Berlin, an upcoming tour stop. He had to have been mistaken, but it rattled him and he would keep an eye on that corner of the room. He made eye contact with Bentley and she saw the alarm on his face. He diffused her alarm by beginning the conference.

"Ladies and gentlemen, thank you for being here today for this great announcement about a band that has taken the world by storm. As all of you can remember, it wasn't that many months ago that we gathered to announce to America and to the rest of the world the formation of superstar band Vasallus and the kick-off of their North American tour. No one in their wildest dreams could have imagined the incredible response by fans around the world to these kids and their music. They are truly special people, blessed with exceptional God given talent..."

There was a commotion at the back of the tent which temporarily cut off Avery as people reacted by turning towards the noise. He caught a second glimpse of Best and he was certain of it this time. He seemed to move like mist amongst the throng of people gathered in that corner. Best was watching him. He could not only catch glimpses of him, but he could also feel his presence. It was evil and it began to permeate the tent. He continued.

"Their talent, combined with their maturity as young people have truly made them superstars and I am honoured to have the opportunity to work with them and to guide them as the glare of the world spotlight beams down on them ever brighter. Their fishbowl gets smaller every day and it is my job to keep them focused and to remind them that they are having fun. The crazy thing is that these kids are having the time of their lives. They give of themselves to their fans and to the media always and they never say no. If it wasn't for me moving them along, they'd still be at the Staples Center where it all began, signing autographs. We are gathered here today to announce the launch of the European tour beginning in Madrid, Spain and the release of the band's second album, *Next Step*. So please if you will, help me welcome, Vasallus!"

The music to their newly released single from *Next Step*, "All Abound", filled the press conference with the upbeat tempo of the song. Everyone stood up as the kids made their entrance into the party tent and took their places at the head table. Camera flashes went off like strobe lights. The kids just smiled and giggled into the cameras. *Much Music* television cameras swirled around the kids like robots. Avery looked down the table at them and marveled at their beauty, style and grace considering all that was going on around them. Chloë looked incredible, her long blond hair filled with wavy curls and highlights, approached the head table first, followed by an equally stunning Brittany. The girls were world class models in how they looked and carried themselves. The two girls were quickly followed by the three boys, Connor, Juan and Patrick. Their arrival elicited a few gasps from some of the female journalists in the crowd. Their astonishing good looks made girls around the world literally faint in their presence and the women in the audience did not hide their delight at their entrance. The three of them waved or nodded their heads to the throng of cameras raining down on them, their flashes blinding. They each had a microphone stand and a water bottle placed on the table in front of them as they readied themselves for the conference.

As the absence of Elizabeth soon began to circulate through the mob, Avery stepped back up to the microphone and continued: "As you can see there is one member of Vasallus missing. Elizabeth Leroux has decided to leave the group and return to Canada for personal reasons. This is the only statement I will make in regards to Ms. Leroux and I will not accept any further questions on this matter at the conclusion of the press conference."

He paused and allowed the shock of this announcement sink in for a few more seconds before he continued: "Thank you and now I would like to introduce to you, Vasallus' follow-up album to *New Beginnings*, aptly named, *Next Step* and the launch of their European tour, *Next Step!*"

A large video screen rose from behind the head table to the top of the tent. The first single, "All Abound", already hitting number one on all of the charts, filled the tent with its upbeat tempo. The video started with shots of the kids on stage performing from the North American tour. It was extremely well done and captured each of the kids in some truly great shots from the tour. The video was exciting and before it broke into the promo for the tour, it paused and Avery stepped back up to the microphone, "The impact on the music scene Vasallus has made here in America has been unprecedented. Now the rest of the world will get the opportunity to see them live with the *Next Step* tour."

Avery stepped back from the podium once again and the video continued with the promo on the *Next Step* tour. The video highlighted each of the cities included in the tour in turn with cutbacks to clips of the kids attempting to speak the language of that city. It was all great fun and the gathered press loved every second of it. It had the effect Avery was hoping for. He needed to take the focus off of Elizabeth and it was working. But not for long.

"Thank you ladies and gentlemen. Please help yourself to an official tour t-shirt and a copy of the *Next Step* CD on your way out at the conclusion of the press conference. Now I am going to open the floor to some questions. Please, one question only per journalist. Ms. Paxton, you have a question?"

Without hesitation, amidst some muted grumbling from the other journalists seated around her, Bentley rose from her chair in the front row, received the microphone from the outstretched hand of the assistant and focused on Patrick before asking: "Patrick, you are the unofficial leader of the group, please tell me and my publication the events and reasons surrounding the departure of Elizabeth Leroux from the band."

The question sent off a ripple of whispers throughout the crowd. A shocked Avery gathered himself and leaned back into the microphone and declared: "Thank you Ms. Paxton, as I said earlier I will not accept any..."

He was cut-off by Patrick who spoke in a controlled, but quiet voice: "That's okay Mr. Johnson. I would like to answer the question if you don't mind."

Avery struggled to maintain his composure. Why did she ask that question? Of all people, she should have known better. Now Patrick put him on the spot. He really had no choice but to allow him to answer it. "Go ahead Patrick. This will be the last question asked regarding Ms. Leroux. Any further questions will result in the press conference ending without any further comments."

He watched as Patrick smiled at Bentley before beginning. The smug bastard was enjoying this and if he dared say anything out of line, he would shut him down. Damn, this was not what he wanted to happen.

"Ms. Paxton, none of us in the band have a sibling. Each of us is from a one-child family. Coming together like we have in this band has made us closer than brothers and sisters. We are all each other's best friend. When Elizabeth decided that she wanted to return to her life back home, we were disappointed, but we supported her decision. She was a very talented singer and musician and we will miss her both in the band and as a friend, but life goes on, we have a new album and the rest of us are very excited about the new music and about going back on tour."

"Wow, where did that sincerity come from?" Avery thought. He couldn't help but notice how he referred to Elizabeth in the past tense. He watched as Bentley thanked Patrick for answering the question and made brief eye contact with him before she sat down. They would talk about this later. He needed to move on.

He pointed to Bill Shaunessey from Dublin's daily newspaper, *The Irish Independent* and watched as Bill stood and asked: "Thank you, Avery. My question is for Chloë. You look beautiful by the way, Chloë. On behalf of your legions of fans back home in Ireland, my question is, will your role with Vasallus increase with the absence of Elizabeth?"

Chloë blushed slightly from the compliment, giggled, then replied: "Please let all my fans know back home, that I think of them often and look forward to our performance in Dublin during the upcoming tour. The new album blends the voices of Brittany and me along with the voices of the boys resulting in beautiful harmonies that I'm sure everyone will enjoy immensely. Elizabeth's magnificent voice will be missed, but I'm very excited about the new songs."

Avery pointed at the very beautiful Aurea Rocio, from Madrid's daily newspaper, *The ABC*, for the next question. In broken English she asked: "Madrid is thrilled to host the opening concert of the Vasallus tour. It will be the first concert ever held in Santiago Bernabeu Stadium with close to 100,000 fans in attendance. Our beloved football team, Real Madrid is praying there will be a stadium left after the concert." After a few chuckles she continued: "Your popularity is so high in my country and all over Europe, the violence that surrounded ticket sales to the concert was unprecedented. I know it is not the fault of the band that there was violence, but let me ask you. How does it make you feel that thousands of people are literally beating each other to death to get a chance to see you live?"

Juan, his sleeveless shirt showcased his newly tattooed muscular biceps, took the question after glancing down the table at the rest of the group and replied: "Ms. Rocio, let me answer the question by saying on behalf of Vasallus, we vehemently condemn the violence and wish to offer our heartfelt condolences to the people and families of Madrid who have been affected by the criminal acts of a few dozen thugs bent on promoting rioting that is resulting in the violence. All of us plan to visit as many of the injured as we can while in Madrid to let them know we care." Looking at the others once again, Juan finished by saying: "If it was up to us, we would perform every single night until every last one of our fans in Madrid and Spain had a chance to see us perform."

The next question was given to the *London Times* Music Scene writer, the flamboyantly famous, Derek Stryper. He thanked Avery then asked, of course, Michael: "Your popularity Michael in England is reaching cult-like status yet you somehow continue to deal with it in such a laid back, aw shucks kind of way. Does the enormous popularity of being in the most popular band in the world ever become too much for you? How do you handle the fishbowl Michael?"

Dressed in his trademark jeans, t-shirt and a hoodie, Michael stood out from the rest of the group if anything, because of his simplicity. His dark hair was now longer, but not long enough to hide his good looks. He came across like he didn't take himself too seriously and it was confirmed when he spoke: "I am thankful to my fans back home and everywhere else. To answer your question Mr. Stryper, I try to stay focused on the music and on being the best musician that I can be. I cannot control how I am perceived; I just try to keep things in perspective. Mr. Johnson has taught me a lot about myself and about how to keep myself focused."

Avery was moved by Michael's comment as he stepped back up to the podium. The press conference moved along with more questions for the band, for him, most of them centered around the violence surrounding ticket sales, but it was time to bring it to an end. It was a weird afternoon; the strange appearance of Best still unnerved him as did Bentley's first question. He gave the last question to an American reporter, *Rolling Stone* magazine's Ted Lisko, a veteran warhorse in the music industry, his aging and grey haired body only reflected the respect he still commanded in the industry. He had seen it all in this business; from the one hit wonders to the legends and Avery anticipated some sharp comments towards Vasallus, but Lisko surprised him.

"Boy and girl bands come and go, leave a few memories and are never heard from again. Vasallus is not only producing great music that I believe will stand the test of time for future generations to enjoy, but your live performances are some of the best I have ever seen. I congratulate Avery Johnson and Robert Best for a tremendous job in managing and producing these wonderfully talented kids. Your maturity and talent belies your age and I commend you for staying grounded and true to your music. I have seen fame crush more careers over the years I have been in this business than you could imagine. So please, as a big fan of Vasallus, don't let the fame define who you are. God has given all of you special talents, reward Him with your continuing commitment and dedication to your craft. The pursuit of fame is the work of the devil. Stay focused."

What should have been a question turned into a speech by Lisko. His words of encouragement were an unexpected ring of endorsement from not only a veteran and respected journalist, but also from his employer, *Rolling Stone* magazine. The fact that their chief rival for subscribers, *Music Talks* had the exclusive deal to tour and follow the band's every movement should have given Lisko the opportunity to shred Vasallus but instead, he enthusiastically embraced them.

****

Three hours after the press conference ended, Bentley and Avery left together for the mansion. After they closed the doors to Avery's BMW and pulled into the early Saturday evening traffic, it was the first time they were both alone and not surrounded by assistants. The tension between the two of them was immediate and Bentley knew he was pissed at her question at the press conference. She decided to put it out there rather than drive along in silence: "I'm sorry Avery, but I had to ask the question."

He looked at her; a flash of anger crossed his face: "Of all the people to not ask that question would be you. The very first question of the press conference asked after I just informed everyone that I would not accept any questions regarding Elizabeth. Why Bentley?"

She paused for a second longer than she should have before replying: "After your explanation Avery, the elephant in the room never left and it was a matter of time before someone asked the question so I felt I might as well address it right up front. I'm sorry I took you off guard. It wasn't my intention to put you on the spot."

She watched as he relaxed somewhat with her explanation: "I guess you're right. It would have come up again and I guess I'm glad it came from you. I was pleasantly surprised by Patrick's response to the question. I was expecting something more mean-spirited from him."

"So was I. We often talk about how much the kids are maturing, but maybe Patrick seems to be changing the most. He is really stepping up as the leader of the group in a good way. They are leaning on him more and more."

He smiled at her, reached out and took her hand in his as he drove, then replied: "Did you notice the look on their faces, however, when Lisko talked about their God given talents? It almost seemed to displease them when they heard that."

"I did see that. It was just a flash of emotion, but I caught it. Very strange. What did you think of it?"

"I don't know what to think." He paused for a few seconds

before he continued: "I wasn't even going to mention it to you because I thought it would just scare you, but in the beginning of the press conference do you remember the commotion in the back of the room?"

"Yes I do, what was that all about?"

"I saw Best at the back of the room. It was a very sinister feeling. He was there, but he wasn't. I cannot be one hundred percent sure I saw him, but if I didn't see him, I certainly felt him. It was the most overwhelming feeling of dread and evil I have ever experienced. The strangest thing was it happened right after I mentioned the God given talents of Vasallus. I shook off the thought of seeing Best as my imagination, but it took me a good part of that press conference to shake the feeling of evil that it gave me."

"That is awful Avery. I wish Father O'Sullivan was here. There are so many strange events going on, we could sure use his wisdom right about now."

****

Ted Lisko pulled his Lexus sedan into his driveway, a comfortable home in the Modesto neighborhood of Los Angeles, thankful that a lot of these press junkets were local for him with the exception of the occasional trip to New York to cover an event. He was tired and thought once again about walking away from a business he had dearly loved for almost sixty years. The kids of Vasallus were special; he felt it with every fibre in his old body. He just hoped he would live long enough to see how big they would become. Their music would change the world. He knew that for certain.

A bachelor for the last fifteen years after the passing of his wife for over forty years, he pulled himself out of his car, closed the garage door as he did so and made his way into the house. He threw his keys on the kitchen counter as he began to undo his tie and head to the bedroom to take a hot shower. These events got harder and harder. When he heard the voice, it damn near gave him a heart attack. When he saw who it was, his heart did indeed begin to squeeze inwardly.

The blazing red eyes of Patrick Benning sitting on the leather recliner in his living room scared him to the core; it was so unexpected; he struggled to find his breath. The boy was nothing like the charming kid he had just witnessed at the press conference. He was evil. Pure evil. He would die here in his home, either by the heart attack or from this creature.

In mere seconds, the Benning kid transformed himself into a hideous and monstrous entity. It flew out of the chair with incredible speed, its talon-like claws slammed into his chest and through his already dying heart. He felt the back of his head crack as the force of the blow sent the two of them into the wall. He felt his own blood erupt from his mouth like vomit. The burning red eyes of the creature from Hell bore into his and before his own eyes closed for the final time, he heard the beast scream out: "This is for thinking my talent was given to me by God. Die you old fool knowing the world you are leaving will never be the same. The Prince of Darkness, my God, will destroy it."

As the final seconds of his life ebbed from his soul, Ted Lisko, the respected journalist from *Rolling Stone* magazine, took one final sound with him into his next life. The roaring and evil laughter of the beast echoed inside of his brain as the blackness of this life ending settled in.

Chapter 8

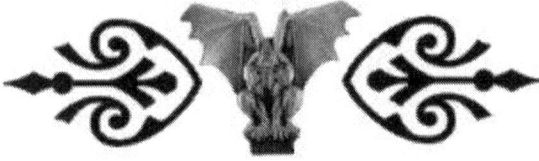

Aanaleeb Varma was fourteen years old and showed signs of academic genius to the point where his father Raakin agreed to send him to a private school for the super smart in a district in North Delhi .. The school was run by the Government of India and was so secret that the parents of the children were not even allowed to visit. It was only recently that the West even knew about this secret school. A suicide by one of the students brought the cameras and notepads of a "60 Minutes" film crew from the United States prying into the super-secret facility suspected of housing a collection of the highest I.Q.'s in children in the world. The "60 Minutes" investigators were given a token tour of a meaningless portion of the school to satisfy their story and fed enough information to keep the journalists happy rather than the school administrators refusing to cooperate and thereby further inviting curiosity seekers and the prying eyes of the world.

In truth, the Muslim school was indeed a collection of the brightest young minds in India. What the outside world wasn't aware of however, was that the several hundred kids housed in the school were being forced to write complex computer algorithms, sixteen hours a day, to be used in a program that would be planted into computer systems in the United States that run the military, transportation, banking and utilities to name a few. The school, completely funded by Islamist extremists, was created solely for the total destruction of the United States of America by bringing the government and its people to their knees by controlling the systems that were the lifeblood of their way of life. When launched, it would make the events of 911 and its aftermath look like child's play.

Aanaleeb and the other students knew nothing of this and were only told that their hard work would allow their impoverished country to leapfrog their economy from third world status to the superpower level. It was extremely important work and they and their families would be richly rewarded for their commitment and diligence.

It was Tuesday and it was Aanaleeb's day off, the only one of the week. He was expected to spend the day exercising and participating in team sports in the school's massive gymnasium complex. After six long and grueling days in front of a computer writing computer code, the day of physical activity was eagerly anticipated. He especially looked forward to the game of basketball this afternoon after a morning of group fitness classes. In the cramped dormitory, he stretched in his tiny bed which barely contained his growing body.. He checked his bedside clock to confirm that he had lots of time. It was 5:45 a.m., still plenty of time to report for breakfast. His roommate snoozed soundly above him in his bunk.

He rose from bed only to be suddenly thrown to the floor. He tried to rise from the floor, but the dorm room was shaking so badly it made standing almost impossible. He heard the thud of his roommate hitting the concrete floor beside him. The impact knocked him out cold. "What is happening?" he thought to himself. He navigated on all fours to the tiny window on the far wall. It seemed like an eternity had passed by the time he finally was able to make it to the window. He began to hear screams from outside his room. The building was shaking so badly that cracks in the walls split open, just a few at first, but then all the walls began to break apart. He needed to get out of his room! He reached up to the window sill and pulled himself up. When he looked outside he knew that making it out into the hallway and out of the building was impossible. The entire building was about to collapse any second. As far as his eyes could see, buildings had either collapsed or were in the process of crumbling to the ground.

Then what he saw next looked like a scene from an American movie. The street in front of the school opened up like a large crevice, sucking all the buildings in the street into it.

He felt the floor beneath him begin to lean forward and then, like a trap door in a theme park ride, the floor disappeared beneath him and he felt himself falling. A second before his head bounced off a severed concrete barrier three floors below his dormitory room, he prayed to Allah, thanking him for how great and loving he was.

****

The devastating earthquake which hit northern India had its epicenter in the fourth most populated city on earth, New Delhi. For that reason, it was catastrophic. The severity of the earthquake was charted with a magnitude of 9.7, which made it the highest recorded earthquake in history. Damage was total and the loss of life during the first day of reporting was in the thousands. By day two, casualty numbers climbed to tens of thousands. By the fourth day after the quake, emergency crews began to reach the most severely hit areas and estimates were reported that put the death toll into the millions, a staggering amount that stunned the world. The aftershocks were felt as far away as Iran, China and Vietnam. Damage to the towns and villages surrounding New Delhi was equally deadly. The world's superpowers moved quickly, sending in aid and supplies to the survivors as well as the military in huge numbers to assist in the search for dead bodies and the injured. The largest humanitarian effort in history was mobilized and the United Nations called for all countries to assist with troops, food, water, medical supplies, logistics or money. Chaos ruled everywhere in New Delhi as the carnage was so widespread and survivors scrambled to get away, fearing follow-up quakes and the raging fires that were still burning everywhere.

****

Safe in his luxurious New York office, Robert Best leaned back in his leather chair as he continued to watch the news coverage of the earthquake in India. He was expecting something big to happen and when it did he was just glad it happened in that part of the world, far away from here and far away from the cities on the upcoming Vasallus tour. He would delay the launch of the tour by two weeks to allow the appropriate time for the world to get over the shock. He could care less about the Indian people and the earthquake, but rather than risk local governments stopping the concerts due to the crisis, he would give it some time. He would instruct Avery that all profits from the tour, and it would be in the millions, would go to a special relief fund he would create and control for the survivors of the quake. He didn't need the money nor did the kids. This had nothing to do with mere money. This enormous gesture of giving to the survivors by Vasallus would eliminate any and all resistance that the tour was -creating because of the violence it generated.

He knew that the earthquake was a signal by God that the time was near for the end of this life and the start of the new Kingdom as was written. There would be more disasters as His fury built and they would come more frequently and they would be even more deadly than the recent earthquake. When one plate meets another plate in the earth's core, it causes a shift on the adjoining plate, creating an earthquake. The scientists who study these phenomena all agree that the science is correct, but they are wrong. What appears to be a natural disaster caused by the earth's awkward movements is nothing but an act of God. Man's belief that natural disasters happen by chance or can be explained by scientific theories or as a series of events leading up to the disaster have it all wrong. It is He that creates these events and it is He who will continue to unleash them in order to reduce this planet to rubble and destroy men who choose not to believe in Him. Mankind was in for a rough ride in the years ahead and he couldn't be happier. The end was near for them and he predicted that it would be in months and not years.

As he leaned further back in his chair, relaxing his physical body even more, he allowed his spirit to swirl around the carnage in New Delhi, feeling the increased levels of misery, suffering and pain that were everywhere. He soaked his spirit and then bathed it in the anguish that existed. He made sure that if a pocket of hope popped up in the chaos, he would quickly douse it with even more pain and suffering. He was adding copious amounts of salt to open wounds that had been created by God. He thought to himself: "When God takes mankind to its knees for repentance, I will kick them till they fall to their backs in total defeat."

His plan would soon reach a new level and everything was going exactly as he had schemed. The immense popularity of Vasallus around the world was predictable, but it was still sweet to see it unfold. The roles of Avery Johnson and Bentley Paxton would soon come to an end. He didn't need them for much longer and neither did the kids. By the end of the European tour, the world would look significantly different.

As he slammed his office door closed and walked past the receptionist on his way to the tower elevators, then out of the office and into the New York afternoon, his chuckles had turned into a full- out laugh fest, drawing stares from onlookers on the busy Manhattan sidewalk. He didn't care. They would all be dead soon anyway. That thought caused him to laugh even harder.

****

The conversation between them was as it usually was, to the point, business only and nothing more. Best's decision to give all of the proceeds to Indian relief was an incredible commitment and he lauded him for that, but something just kept bugging him after he hung up the phone. He knew that Best was up to something. He could have easily decided to donate the proceeds from the concert in Madrid or another city or even stage an India Aid Relief concert with all proceeds going to the relief fund. To donate the proceeds from the entire tour was a bit over the top.

The concert tour being pushed back by two weeks was giving Avery all kinds of fits. He spent the entire day on the phone either with Best or with concert promoters trying to rework the logistics to reschedule the concert dates for each of the stops. One thing was beginning to come clear. Best was no longer interested in profits.

He went from wanting to see monthly profit reports on album, concert ticket and merchandise sales to no longer requesting them, but when Avery brought it up with him, he would quickly dismiss it as unimportant. Concerts were sold out everywhere in minutes. Best was pushing him to add more concert dates and for him to rent recording studio time on days off between the shows to get the kids rehearsing songs for the third album. Avery's protests fell on deaf ears. Best was determined to run these kids into the ground. The question was why? If he wasn't interested in how much profit the band was generating, which was substantial, then why was he so possessed to push them so hard? He wondered if the chief financial backer of the band, Sherman Oakley, was with Best in all of this new direction. He had read that Oakley was driven by nothing but profit.

He walked down the hall into Amber's office, and requested: "Will you do something for me? I don't have any contact information, but can you try and track down a Sherman Oakley of Oakley Steel in London? Let whomever answers the phone know that Avery Johnson of Alive Records wishes to speak with him as soon as possible. Thanks Amber."

He returned to his office, picked up his phone and dialed Bentley. He thought of something he wanted to run by her. She had taken Brittany and Chloë out shopping for the day. The girls wanted to look for some new clothes for the tour and no one liked shopping more than Bentley. She answered on the third ring.

"Hi sweetheart! I heard my phone ringing, but it was buried somewhere in my purse and I couldn't find it. I'm so glad I did! How is your day going?"

He went on to explain the mountain of phone calls and organization involved to shift things around to accommodate the delay in the tour. Her excitement at having so much fun with the girls instantly lifted him out of his dark cloud.

"Let's have some fun tonight with the kids. Let's all dress really dorky or something, in disguise so no one will recognize them and head down to The Brass Monkey on Wilshire. They could use some fun. The tour is about to begin and the pressure cooker for them will be turned right up. Let them blow off some steam. What do you say?"

Bentley chuckled with excitement before replying: "Sorry, Avery, but if you could see these two girls right now you would pee your pants." Her chuckles turned to outright laughter.

"Honey, women pee their pants when they get excited, but men don't. Where are you?"

"We're at the Denim Bar; it's like a lounge that sells high fashion jeans and accessories. You get to lunch and shop at the same time. The girls are loving it! Brittany just pranced around the store in the most outrageous hat." She laughed some more. "I get to sip on fancy cocktails while the girls shop!"

"Okay, well I'm going to let you crazies go back to being crazy. I'm glad you're having so much fun. The girls needed it. Thank you for that. Think about tonight. Love you!"

He hung up the phone and was about to make another call when Amber knocked on his door: "Avery, Mr. Oakley is on line one. He seems very interested in talking with you. I don't mean to pry, but isn't Sherman Oakley Michael's grandfather?"

"Yes and he is a very rich grandfather. How did you get him on the line so quickly?"

"It was kind of strange, actually. When I called the main line for Oakley Steel, the line rang twice, there was a click and then it sounded like the phone was call forwarded. Mr. Sherman answered himself."

"That is strange. A billionaire of a multi-national company, having the company's main switchboard calls forwarded to his personal phone. Okay, thanks Amber, I'll take it from here."

"One more thing that seemed odd. When he answered the call, it was with no formal greeting and I had not yet said anything when he literally yelled into the phone."

He stared at her, waiting for her to finish, his left hand inches from snapping up the phone when she continued: "He said: 'Avery, I'm glad you called. You're in danger.' I informed him that I was Mr. Johnson's secretary looking for Mr. Sherman Oakley. He barked right back by stating, this is Sherman, put Johnson on the phone."

He thanked Amber again and hesitated until she had left his office and closed the door before he picked up the phone.

"Mr. Oakley, this is Avery Johnson. Thank you for taking my call. I..." He was interrupted by Oakley on the other end of the line before he could finish his last sentence.

"Avery, listen to me. Your life and the life of Ms. Paxton are in danger."

Now Avery interrupted: "What are you talking about? My life is in danger? I called you to discuss the financial commitment you made with Vasallus."

The voice on the other end of the line sounded scared and desperate: "Forget about my financial commitment. I could care less. I'm ruined anyway. He made sure of that. He will kill you. He will kill all of us."

"Sherman, get a hold of yourself. What are you talking about? Who are you talking about?"

"Best, you fool! He's destroyed my companies and now he will destroy all of you."

A cold fear zinged through Avery's body as he listened to Oakley. "Sherman, you are one of the most powerful businessmen in the world. How could Best ruin your companies?"

"Haven't you picked up a newspaper lately Johnson? Do you ever read the financial section? The demise of Oakley Steel has been all over the news in the last few months. It all started with one incident a few months ago on a new seventeen-story structure that was built in Moscow. Once occupation of the building occurred, the building collapsed. Stress tests of the steel beams showed that the steel was at fault and never should have passed code."

He remembered that incident. Several dozen people were killed in the collapse. "It's unfortunate, but those things can happen."

"No they do not. Not ever. Oakley Steel has never failed or been at fault in a construction project in the history of this company. That's not all of it. The result of the investigation pointed the blame directly at Oakley Steel and government officials in other parts of the world started scrutinizing other projects under construction using Oakley Steel. Guess what? Every single one of them failed to meet industry standard codes for stress tests on the integrity of the steel. Government inspectors have been all over my plants and smelters and have discovered enough evidence of poor construction using substandard raw materials that they have shut my plants down until their investigations have been completed."

"Jesus Sherman, that is crazy. How could you possibly link all of that to Best?"

"He told me he would do this. It has all happened exactly as he said it would. I visited him during the tour of Vasallus and demanded financial disclosure. I knew the band was making truckloads of money, but I didn't care about the money. It's not why I agreed to work with him. I didn't even really care about the exposure Oakley Steel was to have received as the main sponsor of the tour. Best took millions of my money and never even mentioned Oakley Steel on a press release, a poster, or a napkin for Christ's sakes."

"I'm sorry Sherman; I had no control over that side of the business. I had no idea."

"I knew that. Regardless of all of that, it's still not the reason I went and saw Best. I did all of this, Avery, for my grandson and for my daughter, Ann. I wanted them to be proud of me. I ruined my relationship with my daughter years ago and my grandson barely knows me. I thought that if I could help out his musical career with the only thing at my disposal, my money, then maybe they would see that I truly cared."

"I would think just sitting in a room with them and telling them how you felt about them, that you loved them, would have had more of an effect."

Oakley's voice dropped, Avery could sense the sadness in his voice as he listened: "My daughter despises me and would never be in the same room with me. I have been a terrible father to her over the years. With the death of her husband, I should have been there for her and I wasn't. In fact I pushed her away ruthlessly and for that I sealed my fate and closed the book on my relationship with my daughter."

"So why would Best want to ruin you financially by sabotaging your businesses? He would have known that you could have taken him to court and sued him for the profits Vasallus was earning. How could he possibly pull off the magnitude of the conspiracy to bring down Oakley Steel? He would need people, key people, on the inside to mess with the process that makes your steel. It is a stretch Sherman to think Best could have pulled this off?"

"He is an evil man Avery. I'm not talking about a nasty and cruel businessman. He is up to something and it is evil. I believe the band is a front. A smokescreen to mask his true intentions. We are living in dangerous times Avery. Be careful of him and watch over Bentley and the kids. Keep them safe from him."

"Sherman, I think you need to get a hold of yourself. I'm worried about you. Why don't you come to America? Stay at the mansion. I will talk with Ann and explain to her what you have told me. Maybe she will understand."

"Don't waste your time. That will never happen. You can tell her though when you see her that I cared. I did care about her and Michael. I loved them."

"Sherman, are you okay? You don't sound so good. Where are you?"

His voice had suddenly changed and it sent chills down his spine as he spoke: "Have you ever looked into his eyes, Avery? Have you seen the evil fire that burns in them? He is not human Avery. He is the devil and he is the destroyer. I must go. Be vigilant Avery."

He never had a chance to respond to this ominous warning, as the phone went dead.

He placed the phone back onto its cradle and leaned back in his chair and felt the nerves in his body pulsate with electricity. His mind went back to the day in the hotel room in Denver when he and Bentley were visited by Father O'Sullivan. He had warned them of who Best was and of what his intentions were.

He jumped from his office chair, sending it flying backwards into the wall and headed out of his office without saying a word to Amber as he rushed past her open door. He was headed to the Denim Bar.

As he pushed his BMW towards the freeway and out of the plush neighborhood of Malibu, he turned on his radio and was about to turn it to the channel that monitored traffic congestion when a news update came through with a breaking story on the suicide of one of the world's most powerful businessman. His stomach clenched in anticipation as the newscast spit out the details. He struggled to keep the SUV on the road as the report revealed the identity of the businessman from London who took his life by jumping from his 30th floor condo balcony earlier that morning. The report stated that it was likely the result of the pressure Sherman Oakley had been under in recent times from the collapse of his steel empire.

This time Avery pulled to the shoulder of the road, opened the door and emptied his stomach onto the pavement.

The newscast declared that Sherman Oakley had been pronounced dead on the scene almost five hours ago. His conversation with Sherman had been less than ten minutes ago.

Chapter 9

The pain was unbearable. It was not a physical pain because there was nothing physical about her. She was dead and that reality was her fate in the realm in which she now existed. Her existence was a perpetual Hell because that is where she was and would be for all eternity. Peace would never find her. She had all of her memories intact. Not only did she know where she was and why, but she also knew where she came from. She was born from the seed of the creator of the existence in which she was now trapped. She also had a full memory of her earthly birth mother, Francois Louveneau. Her own birth in the Canadian hospital, where she barely survived the attack from her own mother before Security killed her, played like a movie in her mind along with all of the other events in her short life. It was all she had in her new existence since the fatal blow from her maniac paternal brother, Patrick. She was surrounded by nothing physical, only memories, most of them awful and horrible images which played over and over in her mind. She didn't even know if she could call it her mind, because she was dead; she was entombed in blackness with no sense of touch, smell or taste, only the memories of her time when she was alive. That was her punishment.

The beautiful memories of her making music and sharing it with the world with Vasallus were now nothing but a constant horror show, since she knew she was the daughter of Satan, born into a plot to destroy mankind. She thought of the others and their eventual plight and the pain intensified inside of whatever she was now. She knew they would all come to a horrible ending similar to what she experienced and then be cast into the same abyss. There was nothing, absolutely nothing she could ever do to change her existence. She could not help herself and she could not help the others. She was damned for all eternity.

She screamed. She screamed so hard, that the sorrow wracked her thoughts with an anguish that was indescribable. Then she felt his presence. He was returning. His presence amplified her anguish and pain one hundred fold. He turned her madness into utter chaos when he visited. She felt like she was plummeting from a very high place downward, knowing she would hit bottom any second, but she never did, just kept falling…and falling.

The voice boomed through her realm: "Elizabeth, so sad and helpless. Perfect."

She told herself she would stop begging when he visited because it was the very reason he visited her. Her pain was the fuel that gave him life, but not to beg to be released from this horrible existence was worse.

"Dissolve my soul, Master. Release me from this prison. Let me go, I beg you."

She had heard his hellish laughter many, many times, but it still wracked her thoughts with an unconceivable fear. The fear was that he could cast her into an existence even worse than the one she was already in. She could see, no feel, his hellish red orbs pierce through her darkness, terrifying her even more.

"Your suffering is your life, Elizabeth, now. Get used to it. It is all you know now, forever, for all eternity. Your pain will only intensify, it will never recede. You are alone and you always will be. You will feel the lost souls of mankind pass through your realm, releasing their pain and sorrow onto you as they leave the living world, victims of my final plans. Prepare yourself Elizabeth. Prepare for suffering that will come to you in waves that will plague you for all eternity. The feeling of a damned and destroyed human soul passing through your existence will hit you like a freight train, over and over, forever and ever."

The pain of his words as they passed through her, was

crushing. She felt the rush of wanting to cry out, to sob, to vomit, but of course she could not, and that knowledge further added to her misery.

"Please Master, please. I am born from your blood. Show mercy. I beg you!"

Suddenly her entity was surrounded by his presence. His existence swirled around hers like a cyclone, filling her with a level of dread and despair she had never before experienced. He infused her, as he continued to move furiously about her, images of the murder of her birth father, mother and the grisly deaths of her adoptive parents, the Leroux's. It was awful and it got worse. Images of the future demise of mankind continued to insert themselves into her conscious. She screamed like a lion, but no one would ever hear her screams, not here. She was dead, alone with Satan and powerless over everything. Screaming was all she could do.

"Feel it Elizabeth, suck it in, all of it. Misery and despair are your only companions down here."

Finally his presence began to pull away; he was leaving her. As he moved farther and farther away from her existence, his hellish laughter trailed the fading red pits of the fire of his eyes, leaving her choking from the images that overwhelmed her thoughts.

As her mind thrashed in the black abyss, she was suddenly jolted by a piercing flash of white light, followed by a voice. It was so quick that she barely heard it, but it was unmistakable. It was the voice of God.

"I have not abandoned you, Elizabeth. My love will find you."

It happened so fast, but it filled her with a sense of hope she never thought existed, but now she knew was real. The Master had underestimated her. She was also born through the miracle of God's only Son, Jesus Christ and that beautiful knowledge coated the evil thoughts that wracked her existence like a fresh coat of paint. Her soul had a chance. A chance. He had just given that to her with His words, "I will not abandon you...."

****

Avery tore into the parking lot of the Denim Bar, searching for a parking spot. He was sweating profusely and was still shaking from the news report regarding Sherman Oakley just minutes after his conversation with him. Father O'Sullivan's warnings about Best put him on the defensive and made him wary of his strange behavior, but never did he believe the priest's warnings that Best was a demon or the Anti-Christ himself. He pulled into a parking stall, looked at himself in the rearview mirror and realized that he looked like complete shit. He was spooked beyond anything he had ever experienced before and he did not spook easily. The warnings from a dead man had rattled him. If Best was indeed the Devil, what was he using him and Bentley for? Then the realization hit him like a swift punch to the gut and his breath was expelled from his lungs with great force. Best needed the two of them to launch Vasallus and their music. The band was at the top of the charts and was now the most successful band since the Beatles. Soon he would no longer be needed by Best. Nor would Bentley be needed to write about them. Their days were numbered. He could sense it.

A bang on his window almost caused his heart to stop. He looked out his window to see Bentley and the girls standing beside his SUV clutching shopping bags and laughing. He lowered his power window.

Bentley looked stunning in her strapless, tight fitting sun dress that accentuated every curve in her body. Her makeup was always perfect and today she looked radiant standing in the blazing sun. She was about to say something silly to him when she noticed how stressed he looked: "Hey honey, you look like you've seen a ghost. What are you doing here? We were just leaving to head back to the mansion."

He tried to gather himself before replying, but he knew it wasn't working: "I will meet you there. We need to talk. See you soon."

****

She watched him close his window and, with his tires

100

screeching, he bolted out of the parking lot. What the hell was up with him? She had never seen him like that before. Then she heard Brittany's voice behind her: "What was the matter with Avery? He looked really freaked out."

Bentley turned toward the girls and replied: "Come on girls, let's go. Something is going on. We need to get back home as quickly as possible."

****

By the time he reached the coastal highway which led to Malibu Beach and the mansion, he had calmed down considerably. He cursed himself for rushing out to the mall and freaking out Bentley and the girls. They were still alive which meant that they still had time to try and figure this out. The way he figured it, Father O'Sullivan had the answers and they needed to reach him as soon as possible. He thought about his visit to the mansion a few days ago with Detective Showenstein and how strange he had acted. He left so abruptly. He pulled onto the shoulder of the road and reached for his cell phone. The coastal highway was busy and he wasn't going to risk a wreck. The detective's card with his number was back at his office in the mansion. He Googled the number to the LAPD main line. His smart phone took seconds to give him the number. He dialed it and got the typical recorded directory. He kept pushing the zero button until the response finally said: "transferring to an Operator."

A pleasant speaking voice came on the line, surprising him that it wasn't a preconceived gruff desk Sargent barking, "Los Angeles Police Department. What do ya want?"

"I am trying to reach a Detective Sam Showenstein. Can you transfer me please?"

"Are you calling about an emergency sir?"

"Yes, if that helps get him on the line quicker."

The pleasant voice now carried a slight edge to it: "Sir, I suggest you hang up and call 911."

Avery mentally reminded himself not to lose it. He hated bureaucracy more than anything else on the planet and he instinctively knew where this conversation was going. He neither had the time nor the patience to go down that path: "Mam, my call is not of an urgent nature. Detective Showenstein asked me to call him if I had any further information to pass onto him. Unfortunately I have misplaced his business card and do not have his direct line or his cell phone number. I am hoping you would be so kind as to put me through to the Detective. Thank you."

The edge disappeared and the pleasantness returned to the lady's voice: "It would be my pleasure, sir. May I have your name, please?"

"Avery Johnson."

The voice took on a sudden air of excitement when she replied: "The Avery Johnson from Vasallus? The manager?"

Oh boy, he thought. Here we go, a few more hoops to jump through before he got the Detective. "That is me Mam. Does that qualify me to get the Detective any quicker?"

"Oh my God, I love that band! Absolutely love them! Will they ever play in L.A. again? I can't believe I'm talking to the manager of Vasallus!"

"I changed my mind. This is an emergency. I will call 911."

"Wait a minute. I will transfer you directly to the Detective. My apologies, Mr. Johnson. Very unprofessional of me. Isn't Connor Asker the most gorgeous looking human on the planet?"

"Excuse me?"

"Transferring now, please hold."

Unbelievable, he thought, as the phone rang three times, and then he heard a slight click and then another ring. The call was answered by a man who was obviously having a bad day.

"Bitters."

"I'm looking for Detective Showenstein. I was told this was his direct line when I was transferred. May I speak with the Detective please?"

"This is Captain Rodney Bitters, Sam's boss in Homicide. Who is this?"

"My name is Avery Johnson. Is the Detective available?"

"The Vasallus dude? Doesn't matter. The detective is on

extended leave. Can I have another detective take your call?"

"No, I promised the Detective that I would stay in touch. If you can please pass on a message to Detective Showenstein to have him call me. Thank you Captain."

"Wait a minute Johnson. Let me be frank. Showenstein is on leave for a reason. He was driving himself crazy with events surrounding the kids in that band. Leave him alone will you?"

He knew this was a waste of time and ended his conversation with Bitters. He pulled back into the congested traffic of the coastal highway and thought of another angle. The Detective's wife, he remembered, was a plastic surgeon. He risked using his smart phone to Google Showenstein, plastic surgeon. He immediately found a match. A Dr. Bethany Showenstein, of Showenstein and Roberson Plastic Surgeons in Pasadena. He dialed the number listed in Google.

Another pleasant sounding voice answered the phone: "Showenstein and Roberson Medical Center. How can I help you?"

"May I speak with Dr. Showenstein please?"

"Dr. Showenstein has a patient at the moment. Would you like to book an appointment with the doctor?"

"Please have Dr. Showenstein contact Avery Johnson immediately. It is very important."

"I will have the doctor call you as soon as she is finished with her patient."

Finally, a receptionist who was a professional: "Thank you very much Mam. Have a great day."

His phone rang exactly ten minutes later and Beth Showenstein was on the line:, "Is there something the matter with Patrick, Avery?" Her voice was full of concern as she continued: "Oh my God, I knew something would happen."

He jumped in, cutting her off before she could continue with the notion that Patrick was in some sort of trouble: "Beth, there is nothing the matter with Patrick. I have been trying to reach your husband, but he has become hard to get a hold of. I tried his office, but they said he is on leave."

A sense of relief filled her voice as she replied: "Thank goodness Patrick is okay. I'm sorry Avery; it's been bit of a roller coaster lately around my house. Sam should be at home if you wanted to stop by or give him a call on his cell phone. Do you have his number?"

"No I don't Beth. Thank you."

Saying goodbye to Beth, he immediately called Sam on his cell. The big man's voice boomed into his ear: "Showenstein."

"Sam, its Avery Johnson. You've been hard to get hold of. I finally tracked your wife down at the clinic and she gave me your cell number."

"You have my card, why didn't you just call my cell? It's right there on the card? Is everything okay Avery? I wouldn't expect a call from you unless there was a problem with Patrick. What's that little shit up to now?"

Unlike his wife, Sam's tone regarding Patrick surprised him: "Patrick is fine. What's up with you and Beth? Are you expecting Patrick to screw up?"

"To be honest, yes. To hear you say that he hasn't surprises me. Why else would you be calling me Johnson? You want to take another run at me?"

"We need to talk, detective. When you and Father O'Sullivan were at the mansion a few days ago, you left abruptly. I have some questions regarding the kids and Best."

"Why don't you come over to the house and we can talk."

"I think I'll do that. I'm almost at the house in Malibu. I'll pick up Bentley and we'll come over right away."

****

Two hours after Avery hung up from Sam, he and Bentley were walking up his driveway. He rang the doorbell and looked at Bentley as they waited for Sam to come to the door. She was worried. Fear and anxiety were etched across her face. He instinctively reached out his arm to her, pulled her in close and whispered in her ear: "Everything will be okay sweetheart. I promise."

Just then the door opened and the towering body of Detective Showenstein stood in the doorway: "Great to see you both. Please come in."

Bentley gave Sam a hug and with his long arms, the detective could have given her a hug from his kitchen. The man should have been a professional basketball player, not a cop.

As they stepped into the Showenstein home, Bethany came down the hallway and greeted them both, exchanging hugs and pleasantries with Bentley. Avery was surprised to see another woman come around the corner as well and it took him a few seconds to register who she was: Ann Lockwood.

Sam continued: "You guys remember Ann Lockwood? She is staying with us for a few days."

Ann gave Bentley a hug and shook his hand before saying: "So great to see you both again. When Sam told me you were coming over to talk, I must say I am most anxious to hear about Michael and Vasallus."

Avery was not sure what to say to her as she obviously had not heard about what had happened to her father. He stole a glance at Sam, who understood his discomfort and replied: "It's okay, Avery. All of us are in this together. Please everyone; let's make our way to the kitchen and talk. Beth picked up some cookies on her way home from the clinic at the best little bakery in Los Angeles. I damn near had my hands severed at the wrists trying to sneak one before you got here."

The crack had the desired effect and both he and Bentley seemed to relax as they made their way to the kitchen. The Showenstein home was beautiful and spacious, reflecting the income of a successful plastic surgeon and a LAPD Homicide Detective. They settled in around the kitchen table and after a few more minutes of small talk, Ann asked the inevitable: "Avery and Bentley, please tell me how my son is. I am worried sick about him."

Bentley glanced at Avery, her eyes told him she'd take this one: "Ann, your son is doing just fine. He is working very hard every day in the studio for the upcoming European tour. His school work is way beyond the honor roll level. I must ask you though, Ann. Why are you asking us this? Why don't you speak with Michael directly? I am concerned, to be honest, Ann, why you and the families of the other kids have had no contact with them whatsoever."

Sam cut in: "I guess the two of you haven't heard about Nancy Campbell, have you?"

Avery looked at Bentley, alarmed, then back at Sam: "No, what are you talking about? Brittany hasn't said a word to us about her mother. What has happened with Nancy?"

Sam stared hard back at him before replying: "She jumped from her seventh floor balcony of her Washington, D.C. condo last week."

Bentley gasped out loud and cried: "Oh my God that is terrible. Brittany has no idea. I spent the entire day with her shopping, having a great time. This will devastate her."

Sam continued: "Obviously it has not. LAPD officers, along with Department grief counselors, visited the mansion last week to deliver the news to Brittany. She showed no emotion whatsoever when told of the news. She pleasantly thanked the officers, refused any counseling being offered by the Department, turned and went back into the mansion. I personally spoke with the officer who delivered the news. He said it was very strange. It was as if she already knew that her mother was dead and he felt that they were delivering good news to her."

Avery was dumbfounded and looked at Bentley: "Why didn't Amber tell us the police were at the mansion speaking with Brittany? She would have known. I need to speak to her. Very strange."

Bentley cut in, "Are you sure the police feel it was a suicide? Could she have been thrown over?"

Sam replied, "Her death has been ruled a suicide. There was no evidence of foul play and there was a note."

Bentley reached over and squeezed his hand before she replied to Sam, "She left a note? What did it say?"

Sam paused for a few seconds before replying: "It said simply, 'I am joining my husband who waits for me in the next life'. Investigators feel that Nancy never recovered from her husband's horrible murder and the isolation from her daughter Brittany as a result of the success of Vasallus was too much for her. Taking her own life made it all go away."

Bentley, her voice barely above a whisper, replied: "That is so sad. Brittany must be coping by keeping it to herself. That poor girl. She must be in agony right now. Come on Avery; let's go back to the mansion. I want to see her."

He looked at her; the look of despair and sadness on her face was overwhelming and then took her hand in his and said: "I'm afraid there's more bad news. It's why I called Sam this afternoon and asked to see him." He looked directly at Ann, struggling with the right words to say, and then he said: "Ann, I'm afraid I have bad news."

He watched as she brought both of her hands to her mouth and said: "Oh my God, Michael. Not Michael. Please tell me Michael is okay." She began to rise from her kitchen chair, her grief building when he continued.

"Ann, Michael is fine. We told you that earlier. He is perfectly fine. I am afraid it is your father, Sherman. Have you heard any news regarding your father today?"

She looked at him, her expression not changing and replied: "I am aware of my father's suicide. I received a call from the London authorities earlier today."

Surprised by her non-expression regarding the death of her father, he asked: "Do you remember what time you received the call regarding his death?"

Her eyes slowly narrowed as she replied: "This morning. Over seven hours ago. He had already been dead for five hours before that. Why are you asking me about this, Avery?"

It was now his turn to squeeze Bentley's hand. His breath exhaled from his lungs as he replied: "Ann, I spoke with your father less than three hours ago. Ten minutes after I spoke with him I heard a news report on the radio that his dead body had been discovered hours earlier.

Bentley, with a look of utter shock on her face, stated\: "Honey that is impossible. It couldn't have been him."

Ann once again asked: "Avery, why would you be speaking to my father?" Her voice dripped with growing suspicion.

"When Best was assembling Vasallus, he had met with your father to discuss his financing of the band, the tour, everything including the purchase of the mansion. Best was moving at lightning speed and needed a ton of cash and fast."

Ann took a breath and stared off towards the ceiling for a few seconds, deep in thought then refocused on Avery as she replied: "Best would have played on my father's emotional attachment to Michael, likely telling him that his involvement would bring Michael and him closer together."

Avery continued: "Your father believed he was ruined by Best. The collapse of Oakley Steel due to the multiple investigations of poor quality steel coming from his plants was no coincidence. He warned me Ann, that Best had sabotaged his businesses and that I was in danger."

Sam broke in, "Best killed your father just like he killed Nancy Campbell. He is eliminating us now as his plan to destroy mankind is drawing near."

It was Beth who spoke the chilling words: "Do you think it was Best who was responsible for the earthquake in India and the tsunami in the Philippines?"

No one wanted to respond to Beth's question, the magnitude behind it was too much to bear. The brief silence was broken by Bentley.

Bentley, her voice ringing with fear, whispered: "Where is Father O'Sullivan? We need him now more than ever. He holds the key to all of this. I feel there is something very powerful around him when I am in his presence. Can you believe how much he has changed?"

Sam responded: "He has left for Rome. When we left the mansion a few days ago, he instructed me to take him to LAX at once. He said he would be in touch then climbed out of the car and disappeared into the terminal. Something happened to him at the mansion that forced him to leave at once for Rome."

Avery replied: "I don't know, but things are moving very fast. The tour is soon to begin and then all hell will break loose in Europe. The violence surrounding the ticket sales has been unprecedented. The only reason the tour is still going ahead is Best's announcement that all profits from the tour will go towards relief efforts in India. That act of goodwill has calmed local governments and the critics of Vasallus."

Ann broke in and asked: "How are the kids holding up through all of this, Avery?"

"Remarkably well. They are spending hours in the studio, rehearsing and preparing for the tour. They are also beginning the recording of the tracks for the band's third album which will be released towards the end of the European tour. I have a feeling Best will announce a new North American tour as soon as the European tour ends, along with the third album release."

Bethany shook her head in dismay as she spoke: "How can these kids possibly keep up this pace? Exhaustion and mental fatigue have to be wearing them down."

Ann looked at Beth and then the rest of the group before replying: "These are not ordinary kids, let's remember that. The blood of Satan runs through them. I am the only surviving parent still alive who knows the truth."

The impact of Ann' statement resonated through them all like an electric charge. She continued: "The only reason I'm still alive, is, for whatever reason, God has chosen me to take this stand and fight for these children. Just like He has chosen all of you in this fight, we are all in this together."

The reality of their situation, through the truth of Ann's words, brought a silence to the table. Bentley leaned into Avery, clutching his forearm as the fear cascaded down her spine in waves.

Chapter 10

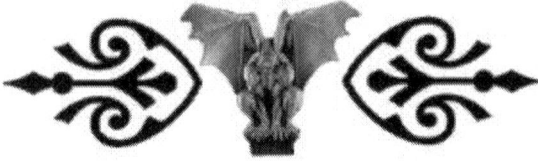

Brittany Campbell, alone in her room at the mansion, changed into a bikini for some relaxing time by the pool. She was exhausted from another day of endless rehearsal. She wasn't exhausted physically, she never was, she was just tired of the monotony and grind of practicing. They didn't need to practice. They knew the music inside and out, and they could do their choreographed dance moves blindfolded and all look completely in sync. She flopped down on the bed, lay flat on her back and thought about the upcoming European tour and how much fun it would be. The songs off of the new album were amazing and the fans would go crazy over them. She got the chills thinking about the crowd's reaction when they hit the stage for the first time with the new music. As much as Patrick creeped her out, his music was the best. She just wished he was a little nicer to the rest of them.

There was a knock on her door, which startled her. She leaned up on her bed and called out: "Who is it?"

"It's me, Michael. I just wanted to see if you were around, maybe we could hang out by the pool for a while?"

She bounced off of the bed, put on her beach wrap and opened the door. "Come on in, I was just going to head down to the pool myself."

Michael walked into the room, shirtless, a towel in his hand. He sat down on a wicker chair by the sliding glass doors that led out onto her balcony. His well-muscled body and aw-shucks looks drove his fans into a frenzy, when on occasion he would take his shirt off during a performance. Brittany noticed something new on his left shoulder. It was the blue and red Union Jack.

"I think people know when you talk, you're British. You didn't have to wear the flag for them to know that," she giggled.

He smiled as he admired his tattoo in the mirror, then back at her: "Yeah, I know. Kind of cool though, huh?"

"I think it looks great. You show Avery and Bentley yet?"

"No, whatever Britt. They're not our parents, you know, where I need their permission to do something."

The remark about the parents hurt her. She thought of her mother's recent suicide and for a brief second, she felt the pain of the loss, but it disappeared just as quickly as it came. She was no longer surprised and she rarely felt any emotion anymore. Michael and the others did not know of her mother's death. They no longer talked about their lives before Vasallus.

Then another voice entered the room. They turned to see Chloë, looking stunning in her bikini, strut into the bedroom.

"Hi guys, I was just walking out to the pool and I heard you talking. Everything okay?"

"Brittany was giving me shit about not asking Avery or Bentley if I could get a tattoo."

She sat on the bed beside Brittany and replied: "You should have Michael. Avery doesn't like surprises. You getting a tattoo will create a media shitstorm for him. The tabloids back home will have front page stories declaring Michael's undying love for Britain and how much he misses home and that you got a tattoo of the flag so it reminds you of home. Then they'll start running stories about how you want to leave the band because you miss home so much."

"I do miss home sometimes, but I just thought it would be cool, you know."

"We cut our hair and it's all over the news. Maybe you haven't noticed, but we're all pretty much the most famous people in the world right now."

Michael shrugged his big shoulders: "I guess you're right Chloë. I'll let Avery know at rehearsal tomorrow."

Brittany laughed: "Well you could doff your shirt in the

studio tomorrow, and then wait for Avery to notice it!"

Chloë joined in: "Better yet, you could make your way to the window of the mixing room, do a crazy guitar solo, lean into the glass and give Avery a bird's eye view of your tat!"

They all laughed raucously, feeling the sensation of enjoying themselves that they had not felt in months. It had been a long time since they had all enjoyed a good laugh. When the laughing subsided, Michael's voice took a serious tone and he said:

"I miss my mother. I haven't heard from her in so long. Sometimes I wonder if I'll ever see her again."

Brittany looked at Chloë, once again thinking of her mother's death, when Chloë said: "Of course you will Michael. Maybe when you explain your tattoo to Avery, you can ask him to make arrangements for you to see your mother."

Michael looked at Brittany and Chloë and asked: "Don't you guys miss your families? Your old friends? Don't you miss Ireland, Chloë?"

The emotions Chloë no longer thought she would ever feel again, suddenly came flooding back. She thought of the Academy back home, of Sister McGarrigle, but mostly she thought about Father O'Sullivan. It was weird, she thought, that she had not thought of him in a very long time. She was about to reply to Michael's question when another voice in the room spoke first.

It was Patrick. He stood just inside Brittany's doorway with Connor and Juan flanked right behind him.

"You can get those thoughts out of your heads right now. All of you. The Master is your family. He gave you life, all of us, don't ever forget that. The thing you love the most, your music, came from him. He demands your complete allegiance and loyalty. Anything less, and you can do all the reminiscing you want with Elizabeth, if you know what I mean."

Brittany, overcome with her emotions from thinking about her mother, snarled at Patrick: "You're an asshole, Benning. I hate you."

Chloë was horrified by Brittany's words, knowing the reaction from Patrick they would cause. She barely had a chance to move before Patrick launched himself at Brittany. He moved so fast, no one had a chance to react. He had his hands wrapped around her throat, squeezing the life out of her. Chloë was finally able to get a scream dislodged from her throat: "Patrick, stop it! You're killing her!"

Michael leapt from his chair to launch himself at Patrick when Connor and Juan stepped in front of him. He stared at them with a look of pure hatred: "Get the fuck out of my way, Asker, before I tear your head off."

Standing behind Connor, Juan pounced like a cat towards Michael. With his fist cocked, he sucker punched Michael across his jaw so hard, that Chloë could hear his jaw snap. She watched as he slumped to the floor. Panic and fear filled her as she turned back towards Patrick. Brittany's eyes had rolled back into her skull; she didn't have much time before she would be dead. With a speed that even shocked her, she threw herself onto Patrick. As she wrapped her arm around his neck, she could feel the power in him and it was enormous. She knew he was a second away from just flinging her off of him and finishing off Brittany. She snapped her right hand to his face, digging her fingernails into his right eye. She pushed them deep into the socket with every ounce of strength that she had. He screamed out in pain. It was working because she should feel the strength in him weaken.

****

While she was working on an article for her magazine, *Music Talks,* about Vasallus' upcoming European tour, she heard the screams. A terrifying scream came from one of the girls. It sounded like Chloë. Panicked, she ran out of her bedroom and down the long hallway towards the scream. She heard more screams and then she heard Patrick's threatening voice. It was coming from Brittany's room.

Reaching that bedroom, she could see all kinds of mayhem. The kids were in an all-out fight. "What the hell is going on?" she thought. As she was about to enter the room and put a stop to it, the door slammed shut in her face. The sudden slamming of the door frightened her because as she tried to open it, she discovered that it was locked. She pounded on the door, yelling at them to open it. She could hear Michael yelling at Connor, then more fighting. She needed to get Avery. She turned and bolted down the hallway, down the stairs into the main foyer, then raced towards the studio.

Reaching the studio in mere seconds, she burst through the studio door to see Avery, slouched in front of the mixing board computer, become startled as she screamed: "Avery, you have to come right away. It's the kids. They are fighting. It's terrible. Please hurry."

When they reached the door to Brittany's bedroom, Avery checked the knob, found it still locked, with the screams piercing through to the hallway, so he pounded his fist into the door and yelled: "Open this God damned door right now, do you hear me!"

He didn't wait; he slammed his big shoulder into the door so hard, it exploded off of its hinges. What they saw next was right out of a horror movie. Chloë, slumped against the bedroom wall, rubbed her head as she tried to get up off of the floor. Connor was standing over top of her, ready to send her flying back to the floor. Juan was standing over an unconscious Michael, ready to level a kick into his stomach. Brittany was motionless on the bed, her eyes were closed and it looked like she wasn't breathing; Patrick's bleeding face hovered over top of her. Avery ran at Connor like a linebacker and tackled him in the chest which sent him flying against the bedroom wall.

Bentley rushed towards Brittany on the bed, screamed at Patrick to get off of her and then pushed him hard off of the bed, while his hands clutched at his wounded face. She could see Brittany's neck was swollen and bruised. Patrick was trying to kill her! She quickly checked her pulse and was horrified not to find one. She screamed: "Avery, she's not breathing. Oh my God. We have to do something."

She heard him yell: "Jesus Christ, what the hell is going on here? Bentley, call an ambulance."

He leaned onto the bed next to Brittany and placed his head on her chest. Looking at Bentley, he said: "I'm going to perform CPR, I need you to call an ambulance right now." He could see that his words were lost on her. She was transfixed by something on the other side of the room. Then he heard a voice that made the blood in his veins freeze. The voice was so evil, so demonic-sounding that he somehow knew instinctively who it was. He felt he had been waiting a long time to hear that voice.

"That won't be necessary, Bentley."

A half creature, half caricature of Robert Best stood on the other side of the bedroom. His eyes shone a deep, deep red. Evil poured off of Him like a waterfall. His skull was disproportioned, like it was at the halfway point of changing into its monstrous entity. His face was covered in deep, fresh cuts. His lips were swollen and horribly cracked open. The guttural words spoken next made Bentley gasp: "Get off of her Johnson. She's already dead. They're all dead, you fools."

They were amazed to hear Brittany gasp for air as they climbed off of the bed. They were horrified to watch her get up as if nothing had happened, walk over to Patrick, wrap her arms around him and start kissing him deeply on the mouth. Avery looked at Bentley and he could see the look of horror in her eyes. He looked back at the creature and whispered: "What is happening here? What has happened to you, to these kids? What do you mean they're all dead?"

In the blink of an eye, Best was inches from Avery, His grotesque face almost touching him. He looked into the evil red orbs and knew he was staring straight into hell. Everything Father O'Sullivan had told them in their hotel room in Denver months earlier was all true. Best was the Devil. For some strange reason he no longer feared Him, even though he was standing inches away from Satan Himself with His hot and vile breath all over him. The words spoken by Father O'Sullivan back then strengthened and emboldened him now. The beast seemed to sense it too as Avery watched his eyes glow brighter. He felt Bentley's grip on his arm tighten.

He stared back at Best and defiantly declared: "Go back to Hell, Best. You don't scare me. Leave these kids alone, you coward. Now get your fucking vomit breath out of my face!"

As Best's hideous face contorted in anger, Avery put his hands on His chest and with all his strength; he pushed Him backwards into the nearest wall. He could hear Best screaming at him as they slammed into the wall, the two of them hitting it with such force that they burst right through the drywall and into the hallway. He rolled onto his back, shook the cobwebs from his brain and looked for what he knew would be an attack by Best. Instead, he found himself alone in the hallway, covered in pieces of drywall. Then he heard Bentley scream. He picked himself up off of the floor and rushed back into the bedroom only to see Best picking Bentley up off of the floor by her neck. He was killing her. He ran towards Best, as a primal scream he had no idea he was capable of escaped his lungs. He hit Best in the waist, sending Him flying backwards. He picked up a gasping Bentley, pointed her towards the bedroom door and screamed: "Run Bentley, get out of here. Go to Father O'Sullivan. He will protect you."

She looked at him defiantly: "I'm not going anywhere without you. I'm not scared of Him either."

She was interrupted by a crazed laugh coming from Patrick, who had moved in front of the doorway to block any escape passage Bentley might have had.

"You stupid bitch, you're not going anywhere. I sh…" His words were cut off by another sound coming from the other side of the room. They turned to look to see that Best had now fully transformed into the beast creature. Any human elements were completely gone. It stood at least eight feet in height; its massive head almost touched the ten foot ceiling. Its huge arms carried menacing claw-like talons at the end of them. They snapped open and closed like a wild animal trap. Underneath its arms and all the way down to its waist, was a layer of skin, purplish-grey in colour and small bones and veins ran through the skin like random roads on a roadmap. Its legs were like large tree trunks, powerful, planted firmly to hold up the huge bulk of its body. Bentley cried out: "Oh my God, Avery. Look at Him!"

Avery looked back at the kids and the sight of them was almost as frightening. He nudged Bentley to see what he was seeing and she immediately brought her hand to her mouth to stifle her screams. The kids, all six of them, were on their backs, floating straight up in the air. They appeared to be in some sort of trance-like state. Then the room suddenly became dark and the temperature plummeted, leaving the two of them shivering in the darkness. A terrible smell filled the room; it was the smell of death. Rotting and decaying flesh would smell like this, Avery thought to himself. Bentley looked up at him and cried: "Avery, what is happening to them? I'm so scared; I don't know what to do."

He looked back at the creature and then back at the kids before replying: "They seem to be in some sort of transitional state. Let's get out of here. We're going to die if we stay. Come on, let's go."

"I'm not leaving the kids here alone with Him. There must be something we can do."

The darkness in the room was suddenly filled with a white glow which surrounded the beast, illuminating its bulk. The two of them took a step backwards. Then the beast began to speak, not in English, but in a foreign tongue, unrecognizable to Avery. Then he heard Bentley whisper: "He's speaking in Latin. An ancient dialect, I presume. It's nothing like the Latin I have heard."

Then the beast roared like a thousand lions, the boom and ferociousness of it sent the fear into every nerve ending in their bodies. The Latin continued: "Satanas timere potestatem magnam. Et revertetur ad principem everyone. Man Rex autem pulverem unde et anima in me, et ipse vivet. Vita aeterna est in me. Peribis in aeternum manus Domini invalida est. Prope est enim mortem timere (Fear the power of Satan. The ruler of all and King of everyone. Men will return to the dust from where they came and their souls will live in me. Life in me is eternal. The powerless hand of God will be destroyed forever. Fear death for it is near).

****

They were in complete darkness, lying on their backs. He could hear Bentley's breathing beside him. "Where were they?" he asked himself. He called out to her: "Are you okay?"

Her voice shook with fear, as she replied: "Where are we? Are we in Hell?" She began to sob and he turned and took her into his arms. He cradled her while his mind raced as he waited for the beast to reappear in front of them to finish them off. Then the sensations guiding him about where they were alerted him. They were in bed. He could feel the softness of the mattress below them. They had to be back in their bedroom. He immediately reached over the side of the bed, looking for the lamp on his bedside table. He found it, reached for the switch and turned it on. The bedroom was filled with light, revealing that they were indeed back in their room. Bentley leaned up in bed, and she reached for the sheets to cover her freezing body. She looked back at him, not saying anything as if she was studying him, then said: "Avery, your hair!"

"What are you talking about? What's wrong with my hair? Who cares about my hair anyway? What just happened to us Bentley?" He leaned up in the bed, instinctively running his hand through his hair. It felt normal, it was still there. What was she talking about? She gazed at him strangely, and then suggested: "Go look at yourself in the bathroom mirror. It's incredible."

Thinking that there must be something growing out of the side of his head, he flew out of bed and into the bathroom. He flicked on the light and stepped in front of the bathroom mirror. He thought his jaw would drop straight to the floor and shatter into a thousand pieces on the hard tile. All he could do was mumble the words: "Oh shit!"

What he found staring back at him was an image of himself, normal in every aspect except for one thing. His hair was completely white. Snow-white to be precise.

As he turned back towards the bedroom, the only thought running through his mind was: "Why was my hair suddenly white?"

Chapter 11

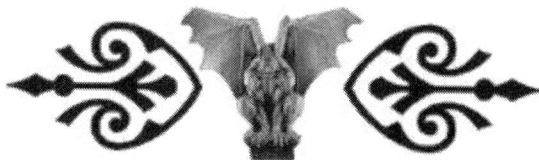

The black spirit of Satan, full of contempt for the human race, spread itself like the black plague over the ruins of New Delhi. The city was still a wasteland of rubble, destruction and death even though thousands of rescue teams from around the globe had descended on the wreckage of one of the most populated cities in the world, looking for any sign of life amongst the thousands of bodies pulled from the disaster on a daily basis.

The Prince of Darkness enjoyed the pleasure of stamping out the little pockets of hope which emerged throughout the chaos. A survivor discovered here and there, would suddenly find a piece of concrete or debris either killing him directly or trapping him for good in his own tomb with all hope lost. The earthquake was the doing of His adversary, but He reveled in its aftermath. The ruined city teemed with misery and despair that fulfilled Him like nothing else. He ensured the biggest natural disaster in history had brought the civilized world to its knees in its attempts to reach the survivors in time. The growing problems after the earthquake revealed a city which was already a humanitarian calamity before the current disaster due to overpopulation, starvation and government corruption. The staggering death toll in the hundreds of thousands was creating a political nightmare for the industrialized countries as the delays in a full-scale relief effort continued to sputter in bureaucratic hypocrisy. Hundreds of new victims died every day, while relief agencies and government officials fought over the supplies that were being stockpiled, but not moved to the field. Confusion was added to the mix of misery and despair, along with heavy doses of greed by private relief agencies, hungry for profits despite the suffering. Greed was good. It fostered more contempt among the people towards authority and government.

The spirit of God, who usually was not far away when He was present, was nowhere to be found in this war zone of suffering. He created this disaster as part of His master plan so there was no need to try and inject hope into the situation. He would ensure that hope never had an opportunity to set roots.

****

Revealing Himself to Avery and Bentley had happened sooner than He would have preferred it to, but it no longer mattered. They were in it too deep, pathetically tied to the kids like they were their parents or something. They were willing to die to protect them and so they would die. The fate of the human race was sealed and they would all die sooner than later and not necessarily by His hand. The two of them would continue to do as He said to protect the kids. He was about to find out if this prediction was still true.

Leaning back in His chair, in His New York office, Best dialed Avery's cell phone. It rang three times before he picked up. After a few seconds of silence, a deliberate and determined voice said: "What do you want?" He made a mental note of Johnson's resolve. This was good; it meant that he was still keeping it together. After all, he had just been exposed to the most evil force on earth, but yet he acted like he was annoyed by His call and did not show the cold, hard fear He knew he was feeling at this moment.

"Good morning, Avery. Glad to see you're in a chipper mood this morning, after what I'm sure was a tough night for you and Ms. Paxton."

"Fuck off Best, or whatever the hell you are. You don't scare me, you monstrous prick. The one thing the history books have always written about you is you're a coward. You're using those kids for your own diabolical plans. You make me sick."

He laughed over the phone, His human laugh not doing justice to the joy He was feeling. He was afraid Johnson might tuck and run, him and Paxton running for their proverbial lives. He now knew they were in it to the end. They wouldn't have to wait much longer. "You're both lucky to be alive and for that you could show me a little appreciation, Avery. By the way, how does the lovely Ms. Paxton like your new hair color?"

He could feel the anger in Avery's voice as he replied: "You or your pet dragon, Benning, lay one more finger on her, and I'll shove that talon at the end of your arm straight up your ass and turn it into a nose picker."

This time his laughter was genuine. He roared with delight at Johnson's bravado. This was even more than He expected. "Calm down Johnson. If I wanted to kill the both of you, you'd already be dead. If you want to keep the kids of Vasallus alive, you will do as I command. The European tour starts in less than two weeks. I want you to organize a benefit concert for India relief aid in Los Angeles by next week. Make it big, bring in as many acts as you can accommodate, but make Vasallus front and center."

Johnson immediately protested: "Are you out of your mind? Of course you are, what am I talking about?"

"I'm not asking you, Avery. I'm telling you. Do as I say, and do it well, or you know what the consequences will be."

"Don't threaten me, Best. You are all encompassing, are you not? You can put together your own benefit concert. I'll look for something better to do, like maybe, finding a way to destroy you."

He was getting annoyed with Johnson and this conversation: "Let me ask you a question. Since you're the best music manager and producer in the industry, can Vasallus excel with five members as well as the six of them? One less female singer shouldn't affect the harmonies, will it? I have been thinking the Irish lilt in the vocals is a bit distractive to the overall sound. What do you think Avery?"

"I think you should crawl back into that black hole from where you come and stay there. I think when you do, the Lord will cover that hole and snap a heavenly lock on it that from which you will never break free."

The mention of His name in this conversation infuriated Him. He was done playing games with this human: "The luck of the Irish just ran out, Johnson. Chloë's death is on your hands."

The panic in his voice said it all: "Wait a minute, Best. You fucking maniac. You're not going to kill Chloë. You do that and you might as well kill them all. The fans will not tolerate another member dropping out of the band. It will backfire on you. Think about it? Besides Connor, she is the most popular member of them all."

"Fine, then I'll kill that British snot, Michael. I hate his fucking mother anyway and it will feel especially good to see her absorb that one."

"Alright, alright I'll do whatever you need me to do. Give me ten days to put this together. I will need to see the availability of the Staples Center and the logistics will be insane Best."

He calmed himself down, He had Johnson where he needed him, vulnerable. "Okay Avery, you make it happen and fast. Forget about the Staples Center. This has to be a much bigger live event than that. Book the Rose Bowl or Memorial. Make it big, Avery."

He listened as Johnson let out an exasperated breath before replying: "I'll do what I can, Best. I still have lots to work out regarding the rescheduling of the dates in Europe and now this. This is crazy and you know what crazy is all about."

The last remark had a little bite to it, but He let it go. "I'm sure you will put on a great show, Avery. Listen I have to run, please say hi to the lovely, Ms. Paxton, will you?"

****

Alone in his mansion office, Avery gripped his cell phone with both hands, almost crushing it as he rested his head against it. He thought to himself: "How did I get myself into this? Why me? Why Bentley?" He struggled to maintain his composure when there was a knock on his door. Before he could reply, it opened and in walked Bentley. Despite what they had gone through the night before, she looked beautiful. She had taken the time to dress herself up and apply makeup and the sight of her right now made his heart melt. He loved this woman so much, that he took a second to marvel at her before he spoke: "Good morning sweetheart. I must say, I didn't expect to see you looking like this so soon after...you know what I mean." He was fumbling for words, to maintain his composure after his threatening conversation with Best.

She walked around his desk, pushed his chair out from under his desk and sat on his lap. She nestled in close to his chest, placing her head just under his chin. He breathed in her scent, the smell of her beauty and touch was intoxicating to him. She lifted her head towards him, her eyes meeting his and it was then that he saw the fear in them. She was terrified and her dressing up was an attempt to hide that fear. He leaned in close and kissed her, tenderly, then stroked her cheek lightly with his hand before saying: "Honey, I will not let him get to you or the kids ever again." He cradled her head close to his chest, knowing his words sounded about as hollow as words could sound. They were powerless to stop Best and they both knew it. They were all in grave danger and nothing he could say would help alleviate that fact. She lifted her head towards him again, her eyes searching his; studying him, it seemed, before replying:

"I love you, Avery. We will survive this somehow. God will intervene and stop Him. I believe that. We have been chosen by Him, Avery, to fight this battle against His enemy. To protect those kids."

He drew her closer, hugging her, feeling her closeness filling him, recharging his resolve. She was an incredible woman, he found strength in her and with both hands, he pushed her shoulders back so that he could look in her eyes and say: "I love you too, beautiful. After what you just went through last night, you are the most courageous person I could ever imagine. The strength in you is incredible. Thank you."

She looked at him for a second before replying: "Why would you thank me?"

"Because, without you, I could never do this, to continue

this charade with Vasallus. Your strength and courage give me the will to take a stand against Best."

He watched her complexion change, fear creeping back into her eyes as she replied: "Has Best reached out to you? He has, hasn't he? That was him you were talking to on the phone when I walked in. What did he say, Avery? Did he threaten you?"

"It's okay sweetheart. I can handle him. It's going to be okay."

Now she sat straight up on his lap, her face etched with concern: "Honey, what did he threaten you with? I want to know, we're in this together, remember?"

He thought about what he would reveal to her, but then he knew he had to tell her the truth, her life was in as much danger as his. He couldn't hide this from her, because it wouldn't protect her. "He threatened me that he would kill Chloë if I didn't put together a large scale benefit concert for India relief by next week. He is fast-tracking Vasallus' performances and I don't know why. If we don't do what he wants us to do, He will kill us, including the kids."

Putting her hand to her mouth, she gasped: "Oh my God, Avery."

"I need you to work with Jenn and put together a press conference to announce the concert to the world. Tell your bosses at *Music Talks* they will get first crack at the press conference so they will stay off your back while we work on this."

"I don't give a shit about the magazine anymore, Avery. We're trying to stay alive and keep those kids safe. Everything has changed now."

"You're right, it has all changed. I'm going to need forty-eight hours to find a venue and line-up enough acts so we have something to announce at the press conference."

She stroked her hands through his now snow white hair and stated: "The stars will trip over each other to be a part of this. It will be epic, Avery."

"We better get moving baby. We are already running out of time."

She climbed off of his lap and headed for the door, then

stopped halfway and turned back towards him and said: "I like it by the way."

"You like what?"

"Your new look. It suits you. It gives you an added element of authority. Very sexy, indeed." She laughed softly as she left his office.

He was amazed as he watched her leave. Just a few minutes ago she was shaking in fear and now she was a determined tigress. Suddenly, Best didn't seem to be as big of an adversary as he thought He was, just a short time ago.

****

Bentley was right. The music stars all scrambled to be included in the star-studded extravaganza. The biggest musical acts in the world knew the globe would be tuned in to see Vasallus and they wanted to be part of the glow shining down from Vasallus on that night. Securing the Rose Bowl in nearby Pasadena was more of a challenge, but convincing city officials there came together when they saw a glimpse of some of the numbers that they would get a piece of from such a huge event. With seats placed on the playing field at the Rose Bowl, attendance would be over one hundred thousand, which was a monstrous gate for a live event. All four of the major networks in the U.S. were willing to shell out record fees to cover the event. Avery made sure that the Indian pop star, Pratichee Ramchandani, was on the card as well as India's longtime favorite, Palash Chauhan. In forty-eight hours, Avery and Bentley, along with Jenn, managed to book the Rose Bowl, sign all of the major television networks and book every major star in the music business to perform. The City of Pasadena and Los Angeles County would take care of police and security for the event. It cost Avery dearly as he would be responsible for the overtime required to pull the manpower together. The revenue generated from this event would cover all costs and hand over a boatload of cash to the Indian government for relief aid.

Only a few weeks ago, they held a major press conference

to kick off the European Tour, but the horrible tragedy in India changed everything and here he was again, getting ready to speak at another press conference. As the minutes to the press conference ticked down, he held one final meeting with Bentley and Jenn. He looked at his longtime assistant and now his partner in his music company, Jenn, to go over the final details. "Is Miley sober? Will Selena share the spotlight with Justin?"

Jenn nodded at him as she replied: "Yes, yes and yes. They will all be on their best behaviour. Sharing the head table with Vasallus is an honour, even for them."

He looked at Bentley, then marveled at her look for the press conference. Her beauty combined with her undeniable sexiness was an incredible package and she looked stunning. "Tell me, Ms. Paxton, how are Vasallus? Are they ready?"

"They are so excited to get going, you can't imagine. I think they are more star struck at the other stars sharing the press conference than the others are of them. If that is even possible. It will be a great announcement, Avery. Let's do it!"

****

It was by far the biggest press conference Avery had been a part of and he had contributed to some awfully large ones in the past. Best was nowhere to be found and he didn't expect him to be in attendance. He had made very few public appearances in the last several months. This was his show now and through it all, he needed to find a way to put a stop to Best. He knew that his life as well as Bentley's life depended on it. He looked out over the assembled press gathered in front of the Rose Bowl main gates and he could see some of the most famous journalists, not only in the entertainment business, but also from the big news networks, *Fox, CNN* and *MSNBC*. This was about as big news as it gets. Journalists from India took up a whole section to the left of the podium and front table and their excitement was palpable. They knew that this event was shining a beacon of light on their terrible disaster and that the rest of the world would be forced to acknowledge their need more than ever now. For that, there seemed to be an air of true appreciation and respect from them for the efforts spearheaded by Vasallus and followed by the rest of the stars.

He looked down the table and he could see that Miley was clearly stoned out of her mind. She was sitting on one end of the Vasallus band members and she seemed to be taking a real liking to Patrick. That was a mistake, he thought. He could see Chloë and Brittany, sitting in the very middle, looking absolutely gorgeous. The events in the mansion a few nights ago appeared to be completely forgotten. This was the first time he had seen them since then. Bentley had been with them since that night and she stated that they seemed to have no memory of the terrible events of that night. They were Best's puppets, he knew, but he held onto the hope that they also knew that they were human and that fact would give them the courage to fight back against Best somehow in the future. Michael seemed to be purposefully reserved, like he was trying deliberately to contain his excitement. Avery knew better. Michael was jacked up for the upcoming concert next week. Connor's incredible good looks and bright smile drew all the stares from the young female writers in the assembled group. Juan's shirt was unbuttoned all the way down his chest, showcasing his collection of gold jewelry as well as his ample abs and that had all of the Latin journalists in a tither. If all of them only knew what dark, cold-blooded killers the two of them really were, they would run for their lives rather than just sit there ogling them. Then there was Patrick. The kid was a demonic, crazed killer and yet there he sat, all smug, staring back at him whenever he had a chance, as if to show Avery who he was and to remind him that, at any minute, he could easily kill him if he so chose. He caught a glimpse of Patrick's hand running up Miley's dress. She offered no resistance to his advance and when Avery looked up at Patrick, he was staring straight at him and his eyes carried a red tinge to them that seemed to flow in and out of his eyes, while a look of total control was printed like a portrait on his face. Avery couldn't shake the feeling that he was the eyes and ears of Best and that

Best was here at the press conference, looking through the portals of Benning's eyes.

He searched the crowd for Bentley. He finally found her, sitting next to Jenn, towards the back of the room. He would not direct any questions towards her, as per her instructions. She had informed the magazine that she would not be participating in the questioning of the stars. The magazine would have to be satisfied with the fact she was mainly responsible for organizing this massive event here today and that would garner them plenty of exposure. Bentley, through her exclusive coverage of Vasallus, had put *Music Talks* at the forefront of the music business and they let her have full rein in what she felt was best.

He started the press conference with a dazzling video presentation put together by Jenn and Alive Records that was stunning, considering the short time frame they had to put it together. It captured the event perfectly. The video showed the plight of New Delhi with the pain and suffering evidenced by the footage of the aftermath of the disaster. Then the video switched to the relief concert at the Rose Bowl. It left everyone in attendance emotionally moved and then when it ended, Avery introduced the head table of stars, choosing to introduce Vasallus last. Miley did not stand when she was introduced and the assembled crowd seemed to take it as a slight, but only Avery had the angle to see why she really didn't stand. She couldn't get her hand out of Patrick's pants in time. He would introduce Vasallus from the other side, starting with Michael, in order to give Patrick enough time to dislodge her hand from his crotch.

When all of the introductions were complete and the clapping and cheering subsided, Avery introduced a myriad of guest speakers, including the Indian Prime Minister, the American Red Cross spokesperson and a prominent New Delhi survivor and then he took the podium again: "Before I open the floor to questions, I would like to thank a few people who helped put this press conference together in virtually just a few short hours. The same group of dedicated folks is responsible for organizing the event which will take place here in a few more days. Let me introduce the beautiful Jenn Steinert from Alive Records, whose incredible talent and determination made this event possible. Next to her is Bentley Paxton from *Music Talks*. She is the love of my life, and she has spent almost every waking minute with the members of Vasallus since the band's inception. She has become their best friend as well as their steadfast pillar of strength and courage as they face the rocky road of music superstardom. She is as much the reason for their success as the talent they were born with."

An unexpectedly enthusiastic round of applause burst from the several hundred journalists gathered there, since all of them had a sense of what she had done and continued to do. A simple acknowledgement turned into an emotional spotlight which he couldn't avoid. It was obvious that Bentley was well-liked and respected within the music industry and their applause was an indication of that.

He then opened the floor to questions and the conference quickly lost control, as the assembled multi-national journalists, and industry professionals fought to get their media outlets in the spotlight. It was pandemonium and Avery fought to bring it under control. At one point, he even heard a comment that Miley had left, but in reality, she was on her knees, under the table in front of Patrick. After a few long minutes, he calmed the throng down to an orderly level and then he handed the microphone to the respected Dermott McShane from the *Irish Times*, who surprisingly directed his question at Patrick rather than Chloë. "Patrick, you seem to be having a good time tonight." He waited till everyone else caught on to the obvious flirting going on between him and Miley and then continued: "You are an accomplished musician at such a young age, but it is your uncanny talent for writing that has people in this industry shaking their heads. You have very quickly established yourself as one of the great writers of our time. You have an opportunity to use that talent to lift up and inspire the youth of the world, but instead you choose to write music that encourages and demands disobedience and promotes mayhem and violence. Why is that Patrick? Can you explain that to the world listening here tonight?"

The question caught everyone off guard, except perhaps Patrick, who quickly shoved Miley to the side, almost toppling her off of her seat and replied directly to McShane: "You're a pompous prick, McShane. What the fuck do you even know about music anyway, huh? You're a news reporter and not a very good one. How did they let you in here tonight anyway?" Patrick ended his verbal abuse of McShane by leaning back in his chair and grinning from ear to ear. The networks were in a complete scramble as they attempted to beat the few second time frame to bleep out Patrick's choice of words.

"This event is news, Benning. Do you even know why you are even doing the concert in the first place? I bet you think it's just another performance. Do you know what happened in India?"

The sound of chairs, tables and microphones flying everywhere drowned out the reporter as Benning rushed from his chair to reach him, quickly followed by Connor and Juan. Avery was unable to grab Patrick as he flew past him. He ran around the podium and rushed Patrick from behind, but not quick enough to prevent him from tackling McShane and throwing him, hard to the ground. He got in two devastating shots to McShane's face before Avery was able to tackle him with a hard shoulder to Patrick's back, sending him toppling off of him. A dozen or so security guards pounced on Patrick and prevented him from doing further damage. Others secured Asker and Jimenez before they could come to Benning's defense. He knew that only he and Bentley understood that Patrick could have flung those security guards off of him without any hesitation, but he also seemed to understand that he had already gone too far.

Soon control was returned and the press conference resumed, albeit without Patrick, Juan and Connor. McShane was taken to the nearest hospital with severe blunt trauma to the face. No doubt a lawsuit would be coming at him and Vasallus for Benning's outburst. The world finally got a firsthand glimpse of the violence which seemed to follow Vasallus wherever they went.

It was only a sign of what was yet to come.

Chapter 12

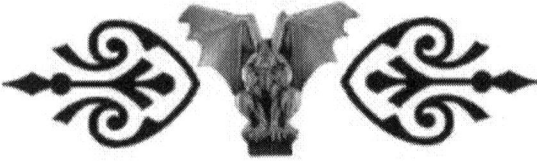

Despite the catastrophic earthquake in India, that country and the rest of the world were able to find some small element of enjoyment in the monstrous benefit concert taking place in Pasadena, California. The concert was planned to run for twenty-four straight hours with a total of thirty-two of the biggest music acts in the world performing one after another. Some would perform a few songs and others would be given a set of forty-five minutes. Prime time television on all of the U.S. networks would carry the first four hours and the final four hours of the event live to an expected record-setting viewing audience. Millions and millions of dollars would be raised for the earthquake victims as the artists would continually deliver the message that all of the viewers should open up their wallets and donate.

The main event of the extravaganza was Vasallus' performance and they would close the marathon show with a full two-hour set which Avery and the organizing team hoped would bring in an astronomical amount of donations. The mega concert began and the entire world watched. The fans inside the Rose Bowl behaved themselves for the most part, seemingly knowing they were part of an historical event, but as the bands and single acts came and went, bringing Vasallus closer to taking the stage, the fans inside and the tens of thousands watching the giant screens outside the stadium seemed to sense that the mega-superstars, Vasallus, would soon be performing live. News helicopters buzzed in the air overhead, feeding live updates to their networks. Fans, fueled by adrenalin in the alcohol-banned concert, began to chant Vasallus, Vasallus inside the stadium as well as outside of it. Big time stars slotted in the run-up to Vasallus found themselves being drowned out by the fans booming the name Vasallus like it was a soccer match.

****

The six members of Vasallus gathered in one room to await their cue to take the stage. All six of them were trying to remain calm and focused as they waited, with the excitement building in the room as they heard the deafening roar of their name coming down the corridors behind the stage and through the walls into their dressing room. Connor Asker jogged in one spot, his perfect looks and expertly styled hair not moving as he let out some of the energy building within him. Patrick and Juan joked back and forth between each other with Patrick teasing Juan: "There are no Spanish people in the stadium Juan. You might as well wait for us here until we're done and we come back," he laughed and followed it up with a friendly slap on Juan's back. Juan replied just as quickly: "Oh really and why would that be?" He realized too late that he had walked right into Patrick's joke: "They have no money to donate stupid! They're in the cheap seats in the parking lot watching on the big screens!" roared Patrick with laughter. This latest zinger by Patrick brought smiles to everyone in the room.

Michael smiled, more because he could see that Patrick was in a good mood. This was better for everyone. If Patrick was in good spirits, it would make for an even better show. If he was in a bad mood then it affected everyone's performance. Michael looked over at Chloë, who was watching him intently, no doubt thinking the same thing about Patrick that he was. Her beautiful smile lit up as she said: "I see you dressed in a sleeveless shirt so you can show off that new tattoo! The Brits are going to love it. I can just imagine the London tabloids tomorrow, splashing that Union Jack on top of a bony bicep all over their entertainment sections."

Michael moved closer to her before shooting right back: "First of all, these pipes are not bony; they're perfectly big and sexy. Just watch the girls' reaction when I flash the tat in their faces when I get down low during my guitar solo." Chloë giggled, enjoying this immensely, then she replied: "Oh, now that you came closer Michael, I can see they're not so bony after all."

He laughed at her playfulness and stood in front of her in a bodybuilding pose, flexing his biceps, showing off his impressive physique when he noticed that the others were all watching. He watched as Connor, Juan and Patrick all moved to the centre of the dressing room, posed in bodybuilding stances and made their muscles taut as they made fun of him and his antics with Chloë. It didn't take long for Brittany and then Chloë to join them in the middle of the room, and then all five of them began to flex their muscles and look completely goofy.

Michael laughed even harder at their antics; it was a rare moment for all of them where they shared some good laughs together. "Alright, alright I get it. You're all jealous of the tattoo. I understand."

The fun was interrupted by a knock on the door and then Bentley, followed by Avery, came into the dressing room. The roar of the crowd was deafening in the room when the door was briefly opened. It was time to perform.

****

The six of them exited the dressing room after the pep talk from Avery and Bentley. It was still weird seeing Avery with his hair the colour of snow. "How did he go from dark hair one day to bright white the next? He must have coloured it. But why? What man would dye his hair from his natural dark colour to white?" Chloë thought this to herself as she followed Michael along the narrow hallway leading to the stage. He was dressed in black leather pants, a red sleeveless shirt, black high top running shoes and a black leather jacket that she knew wouldn't stay on beyond the first song. She watched as Patrick led them down the hallway. He was dressed simply in blue jeans, a white t-shirt and black boots. His dark moods used to frighten her, but he no longer scared her or the others. He was followed by Brittany, with her supermodel good looks; her shoulder-length hair was now more blonde than she had ever had it before. She was wearing a short black dress that accentuated her body perfectly and black high heels. Juan, the Latin mega-star, was quiet and focused as they made their way closer to the stage. His solo performances tonight would set the Latin world on fire with excitement. They loved him and he was a national treasure in his home country of Venezuela. Behind her was Connor, the uber-confident heart throb that the majority of the girls in the stadium tonight had come to see. He had an effect on them like nothing ever seen before. Not even Elvis Presley and his gyrating hips could do this to screaming girls in the 50s and 60s. When it came time for Connor to step forward to the front of the stage to perform lead vocals, the crowd would go insane. She smiled to herself at that thought. He had it all, incredible looks, a voice like no other and the charisma to bring it all together. She was excited to get on stage and perform and she knew the rest were too. The world would be watching and they couldn't wait to perform their new songs from the second album and some select songs from their soon-to-be-released third album. She felt amazing, powerful and beautiful. She would sing her heart out on stage tonight.

They were one now with one purpose. To fulfill the Master's plan. They all knew their music was changing the world and creating a following that spanned the globe. The songs Patrick had written would, in the very near future, bring the world to its knees. It was their destiny. It was the reason they were born. She knew that now and she was at peace with it. If she could only find a way to put a stop to that annoying little voice in the back of her head that wanted to speak to her all the time. She sometimes wondered if the others heard the same voice. The voice and the message it carried was dangerous to all of them if the Master somehow found out. She was so deep in thought that she barreled right into Michael, who had come to a stop as they had reached the stairs leading to the back of the stage.

"Hey Chloë, watch out girl! We can't have you turning an

ankle in those big stilettos before we even hit the stage. Everything okay?"

"I'm fine Michael, just excited to get out there, that's all!" She watched as he gave her a curious look, as if he knew what she had been thinking about. Their thoughts were interrupted by the roar of the crowd beginning to go ballistic as the final act finished up and the audience realized that Vasallus would soon be hitting the stage. They all looked up towards Avery as he shouted above the crowd, asking them to move in close. They were completely surrounded by plainclothes security and uniformed policemen. The stage hands were milling about at the top of the stairs, preparing for their entrance. Avery spoke.

"Remember why we are here. We are here for the terrible tragedy in India. This is for them. Be the best you can be. There are millions and millions of people watching from all over the world. Let's give them the greatest show they will ever see. Stick to the song list and you'll be fine. Watch for the assistants between songs as they will guide you regarding the placement of the props. You will be great because you are great. Now go get em!"

Just then, there was a commotion as Miley came down the stairs in front of them. She was pissed and before she brushed past Vasallus, she glared at them all and hissed: "What a fucking waste of my time out there. Their chants of your name drowned me out completely; I might as well have stayed home. Go on get your asses out there! It's obvious they are here to see you and no one else." She turned and stomped her way down the hallway, with security guards doing their best to get out of her way. She could then be heard cussing out her manager for putting her behind Vasallus in the lineup.

Avery looked at them one last time and said: "She obviously missed the point of why we are here. You heard the lady, now go and have some fun."

The six of them embraced each other and gave each other well wishes for a great performance, which was something they had come to do before every show. They climbed the stairs onto the back of the stage and made their way to the holding area where the stage director, clutching a clipboard and wearing microphones, stood waiting for them. Michael, Connor and Juan took the guitars handed to them by the guitar techs. The wireless remotes which would carry the sound from their instruments were checked one final time. Each band member was given a wireless, almost invisible boom microphone which clipped onto the back of his or her head and a thin, skin-coloured boom mic came down the side of his or her face to the mouth. The stage director gave them last minute instructions before they turned their attention to the P.A. system that boomed throughout the massive stadium. "Ladies and gentlemen are you ready?" The 100,000 plus fans were going crazy, stomping their feet, clapping their hands and shouting in complete unison: Vasallus, Vasallus. The moment was surreal for all of them and the six of them held hands and waited for the P.A. to announce their entrance. "Please welcome, multi-platinum selling recording artists, VASALLUS!"

They all turned, waved at Avery and Bentley standing towards the back of the stage and made their entrance. The stage lights came on as they entered and the crowd surrounding the stage went crazy. Dozens of armed security guards and policemen created a twenty foot buffer zone between the first row and the stage. The buffer zone lasted less than ten seconds, as the fans rushed towards the stage and pressed the security people up against it. They scrambled to keep control and it seemed to be working, but the stage director quickly went to work backstage to direct more security to re-establish the buffer zone.

Patrick took his position behind the elevated drum set which spanned almost the entire width of the stage. He was on a pedestal above everyone else and the music began as his sticks beat down onto the drums for the first time. They started the set with one of the up-tempo group number hits from their first album. That got the crowd dancing in front of their seats and jumping up and down. Connor and Juan playfully came together in the centre of the stage and worked their individual guitar pieces. Brittany and Chloë stood in front of their microphone stands belting out the song. Michael worked the bass guitar along the side of the stage to the delight of the fans as he dipped down close to them, giving them a bird's eye view of the blue and red tattoo. Chloë flashed him a big smile as he regrouped in front of his microphone stand along with Connor and Juan in front of theirs and the five of them joined their incredible harmonies into one to the delight of the crowd.

At the back of the stage, Avery and Bentley stood side by side with their arms around each other, soaking it all in. Bentley turned towards him and shouted into his ear: "Isn't it incredible! To see them now on stage and how much fun they are having together and how much the world loves them, it is just so hard to imagine the evil intentions behind their existence."

He leaned down towards her so she would hear his reply: "I agree and it's so hard to separate what just happened the other night and how close Patrick came to killing Brittany and with Juan and Connor close to doing the same to Michael."

She shouted back: "Do you think they even remember what happened? They look at us like nothing happened. They almost killed the two of us and yet they act like it was nothing. This is crazy Avery and I don't know how much longer I can keep it up. I'm really afraid for you and what Patrick is capable of doing to you."

He pulled her closer to him and reassured her: "All we can do is try to hang in there. We have to keep an eye on them until Father O'Sullivan and the detective find a way through this. We need to keep them safe from each other and the best way to do that is keep them immersed in their music. Whether it's out here on stage or in the studio, when they are performing they are safe from each other and the world is safe from them."

He watched her look at him, with her eyes glowing from the sparkle of the stage lights, when she declared: "We could just run. Get away from all of this. Go somewhere far away where we cannot be found by Best. Please Avery; let's just go, right now."

The chaos of the music and the crowd swirled around them

while he held her close and looked deep into her eyes before he answered: "You know we cannot do that. We cannot leave them. We are their only hope until the others get here. We will be safe till the end of the European Tour at least. Best needs the both of us to keep this thing going and only we can ensure that it does so we are safe for now. Trust me sweetheart, we will be okay and somehow we must trust that Father O'Sullivan will find a way to defeat Best and end this horror and set these kids free. We have to believe in that."

She squeezed him back and said, "You're right. Let's enjoy the show and not talk about Best anymore tonight, okay?"

The band was into their fifth song of the set when there was a huge commotion at the back of the stage. Stage hands were running everywhere, yelling into their headsets. The stage director was barking out orders. Something was happening on stage. He and Bentley made their way closer to the stage, keeping out of sight from the crowd by hiding behind the pieces of equipment which ringed the sides of the stage. When they got close enough that they could see what all the fuss was about, they were stunned by what they saw.

Patrick, positioned behind his drum set, was elevated in the air in the centre of the stage. The rest of his extensive and extravagant drum set was still in place on the elevated platform. Patrick and his drums were floating in midair in the middle of the stage. The crowd was going nuts, soaking in the great special effects like it was part of the show. However, this was no orchestrated and choreographed effect. The two of them just stood there, as their jaws gaped open while the unthinkable happened. Patrick and his drums floated further out, past the centre of the stage and above the rest of the band members' heads and out into the crowd. The tens of thousands of people inside the stadium were going berserk as Patrick floated above them, pounding on his drums as he did so. Avery and Bentley were joined by the stage director, who looked at them, his face filled with wonder as he spoke: "What is happening here, Avery? I don't understand. How can he do that?"

****

Chloë knew it was coming, but she didn't know when he would do it. They never discussed it as a group, but Patrick had brought it up in the studio that he wanted to try it. She could see as she looked out into the crowd that they loved it, thinking there were high wire cables whisking him around them. It was an incredible sight and she wondered what the people watching on T.V. around the world were thinking. She was about to give them a lot more to think about.

Patrick and his drum kit floated back onto his elevated platform behind them. The lights softened and the music slowed as the first ballad of the evening began with Chloë. She moved to the front of the stage where the lights focused on her. Her long blonde hair hung straight down onto her shoulders. She looked radiant as she began to sing. She was singing one of the new songs, *It's Time* from the unreleased third album, so the crowds were hearing it for the first time. Her angelic voice came out and seemed to mesmerize the crowd into a complete silence. To compare her voice to anyone else would be impossible. Her magnificent sound was her own and the effect it was having was incredible. The rest of the band hummed in some quiet harmonies in the background as Chloë pushed her beautiful voice into every nook and cranny in the stadium. As she completed the first chorus, something incredible happened. She began to float, slowly at first, straight up until she was about ten feet in the air. She then started the soft and tender lyrics in the song and as she did so her floating body with the microphone stand still in front of her moved out and over top of the crowd, it rose slightly as she moved farther out. She stopped about halfway down the rows of seated fans on the playing field of the Rose Bowl and rotated in a circle; her voice reached each and every one of them individually and touched them with an incredibly moving and unforgettable moment. . She was suddenly joined by Brittany and Juan and the three of them floated above the crowd, the power of the harmony of their three voices singing the chorus enhanced the hypnotic sensation of seeing the three of them

140

floating in air.

When the song ended and they were all back on the stage, they broke into the big hit from their first album, "Don't Look Back". The song seemed to snap the crowd out of their trance and they once again jumped up and down with the beat of the music. Avery and Bentley gathered themselves to return to the back of the stage, but the stage director stopped them.

"Johnson, what the fuck just happened out there? I just spent the last few minutes grilling my guys about why I wasn't informed of the high wire cable act when they swore they knew nothing about it. Now I'm asking you. If that wasn't cables and wires, then what the hell was it?"

Avery stuck his finger into his chest and said: "I was just going to ask you the same thing Jim. We're both in the dark okay? The kids will have to answer that question. Now get to work, because in case you haven't noticed, there's still a show going on."

They turned and walked away when Jim called out to them: "There is definitely something spooky going on here. First, you show up with your hair all white like you're an albino, the kids are floating in the air like Peter Pan and then when I directed the stage hands to try and get Benning back on the stage, some asshole with eyes glowing like red stop lights threatened me. He said if I did anything, he'd hang me by my neck off of the lighting racks."

Chapter 13

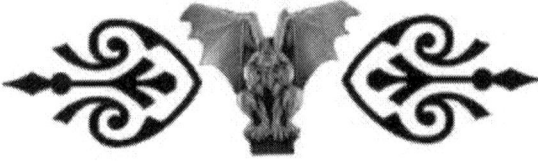

Patrick giggled as he pounded the drums. He had the best seat in the house to see the reaction created by the performers' levitation act. Fans in the stadium were thrilled at what they were seeing, and the fans were delirious at the over the top special effects. He was surprised that a pilot, navigating one of the floating helicopters above, didn't drop from cardiac arrest at what he was seeing. He could see the stage hands below and behind him shouting. They would be searching for the rigging equipment that controlled their movements, but they wouldn't find any. What he and the others just did was the most enormous live stunt ever performed in concert. He envisioned Avery and Bentley attempting to downplay the stunt to the hordes of media that would descend on them after the concert and the days ahead. He was keen to see that camera shots from the helicopters offer the television audience world-wide an incredible view of him and his drum set floating in mid-air. Those same camera angles would also show there were no cables or wires hoisting them into the air. This brought throngs of new and devoted fans around the globe to their music. The Master wanted Vasallus to take the performance to the next level. They did just that. When the European Tour began he unleashed a bevy of new music. The lyrics would create unprecedented global social upheaval.

He watched as Michael moved along the front of the stage making life hell for security as the girls tried to crash through the human chain of muscle. Connor had two girls' bras around his neck with several others scattered on the stage floor around him. Son-of-a-bitch; this is great fun! He looked out over the massive stadium. What a beautiful sight to see: a hundred thousand people on their feet going crazy. The Master was right! It was time.

He moved his head from side to side in tune with the music. His sweat soaked hair whipped across his face. Out of the corner of his left eye, he caught a glimpse of an intense glimmer of something shiny. It was like a reflection of the sun bouncing off a mirror in the desert heat into his eyes. Surrounded by pandemonium and chaos, the flash of light from that section of the stadium startled him, and he struggled to maintain his focus on the drums as he searched the crowd for the source of the light. "What was that"? Why did it unsettle him so much? He returned his attention to the group harmonizing a dance number. All five of them moving and gyrating in unison. He had almost forgotten about the intense flash of light when he caught sight of it again. This time it was to the right of the stage. It lingered a millisecond longer giving him a better sense of it. It was a shimmering and brilliant light that pierced through the crowd and into his vision. He scanned the area, desperate to find the source of the weird light that was so much in contrast to the multitude of lights sweeping across the stage. He looked back towards the front of the stage and could see Juan approaching him from below. He danced to the music, working his guitar as he moved towards him. When he was close enough, he looked up, shrugged his shoulders and made a face. Shit, he had stopped playing the drums! Then he could see Michael furiously trying to keep the song intact and working his bass guitar to keep the beat going. He paused and waited for another second and then began hitting the drums once again. That light frightened him, and the thought that something frightened him scared him even more.

Patrick was captivated by the rhythm of the song, an anthem from their second album he wrote in the days following his first human kill: the Crittendon's! The rage he felt was evident in the song and he knew the world's youth would express great defiance and violence. This concert and

143

the upcoming European tour was designed to put the young people everywhere mad with excitement, and their parents and peers along with them. He was trying to imagine what the crowds would do in the streets of Los Angeles and the surrounding cities after this concert. Whatever it was, it would be epic!

Then he saw it again. The light was directly in front of him this time. It was more than a light.

A man, very large in stature, stood tall, above the layer of security in front of the stage. He was standing in the buffer zone between the crowd and the security. He was covered in gold armour topped with a shiny gold helmet on top of his head. He was pacing back and forth in front of the stage, threatening to take out his sword as his hand gripped its handle. "Why wasn't the security apprehending this man"?

The soldier was staring directly at him. Paralyzed with fear he no longer played the drums. The other five scrambled to save the song without the percussion. Something inside his head was telling him to go to this soldier. Confront him. He slowly stood up behind his drum set, never taking his eyes off the colossal soldier. He climbed down the narrow winding stairs at the back of his platform. The stage lights had silhouetted his drum kit in blackness, and he sensed but did not hear the voice in his head instructing him to go to the soldier. As he exited off the staircase, he was met by the stage director.

"Benning, what the fuck are you doing? Get your ass back up there and get playing those drums. You're ruining the set. What the hell is the matter with you, and what is wrong with your eyes? Jesus, I've had enough of this bullshit. Johnson can deal with you."

He never even heard the dick with the headphones talking. He just needed to move to the front of the stage and confront the man in the shiny armour. He could see Avery talking with the headphone man. Fuck them. He looked out on the stage and saw Connor singing a ballad at the front of the stage. The rest of the band was cast in darkness as Connor worked his magical charm on the girls. He walked towards the front of the stage, when a hand gripped his arm. He was twisted around backwards and found himself staring into the eyes of an extremely pissed Avery.

"Would you like to tell me what the hell you're doing Benning? Maybe you haven't noticed that we're in the middle of a performance. You out for an evening stroll maybe?"

The dark power was building inside of him. His rage was close to taking over. "Fuck off Johnson. Get off this stage; you don't belong here." He turned to continue his walk to confront the man in gold.

"I could shut you down in a heartbeat Benning. Shut down this whole band as quick as it started."

Patrick whirled around so quickly their faces almost touched. His eyes were on fire, and the dark rage was coursing through his veins. He snapped his hand over Johnson's throat so fast he could see the surprise in his eyes. Surprise, but no fear. That was unusual. He was getting more emboldened. He'd be dead soon Master almost finished with him. "Oh yea, Johnson, well I could kill you right here. Crush your neck in front of 100,000 people and millions more on live T.V. You're a smart man Johnson and you know you're still alive for one reason. Your babysitting days are numbered and soon you and that hot bitch Paxton will be dead."

He felt an object jam into his rib cage. The urge to squeeze Johnson's windpipe and rip it out of his throat was overwhelming when he heard him hiss, "Get your fucking hand off of me Benning or I'll blow a hole right through your chest. You really think we're afraid of you and Best? If we were, we would have high- tailed it long ago. You're a punk Benning, and nothing but a little bitch for Best. You even think of laying a hand on Bentley again or the other kids I will fill you full of holes, even if I have to use a cannon to blow a hole massive enough to kill you. Now get your shiny red eyes behind that drum set or get out of here. Take your elevator to the basement floor from where you came and don't ever come back here! Do you hear me?"

"That motherfucker," he burned as he watched Johnson turn and walk to the back of the stage. Killing him would be his priority, when the Master gave him the green light. He would torture the bitch in front of him first. He was right, as much as that angered him into a blinding rage, he needed to get back to his drums. Wait a minute. The soldier. He turned back towards the front of the stage. Connor was finishing up his ballad, but the shiny soldier was gone. He scanned the stage from left to right hoping to see the blinding light again. Fucking asshole Johnson. His rage was building once more and if Johnson was stupid enough to come out on the stage again he didn't think he'd be able to control himself. He walked back to his massive drum set as the song was ending; they would need him to lead into the next song. It was when he walked past the front of his drum set to the back that he almost walked into him.

The giant was blocking the narrow metal stairs leading up to his drums.

Patrick braced himself. Fear gripped his chest. Who was this menacing looking beast of man covered in gold plates that carried a hideous scar above his eye? Then he took notice of the brilliant blue eyes of the man and he knew. He was a soldier of God. His fear quickly turned to rage. It burned so intense it felt like an inferno inside of him, melting his organs to stew. He prepared to attack him when the soldier pulled the enormous sword from its scabbard. The light that escaped it as it was pulled further out was blinding. He struggled to shield his eyes from the light. He watched as the soldier maneuvered the huge blade up and over his head. The brilliant light that swirled around the steel blade paralyzed him, as he found himself transfixed on the sword and the giant that held it above his head. He could not move. The power emanating from this man was too strong and held him frozen in place. He could only watch as he lowered his massive blade towards him, knowing he was about to die from its blow. Where was the Master? He searched around, looking for him to step in and waste this cocksucker.

A voice as enormous as the man boomed, "He is not here Patrick. You are alone. It is just you and me."

He snarled at him, "If you're going to kill me, then do it,

before I kill you."

The giant expressed great mirth, the large heavy plates of armour shaking up and down as he laughed. "I am not here to kill you, Patrick. I am here to warn you."

"Warn me about what? Who are you?"

The energy flowing from the massive blade flowed through him, completely immobilizing him, powerless to resist. The soldier continued, "I am Babken, son of King Tiridates, soldier of the Lord, Our God. Your mother Patrick, and you, are the direct descendants of the great King."

Patrick was in disbelief, "I am your lineage?"

The soldier in gold took a step back, lifted the sword away from his chest and returned it to its massive scabbard and then replied, "You have the blood of your mother, and of me, flowing through you. You also have the blood of the wicked one. Resist his evilness Patrick. He will destroy you and all of mankind."

Patrick felt the strength in his body leave him completely and he fell to his knees. The music had stopped and he could see the band members standing in confusion in front of the stage. He looked back up at the soldier, but he no longer stood before him. He was gone.

****

Avery and Bentley, standing at the back of the stage, watched in disbelief as Patrick stopped at the stairs that led up to his drum kit. He appeared to be suddenly frozen in place. He was talking to someone or something; yet, he was all alone. Something was happening to him. Bentley let go of his arm, turned towards him, and said, "There's something wrong with him, Avery. I'm going out there to check on him." A strange feeling overcame him as he watched Patrick confer with an invisible entity. A tiny voice in the back of his head whispered to him, "Leave him be. He will be okay." He had not told Bentley the details of his confrontation with Patrick minutes earlier, not wanting to scare her even more. There was definitely something happening to him as he continued to remain on his knees. He decided to hold her back, clutched her arm and said, "Wait a minute, Bentley. Leave him be. He will be okay." He motioned for the stage director to dim all of the stage lights and bring in the kids for a wardrobe change. He nodded, turned and barked instructions to his assistants to start the video show depicting an entertaining and fascinating behind the scenes movie of the kids of Vasallus. The video immediately started and a hush spread through the crowd as the thousands instantly became drawn to the giant video screens on stage and positioned around the stadium. The video, scheduled to be run at the end of the concert and before Vasallus's first encore, highlighted the personal voices of Vasallus in candid and casual interview pieces with Bentley. The interviews were one on one with each of them, as a group, and interlaced with images of behind the scene antics of the kids in lighter moments backstage, around the pool and on the beach with their fans.

They watched as the kids walked off the stage and gathered around Patrick. Juan and Connor lifted him up, and together they left the stage for their dressing rooms. He looked over at Bentley once again, "Let's leave them be. Whatever happened out there is between them and they will figure it out. Come on let's catch our breath backstage in the lounge before the second set starts up. What a night."

****

The Quake Aid Concert for India earthquake victims was an overwhelming financial success. Records were shattered for the most money ever raised in one single event. The tens of millions of dollars raised around the world made similar events like "Farm Aid" and "Artists Against Apartheid" pale in comparison. People from around the globe embraced the message and gave generously..(Not clear. Provide clarity by dividing into two sentences.) For all the good that was accomplished by the concert, it was overshadowed by the unprecedented outbreak of violence when the concert ended. The Rose Bowl was damaged severely due to rioting by fans inside and out of the stadium. Bleacher seats were broken, bent or ripped. Concession facilities were broken into, looted and smashed. Dozens of fans were killed outside the stadium by growing and angry mobs. Around the stadium that held the army of T.V. cameramen covering the event, scaffolding was pulled down and destroyed. Cars were lit on fire in the parking lot. The tens of thousands pouring out of the stadium into the parking lot were confronted by the mobs and angry crowds still seething because they were the ones not able to secure a ticket inside. Full scale fighting broke out, quickly overwhelming security and police. They watched in horror as the crushing mobs pushed past their secure lines and systematically began beating officers unable to retreat fast enough. Fans were on a rampage, fueled by the lyrics sung by Vasallus and the multiple deaths that occurred caused the Governor of California to call in the National Guard to take back control and put a stop to the violence.

T.V. camera crews from all major networks moved in and out of the mobs, capturing the violence up close and sending the live images back to their network stations. The world watched in horror as the violence reached unprecedented levels, eclipsing the mayhem during the Rodney King riots of 1992 that brought the city of Los Angeles to its knees. The network helicopters continued to buzz overhead, beaming the live images instantly back to their stations and into the homes of everyone who tuned in. Coverage by CNN had the world in disbelief of the events unfolding as their state of the art method of covering horrendous events was unparalleled by any other network.

President Stanley Kipshaw of the United States of America was one of those sitting in disbelief. In one minute he went from basking in the spotlight as the head of the nation hosting the largest musical spectacle since Woodstock to the worst civil violence in the history of its nation. Tucked away in the Presidential Camp David retreat, he looked at his wife, Leah, and shook his head in incredulity, "Jesus Christ, what in God's name is happening to this bloody world. What should have been the celebration of the biggest event that showcased hope and generosity has turned into this," he disparaged, pointing at the T.V. screen. "I hope Alexis wasn't watching this?"

Before his wife could respond, there was a knock on the door. Kipshaw yelled , "Come in."

A Secret Service agent pushed the door open, apologized for the intrusion, then stepped back as the President's Chief of Staff, Adam Linker, stepped into the room. He looked at the First Lady first and then to the President before replying, "My apologies Maam, Mr. President, for the intrusion. The outbreak of violence in Los Angeles is rapidly deteriorating and the Governor has called in the Guard."

Kipshaw looked up at him from his sitting position on the couch he shared with his wife and replied, "Okay Adam. That is standard protocol. What else is the matter?"

He hesitated slightly looking at the First Lady then back at the President. He was interrupted by the First Lady who looked at her husband and said, "I'm going to check on Alexis. You finish up here and I'll meet you in bed." She bent over, gave him a kiss on the cheek, and then stood up and left the room.

Linker watched her leave and then turned back to the President and replied, "Mr. President, Los Angeles is not the only city burning right now. Reports are coming in from around the world. There is full scale rioting against local governments in almost every major city by the youth of these countries. Hundreds are being murdered in full view of authorities. Anarchy is taking over Mr. President. Local police forces are not using tear gas or water cannons to control the crowds; they're using bullets, Mr. President. People are dying tonight by the hundreds and more likely by the thousands."

"Jesus, Adam! What's the situation here in our cities besides L.A. What's happening in Washington?"

Linker pointed back to the television, "Take a look for yourself, Mr. President."

Stanley turned his attention back to CNN and watched in horror as the network was switching between reporters from different cities around the country and it wasn't pretty. Then the

Washington Bureau Chief from CNN came on and reported the rioting in Washington. Mobs were gathering by the thousands in front of the gates to the White House. People were fighting everywhere; others were chanting and provoking the police guarding the gates. Pandemonium. Perhaps one word such as mayhem or pandemonium would work better.)

He cursed under his breath, and then looked at Linker and said, "Convene an emergency meeting with the Joint Chiefs. Bring in Secretary of State, Clover and her cronies. We need to put a stop to this as quickly as possible. The longer this mayhem goes on, the more momentum it picks up.. They're destroying their own cities for shit sakes! A fucking rock concert is making people go nuts?"

"It seems to have been triggered by the final performance of the benefit by Vasallus. We are analyzing the words to the songs from Vasallus's second and third album they sang tonight."

"Good, and anything there that would trigger such an outbreak of rioting?"

He paused for an extra second before replying, "I've been told, Mr. President, the lyrics are incredibly clever and contain hidden messages that seemed to have been unlocked by fans and it has taken on a life of its own. The songs appear to be a call to fight back against all forms of authority: government, police, teachers, anyone in a position of power seems to be targeted by these songs."

"Jesus, Linker, they're songs. You're saying that within hours after they've been played, people are rioting in the streets in defiance? That seems a bit of a stretch, Adam."

"Maybe, but they're working. Kids everywhere are going nuts, turning into killing machines. There's something else, Mr. President."

He looked at his Chief of Staff and said, "What else?"

"It appears the message is also being heard by the parents and adults. They are joining the riots in droves. All over the world."

"Holy shit."

****

Leah Kipshaw knocked on her daughter's door, but there was no response. She looked down the hall at the Secret Service agent standing dutifully halfway down the hallway. She called out, "Has Alexis come out of her room?"

The agent replied, "No maam. She went into her room, excited to watch the performance by Vasallus, and she hasn't come out since."

She has probably fallen asleep. There are no locks on her bedroom door; it is forbidden by White House security. Leah turned the knob and opened the door slightly. She could see the shape of her teenage daughter lying on the bed. A slight panic began to build as she threw the door open. She could see Alexis on her side, her iPod earplugs in her ears, her eyes closed. The T.V. was still on, tuned to CNN, the screen full of the reports of worldwide rioting. She moved to the T.V. and turned it off. She went to her daughter on the bed to pull the blankets up and remove her earplugs out of her ears. She reached down and suddenly her daughter's eyes snapped open and she lifted herself up quickly in the bed, startling Leah. Her daughter glared at her, her eyes blazing. She looked at Alexis and said, "Sorry honey for scaring you. I was just checking on you, saw you were sleeping, so was going to tuck you in."

Leah was utterly shocked at her daughter's next words, "I wasn't sleeping, you stupid fucking bitch. Get the fuck out of my bedroom right now."

Chapter 14

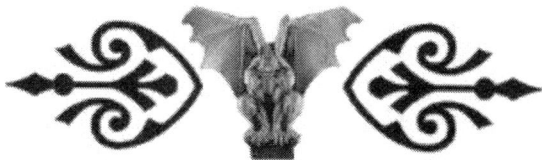

Thomas relaxed and leaned back in the seat of the airplane as it climbed to its cruising altitude of 40,000 feet. The non-stop Ryanair flight from Dublin to Fiumicino in Rome was a short three hours and he would take those hours to rest. He could not remember the last time he slept. It had been days and even though his body felt strong, his mind yearned for rest. Thomas knew that Robert Best would continue destabilizing the world through the growing violence and chaos surrounding Vasallus and their music. He also knew that the Lord Almighty would not stop His plan to bring mankind closer and closer to Armageddon. It had been written and that time was drawing near. He was the one man who knew more about this catastrophic event than any other person on earth. It was why he spent so much time in Rome.

He had been chosen. The Lord had chosen him to stop the Demon from destroying mankind before He had an opportunity to give every man; woman and child on this earth a choice. The Lord would save man, if they made the choice to be right with Him. To accept His son, Jesus Christ, as their Savior. If they chose Christ, they would be saved; if they did not, then Hell would find them. Satan would never allow them that choice. He was in a race against God to turn them away from Him and take away their choice.

He thought about his beloved Chloë and how horribly frightened she must be. The world was coming apart all around her and she was all alone. He knew she was aware of her origins and that she was a pawn of the Devil. What he could not determine is how much Best has revealed to her and the rest of Vasallus. He wondered to himself, "Was she aware the violence surrounding their performances was by design? Did she know the music created by Best and Benning was to poison the minds of the youth and turn them against society?" He continued to wonder inwardly "Was Chloë and the others aware of Best's plan to destroy all of mankind? Would Best kill Chloë and the others when his plan was complete"? All these questions and more raced through his mind as he leaned towards his window, looking out at the clouds that gathered like a large fluffy white comforter well below the level of the plane. He willed his eyes to sleep. Soon he was fast asleep.

****

Thomas was jarred awake when the wheels touched down hard at the Fiumicino airport. Momentarily hazy from his deep sleep, he quickly glanced out his window to ensure they were indeed on the ground. He watched the multiple hangers and buildings,surrounding the terminal in Rome's largest airport, whip by as the plane engaged the thrusters to slow it down. This flight he was fortunate to have two empty seats beside him as the plane was half empty. The stacks of papers he had placed on the two empty seats were now thrown to the floor and scattered beneath the seats in the next row. As the plane found its gate, passengers immediately began to rise from their seats, retrieve their overhead baggage and proceed to block the aisles while the compartment door was opened. He scurried out of his seat to retrieve his files when the aisle beside his row was blocked by a passenger. Thomas looked up at the passenger and asked if he could sneak past him to retrieve his fallen paperwork. The passenger, a middle aged, well-dressed professional beat him to it. "Please, allow me Father." The man scooped up the paperwork and handed the pile of jumbled papers to him before saying, "I'll let you sort them out, Father. Do you mind if I take this aisle seat? It looks like it's going to be awhile before they let us off this plane." Thomas motioned him to sit, "Most certainly. I would think you'd be glad to stand after that long flight. I need a few minutes to orientate myself before I get up and join the rush. My eyes close the second the wheels come up and don't open till they touch down."

The man smiled at his remark as he took the aisle seat and commented, "I can never sleep on a plane. I don't know why, because I'm usually dead tired when I fly."

"It's likely you have too much on your mind young man. Maybe an important meeting at your destination keeps your mind from relaxing?"

Suddenly the young man quickly moved over to the middle seat, beside him and leaned in close. Thomas found himself staring into the man's eyes, recognition crystalizing in his brain before the man hissed, "You're calling me a young man, O'Sullivan? What are you now, eighty years old? Yet, you look forty. Preparing for battle, priest?"

Thomas was stunned, as once again he was cornered on an airplane by Robert Best. His eyes burned a bright fluorescent red, and the wickedness danced freely within the red orbs. Best was pushing his weight against him into his side window, drawing the attention of passengers standing just a few feet away in the plane's aisles. Thomas focused once again on the eyes of the Demon and replied, "What is it about airplanes and airports you find a need to seek me out for a discussion? You know you can make an appointment at the Vatican for a sit down meeting."

The eyes of Best narrowed.His eyes burned slightly brighter at his remark, "Cute, priest, your new look has loosened you up somewhat. Not so stuffy anymore. I like that. Makes our encounters more light and not so formal, what do you think?"

Now Thomas narrowed his eyes and with a steady and authoritative voice replied, "I'm not interested in conversation Best. You're seconds away from having airport security pull you off of me. You're making quite the scene. Know, Demon, I'm not afraid of you; I know what you're trying to do, and why you're using Vasallus to poison the minds of people. It won't work. Believers in Christ will not be fooled. Your days in this world are numbered. Understand that the armies of the Lord God are marching towards you for one final conflict that will destroy you for all eternity."

Best's hand shot straight into his chest knocking the wind out of his lungs. Thomas could hear the shouts of airport security coming onto the plane and the hurried comments from the surrounding passengers directing them to the assault on a Catholic priest. He gasped for air and continued, "God's armies will be led to your ultimate demise by the kids of Vasallus; the blood of Christ that flows through their veins will prevail and together they will lift His mighty sword and swing it, slicing your monstrous head from your neck, sending you to an eternal damnation specially prepared by God." The Beast, his demonic face inches from his, shook with rage, and shocked at his words, drove his fist deeper into his rib cage, threatening to break through it when he screamed, "Your faith will kill you and all of mankind. Faith in a God that is willing to destroy this world and millions of your people? Tell me priest, is there a difference between Him and I? How many people perished in His earthquake in New Delhi? A few thousand music fans throwing Molotov cocktails at police is the same, priest?" Two burly uniformed security officers of the Aeroporti di Roma reached over and grabbed Best by the shoulders, pulling him away, barking out commands in Italian. Before he was led offthe plane, Thomas leaned over the middle seat and spoke, "The final conflict between my just and loving God and his adversary, Satan, is upon us. Prepare to die, Beast. Your death has been written and so it shall be!"

****

After Thomas finished giving his statements to police, he quickly left the airport in a taxi for the Vatican. If he hadn't already, Best would disappear like the mist, leaving the police wondering what happened. In the backseat of the taxi, he rubbed his sore chest and reflected on his conversation with Best. He thought about Best's reaction when he said it would be the kids of Vasalluswho would lead God's armies to his ultimate demise. "I don't believe Best has ever considered that the kids could turn and fight for the Lord," thought Thomas. "The idea of the kids turning towards their human origins and to God, likely scared Best more than if God Himself stood before him with a mighty spear ready to thrust it into his chest," he thought, as he watched the pounding rain hit the taxi's side window. Soon the Church would make a move against the kids of Vasallus. Their protection and safe-keeping was a direct command from God, and it was bestowed upon Thomas to fulfill that command.

The taxi rolled up in front of Thomas's private entrance of the southeast wing of the huge structure making up the Vatican. The entrance was unknown by most who inhabited the Vatican and was invisible from the street. The taxi driver paid no attention to the location where he was dropped off. Just another black robed clergy fare that came and went to the Vatican almost every day. The driver was anxious to get back to Fiumicino airport and the throng of ever waiting tourists eager to see the ancient city of Rome. The driver thanked him for his generous tip before he sped off, clearly appreciative of the normally nontipping priests whom he usually had in his taxi.

Thomas turned to enter the entrance when it suddenly burst open and a young clergy member stepped out, "Father O'Sullivan, you are wanted at once in Father Ricci's office. Please you go, I will handle your bags and have them placed in your room." Thomas handed his two bags to the young priest, "Thank you. Just place the bags on my bed if you will." He made his way down the long hallway from the street entrance towards the staircase that would bring Thomas to the second floor and to Father Ricci in the the south-east wing offices. Within a few minutes he was sitting down in front of Father Ricci, a much younger member of SOSL who was permanently stationed to the Vatican. His office reflected the décor and untidiness of someone who spent every day and many hours there.. "Tell me Father Ricci, what is it that caused me to forego at least an opportunity to prepare a cup of tea after a long flight"? He watched as Father Ricci folded his hands in front of him on his desk, a clear sign that something had happened and he was about to reveal some bad news. It was something that Ricci only did when he was greatly bothered. "Thomas, there has been a sign. This morning it came. It was discovered by Father Moretti, as he prepared for Mass. The same sign as before."

A signal from God had been received by the Vatican for Thomas. He had been chosen by the Lord to lead His fight against His enemy. He communicated with Thomas through confession in a special confessional room in the Vatican built hundreds of years ago for priests visiting or dispatched to the Vatican to pray to God in what was believed to be a direct link to the Lord. It was, symbolic, of course, but considered a very holy and privileged place. The Lord had chosen this room for His communication with him. The venue was discovered when Thomas had been praying in the special confessional room several months ago when He gave him His instructions. "Thomas, listen to my words. You will come to Me in this room when I call for you. It is here I will command you, Thomas. Do you understand?" He did not understand so he asked God, "How will I know Lord, when you want to speak with me?" The Lord replied, "The tears of My Son will echo like bells. It is then you must be summoned to this room. You must come quickly." The wonder of the Lord left him with more questions than answers that day. Among those questions was the sign of tears of His Son echoing like bells. What did this mean? He did not have to wait long for this sign, to find meaning. Exactly two weeks after the Lord had spoken directly to him, he was back at his parish in Balbriggan when he was urgently summoned to the Vatican. Once there, he was ushered into St. Peter's Basilica to witness the miracle of God. The Vatican priests brought Thomas to the statue of 'Pieta' to witness the miracle. The body of Christ, in the arms of Madonna, his head hanging limply to the side in her arms was crying. Tears from the sculptured eyes of Christ slowly dripped to the base of the Michelangelo sculpture where a steel goblet had been surreptitiously placed in the exact position to catch the tears as they fell the distance of approximately three feet. The sound of the tears hitting the rim of the goblet was eerily similar to a bong of a bell. It was the sign Thomas had warned Father Ricci about.. This was the second sign Thomas had received.

He followed Father Ricci to the special confessional room, both of them quiet as they walked. The fact that the Lord was communicating directly to them amongst all of the chaos happening around the world was not lost on them. The Lord was moving quickly now, and he was preparing His people. As they arrived at the large, heavy wooden doors of the confessional room, Father Ricci placed his hands on Thomas's shoulders and declared, "You carry a heavy burden, Thomas. Your strength and courage is also a miracle from God. Go my friend and I will be here waiting for you when you are done."

Thomas entered the shadowy confessional room and made his way to the tiny cubicle in the middle of the room. The room was devoid of any décor with the exception of a large crucifix attached to the wall opposite the confessional booth. The only light in the room was from a few candles burning that served only to cast shadows, rather than provide meaningful light. He squeezed into the darkened confessional, sat down and dropped his head in prayer. It was only a few minutes when the booth began to fill with a brilliant light that burst through the tightly woven lattice of the booth walls and splintered in every direction inside the room. It was exactly as he remembered it the first time. Thomas felt the power of the Lord surge into the room and his tiny confessional. He called out to God, "I am here Lord, as You command. I await Your word."

A deep voice boomed through the entire confessional room, as if the voice carried by loudspeakers. There were, of course, no loudspeakers in this room. It was the sound of God and His mighty voice echoed, "Thomas, you will leave at once to warn the leader of the world's most powerful nation of the coming arrival of the deceiver. Tell him to be vigil and to not make war with other lands. Stand up to the Anti-Christ and he will be rewarded. Go Thomas." He understood what God was asking but he knew he could not approach the man He was asking him to warn, "Lord, the man You suggest is very powerful and I am but a priest. How will such a man know to meet with me?" The voice of the Lord boomed again, "He is but a man, Thomas. Meet first with his underlings, and the truth will open their eyes to who you are. They will gain you an audience with this leader."

Before Thomas could ask another question, the light faded with the voice of God diminishing with the light, instructing him one last time to leave at once.

****

The long flight to Washington was over ten hours and Thomas was on guard for another appearance by Best. He doubted Best would choose to engage him once again. The Beast was powerless to stop him, and his threat that the kids of Vasallus would join forces with God and destroy him struck a chord with the Beast. He knew the kids would be safe until the end of the European tour before Best would bring any harm to them. The upcoming tour was a critical stage in the Demon's plan to create complete chaos and a total breakdown of civil obedience in all of the cities on the tour, setting the stage for his arrival to bring back a sense of sanity and control once again to a world teetering on civil unrest unprecedented in modern times. He was able to gain a meeting first thing tomorrow morning with help of the influence of the Vatican with Robert Ramirez, Deputy Secretary of the U.S. Department of Health and Human Resources. It is with him that Thomas would begin his quest to meet with the President of the United States.

As usual, he slept the entire flight, arriving in Washington feeling rested but with a hunger that growled deeply at him. Father Ricci insisted that he would accompany Thomas after he was briefed on what Thomas was tasked to do. He also insisted that Father Whitscomb, a Vatican expert on the Book of Revelations and its interpretations, also accompany them to help clarify the language of the many mysteries that made up the Book of Revelations. It wasn't long before the three of them had their luggage and made their way to the Marriott, just minutes away from the airport. Eating a hearty meal in the hotel's restaurant, the three of them said goodnight and retired to their rooms. As Father Whitscomb disappeared into his room, Father Ricci turned back towards Thomas's room and knocked on the door. The door opened immediately and Thomas smiled back at Father Ricci and said, "You need to borrow some change for the vending machine Father Ricci?"

"I wanted to make sure you were okay Thomas."

"I couldn't be better Father. Why do you ask?"

"Every time you come out of the special confessional room you're different somehow. How are you feeling Thomas, for real now"?

Thomas took a step towards Father Ricci and placed his hand on his shoulder. He replied "Don't worry about me Father Ricci, I am perfectly fine. Now get some rest; we have a big day tomorrow."

"I know you're right; it's getting late. I'm just worried about you. May I ask you one more question?"

"Certainly."

"Why is it that you never call me Enrico? I know the formalities of the priesthood and the Vatican, but I have called you Thomas when we are alone for as long as I can remember. You never call me Enrico, but you always address me by the formal Father Ricci."

This time Thomas smiled and patted his shoulder when he replied, "I always respect my elders Father Ricci and choose the formal name out of respect. Have a restful sleep, Father."

Father Ricci turned and headed towards his room, shaking his head at Thomas's reasoning. The priest, Father O'Sullivan, touched personally by God, looked years younger than him, but in fact he was thirty eight years his senior.

Chapter 15

Social media took on a life of its own in the subsequent days of the Quake Aid concert. Rioting around the globe intensified, fueled by the growing social media storm. The Vasallus members took to Twitter and Facebook , posting comments that bordered on anti-social. Their followers were consuming it in mass quantities and taking to the streets by the tens of thousands. Governments everywhere scrambled to contain the rioting and the crowds. In Sweden, of all places, people of all ages took to the streets of Stockholm in protest of the Government's recent increase in personal income taxes. Already one of the world's highest taxed countries, they have traditionally gotten away with it in return for the high quality of life provided to the Swedes.. The increase of the super-rich in Sweden and the anonymity from these increases has turned the working class bitter and resentful, Taking to the streets, they are fueled by the music and words of Vasallus, inspiring them to take a stand. Protests turned into riots and riots soon turned into looting, mayhem and violence.

****

Robert Ramirez, Deputy Secretary of the U.S. Department of Health and Human Resources, silently cursed himself for not getting out when he had the chance. He was supposed to have retired months ago, but he hung around to ensure Bruce would acquire his job before he left. Stupid. Now he was front and center to a mushrooming social upheaval mess that was out of control, threatening to bring down the nation's most basic and humble of institutions, the public school system. The majority of kids across the country refused to go to school anymore. The dwindling population of parents who still cared was powerless to stop it and get their kids back in school. They looked to the government to restore order and put a stop to their crumbling children's educational disaster. The only schools in the nation still running classes were the private schools. They fell under a different set of regulations, and were so far able to keep the kids in the classroom. It wouldn't last, however, and everyone in the room knew it.

They moved over to the conference table in the middle of the Secretary's office. Bruce Petersen, of the ACYF or Administration on Children, Youth and Family was one of the up and comers in Washington circles. He was young, smart and aggressive. Ramirez liked him immensely and his research on Vasallus was impressive. He watched him open his iPad, plug the cable to the projector into it, then another jack from a small sound system at the end of the table. Seconds later, the song began, and the beautiful voice of Chloë McClosky filled the room. All three of them sat in silence as the song played. When the song ended, Ramirez looked over at the Secretary, watched as she collected herself before he asked, "What did you think?" She looked at them both before replying, "I don't know other than to say it was beautiful."

Ramirez nodded at Petersen, and as he moved to bring up the next slide on the screen he looked back at the Secretary, "Now take a look at the words of the lyrics you just heard McClosky sing; now tell me what you think."

Petersen slid his finger across the face of his iPad, bringing up the next slide on the big screen. The room was cloaked in silence for a few minutes as the Secretary re-read the words several times. Both Petersen and Ramirez waited in silence, letting the words sink in fully before they commented. An audible gasp escaped the throat of the Secretary, as the reality of the words crystallized in her mind; "Mother of God."

We are not shackled or chained

Yet we cannot speak or do

Our leaders enact new laws to control us

To limit you and me
Will you tear down what is theirs and put up what is ours
Chorus:
It's Time
For you to have a say and be heard
It's Time
To say no To say no
It's Time
For a new beginning a new voice
Second verse:
Do you see what I see, everyone
Walls closing in erected by them
I want to see everything not just what's in front of me
Boundaries everywhere dictate what I see
Why is this happening to you and me?
Chorus:
It's Time
For you to have a say and be heard
It's Time
To say no To say no
It's Time
For a new beginning a new voice
Third verse:
We can fight the tyranny you and me
We stand we hold hands and together
We kick down the walls surrounding us
Say no to living in their cage
Break free from their control break free
Final chorus:
It's Time
For you to have a say and be heard
It's Time
To say no To say no
It's Time
For a new beginning a new voice
It's Time

For you to have a say and be heard
It's Time
To say no To say no
It's Time
For a new beginning a new voice

Ramirez continued, "The words were clear in the ballad, but combined with the magical voice of the McClosky girl and the background harmonies, one did not hear them and that is the aura of Vasallus. It is what has kept the group under the radar thus far. Our office has received complaints from concerned parents since the day Vasallus performed its first song, but the lyrics and message have steadily increased in dogma from the first album to the second. Songs performed from the upcoming third album are even stronger yet. These lyrics from "Its Time" are blatant anti-government hyperbole. We believe Vasallus is purposely poisoning the minds of our youth for some sort of a cause." The Secretary returned her attention to the screen once again and studied the words as if she were intensely analyzing an intelligence briefing memo from the CIA, and carefully taking her time. She then leaned back in her chair, straightened out her pant suit that seemed always to rise up, creating an uncomfortable gap between her jawline and her neck. She replied, "I would agree in the theory of anti-establishment rhetoric, although it's blatant, it's harmless to me, Bruce."

Petersen, mostly quiet to this point, spoke up, his voice tinged with sarcasm, "It's hardly harmless, Secretary. Look what is happening on our streets. The kids that listen to this shit and it's pretty much all of them, are destroying our cities. Vasallus's message is being heard and they're acting on it."

Candace Jenkins, Secretary of the U.S. Department of Health and Human Resources had heard and seen enough. She glared at Ramirez, from across the expanse of the conference table, then addressed Bruce Petersen, Commissioner of the Administration on Children, Youth and Family sitting beside him, "Jesus Christ, Bruce, these fucking lyrics should have been censored the minute they hit the airwaves. Come down hard on the NAB, set an example for the rest of the world to do the same." Looking back at Ramirez, she continued her tirade: "Bob, how did we miss this? The National Association of Broadcasters are to blame for this mess. Its job is to police its own industry. Well if they won't, then we will. Make the fines hurt, Bob. I'm scheduled to brief the President this afternoon on how we let this happen. How did we let this happen?"

"It completely flew under everyone's radar, from the NAB, to the people running the radio stations, music television and record stores who decide what content they want on their shelves. Everyone was blinded by the incredible popularity of Vasallus and no one took a hard look at the lyrics of the songs these kids were singing," he sheepishly commented.

"You still haven't answered the question, Bob. How did this happen? Who is to blame? Do we fine them all? Do we shut down Alive Records and Blackstar Studio's for producing this shit?", fumed the Secretary.

Ramirez took in a breath, the hot seat uncomfortable, as he watched the Secretary lean over her desk towards them, her immaculate pant suit rising up her neck as she did so and spat, "Were the songs written deliberately to cause this reaction? If they were then we will not only shut down the studio's we will go after Best and Johnson criminally for citing the violence and riots. We'll then go after the Benning kid who wrote this shit. Short of breaking every finger on his hands so he'll never lower a pen again to paper, we'll shut him down too."

He cursed his stupidity once again as he thought of a quiet beach he should have been lying on and sipping a cocktail. He looked at the Secretary and replied, "The Benning kid is brilliant, beyond brilliant when he wrote these songs. His talent Candace, is unheard of and borders on mystical. The kid is a freak from all accounts. Word has it he has written thousands of songs, all of the hit variety that could potentially keep Vasallus well stocked with hit material for decades. In fact, they could release a new album every few months and never run out of material."

"I don't give a shit about Benning and how talented he is. Shut them down, Bob. Do it now! End these fucking demonstrations, riots, or whatever the hell they are."

"It's not as simple as that, Candace."

Her face turned red, as she shouted, "Excuse me? What are you talking about? That is your job, Ramirez. I don't care about the public reaction to government censorship. The violence needs to be stopped. Stop the music of Vasallus, the rioting will disappear."

Petersen interceded, "To the contrary Secretary. Censoring Vasallus now will cause an all-out tornado of backlash, far worse than what is happening now. People idolize this group and when they discover the government has censored them, they will burn the country to embers. Vasallus represents a voice for the people that individually they could never have. Their music is changing this country, whether we want to stop it or not."

Ramirez continued, "If we censor them now, their music will go underground, making them even more notorious than they already are and their music even more popular."

Candace dropped her face into her hands, pulling her impeccably done shoulder length hair behind her ears. Frustration showed through her wrinkles making them more pronounced. She exhaled a breath of air, then looked up, "They're a bunch of kids who can sing, really good. They're not the Black Panthers marching for equality for Christ's sake. There has to be more to this than provoking lyrics causing our youth to rise up so violently."

Ramirez paused, knowing what he was about to say could blow up in his face, either the Secretary will think he has gone nuts or she will fire his ass, complicating his upcoming retirement more than it needed to be. "Candace, there is another explanation to all of this. I wasn't going to introduce this theory to you, because, well you'll know what I mean after you hear him out." Glancing at Bruce he instructed, "Bruce, would you bring in Father O'Sullivan please

****

On the instructions of Deputy Secretary Ramirez, Thomas took a guided tour of the White House along with his three colleagues from the Vatican. It was a fascinating piece of American history, and he wished he had more time to visit other institutions in Washington, but time was not something he had in abundance anymore. They were about to enter the Lincoln bedroom, when they were interrupted by a young man dressed smartly in a business suit and seemingly in a hurry, "Excuse me gentlemen, I have been sent by Deputy Secretary Ramirez to bring you to Secretary Jenkins's office immediately. Please follow me." Nodding at the White House Tour guide, as he held out his hand to direct Thomas and the others down the hallway and away from the Lincoln bedroom, he felt a twinge of disappointment in not being able to enter the Lincoln bedroom. He comforted himself in knowing he was receiving the opportunity to speak directly to an important official in the United States government that hopefully would result in a meeting with the President.

Minutes later they were rushed into a large and richly decorated office. The Deputy Secretary stood to greet them, shaking their hands and introducing Petersen once again to them, whom they also met yesterday.

"Father O'Sullivan, gentlemen, may I introduce Secretary Candace Jenkins."

Thomas shook the Secretary's hand, pleased by its warmth and strength. That was a good sign. "Secretary Jenkins, my pleasure. Thank you for taking the time to meet with us today. I know you must be busy."

She had a curious yet fascinated look on her face, another good sign. It meant that she would listen. For how long would be determined.

"It has been a very interesting day, Father O'Sullivan. Now I have four clergy from the Vatican in my office. Please tell me Father, the Pope isn't waiting outside my door to come in next because if he is he can come in now."

Smiling, he replied, "I can assure you he is not and if he was, he'd likely be taking a nap on Lincoln's bed, I'm sure." They all laughed at the unexpected expression of humour by Thomas. Taking the Secretary's invitation to sit, they all took a seat around the conference table.

"Your Irish is very Irish, Father. You haven't been in Italy for long I gather. How magnificent an Irish accent would be with an infusion of Italian?"

"Unfortunately my time in Rome is limited to the Vatican. You would be surprised to know that Italian clergy are a minority in the Vatican. If it wasn't for the support staff and administration, one would never know one is in Italy, based upon the language while in the Vatican."

A smattering of light laughter made its way around the table until Ramirez spoke, "Father O'Sullivan, Commissioner Petersen and myself have finished discussing the lyrics of Vasallus's music to Secretary Jenkins in relationship to the outbreak of violence following Quake Aid. We have discussed the possibility of censoring Vasallus and the management behind them. Please explain, and take your time if you will, your story, theories and personal connection to Vasallus." He watched as the Secretary shot him a look, a cue his time was limited. Government censorship would be disastrous and would only cause untold violence and death as Best moved to clear the people responsible for the censorship out by murdering them.

Thomas cleared his throat, gave his colleagues a reaffirming nod and began, "Secretary Jenkins, thank you for taking this time to listen to a few aging priests. What I am about to share with you, very few people in the world know about. It has been kept a secret within the walls of the Vatican for decades and there are very few in the Church who is aware of the details. Let me start by asking you a question."

He watched as Jenkins face took on an immediate look of fascination and likely was a little confused with his comment about 'aging priests.' She did not hesitate to answer his question, "Certainly Father, you may ask me anything you want. No guarantees, however, that I will answer them." She finished with a smile as she made her last comment. Thomas continued, "Do you believe in God?"

"I do, Father. You will be happy to know I was born and raised Catholic. We can end the formalities in this room. Please call me Candace."

"Thank you. I am happy to hear you have faith in your heart, Candace. You will need it in the coming months. What you are going to hear has no denomination. We have come to you under the guidance of the Eminence, who wanted me to tell you that if he needed to travel to the United States to personally speak with the President and your government, he would. It is my hope that it won't be necessary."

He received a reassuring smile and nod from the Secretary so he continued, "The day I had taken my vows as a young priest in a small village in Ireland, I was summoned to Rome. It was disappointing for me because I was eager to begin work and serving God in my village. Father O'Malley, who I had been under his tutelage for six months before accepting my lifetime commitment to the priesthood, reassured me that I was being summoned for a great purpose and I had been chosen by God for something great. I scoffed at his encouraging words, but he was right. I have been chosen by God for something great."

He could see the Secretary's patience was waning, he noticed her glancing at her watch as he spoke. He was sure her daily agenda did not allow for deviations to her tight schedule so he decided to shock her. "The spiritual warfare raged between God and Satan since the beginning of time has now manifested itself in real time. The predicted Armageddon, written in the Book of Revelations is upon us. The world as we know it will end soon. Not years, but in months or even days. Satan is in a race with God for ownership of the souls of mankind prior to the cataclysmic event. Satan is using the kids of Vasallus to influence the youth of this world by poisoning their minds to God through their music."

He watched the predictable reaction he knew was coming. The

Secretary looked back and forth between Ramirez and Petersen, anger swelling in her face and body movements. She glared back at him as she spat, "With all due respect, Father. I am sorry you and your colleagues have had to travel so far, but the United States government is not interested in the spiritual warfare between good and evil and the impending end of the world. If we listened to all of the religious zealots, Father, who have predicted the end of the world and felt compelled to take some sort of action, then I'm afraid we would lose the ability to govern the people of this great country through the sheer madness of our actions. Now if you will excuse me I must get back to work." She rose quickly from her chair and addressed Ramirez, "Please have security escort our guests to wherever they need to go. You and Petersen can remain in my office until I return." Turning back to him she continued, "I'm sorry your trip was a waste of time. Please give the Pope the warm regards of the United States government."

Thomas did not make a move to stand and accept her out stretched hand. Instead he replied, "Secretary, would you believe if I told you I was seventy five years old?" She pulled back her hand, temporarily stunned by his admission, but she quickly recovered, "Well, I'm impressed with the Vatican's commitment to fitness, Father." She then turned to leave when he continued, "I was in the delivery room, Secretary, seventeen years ago in Dublin to witness the birth of Satan's child." He was quickly interrupted by the Secretary, "I am not interested in the Church's stories, Father. Now, my apologies, but I must move on to my next meeting."

Thomas kept going, "The baby girl, Secretary, was Chloë McClosky. The same Chloë McClosky of Vasallus. I watched her mother die, but before she did, she pleaded with me not to let the baby live, that the baby was the child of Satan."

****

Candace slowly returned to the table, the priest's words were not making any sense, but it was his eyes that shone a beautiful blue, drawing her back. There was something in them, she struggled for the right words that spoke to her. There was an incredible presence surrounding the priest and she found herself sitting back down in front of him. "Continue Father."

"The Devil was in the room, disguised as a doctor, laughing as the life of baby Chloë's mother, Katherine slipped away. I turned and attacked the doctor, pummeled him with my fists, my rage at the Beast uncontrollable when I heard a sound distract me. The baby did not cry out like babies do when wrapped in a towel. She began to sing, Candace, like an angel. She filled the delivery room with the sound of beautiful angels singing. Everyone in the room knew it was a miracle from God. I knew that God had saved this baby from Satan and I was overjoyed with happiness. I was horribly wrong. The doctor I was seconds away from killing had disappeared into thin air. I was summoned into the next room where they had moved Chloë and shown the baby's birthmark that convinced me this was no miracle baby from God. It carried the mark of the Beast in three backwards sixes on her upper right thigh."

She stared at the priest, unable to speak as he continued his remarkable story, "The Beast had slaughtered Chloë's father and his parents just prior to Katherine coming to the hospital. He attacked and revealed himself to me in the elevator as I arrived at the hospital, but he did not kill me. With the approval of Katherine's parents, the Church took custody of the baby. I watched as she grew to the young lady she is today. I have seen her incredible music gifts since she was a young child."

She looked at him, unable to put things together so she asked, "What does this have to do with God's plans to end our world, Father?"

"The other six members of Vasallus also carry the same mark as Chloë. They were all born on the exact same day, the very same minute in different parts of the world. All seven of them were born musical prodigies. All seven fathers were horribly murdered. The murders were never solved as the investigations in each and every one of them stalled because of a lack of evidence. The copious amounts of blood retrieved at the murder scene that was not the victims carried no DNA known to man. Key people in the investigation of these murders over the years have themselves been murdered or have disappeared."

He continued, "The Devil has spawned these children for one purpose only. He is determined to darken as many souls as he can before the Rapture occurs. It is written in the Book of Revelations. He is utilizing the one thing that is a universal language. Music. He is using Vasallus to poison the minds of the youth and then everyone else through their music. Then he is extending his message into the long tentacles of social media. It is working as you can tell. The youth around the globe are revolting. Inspired and emboldened by Vasallus's music, they are taking to the streets. It is not only your government, but governments around the world do not know how to control it. Some countries have moved their riot police in with tear gas, water cannons and real bullets; it will only fuel their rage to greater heights."

Stunned by what she was hearing, overwhelmed by the presence of God inside of Father O'Sullivan, she was sure of it. "Why are you telling me this, Father? Why the United States government?"

"It is the belief of the Church that Satan will continue to create further chaos and upheaval in the coming weeks, further weakening governments' ability to deal with the revolts. When the world is too weak and too late to stop the people and social anarchy is in place, only then will the Beast reveal himself. He will appear as a savior, a calming and effective leader with the ability to pull the world out of its self-destruction. The world will quickly move to embrace him. Once he is in power, he will cut off the heads of the world's leaders in a show of complete power further sealing the fate of mankind. His first target will be the President of the United States."

The priest's incredible blue eyes radiated like beacons, and she struggled with the priest's admission that he was seventy five years old. He could easily pass for thirty. He was youthful, strong and handsome. His story was astounding; yet, she found

173

herself believing him. There was a power and authority to him that she couldn't put her finger on. She then understood why he was here to speak with her. He needed to reach the President and warn him, and she was the conduit. She asked, "How will we know who this man is?"

"You already know him."

"I do? How would I know him?"

"Who is the driving force behind Vasallus?"

She gasped, "Avery Johnson is the demon?"

"Avery is much of a pawn in this as the kids are."

She thought back to the press conferences of Vasallus and then it clicked, "Robert Best?"

He never responded. The look in his ocean blue eyes confirmed it. "He is just a man, Father. He can be stopped. I will have him picked up and arrested. We will lock him up. We will have Vasallus rounded up and arrested." She glanced at Ramirez for the first time in a long time. "Robert, have the FBI pick up Best and haul his ass in for questioning."

She was taken aback by his sudden laughter. He replied, "You cannot pick him up, Secretary, as you will never find him. You cannot stop him either, nor can you stop the kids of Vasallus. Robert Best is the Anti-Christ and the members of Vasallus are his children!"

The revelation of Robert Best as the Anti-Christ was astonishing. She remembers the man from the televised press conferences. He appeared handsome, dashing and came across as a powerful music executive in his interviews. To picture him as the Devil was a stretch for her, even after all she had heard. She asked Father O'Sullivan, "How do you know all of this, Father?"

She watched as he reached across the table with both hands, palms up, inviting her to place her hands in his. She did not hesitate. It felt like there was an unseen force moving her hands for her. When she placed her hands in his, she was instantly overcome with a sense of an overpowering force emanating from the body of the priest. She closed her eyes, and the vision that flashed through her mind was immediate but long enough for her to see and feel the holiness in the touch. She knew with every shred in her body that she had been touched by the hands of God.

Chapter 16

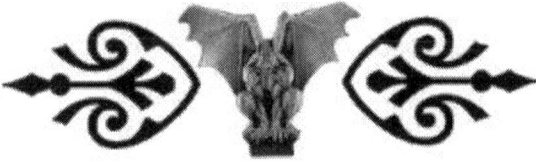

Patrick sat alone in his room in the mansion, refusing to join the others in rehearsal. It was a few days after the concert at the Rose Bowl, and the appearance of one of God's soldiers still left him unable to shake the encounter. Where was the Master? There was not one word from him in this world or from the dark realm. He needed him now more than ever. He wanted to go out into the spiritual world and search for this soldier, engage him, then destroy him. Who was he, claiming to be the son of the King Tiridates? It didn't matter to him, but it probably would to the Master. He claimed that his blood flowed in me! Preposterous! The Master would go galactic when he learned of this encounter. Together they would seek out this tin man and cut him to ribbons with his own sword.

"Have any of the others had a similar encounter?" he wondered. He thought about approaching Juan or Connor to see if they did, but if they hadn't the Master would be furious with him for planting that seed in their minds. They're being watched. Maybe they are being watched? The spiritual battle the Master has often talked about and warned us all to prepare for what might finally be imminent. He hoped so, because he was sick of waiting for God's armies to descend down on them in battle. The final destruction of mankind was upon them. This is what this was, and he concentrated his mind to will the Master into the dark realm to discuss their strategy.

He could no longer take the waiting. It was driving him crazy. Confused and angry at the Master's mysterious absence, he turned his thoughts toward something he could control. He needed to get out of this mansion and go on a murderous rampage tonight. Kill at least a dozen people, place the city into a state of catatonic fear. Maybe that would be enough for the Master to take notice and return. He would bring the rest of them with him. He felt it was time that the girls felt the rush of a human soul pass through their bodies on their way to Hell as they snuffed out their lives with their own hands. Connor and Juan were seasoned killers themselves but preferred to murder and wreak havoc far away from Los Angeles. The girls resisted the forces that tugged at their dark souls, but it was time for them to embrace the evilness that licked their very consciousness.

****

It was 3:30 a.m. and the five members of Vasallus stood in the quiet darkness of the hallway outside the bedroom of fourteen year old Alexis Kipshaw. The daughter of the President of the United States slept undisturbed as they stood looking at each other, all of them unsure why Benning had brought them here to the most secure building in the United States, the White House. It was not secure enough, however, to stop the entrance of the darkest spirits on earth. The Secret Service, stationed at each end of the hallway that also included the bedroom of the President and the First Lady did not flinch at the spiritual commotion that happened just a few feet away. Brittany knew this was not going to be good. She glanced at Chloë, getting a stare back that read, "What the hell is going on?"

Chloë took a step towards Patrick, who was about to open the door leading into the bedroom, and warned, "What are we doing here? We leave for Europe in a few days, and we can't have any problems. Do you hear me Patrick? You might not have noticed the two agents down the hall? They might not be able to see or hear us, but we could bump into something or something could fall on the floor that will send these guys running over here."

He whirled around, eyes blazing, retorting, "I think it's time, my little Irish lass, to shed your good girl image and accept who you are and why you were born." Looking at

Brittany, he continued, "That includes you Britt. I'm tired of covering for you two. Tonight you will wreak havoc in this house and introduce death into it. Do you hear me? Now follow me."

Chloë protested, "Forget it Benning. You're not forcing me or anyone else to do anything we don't want to do. You think you're some bad-ass but all you are is a ruthless killer." Staring at Connor and Juan she continued her tirade, "You two can continue being his whipping boys but Brittany and I are out of here."

Benning, his anger out of control, threw himself against Chloë, the force and swiftness of his attack sending them both crashing into the wall adjacent to the entranceway door. The sound of their impact echoed through the stillness of the dark hallway. Both agents from opposing directions raced down the hallway towards them, guns drawn. Benning pressed his body hard against hers, trapping any escape. His voice, guttural boomed, "Don't you ever challenge me again McClosky! In case you haven't noticed, the Master hasn't been around for days. We're on our own. Now you will do what I say, otherwise there will be no tour for you, you pathetic bitch; instead you'll be exchanging bedtime stories in the dark with Leroux. We are all going inside this room. Now let's get going!"

Chloë felt the dark power seep into her soul like a pool of mercury on a hard surface flowing in one direction. Like a vampire thirsting for blood, she fought against it and willed herself to resist the urges that would soon come. The agents raced back from the President's bedroom, searching for the source of the noise. They reached the bedroom door of Alexis Kipshaw and entered, completely unaware of the evil presence surrounding them. Soon the hallway lights came on , and they heard the panicked voices of the President and his wife rushing towards the bedroom, alerted by the agents.

Instinctively, Chloë knew why they were here and the fear in the human half of her soul began to cry out, desperate to stop Benning. She and Brittany could only watch in horror at what was taking place on the bed.

The spirit of Connor Asker, on the direction of Benning had

entered the soul of the young and naive, Alexis Kipshaw. At first it was just a rush of air being sucked from the room as Asker entered her body followed by the physical change in the young girl as the malevolent spirit worked its way through her.. Michael had seen enough and turned on Benning, his smaller body forcing Patrick hard against the dresser-drawer chest beside the bed. The impact lifted the large dresser backwards on to its back legs, then forward pulling the dresser off the wall slamming it back onto the floor. The two Secret Service agents along with the President and the First Lady reacted to the invisible force seemingly picking the dresser up before crashing it to the floor.

President Kipshaw, hovering above his daughter, startled at the loud sound, yelled at the closest agent, "What the hell was that?"

The agent just stared at his boss, unable to say anything. The brief silence was interrupted by a loud scream from the First Lady, "Jesus Christ, Stan, our daughter!" The President turned back towards his daughter, stunned at what he was witnessing. Alexis, her eyes rolled back into her sockets revealing white blanks arched sharply towards the ceiling above her bed. Her back bent at a severe angle. He instinctively jumped on the bed, reached up and tried to pull his daughter back onto the bed, but he couldn't. She was locked in a rigid position. He cried out to the agents standing beside the bed, who stood horrified at what they saw happening to the young girl, "Call the medics now!" Looking up at his panicked wife, he instructed, "Leah, her body is in a seizure. We have to get her to lie flat on the bed before she hurts herself. Grab her by the ankles and slowly lift them and see if we can get her to lie down." He jumped on the bed and took a position behind his daughter's head while his wife leaned over the foot of the bed and reached for Alexis's ankles.

Suddenly Alexis's ankles shot upwards and wrapped themselves around the First Lady's neck. The ankles moving into a locked position at the back of her neck. The swiftness of his daughter's movement shocked the President, and he hesitated for a second before the choking sound from his wife snapped him back to reality. He glanced at the face of his daughter, devoid of any emotion before leaping off the bed and wheeling towards his wife. He grabbed his daughter's ankles and tried to free them from around her neck. Her grip was astonishingly strong and he struggled to no avail. He could hear Leah gasping for air, and the thought of her dying at the hands of their fourteen year old daughter flashed before his eyes. He used all the strength he had to pry open her ankles, but the seizure had locked her muscles. The medic would need to give her an injection to relax her muscles. "Where the hell was the medic," he thought. Panicking, he moved to position his shoulder beneath her legs so he could gain better leverage in forcing her feet apart. Leah's face began to turn purple from the asphyxiation. She couldn't hold on much longer. Out of nowhere a new set of hands joined in the effort to pry open Alexis's ankles. While the others left in search of the medics, the agent who stayed behind strained to move the girl's ankles apart. The sheer strength of his daughter's locked legs was staggering. The two men couldn't budge them.

A guttural roar erupted from his daughter, and he turned to see Alexis launching herself forward with her ankles still locked around his wife's neck. She planted her fist into the face of the agent, and his nose exploded upon impact. He could hear the bones shatter in the agent's face. His daughter began to whip her upper body up and down savagely, while turning her ankles over and twisting her mother's head down onto the bed with such force it threatened to break her neck.

****

Michael and Patrick bounced off the dresser and =to the floor. Rolling on top of Benning, Michael pounded his fists into his face, screaming, "You're killing her mother, Benning! Stop Asker or I'll kill you, I swear!" Benning, his mouth bleeding from Michael's blows, laughed like a crazed psychopath, "What's the matter Lockwood? Are you jealous Asker's having all the fun with the little bitch!" Michael wrapped his hands around Benning's neck, in a rage, squeezing the sneer coming from Benning while he yelled back at Chloë, "Help the girl, Chloë. Stop him from killing the First Lady!"

Chloë instantly reacted, jumping on the bed, screaming at the young girl as she did so, "Connor, stop it! Don't do this. Don't listen to Benning. He's out of his mind crazy! This isn't what we are Connor, please! Let her go!" She sobbed as she begged Connor to stop. She knew the lady would die when suddenly the cacophonic sounds coming from the girl abruptly stopped and she rose to a sitting position, releasing her ankles from the neck of the First Lady as she did so.

****

The roar of his daughter's screams was horrifying to hear, and he desperately tried to unlock his daughter's ankles. His daughter's bedroom had turned into an unstoppable nightmare. He was losing his wife; she only had a few seconds left to live. He cried out, "Leah, hang in there baby, hang in there." Sobbing, his own strength was ebbing away, and he desperately tried a final time to save his wife when suddenly his daughter's ankles went limp and fell away from around his wife's neck. His wife fell backwards onto the floor at the foot of the bed, gagging as her lungs sucked in short gasps of welcome oxygen. His daughter fell straight back onto the bed, the end of her seizure leaving her limp and crying. There was a commotion behind him and he looked to see medics and agents pouring into the bedroom. "About fucking time," is all he could say," as he too fell back onto the bed, landing beside his daughter. He put his arm beneath her neck and pulled her close as sobs wracked her body. He watched the medics begin an oxygen flow to his wife's starved lungs, while as they quickly loaded her onto a stretcher and carried her out of the room.

****

Benning, blood covering his mouth, glared at Lockwood as the six of them gathered in the corner of the room, witnesses to the chaos in the bedroom while the flurry of people tending to the President's family swirled around them, oblivious to their presence.

Benning, flanked by Juan and Connor, seethed, "You ever do that again Lockwood, and I'll kill you."

Michael clenched his fists, ready to launch himself at Benning, when the touch of Chloë 's hand on his arm, stopped him. He glared right back at Benning, "You don't scare me, Benning. I'd relish the chance to rip your heart from your chest like you did to Elizabeth."

"I wish you would. I wish all of you would. The Master demands it, and soon he will lose his patience with your fear to embrace your true purpose."

Chloë took a step towards Benning before answering, "It's about choice, Patrick. You have the blood of your human mother that flows through you, like all of us do. You three ignore the fact you are half human and choose to pursue your dark side. We choose life and I will die fighting for that gift."

Benning's rage began to resonate through the room as McClosky's blasphemous words echoed. Pictures flew off the walls and crashed into the opposite walls, clothes ripped off the hangers in Alexis's closet and were flung across the room. The stunned looks on the medics and agents still in the room as the objects soared around them belied their fear.

"The Master will rip you to pieces, McClosky, for your traitorous words. What is the matter with you? You're lucky the Master didn't kill you at the mansion when the priest pierced the door with his Holy sword. This is our destiny, all of us, together. The European tour will culminate in the final fury against humankind and their ultimate destruction. There will no longer be life to fight for Chloë. The God you believe is so gracious and loving will destroy man once and for all."

Brittany, quiet to this point, raised her voice defiantly to Benning, "What the hell was this fiasco tonight? What are we doing in the bedroom of the daughter of the President of the United States? Why would you allow Connor to hurt that girl?"

"I didn't tell him to do anything, Britt. Like Chloë said, we all have a choice. Connor chose to enter the soul of the girl, take a peek inside and stir things up?"

She looked at him, disgusted, "Why? Why bring the three of us here to this?"

The three of them stared at Benning, waiting for an answer to Brittany's question when he replied, "In time you will come to understand why we are here tonight. Soon you will see."

****

President Kipshaw, alone with his wife, sedated so she could sleep, reflected on the bizarre series of events just hours earlier in his daughter's bedroom. Thankfully, Alexis had no serious injuries from her seizure and would go through a battery of tests in the coming days to determine the cause of the powerful seizure. His body shook slightly at the memory of the events. "Where did the strength of her grip come from?" He thought. Her muscles, locked in a death grip, could not produce that kind of power or could they? He would hear from the doctors soon and he hoped their diagnosis would show nothing serious and that it was just a freak accident that his daughter had attacked her mother. His body began to succumb to the exhaustion of the evening's events and the lateness of the night. He needed to get a few hours rest before the day began as it would be a busy one. The thought of the day's schedule made his shoulders slouch even further.

****

Patrick stood outside of Michael Lockwood's bedroom, his rage over his attack earlier in the night not diffused. He wanted desperately to kill the British punk who defied his authority. He was superior over the rest of them, because he was the only one who truly embraced their dark side. Sure, Juan and Connor didn't shy away from theirs, but they also didn't completely buy in. Usually he had to prod them to flex their demonic power and that infuriated him almost as much as the bitch McClosky did when she extolled her human side. He knew the Master had not interfered or made an appearance lately. He needed Vasallus to complete the European tour to close the loop on his diabolical plan. The only plausible explanation the Master did not punish McClosky and the others is because the power that came from their human soul was more of a threat than he thought.

He was not afraid of their belief in God. He despised Him and those that believed in Him. The sudden appearance of a soldier of God the other night at the Rose Bowl only emboldened him further to what lay ahead. He would destroy McClosky, Lockwood and Campbell and maybe the other two as well, if they did not change and accept their demonic gift fully. He would stand beside the Master and together they would wield a power too great for God and his soldiers to withstand.

That day was near and he would be ready.

Chapter 17

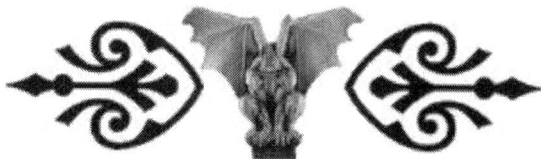

The world had gone to shit and all eyes were on America to fix it, just like they have for decades. Previous President's had just begun to feel the sting of American people's disdain for military intervention. The current President of the United States was feeling that contempt full on.

Stanley Kipshaw was the 44th President of the United States and the current crisis in India had his administration in complete damage control. He had been criticized from the rest of the world for his administration's handling of the numerous catastrophes: the aftermath of the horrible earthquake in New Delhi and the tsunami in the Philippines. The Chinese government had sent thousands of troops into India to assist the Indian government in stabilizing the region. The arrival of the US troops was viewed by the Chinese as unnecessary and a deliberate attempt by the US government to undermine their efforts.

President Kipshaw wasn't worried about the Chinese and any political fallout from them, but he was worried about Pakistan's intentions. Kipshaw was still very popular to the American people, winning his second term by a landslide, but he knew that trust and popularity was wearing thin. He also knew the Pakistan government was directing the rebel movement to continue to destabilize the region in the hopes of a political overthrow of the current Indian government. The collapse of the Indian government and its President would pave the way for a Pakistan invasion, and the United States could never allow this to happen. To make matters worse there were indications from satellite intelligence reports that Iran was suspected of troop movement from their largest military base located in Hamadan towards the Iraq border. His military commanders strongly sensed or suspected the Iranian government was trying to take advantage of the world's spotlight on India to amass an army and heavy equipment along their borders with Iraq and within missile range of Tel Aviv. Iran's suspected new medium range ballistic missile, the devastating Shahab – 3 was feared part of this arsenal buildup along the Iraq border. If Israel intelligence were to confirm the missile's presence they would surely pressure the United States government to support an all-out air strike by Israeli Air Force jets.

To top it off, his mind constantly crept back to the frightening events from last night in his daughter Alexis's bedroom. Why had a terrible seizure wracked her body with spasms, causing her to hurtle herself into the walls of her bedroom, completely destroying the room, he queried to himself. Heavily sedated she was at this point sleeping peacefully in hospital, his wife keeping a close vigil. The demands of his office kept him from where he needed to be.

The President made his way through the hallways of the West Wing of the White House, his usual Secret Service detail close by, to a meeting with the Joint Chiefs in his Oval Office. The door to the Cabinet Room suddenly opened. His Chief of Staff, Adam Linker, stepped into the hallway and asked, "Mr. President, may I have a word?"

Stanley picking up on Adam's agitated state, replied, "Adam, I am off to the meeting with the Joint Chiefs. A meeting you are also attending. What's up with you? You look a little frenzied. Is there a lineup to the bathroom in there?"

He noticed that Adam wasn't impressed with his feeble attempt at humor, and his face grew even grimmer as he spoke, "Mr. President, my meeting with Jenkins and her people from Health and Human Resources has gone much longer than I anticipated, and they have something I think you need to hear. Can you give me ten minutes to hear them out?"

Now he was getting annoyed with his assistant, "Adam, for

Christ Sakes, I am off, no, we're off to an important meeting to discuss how we can keep the Middle East from annihilating each other and you want me to take time to talk to Jenkins about how much of a hypocritical prick I am when I cut back on her education funding for this budget?"

"Mr. President, I know, I know. It has nothing to do with cutbacks, I promise you. There is a group of priests from Rome, dispatched by the Vatican, who have some news that affects our national security."

"You're not making any bloody sense, Adam. You want me to meet with some priests from Rome or Jenkins?"

"Mr. President, the priests are here at the request of Jenkins. This incredible story you are about to hear, somehow found its way to her and then to me. Please, Mr. President. This is important."

He stared into his Chief of Staff's eyes for a few seconds, seeing how serious he was, then turned to his security detail and instructed, "Give me ten minutes, then come in and get me. Adam, you let them know in the Cabinet Room we're going to be late. This better be good."

****

Candace Jenkins, Secretary of the U.S. Department of Health and Human Resources, jumped from her chair to greet him as he entered the room. He quickly greeted her and shook hands with her Deputy Secretary, Robert Ramirez and another bureaucrat named Petersen he did not recognize. He was momentarily taken aback with the presence of the three Roman Catholic priests, who all rose to greet him. "This was going to be a strange one," he thought to himself as he took a seat directly across from the three priests. The presence of the clergy unnerved him somewhat. He felt a sudden sense of guilt that came with occupying the Oval Office in the eyes of many including the Vatican, who were often both privately and publically critical of his administration.

He turned to Jenkins and Ramirez and in respect to the clergy stated, "My time is limited. I'm afraid Candace; the

187

Joint Chiefs are all strapped in and loaded to tear a much bigger piece off of my hide this morning."

Everyone in the room laughed, the necessary ice breaker out of the way, except for one of the three priests - the one called O'Sullivan. He acted like he never heard him, or maybe it was because he didn't much care for what he said.

He thought he would try another ice breaker, "Adam, you never told me I'd be attending Mass on a Thursday morning."

After the laughter made its way around the room, Jenkins immediately brought a serious tone to the room when she said, "Mr. President, thank you for taking the time to meet with us this morning."

Stanley interrupted the Secretary, "Once again Secretary Jenkins, and my apologies gentlemen, I am in the middle of an escalating situation that requires my full attention. We only have a few minutes, Candace, so please, tell me why I am meeting with the Catholic Church this morning."

Not fazed by Stanley's interruption, Candace rose from her seat and began to pace as she spoke, her usual routine in meetings.

"Mr. President, before I introduce the clergy who have travelled all the way from Rome, they have shared with me this morning, an extraordinary story that you must hear. Let me explain to you a phenomenon that is emerging amongst not only the youth of the United States, but around the world and is now spreading into the adult population. We are seeing unprecedented violence and mayhem surrounding the music of the super-group Vasallus."

Now it was the President who rose from his seat, anger building inside of him. He flashed a stare at Adam before addressing Secretary Jenkins, "Candace you can't be serious. You had representatives from the Vatican come all the way over here to tell me that the kid band Vasallus, who my daughter is crazy about, is polluting the minds of our youth?"

Still unfazed and expecting the reaction, "Mr. President, approximately ninety minutes ago my reaction to that opening statement was exactly the same as yours. Please hear me out."

His impatience clear, he replied, "This is not the problem the

President of the United States needs to solve. Draft a censorship order. I'll take a look at it and if it's reasonable I'll sign it. Now if you don't mind, I must move onto another meeting."

He gave Linker one last look, then turned to leave. He heard a voice behind him that caused him to stop. He didn't know what it was about the voice that caused him to stop, but it just did. The voice had a tone that was captivating and meaningful. He turned to see the youngest of the three Catholic priests standing. He was immediately drawn to his incredibly blue eyes staring back at him, boring into his. His eyes were so vividly blue, so engaging, he found himself unable to speak for a second. Then the voice continued.

"Mr. President, if I may be so direct. Please give us a few more minutes of your time. I promise you, that what we have to tell you won't take long and you will want to hear it."

Secretary Jenkins introduced the priest by name, "Mr. President, this is Father Thomas O'Sullivan. He is head of a secret office within the Vatican, called SOSL. What he and the other priests from the Vatican have to say is important for you to hear. It could very well direct the decisions you must make in regards to the growing conflict in the Middle East."

There was an aura about him that he could not explain, but instinctively he felt he needed to listen to him. He nodded to his Chief of Staff then took a seat on the leather chair across from Father O'Sullivan.

"Please Father, continue."

For the next hour he listened to a story from O'Sullivan that took many twists. From outright bizarre to eerily frightening the story of the seven children from Vasallus took shape. He heard about the rapes and attacks of the seven women around the world at the exact same time by a so-called demon. Then all of them giving birth at also the exact same time to seemingly miraculous babies that grew to become musical prodigies and eventually formed Vasallus. He looked at Candace and asked, "How long have you known about these kids?"

"Deputy Secretary Ramirez here and the Commissioner of the Administration on Children, Youth and Family, Bruce Petersen, approached me several weeks ago with their theory."

"I understand the violence surrounding the band, but tell me why has it continued or better yet, why has it been allowed to escalate?"

Ramirez stepped in to answer the President, "If I may, Mr. President, the popularity of Vasallus was so enormous when they were originally formed simply because of the incredible popularity and diversity of the kids that form Vasallus. They are all unique in their own way with a different style of their own; half of them are from different parts of the world giving them instant international appeal."

Ramirez kept going, "We strongly believe Mr. President, that the lyrics of their music are specifically designed to site hatred, violence and outright defiance to the rules of society. Their lyrics completely slipped through the radar of this government, even though protest groups of parents and religious leaders from around the country and the world for that matter have strongly denounced their music and lyrics. The message in their music is subtle but very clever in delivery. They are releasing one major hit after another, building a frenzied and loyal following around the world that grows exponentially every day.

Stanley looked at Ramirez and said, "Censor them. Plain and simple. Inform the industry the music incites violence and anti-social behavior detrimental to the good of society. Have their music taken off the shelves and haul Best's and Johnson's asses into your office and hit them with heavy fines and outright banishment if they do not comply."

It was Jenkins who replied, "Mr. President, with all due respect, this is not the 50's. We're not talking about Elvis's swinging hips throwing young pubescent girls into a crazed state, even though they seem to be doing that over Asker and Jimenez. The lyrics mask subliminal messages that are reaching the youth and turning them against all forms of authority in an ever increasing violent manner. It is no longer getting out of control; it is out of control, Mr. President."

"Does it change what I just suggested you needed to do?"

Another voice entered the conversation. It was Father O'Sullivan. "Mr. President, let me clarify what the Church believes. The music of Vasallus is just the beginning of a plot by the Anti-Christ to destroy mankind. Satan gave birth to these children, all of them musical geniuses, by design. It is as if he manufactured them for a sole purpose. He wants to blacken the souls of the youth of the world, turn them away from God and His teachings."

Stanley looked at the Father O'Sullivan, his dazzling blue eyes drawing him closer, inviting him to look through them, like windows to Heaven. It was mesmerizing and he had to tear himself away from his stare in order to respond, "Father, with all due respect, what my people are saying is about social upheaval that an enforced censorship would alleviate. You are talking about a demonic plot by Satan to destroy mankind. I don't see how the two theories become one."

Father O'Sullivan stood, walked slowly around the leather couch he was sitting at, then turned back towards the President before saying, "Mr. President, how old do you think I am?"

Surprised by the question, the President fumbled before answering, not sure what to say, "I'm sorry Father, I'm terrible at guessing an age. Why would you ask me that? Besides, I am long overdue for my meeting. Adam, please inform the JC, I am on my way."

As he was about to get up from his seat, he heard Father O'Sullivan speak, the words he was speaking did not make any sense. He looked up at the priest and replied, "Excuse me Father, what did you say?"

The priest's eyes seemed to fill the room with a presence he had never felt before. He was overcome with an overwhelming feeling he was standing in the same room with the Lord himself. It was incredibly eerie, but wonderful all the same.

"I am seventy five years old Mr. President."

He stood for a long minute, stunned by what the priest had just said. He couldn't have been any older than thirty in appearance.. It was an incredible revelation, but he knew it to be true; he just felt it.

"Father, that is impossible. You are the youngest looking priest I have ever met. You barely look old enough to have graduated from seminary school."

Ramirez spoke next, "Mr. President, with Father O'Sullivan's permission, I would like to show you something." Receiving a nod of approval from Father O'Sullivan, Ramirez handed the President a book. The book was a large, worn leather-bound book. A scrapbook of sorts, filled with articles and photographs.

The President fell back into his chair and began to leaf through it. He was speechless as he recognized pictures of a younger looking Father O'Sullivan, shaking hands with a man as he received his Bachelor's Degree at the University of Dublin. The caption, handwritten   below the photo also included the date, 1958. Four years later, a more mature looking O'Sullivan receiving his Master's Degree in Psychology. Another photo and caption had him embracing an elderly priest by the name of Father O'Malley.

As he continued to turn the pages, he keenly felt he was witnessing a miracle. The photos covered an extraordinary career for a small town priest from Ireland. There were photos and captions of a group of priests in what was obviously the Vatican, with the word 'Paratus' written below the picture. As the pages turned there were many more photographs and handwritten notes describing the evolution of Paratus. It was the photograph of a much older looking Father O'Sullivan, standing beside a Cardinal by the name of Zorn. The hand written note underneath read, 'SOSL', 2007. He made a quick mental calculation in his mind and figured the priest had to be in his late sixties when the photo was taken with the Cardinal. He had seen enough. He looked up at Father O'Sullivan, his face reflecting his complete astonishment and shock. Here was a youthful, handsome and powerfully built man underneath the black clergy clothing, standing just a few feet away from him.

He looked over at Jenkins and Linker, their faces also etched in wonder and asked, "How long have you known about this? Forget it. Adam, cancel my meeting with the Joint Chiefs. Clear my entire calendar for the rest of the day." Turning back to Father O'Sullivan, he asked, "Father, tell me more about these children, Robert Best and SOSL."

Hours passed, and trays of food, coffee and tea came and went. Father O'Sullivan, described the seven children born by Satan, all at the exact same time and all borne with the distinctive birthmark of three musical notes that looked like backward sixes, the mark of the beast. His description of his encounters with Best and the beast over the last seventeen years sent chills down his spine, his admiration for the priest growing by the minute. The other two priests, members of SOSL, described the doctrine of the task force. He found it unbelievable the Vatican and the leader of the most powerful Christian religion in the world was mobilizing for the event the world would soon come to an end, brought on by God himself.

He asked the priests the question, "Why would Satan, the Anti-Christ or whatever he's called, be present on earth, hatching a plot to destroy mankind? Isn't that exactly what God is doing anyway? I don't get the logic?"

Father O'Sullivan interjected, "The teachings of the Apostle Paul, revealed in his writings in the Book of Revelations, is clear on this. Once the Lord Almighty has washed away the sins of man through their destruction, He will return His only Son, Jesus Christ, to establish His Kingdom on earth, filled with the people who held onto their faith till their death, resurrected to begin a new life, with Christ, on earth. Satan, we believe is now active on earth, in a race to darken as many souls as possible before the end arrives."

The President finished his thought for him, "When Christ returns to rule the new Kingdom, there will not be one. The souls of man would also have been destroyed along with their bodies when they pledged them to the Anti-Christ."

That realization, now spoken, reverberated off of the walls and through the minds of everyone in the room, like a cold hard slap in the face.

The President continued, "Can Best be stopped? Can we bring him in, contain him?"

Father O'Sullivan replied, "Best is an entity; he is not real. He appears in physical form to further his charade only. He is appearing less and less in his earthly persona of Robert Best. Mankind is in grave danger, Mr. President."

He stared back at the priest and asked, "Why are you telling me all of this. What can I possibly do? There is no weapon in the arsenal of the United States to stop what has been written by God."

Father O'Sullivan took a step closer to him when he said, "Mr. President. The next step in the demon's plan is to take you out. Take out the leader of the free world. Not just by putting a bullet in your head or appearing in your bedroom at night and tearing out your heart with his claws. He needs to destroy you publicly in the eyes of the world. Make you an enemy of the people. He will turn country against country, wars will increase, and mayhem and chaos will be the norm. It is then that he will step in as the savior, embraced by the world and put into a seat of ultimate power. The final piece of his plot to destroy mankind will be complete. The world will be falling apart, self-imploding when he appears in his true form offering salvation through allegiance to him."

The door to the meeting room suddenly opened, Defense Secretary Bernard McKutcheon stepped in, unapologetic, "Mr. President, there is a situation happening in the Middle East that requires your immediate attention. It cannot wait, sir."

Stanley rose from his chair, acknowledged McKutcheon, and then he turned to Father O'Sullivan, "Father, I must leave. Thank you for coming here. My office will be in touch." He then took a step towards the priest and whispered to him that no one else in the room could hear, "Father, what has happened to you? Physically, I mean?"

He watched as the priest reached out and took his hand in his and held it tight. He stared back at him, intently for a second, into those amazing blue eyes, until the realization hit him like a sledgehammer. As he turned away, he staggered briefly, his feet light, and he could catch glimpses of bodies rushing towards him from his peripheral vision, ready to catch his fall. He didn't fall, however. He stood tall and before turning and following his Defense Secretary out the door, he looked back at the priest one final time.

Without a shadow of a doubt he knew he had just shaken the hand of God himself.

Chapter 18

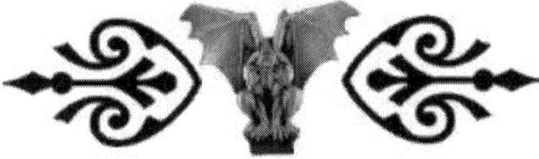

Ann Lockwood, amidst the chaos in Los Angeles after the Quake Aid concert, slipped away in her private jet back to London. She could not sit around any longer with little or no word from Father O'Sullivan, and no opportunity to see Michael.Sam was called back into duty by the LAPD as it was all hands on deck to try to contain the violence still raging after the massive concert. Beth needed to return to her practice, because her clinic was seeing a rise in patients requiring facial reconstructive surgery from injuries caused by the riots.. There were terrible wounds from bullets, glass shards and stabbings. Ann remembered the violent riots of 1992 that turned L.A. upside down. Sam had said the 92 riots were a walk in the park compared to what was happening after Quake Aid.

She arrived at her mansion after being whisked away by limo from the Heathrow VIP service. Standing in the vast openness of her main entrance, the huge chandelier shimmering above her she took a few minutes to reflect. A few weeks had passed since she had last stayed here, and she was essentially alone. Staff was minimal, just enough kept around to maintain the grounds and keep the place clean. She looked around her and down the hallways. She could envision her son Michael, six years old, flailing away at the open air on his air guitar as he played in these hallways. She missed him terribly. The last two years she could count, on one hand, how many times she had seen her son.. His career took off in London and now had exploded with Vasallus.

She made her way into her study off of the main entrance and recalled the visit in this room two years ago by Avery Johnson and

Bentley Paxton. They had come all the way here from the United States at the request of her father, Sherman, to talk her into letting Michael leave for America and join the new super-group. Now even her father was dead, killed by the Beast. Soon it would be her and then Michael. Where was the Lord in all of this? When would His love and compassion strike down this threat against His people? Maybe He, infuriated with man on the destruction of His planet through our pollution and flagrant abuse of the precious resources He put on this earth, was now turning his mighty back away from His people. So many people dead in her life and she decided on the plane on the way over the Atlantic, she could no longer wait for Father O'Sullivan and the Church. Her son's life was in grave danger and she would do everything she could to save his soul from the demonic Beast who had claimed him as his own. She knew she would die in the coming weeks and she was at peace with that knowledge. She was determined to live long enough to see Robert Best cast back into the Hell from where he came. She also knew in order for that to happen, her Creator would have to step up and condemn the Demon to Hell for all eternity.

After a long hot shower, the first stop in her quest for understanding was the British Library on Euston Road. She wanted to understand more of the great battle lost by Satan so many centuries ago. She made her way up the stairs towards her bedroom and was once again struck by memories that came flooding back to her. Often the walk up these stairs reminded her of Dalton and their time together. How they would stay up late, wrapped in each other's arms on the couch, watching a TV program, then crawl up the stairs to bed, exhausted. This time, the images flooding her head were terrible ones, reminders of the graphic violence of which he died. Images of his severed head hitting the floor only inches from hers made her body shake with the memory. "What was the matter with her," she thought to herself, as she made her way up the stairs and onto the hallway. She entered her bedroom and froze. Lying bare chested under the covers of her bed was her husband, Dalton.

"You're home honey! It's about time. I have been waiting for hours for you to get home. Get in here will you. I've missed you."

Ann felt her knees wobble and the strength in her legs turn to jelly. This was a mirage; it was not real. Her husband was dead. "Who are you? My husband is dead. He's been dead for eighteen years. If you think this is funny, you're wrong. Now whoever you are I suggest you get out of my bed and my house right now before I call the police."

"Jesus Ann, it's me! It's Dalton, your husband. What is the matter with you? I took the afternoon off work to surprise you and you come home and start acting all weird."

He looked real, though. He looked alive. He had come back to her. Maybe eighteen years ago was a dream and he's been here the whole time. Maybe she was dead? The room began to spin out of control around her. She reached out to keep her balance but her hand felt nothing solid, only air. She felt herself falling to the floor. Oh my God, what is happening? She opened her eyes, prepared to see blood pooling around her, thinking she bounced her head off of the dresser, but instead she was lying in bed, under the covers. She gasped and quickly looked at the other side of the bed. Dalton, now fully exposed, moved up against her, his breath hot against her shoulder as he kissed her skin everywhere. It was Dalton; it really was him! As soon as he touched her, she knew. He had somehow returned to her! She pulled his head up towards hers, their mouths finding each other in a passionate kiss, the heat from their two bodies quickly building. The rush of emotions cascaded down her body like a waterfall. She kissed his face like a dog missing his master. "Dalton, I have missed you so much. I can't believe it's you! I love you, baby." Her words spilled from her in a rush. Her emotions were overwhelming. Suddenly she remembered Michael.

"Dalton, you have a son. His name is Michael. You have to meet him. Oh my God, I can't believe this. I'm so happy." He never replied when she mentioned their son, he just kept giggling as he continued to caress her skin with his mouth on her flat stomach, threatening to move further down. The next thing she felt was her body building to a climax she had not experienced since before his death. Her breathing turned to shallow gasps as the climax came roaring to the surface. Her body shook with the pleasure that coursed through her body. Collapsing backwards on to the stack of pillows, she called out to her husband, "Come up here baby, there is so much I need to tell you."

She felt his body shift on the bed, as he made his way towards her. She was basking in the warm waves rippling through her body. She couldn't believe this. It was a gift from God. Once again. His love came for her. Her mind had completely accepted that this man was her husband, dead and gone for eighteen years, but somehow here right now making love to her. She just wanted to spend the next several days lying in this bed with her husband, rediscovering each other after so long apart. "Or were they ever apart?" she asked herself. Her mind could not decipher any of this right now and she didn't care; she wanted Dalton beside her. She smoothed down the fluffy blankets in front of her, as Dalton moved up the bed.

She screamed.

Rising above her was the Beast. His hideous body seemed to block the entire ceiling of her bedroom. His wings hummed as he hovered. His face was contorted in an ugly grimace, laughter escaping its badly scarred mouth. "Did you enjoy our little romp, sweetheart?" Laughter boomed above her, and streams of saliva dripped from the creature's mouth onto her chest. The revulsion from the knowledge she had succumbed to the trickery of the Beast made her stomach lurch upwards to her throat. She cried out, "Why are you doing this! Leave me alone!" Her body shook with the sobs rifling through her. She was finished with the evil entity that had made her life and that of her son a living Hell. She looked into the burning red orbs of the Beast's eyes and screamed, "Kill me! I don't care anymore! I would rather die than have to live to look into your eyes any further. Kill me and do what you have to do with Michael!"

The Beast flung himself upwards away from her until it smashed into the ceiling above her. Ann's eyes took in the full magnitude of the creature and were stunned at the pure evilness that floated above her. The huge wings were fused into the creature's massive torso. The torso was covered in muscles, purplish grey in color, shiny with slime, and the shoulders looked like boulders that housed powerful arms ending in claw-like talons. The head was gigantic in size, round with pointy little ears. The eyes projected an evil so horrible she desperately tried to look away but found she no longer had the will to tear them away. The bizarre looking shape was designed to crush, cut and kill. It was preparing to fall from the ceiling onto her and do just that, crush and cut her to bits. She waited for it to descend, wanting this horror to be over with, once and for all.

Then a voice called out to her in the back of her mind. "Fight, Ann! You are not alone. For I am with you! Don't give up. I need you to fight this evil that claims you for himself. Rise up Ann, and resist the Beast!"

She gasped as the voice disappeared and the Beast above her dropped from the ceiling like a giant bug, hurtling itself towards her, its evil claws fully exposed to crush her. In that split second before impact and the end of her life, she heard a second voice. This one was the voice of her son, Michael. He shouted out to her, "Mother, move, now!" Instantly, she rolled hard to her left, narrowly missing the impact of the Beast as he fell onto the bed. The bed imploded on the impact of the huge creature, sending her flying off it onto the floor. She quickly rolled onto her side to brace for the next attack. She was not quick enough. The Beast was far quicker than she was and was already on top of her on the floor. It snapped one of its huge claws around her throat, choking all air into her lungs. She could see the darkness creep into the corner of her eyes as the life began to ebb from her. She looked into the red pits of the creature and could see the joy in them as he squeezed her throat tighter. The pathetic lips spread wide in a mock smile, exposing huge fang teeth, saliva pouring through them and onto her face. It screamed a grotesque roar, "Finally your death is my reward, bitch. The legacy of Davit ends with you. My son will never remember he once had a mother. Michael will sit on my side for all eternity and together we will destroy man and their beloved God. Die, Ann, knowing you gave birth to the son of Satan, ruler of man, destroyer of all that is good. Your God abandons you, Ann. He claims His love for you, but He lets you die here now." The Beast roared with laughter, its body shaking.

The claw around her throat squeezed even harder. The darkness in the corner of her eyes moved towards the center of her eyes. The life in her was almost gone, when the bright light pierced the closing darkness in her eyes. Her eyes opened wider at the intense light quickly filling the room. She could feel the grip of the Beast's claw loosen around her neck. The coolness of the air as it made its way down her windpipe was soothing, breathing the life back into her exploding lungs. The Beast screamed above her, and she could feel the air whipping around her as its wings lifted the creature away from her. She rolled her head to her left and saw a giant of a man standing in her bedroom, covered in gold armor. A bright light surrounded him, making his gold plates sparkle in the light. He gripped a sword so large and shiny that from her position on the floor it looked eight feet long. She watched as he swung the sword high above his head before his booming voice echoed through the room like thunder, "I am Davit, son of King Tiridates, destroyer of Satan and angel of God. I command you evil one, in the name of the Lord God Almighty, to leave this room at once and go back to Hell. You will not have your vengeance this day. My bloodline, Ann Lockwood, will live to fight another day, wicked one. Now go before my mighty sword cuts you in half!"

Ann tore her eyes away from the soldier to see the Beast pinned against the wall by power of the soldier's sword. Its face was twisted in agony, pain coursing through its body. The huge wingspan kept its body erect. She didn't understand why the soldier, dispatched by God, did not finish the Beast off by swinging his mighty sword and cutting the creature in two. She looked back at the soldier and cried out, "Kill him, soldier! Do it now before it escapes! You must! You must kill it!" Ann was sobbing and she didn't even know it, "Please swing your sword, Davit! If the Beast lives, my son will die!"

The mighty soldier looked at her intently as she cried out. He acted as if he were confused at what she was asking. She screamed again, "Swing your sword! Kill the Beast!" The confusion of the soldier was all the distraction needed. Ann turned her head to see the Beast, a triumphant grin across its face, perched on the sill of her bedroom window and shouted, "Your sword will not penetrate my armor soldier. You live another day, Ann Lockwood. The Lord has spared you again. I will be back. Know that in your soul, Ann. Soon the cries from the damned soul of your son Michael will reach your ears and when that does, I will strike you down and into damnation for all eternity."

Ann rose to her feet and approached the window where the creature perched. A strength coursed through her veins she did not recognize, but she knew it was placed there by Him. She looked defiantly into the burning red eyes of the Devil and shouted, "You do not scare me evil one. I have the power of God's grace by my side and that makes me fearless. Before you fly off that window and into the darkness from where you came, understand one thing, Demon. My son Michael is a child of the Lord and I am coming for him. You will not stop me. When I come for him I will also becoming for you. I will destroy you once and for all. I will have my vengeance Beast for what you did to my husband."

The sound of laughter from the Beast as he leapt from the windowsill into the night mixed with the sounds of its wings unfurling like masts catching the wind at sea. Almost forgetting about the mighty soldier, dispatched by God to save her life, she quickly turned around, only to see she was alone in her bedroom. The soldier who called himself Davit was gone. Feeling her strength leave her, she dropped to her knees. Closing her eyes, she raised her hands high to the ceiling and called out in prayer to her Lord, "Heavenly Father, protect my son from the evilness that controls him. Your love, Father, is shielded from him by the Demon who is your enemy. Let the light of your soldier's sword reach him, Lord. Let him know he is not alone, that You are there with him. In the name of your beloved Son, Jesus Christ, I pray, Amen."

Ann collapsed onto the floor, all strength gone and fell into a deep sleep. She dreamed of a place, full of the greenest grass she had ever seen, flowers and beautiful plants growing everywhere. There were snow covered mountains far off in the background. A breath taking valley of open fields stood before her. Wild animals frolicked on the vast open grass, and the different species of the animals did not stop them from having fun together. Coming out of a field of mature crops, on the other side of the open valley, was a young man that she did not recognize, the distance too great to bring clarity. The young man had long brown and wavy hair, his facial features framing a broadening smile. Then she recognized the smiling face of her son, Michael. He was coming home to her at last. She ran as fast as she could towards him, the animals moving wide, giving her a wide path unimpeded. She reached her son and embraced him, not wanting to ever let him go. Eventually he pulled away from her and stared into her eyes, a beautiful shade of blue in his eyes that carried the love of God in them, spoke out, "Mother, it is so wonderful to see you. Do you know where we are?" She knew instantly that they were in Heaven. She nodded at him and he continued, "Mother, I need you to stay strong and stay alive. There is a great battle ahead\ and we must be prepared. Our God will not forsake us. I miss you so much. I love you, Mom and we will be together soon. I promise."

She protested as he turned to leave and walk back across the valley of green grass and wild animals to the field of tall crops. Before he entered through the tall wall of crop, he looked back at her and smiled one last time. His smile was beautiful, and she smiled back in return and waved to him. With one leg in the field and one out, he reached out with his one hand and waved back.

****

When she awoke hours later in her bedroom, lying on her side on the floor, she tried to raise herself up but the stiffness of the hard floor made it difficult. Instead, she continued to lie there, opened her eyes fully and looked through the open window of her bedroom.

The sun's morning rays poured through the window bringing the warmth of a new day to her chilled body.

Chapter 19

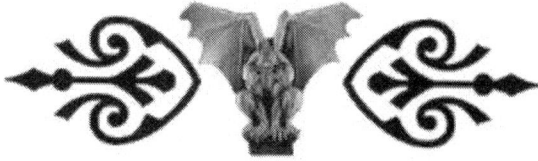

Connor Asker sat quietly in the corner of the bedroom. He was afraid for the first time in his life. He always had his music to fulfill him. It was his joy, his everything, and he loved to sing and perform. The reaction of his fans when he stepped up to the microphone on the stage was like no other feeling in the world. He could sing twenty-four hours a day for the rest of his life. He knew that was no longer possible. His life had spiraled out of control since he joined Vasallus. The Master controlled all of them, using their talents to spin his plan. He worshiped the Master for what he did for him and his music career and then what he has accomplished to bring all of them together to form Vasallus.

He always knew he was special, born into this world from supernatural events. He did not remember his parents or much of his childhood. He always remembered the music and the extraordinary times growing up. He remembered when he was thirteen years old and winning the America's Got Talent competition. That was so much fun. He missed that fun. It ended when the Master entered his life. The truth was revealed to him. He was born of him, to fulfill his plan of complete domination and destruction of humankind. They were all born for this purpose. His music would be a vessel for destruction and this made him extremely sad. The Master, in the beginning, showed him that his musical abilities would change the world; he just didn't know it would be for this. He remembered convincing an extremely frightened Juan so long ago that he would not need his mother, to come and embrace the Master and the beautiful world revealed to us.

Even though the Master led him to the truth, his music took away the frightening thoughts of what he was. He was a murderer and a purveyor of evil and he hated himself for it. What the music gave him was taken away when Patrick Benning joined Vasallus. He was a monster and the most violent person he had ever known. Patrick rarely let him and Juan out of his sight; he was afraid we would collaborate with the others and conspire against him. That was impossible as the Master was all knowing and knew their every movement. Patrick forced his will on them because the Master was instructing him on how he used them to impress the Master. The attack led by Benning on the girls and Michael was horrible and he hated it.

Death and despair were foreign to him before Vasallus. Now it was all he knew. He was here in the bedroom of the daughter of the President of the United States, because Benning wanted to elevate the pain and fear for the girl. "Was this because Benning was getting his jollies wreaking havoc on the President's daughter, or something else?" he thought. He glanced over at the girl on the bed, sleeping, snoring softly, her body comfortably twisted into the blankets.. He stood up and walked over to her bed. He looked down at her, knowing in a few minutes her consciousness would fill with utter dread and cold hard fear. She would be aware of his presence when he entered her body, first through her sub-conscious, stepping into her dreams and waiting until the recognition of who he was and what he was registered in her conscious mind. He needed to get this over with; otherwise Benning would be here, dragging Juan along with him. Benning would pounce on his fear, and his anger and rage could result in the girl being seriously hurt if not killed. He closed his eyes and prepared to enter the all too familiar black space when a voice knifed through his conscious conscience and snapped his eyes open. He whirled around to the unfamiliar voice coming from behind him.

"Do not be afraid, Connor."

A man, huge in stature, dressed in heavy and glimmering

golden armor stood at the far end of the bedroom. His hair was dark and long and included braids of hair mixed in. He moved towards him a few steps, but he did not make a sound. Even his armor did not give off a metal sound. Connor knew he should be afraid of this intruder, but strangely he was not. He had already decided the man was not human; otherwise, he would have detected him entering the room. The man bore a handsome, but battle weary face. He finally snapped out of his bewildered state and asked, "Who are you? What are you doing here?"

The man spoke again, "I am Edil, son of King Tiridates and soldier of God. You, Connor and your birth mother, Lori Weston, are direct descendants of the great King of Armenia and in turn, mine. I am here to warn you Connor."

"Warn me of what?"

"I know what you were about to do. The soul of that girl must not be sacrificed, Connor. Do not bow to the darkened soul of the Benning boy or the Demon, Robert Best."

Connor's mind circulated thoughts of violently lashing out at the soldier and was then quickly replaced by these thoughts of being repulsed by what he going to do to her soul. He found himself becoming weak, unable to stand and suddenly he dropped to one knee. He quickly braced himself with his hands on the floor to prevent from falling over.

"Resist the power of the Beast, Connor. You have the blood of Christ, Son of God, flowing through you. Reach for that love, Connor. It is beautiful and it will protect you from the evil one. Do not resist Him when he calls for you. Do you understand?"

Connor, looked up at the soldier, the love and goodness that radiated from him was overpowering. He whispered, "I am afraid, Edil. Not for my life, but my friends. How can I help them?"

The soldier took another advance towards him. Connor didn't back away. He was close enough now that he could see into his eyes and it is then he saw and felt the incredible power of the Lord. The soldier's eyes sparkled a deep blue, like a bright afternoon sky. Then he spoke: "Your friends are your brothers and sisters. Leave this innocent girl sleep. Go home and when you are alone, pray to the God who loves you, Connor."

"Patrick will know what I have not done here tonight. He will tell the Master. I will die, Edil. Maybe that is what I deserve."

The soldier paused before speaking again. Connor watched as his attention was distracted by something else in the room. There was no one else in the room, except the two of them. The soldier turned back to him and declared, "Quickly Connor, you must leave here at once. It is no longer safe. Now!"

Connor began to panic. He did not know what to do. He would surely die, if he returned to the mansion. Then he heard the voice and it was too late. It was the voice of Patrick. He appeared at the entrance to the bedroom. His face was twisted and contorted into a hideous rage. He screamed, "Asker, what the fuck is going on! Who are you consorting with! Destroy him. He is your enemy! He will kill you!"

Connor could not move. He could feel the rage of Benning pour over him like an angry storm. He felt compelled to take action against the soldier, but an unstoppable voice in his head told him not to react. Instead, he slowly backed away until his back made contact with the wall. He watched as the soldier, Edil, reached to his side and placed his armored hand on the handle of the huge sword. The soldier pulled the sword out, the biggest blade of steel he had ever seen. It shimmered in a darkened room it had its own light source. He stepped back, swung the blade over his head and pointed it directly at Patrick, inches from his chest. His voice boomed throughout the bedroom, "The power of the Lord will leap from this blade into your chest like a bolt of lightning. Do not tempt His patience."

Connor was horrified as he watched Patrick. He was going insane with rage, "A soldier of God does not strike fear in me. Your blade fizzles like a shorted toaster. You will die in this room, soldier. When I'm done with you, I will stick Asker..." Patrick was cut-off by the soldier, "I will leave here and let you live. The

Asker boy must die. He cannot be stopped from taking the soul of the girl. I will not let that happen. Let my sword cut him in half and then I will leave."

Connor was stunned at the sudden turn of the soldier, Edil, demanding his death in return for Patrick's life. "This is insane, he thought! What was he doing? How could he offer to kill him after just offering him the Love of the Lord?" Then he understood. The angel from God was saving his life! He turned to Patrick, "Kill him Benning! He's trying to stop us from taking the girl!"

He could only watch as the soldier, the plates of armor shaking, the sound of steel now audible, rubbing against steel, echoed in the room as the mammoth-sized man swung his sword over his shoulder in a circular motion with great speed. A source of light began to leap from the tip of the blade, filling the room with an intense brightness. Connor moved his hand to his eyes, shielding them from the fierce light that blinded him. In the chaos of the light, he could hear Patrick scream. He fought the light that was blinding him when he heard another voice, a whisper that pierced his conscious, "Occupy the girl's soul to save yourself, but do not destroy it. Remember what I said, Connor. The Lord will come for you soon. Be ready for Him for He is your true Master! Now move!"

As the light diminished in the room, the cries of the daughter of the President of the United States, Alexis Kipshaw, reached the secret service agents, who were sitting quietly at the end of each hallway. They flew out of their chairs and raced down the hallway. The bedroom door of the President and the First Lady opened simultaneously, the two of them ran down the hallway towards their daughter's screams.

When President Kipshaw and his wife ran in their daughter's bedroom what they saw was beyond comprehension. Alexis, her body completely naked, floated five feet above the bed. Her arms and legs were covered in deep cuts, blood oozing from the wounds. Leah Kipshaw, cupped her hand to her mouth as she screamed, "Oh my God. What is happening! Stanley, do something! Jesus Christ, she's floating in the god damned air!"

Temporarily stunned by the sight of his daughter, the President turned to the agents, both of whom stood paralyzed in disbelief at what they were witnessing and cried out, "Call an ambulance. Secure the White House! Someone is getting in here and they could still be in here! I want whoever did this, found. Do you hear me?"

The two agents snapped to attention and bolted from the room. Suddenly it was just the two of them. Stanley moved to his daughter, picked up a blanket off of the floor and threw it over his daughter and put his weight on top of her to move her back down onto the bed. She did not budge. She was locked in the elevated position. "What the hell is going on," he thought. He used all of his weight this time to try and move her back down to the bed. He could not move her. Suddenly, her arm came to life and wrapped around his neck with incredible speed. His daughter gripped his head against her chest with a force that was beyond that of a fourteen year old girl. He tried to pull away but her grip was too powerful. He cried out, "Alexis, let go baby! You're hurting me!" Rather than loosen the grip, she squeezed his neck tighter. He could not breathe and struggled for air. No matter how hard he struggled to free himself from his daughter, her grip held him tight. Then he heard the panicked voice of Leah, screaming, "Alexis, let your father go. You're choking him. Alexis, please!"

The next thing he heard was the impact of Alexis's fist hitting Leah square in the face, sending her flying to the floor. His lungs were burning for air and he didn't know how much longer he could stay conscious. He couldn't believe his daughter was choking him to death. He thought, "Something terrible has happened to her. But what?" Then with a force unimaginable, his daughter flung him against the farthest wall in the bedroom, a distance of at least twenty feet. The impact sent pictures tumbling off the walls and onto the floor around him. The pain shot through his back and shoulder like ice picks. His neck muscles where she had the iron grip were painfully sore. He lifted his head, knowing they had left earth and stepped into Hell.

The room had gone completely dark except for a glow of light around Alexis, as she began to lower back onto her bed. Her tongue was protruding from her mouth at least six inches and thrashed at the empty air as if searching for something. A sound, harsh and rasping screamed from her throat. It was in a foreign language, Latin perhaps, "Yo soy el verdadero gobernante del hombre. Más allá de mí no hay nadie más. Pronto todo el hombre va a arrodillarse delante de mí" (I am the true ruler of man. Beyond me there is no one else. Soon all man will kneel down in front of me).

Stanley lifted himself off of the floor and in the blackness of the bedroom, he moved towards his wife, whose moans directed him to her. The blow she received by Alexis had broken her nose, the blood was still flowing. She was knocked unconscious, but was now coming to. She opened her eyes and looked up at him, "Stan what is going on, what is wrong with her?" He whispered back, "I'm not sure baby what is going on, but she will get all the help she'll need." Then a horrible sound filled the room, jarring the two of them. It was a demonic cackle from their daughter, the light still shrouding her in the darkness that sent shivers down his spine. He heard Leah gasp, "Oh my God, Stan. My poor baby!" The cackle turned into a series of undiscernible gibberish. The room had become sub-zero in temperature and the two of them shuddered in the cold. He knew, that somehow Hell had found their little daughter. She would never be the same again.

They could hear banging on the door of the bedroom as the agents and medics tried to get in. A few seconds later the door broke off of its hinges, but before they could charge into the room, the dresser drawers on the far side of the room came hurtling towards the open doorway with impossible speed. They slammed into an agent who was just coming into the bedroom sending him flying back into the hallway. They could hear his muffled screams from behind the blocked doorway.

Stan reached over for the other blanket on the floor beside Leah and stood up, placing it on his daughter. He looked into her eyes for the first time and knew that this was not his daughter. Gone were the soft and friendly eyes, replaced by an evilness he could not describe. His daughter then vomited in his face and chest, the putrid stench all over him. He never stopped looking into her eyes. His daughter's lips were dry and split open as she hissed at him, "The slut will die! First, I will have some fun with her, Mr. President!" His daughter opened her mouth and cackled uncontrollably. Her teeth had become black and her immense tongue moved around inside her mouth as she laughed. A scream building inside of him exploded, "Leave her alone! Leave my daughter alone, you coward, whoever you are! Please, she's just a girl." He pleaded with whatever evil spirit was inside of his daughter. She laughed even harder before cocking him with a closed fist so hard and so fast into his cheek he never saw it coming. "Fuck off, motherfucker!" The punch sent him sprawling backwards onto the floor. He turned over onto his side instinctively, the pain unbearable. Fireworks were exploding inside of his head. as he struggled to lift himself off of the floor. "This bedroom, the White House had descended into Hell," he knew.

Without warning, the darkness disappeared and light returned. A sound of a teenage girl's crying filled the room. As he and Leah raced back to their daughter's bedroom, he could hear the sound of the large and heavy wooden dresser crash down onto the floor. He could hear the sounds of people's voices everywhere around him. He could even make out the shapes of people milling about. He didn't care. As he and Leah looked down at their daughter, crying, all they could think about was the tears streaming down her face were coming from his daughter's eyes, hazel and beautiful. The thing that was occupying Alexis's soul was gone. It had done its business and now it was gone. Gone for good he hoped. He thought of his meeting with the priests from the Vatican and the words of Father O'Sullivan. He knew whatever had terrorized his daughter would be back.

****

Connor Asker lay in his bed at the mansion. He feared what Benning would do to the President's daughter. After the angel of God, Edil, had left the girl's bedroom, Benning insisted that he was the one who would torment the soul of the girl. He knew he had barely escaped the suspicions of Benning and the Master thanks to the soldier. Dangerous times lay ahead for him and the others from Vasallus. He hoped the angel, Edil, would be nearby. He wondered if any of the others also had an encounter with an angel. He hoped so. To defeat those who now bound them, they would need all the armies God could muster.

Chapter 20

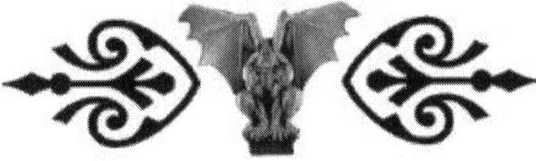

Alexis Kipshaw was rushed to George Washington Hospital with the President and the First Lady close behind in a heavily secured motorcade of Secret Service vehicles. Stan had contained the events in his daughter's bedroom earlier that evening as best he could. He gave the head of his security, Senior Agent-in-Charge, Darren Brighton just enough information to keep him from asking more questions. The two agents who entered the bedroom ahead of them reported seeing Alexis Kipshaw elevated several feet off her bed in a bizarre and frantic scene. Stan informed Brighton that Alexis has suffered two seizures in recent days and would remain in George Washington for extensive testing before returning to the White House. He knew Brighton had more questions than answers and backed off for the moment, but Stan knew he would be pushing for more answers from behind the scenes. "Where would it lead him? Nowhere is where it would go," he knew. An evil spirit had found his daughter's bedroom. That was certain. Both he and Leah grew up in strong Catholic backgrounds and the possibility of something like this occurring was not foreign to them, but the reality of it was incredible. Down the hall, Alexis was resting comfortably under sedation, her wounds bandaged and her mother standing vigil. The family priest, Father Nichols, would arrive any minute at the hospital. The two would meet with him in private. He and Leah would share their nightmare with him in the hope the priest would secure the help their daughter needed. This was an extremely private affair, but Stan knew he needed to tell his Chief of Staff something; otherwise, security and the Secret Service would never cease investigating. They desired privacy now more than anything.

President Kipshaw stepped aside from the throng of Secret Service agents and stood in private with his Chief of Staff, Adam Linker. His Chief of Staff and good friend was a mess with worry and he asked, "Stan, what the hell happened? I'm hearing Alexis is covered in wounds and the agents who found her stated she was elevated five feet in the air? Jesus, is she going to be okay?"

"She is heavily sedated right now. She has been through a nightmarish night, to say the least, Adam."

"What happened to her? Was she attacked? How could that have happened?"

Stan took half a step towards his chief aide, "Alexis is suffering from extreme emotional issues that have caused her to hurt herself. She cut herself. All over her body. She needs help by the best doctors and psychiatrists we can find. She is sick, Adam, and we never even saw it coming. Leah is really shaken by the whole experience. She feels she wasn't there for Alexis, so never saw the signs."

He watched as Adam absorbed the information. He was close to Alexis, like an uncle to a niece. He felt bad spinning this all onto Alexis, but it was the best he could do for now to mask the horrific truth. "Oh my God, Stan. This is terrible. Let me know what I can do. I will have Rachel come by when things have calmed down to see Leah."

"That would be great, Adam. Thank you. I will talk with you soon. I need to get back in the room."

****

Adam watched the President disappear into the hospital room, followed by Father Nichols. Adam felt an enormous and overpowering sense of dread. He knew there was more to this than the President shared with him. He shook the evil thoughts from his mind, pulled himself together and moved back into the gathering throng to begin taking charge of the situation. He would start by getting most of these people off this floor and give the President, his family and the hospital staff some space.

****

Thirty minutes later, Father Nichols met with the two of them on the other side of the private hospital room. Alexis continued to rest under a deep sleep of medications. He looked at the two of them, his advancing age framed in a burden of worry and concern, "I've examined her wounds, the location of them and it caused me to ask the attending physician, Dr. Hemmerlock, to look closer and after closer examination he confirmed my suspicions."

Stan looked over at Leah, concern causing her brow to shrink, and then asked, "What suspicions are you talking about, Father?"

"Before we talk about my suspicions, I want the two of you to tell me what happened in Alexis's bedroom tonight. Do not leave out any details, please."

For the next thirty minutes, they shared with Father Nichols, the harrowing story of the demonic events in their daughter's bedroom. When they were done he asked for the three of them to join hands in prayer.

"Heavenly Father, Creator of all that is good, Conqueror of all that is evil, place your protecting arms around this family. Shield Alexis from the evil that stalks her. Give the Kipshaw's the strength to endure what is in front of them and the courage to stand strong against the evil who is trying to claim their daughter. Pray this in the name of your Son Jesus Christ, Amen."

Leah, fighting tears, asked, "Father, what is happening to our daughter?"

Father Nichols reached out and took Leah's hand in his before replying, "Leah, how long have you been coming to my boring sermons every Sunday?"

She replied, "As long as I can remember, Father, since I was a little child?"

"I've been giving confession to your father before you were even born, my dear. Do you trust me?"

Between her tears she managed a smile, "Of course I do, Father."

Father Nichols continued, "I've witnessed a beautiful young

woman grow into the courageous and intelligent woman who sits in front of me now. You introduced me to the brash, up and comer Stanley Kipshaw that you had fallen madly in love with. What did I tell you all those years ago when you asked me whether or not marrying Stanley was a good idea? Two powerful and political families coming together through the marriage of their children. Do you remember what I told you?"

She looked back at him, the memories of that time coming back to her, "I remember, Father. You told me to follow my heart. You said that our union would be followed by stormy seas and that many people and outside forces would try and destroy our love for each other. You told me to let our love conquer all, let no one get in between our love."

Smiling at the two of them, he continued, "Exactly, my dear. The three of you find yourself in stormy seas. A terrible evil is trying to tear the three of you apart. Let your love for each other conquer all. Be strong and vigilant for each other and you will prevail. Pray for God's love always, and He will fight for you. Do you understand?"

Leah nodded her head and Father Nichols looked at the two of them before continuing, "Alexis's wounds were not self-inflicted. They were not incisions caused by a knife or any other instrument. They seemed to have burst open from the inside out. The doctors seem to think it may have been caused by the severe seizures her body was inflicted with, and her muscles contracted so violently it caused the surface of the skin to break open. It's a lot to wrap your head around, but without further tests they cannot give you anything more than that information."

He looked at Father Nichols and said, "Father, the three of us know exactly what has happened to Alexis. She had super-human strength in that bedroom that does not come from a seizure. She was talking in Latin! Her physical changes, Father? She has been possessed by an evil spirit and I want to know how we can help her?"

The priest stared at them both for what seemed an eternity

before he replied, "There is one more thing I need to tell you both. When I was alone with Alexis earlier and I was examining the wounds she spoke to me."

Leah gasped and could barely contain the moan that tried to escape her throat, "What? What did she say?"

Father Nichols continued, "It was not her, you must understand, that spoke to me. It was the entity that resides within her that spoke to me. It switched from Latin to English and back. I understand and speak Latin fluently and she was impressed that I could speak Latin. She or the thing that is inside of her was content in just talking small talk. It wasn't until I splashed some Holy Water on her that she reacted, anger coming out of it. He, not her, told me I would die. He said the world was too late to stop him and all of humankind would also die."

He was stunned at the words coming out of the mouth of Father Nichols and asked, "What else did she say, Father?"

The priest paused, then continued, "He switched to Latin and spewed a tirade of hate and discontent for a Father O'Sullivan from Rome. Instructed me to summon Father O'Sullivan so he could shred his soul into pieces and feed it to his dogs in Hell."

Stan felt the bile rushing from within his stomach, threatening to explode all over Father Nichols. He stood up to try and calm his stomach. His mind was spinning out of control. Father O'Sullivan. Of course. He had come from Rome to warn him. "How did his daughter fit into this? Why had the Demon chosen her?" he asked himself. Then he knew. The realization hit him like a swift punch to the solar plexus. He turned to the two of them, both of whom were staring at him concerned, "Father O'Sullivan came to the White House a few days ago. He had been dispatched by the Vatican to warn me."

It was Leah who asked, "Warn you, Stan? About what?"

He began pacing the room as he spoke, "He warned me that the enemy of God was out to destroy me. He said Satan was unleashing his Hell on earth, as written in the Book of Revelations, and that he would destroy the most powerful man on earth, me, in order to instill himself as leader of the free world, tricking humankind into believing he was the one to lead the people back from the brink. I thought he was crazy until…"

Father Nichols replied in a stern voice, "Until what, Stanley?"

"Until he reached out to hold my hand and I stared into his eyes did I know."

Father Nichols and Leah both in unison asked, "Know what?"

"That I knew that I had been touched by God Himself. Father O'Sullivan carried the presence of God inside of him."

Suddenly his words were interrupted by a sound coming from Alexis's bed. They all turned around to see her sitting up in bed, staring at them with eyes that were a bright red in color. She tilted her head back on her shoulders and began to laugh, cackling then moaning, a sound so horrific and demonic it sent chills down their spines. Stanley moved towards her bed, and this led her to scream out: "I'm coming for you motherfucker! Maybe I should take you now. Get it over with!" He never even seen his daughter's fist before it was too late. The blow to his face sent him sprawling against the wall. He heard Leah cry out, "Oh my God! Father, please help her!" He watched in horror as his daughter turned towards him in the bed, her tongue thrashing wildly, her screams piercing the room. Alexis pulled a fistful of hair with each hand violently from her head then roared, "The time is near Mr. President. I'll kill your slut wife and your fucking daughter first." The Demon's last words were cut off by Father Nichols as he moved towards his daughter.

Before Stan could react, Father Nichols brushed past him and took a small bottle from his pocket. He stood at the end of the bed, in front of her, and began to recite a prayer. She laughed loudly in her hoarse sounding voice, then spat, "Go fuck yourself priest. Why don't you tell your President you've been fucking altar boys since you took the collar? You'd fuck the Kipshaw girl if she was a boy, wouldn't you Father!" Her demonic laugh filled the room. Father Nichols bellowed, "Stop it Demon. You are the carrier of lies! You use the weak and defenseless to strike fear. You are a coward!" He then lifted the bottle of Holy Water high over his head and declared, "In the name of the Father, the Son and the Holy Ghost, I command you to leave this girl at once." He brought the water down in a striking fashion, spilling the water across Alexis's chest. She fell backwards onto her back and screamed. She arched her back and thrashed on the bed. Father Nichols continued, "Purveyor of lies, master of misery, go back to the Hell where you belong." He splashed more water on her, causing her to thrash and scream. It was a nightmare scene. He heard Leah cry out from behind him. He turned towards her and then he heard Father Nichols call out, "Stanley, take Leah out of here at once. Leave me alone with her."

He agreed. He knew Leah could not bear witness to the terrible things happening to their daughter. He took her by the arm and began to lead her out of the room. Suddenly, the room went instantly quiet and dark except for their daughter on the bed, lit by an unknown light. Except it wasn't Alexis. It was an elderly Samantha Boxton, Leah's mother, lying on the bed, her arm stretched towards her daughter in a sign for her not to leave, "Leah, darling, please don't leave me here. Take me home. I'll be good, I promise. I'll bake you and Stanley your favorite pot roast every night; just don't leave me in this place, honey."

The memories of putting her mother in a home when her care had become unmanageable had always left his wife feeling terribly guilty. The pressure of the campaign for President left her little time to care for her elderly mother. His wife began to lose her balance as the sobs rose out of her in waves. He struggled to help her to her feet as she pushed towards the bed. The room had become an absurd nightmare. Then he heard the voice of Father Nichols boom out, "Do not listen to the lies. That is not your mother, Leah. It is the Demon using his lies to trick you. Stanley, get her out of here!"

After a few minutes he was able to usher his wife out the door and into the throng of nurses and doctors, shocked as the crying First Lady and the President came out of the room. Linker and half dozen agents quickly moved towards them.

"Mr. President, what's going on? Is the First Lady okay?" Before he could reply he instructed agents into the room. He shouted at them as they were about to burst into the room, "No, stop. Leave her alone. She is with Father Nichols. He needs to be alone with her." The agents hesitated, not sure, exactly what they should do when Linker spoke, "Do as the President commands. Do not go inside." Turning to the President he asked, "Mr. President, should the doctors not go inside? Your wife is hysterical."

All he could think of to say was, "There's nothing a doctor can do for my daughter. Father Nichols must be alone with her, Adam. I need to get Leah into a room to rest." Adam instinctively motioned for the doctors and nurses to take the First Lady. They took Leah by the arms, helping her into a wheelchair, and then whisked the sobbing First Lady to a nearby room.

Adam leaned in close to the President and whispered, "What the fuck just happened in there, Stan?"

He locked eyes with his Chief of Staff before replying, "Do you believe in God, Adam?"

Confusion in his eyes, he replied, "Of course I do. Why?"

"Because I need you to pray. Pray for the salvation of Alexis's soul. I need you to pray for the salvation of all of humankind."

"What the hell?" Adam could only shake his head as to the strange request from the President, as he watched him disappear back into his daughter's room.

Stan opened the door to his daughter's room expecting Leah's mother to scold him upon his entrance, but instead he fell back in shock against the door. The room was completely white. Everything from the walls, windows, tables, T.V. all were white. His daughter sat up in bed, laughing hysterically, her face etched in the evil spirit that had invaded her body. Then he saw Father Nichols. He was lying on his back at the far side of the room. Except he wasn't lying on his back, he was lying on his stomach. His head had been twisted 180 degrees to where it was staring up at the ceiling. The Demon had killed Father Nichols. Rage surged through his body like an inferno. He could no longer see his daughter anymore, only the evil monster sitting on the bed. He rushed towards her in a fit of rage and as he reached her bed, the Demon laughed harder. He slugged the Beast across the face sending it flying back onto the bed. He jumped on the bed and wrapped his arms around his daughter's throat. He was out of control, he knew, but he didn't care. He just wanted to kill the source of so much pain and get his daughter back.

He screamed at the hideous face, "You fucking coward! Leave her alone. I'm the President of the United States. Come into me you fucking prick. You want control then take me and leave my daughter alone!"

Suddenly, the door to the room burst open and Stan could hear the voice of his Chief of Staff holler, "Stan, what are you doing! Jesus Christ, get off her!"

He felt the arm of Linker wrap around his throat as he was pulled away from his daughter. The Beast was no longer laughing but instead replaced by his daughter, bruised and battered, crying for her mother. "Jesus what had he done?"

He found himself being pulled to the ground and then the door opened again and he could hear an army of nurses, doctors and agents pouring in and with Adam's hand firmly pressed into his chest to prevent him from getting up, he heard him shout, "The President has been attacked! The priest is dead. Secure every entrance at once."

He knew what his good friend was doing. He was ensuring all suspicions of what happened to Father Nichols would not come back to haunt him. He moved from underneath his Chief of Staff. He needed to get to his daughter. She was crying his name!

Chapter 21

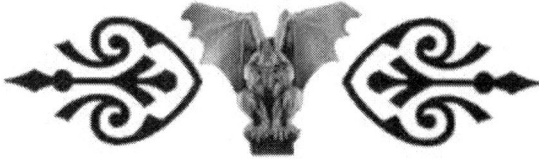

Madrid, Spain, readied for the largest and greatest rock concert the country had ever seen, because Vasallus was in town. The opening concert in the massive Vasallus European Tour was hours away. Heavy security forces mobilized in and around Santiago Bernabeu stadium. Thousands of fans, ticket holders and non-ticket holders were already gathering in anticipation of Vasallus's arrival. Prime Minister Eli Lopez was taking no chances, ordering thousands of troops, armed with crowd control weaponry that included water cannons, tear gas and rubber bullets in a multi-layered security ring in a five kilometer radius of the stadium. Commanders were ordered to use force to subdue any uprisings before, during and after the concert. Prime Minister Lopez may have avoided a full-scale riot by not cancelling the concert, but he would use whatever means necessary to prevent another repeat of the Los Angeles riots that nearly destroyed the city. Youth around the world were empowered against society and its rules, and Vasallus fueled their passion.

In truth, the country was on the brink of an economic meltdown as were many other countries in Europe and the needed revenue the concert generated for Madrid was in the tens of millions, and Lopez had felt the pressure from the Mayor to allow the concert to go ahead. Vasallus was paying for the bulk of the security, so all they needed to do was to hold order for a few hours, wait till Vasallus moved on to France for their next show and hopefully take the economic shot in the arm to pay for a few civic bills: two badly needed hospitals, half completed when the money ran out and construction was halted, back on schedule. The press conference by the members of Vasallus and its management team opted out at the last minute. The fears by army commanders in their readiness for the anticipated violence that would surround the event was too great as they needed to focus their efforts on the concert itself.

****

Two men, dressed in dark clothes, sat quietly in their SUV, perched on a hillside driveway, three kilometers from the Santiago Bernabeu Stadium with a direct view of the stadium and the surrounding area. The older of the two, his face unshaven, eyes covered by dark sunglasses looked over at the other man in the passenger seat, binoculars resting against his eyes and asked, "Have any of the television crews showed up yet? We can't do shit until the world is watching," spoke the man in broken English. The younger man, dropped the binoculars from his eyes, looked over at his older partner and replied, "Jesus Christ, Sosa, do you think I would not tell you if the media crews showed up? It's why we're sitting here in this fucking heat. How about you hold these fucking binoculars and maybe I'll catch some sleep behind a pair of sunglasses, which you've been doing for the last hour. The concert is hours away and you're not going to see the media for a long time. Plus we're under strict orders to wait until the concert is under way and we have confirmation that it is received worldwide on live television before we strike."

The owner of the multi-million dollar mansion whose driveway they were parked on was unknown to the two men. They'd been hired by a middleman; one they have used many times in the past for previous hits and they were being paid an extraordinary amount to fire an anti-aircraft missile into the gathering mobs outside of the soccer stadium. The mansion was empty except for the Humvee tucked inside of the four car garage attached to the main house .When they received the word to fire they would drive the Humvee out onto the sloping driveway that was pointed directly at the expected gathering point for the main crowds. Huge video screens had been built in this area to accommodate tens of thousands of fans unable to get a ticket inside. It is here where they would fire their arsenal. The Humvee mounted SL-AMRAAM, contained a launcher capable of firing six Raytheon AIM-9X Sidewinder missiles with a range of over ten kilometers that would deliver devastating ferocity to the throng of unlucky fans.

The two of them were chosen because of their experience with the missile launcher in the rebel forces in the Syrian conflict for the past two years. The launcher held only three missiles, already two more than needed, but their contact wanted maximum carnage. They would obtain that. The designated area for the fans expected to number twenty-five thousand plus would be reduced to a crater after the three Sidewinders made impact. The rich bastard behind this act of terrorism was a sick fucker, to say the least, they thought. They had already received one half of the one million dollar fee, wired to an account they controlled in Damascus with the remaining half wired within sixty minutes of impact of the three missiles.

****

The six of them had been moved into the tight security off-stage dressing rooms hours in advance of the concert. Security officers were taking no chances and wanted to make sure they were safely inside of the stadium before the crowds began to build outside making it more difficult and dangerous for Vasallus. After the chaos surrounding the benefit concert in Pasadena, host cities in Europe were treating the concert security as if it were a G20 summit.

Chloë McClosky stretched out across the large leather chair, her legs dangling over the sides, listened to her iPod, killing time until Avery came in and gave them the sign to begin preparing for the show. The lounge where the six of them gathered plus a few assistants coming and going, had everything. Large screen TV's hung from the ceilings everywhere, each of them equipped with Xbox, PlayStation and Apple TV. There were stocked refrigerators with all kinds of juice and soda plus fresh fruit to accommodate individual tastes, but all liked the same stuff so variety was not really required. Chloë noticed Connor was unusually quiet, keeping to himself off in the corner of the room with a pair of large headphones keeping him preoccupied. Normally, Juan and he would be hanging out together, while they waited for the concert, immersed in video games or chatting. Juan and Patrick dueled it out on a violent combat video game. Something was up with Connor and she decided to go and talk with him.

Pulling her ear plugs from her ears, she rose from her lounger and walked towards Connor, "Hey Connor, what's up?"

He lifted the big noise cancelling headphones away from his ears and replied, "Hey Chloë. Big show tonight, huh?"

She sat in the large arm chair opposite his and replied, "Something up with you Connor? You don't seem yourself? Are you nervous about tonight's show? It's okay you know, it's probably the biggest venue we've ever played so far and certainly the biggest television audience. I think all of us are a little on edge."

He smiled weakly, and then replied, "No, nothing up Chloë. Just getting myself psyched up, you know."

She was about to reply, but the door opened and Avery and Bentley entered. Seeing Avery with his styled white hair no longer made her look twice. She had a hard time remembering when it wasn't white.

"Okay, listen up gang. It's getting to be that time. Show time is in two hours. I need you to head into your individual rooms within the next thirty minutes. We meet back in this room at 7:30 p.m., alright? Lots to go over in regards to the sets, song lineup and costumes. Everyone good? We'll see you in ninety minutes."

After a few minutes of pep talk from Bentley the two of them left. Chloë turned back to Connor and said, "If you need to talk to someone about anything, you know you can talk to me anytime, Connor."

He was about to reply when Patrick and Juan had walked over and joined in, with Patrick snorting, "Doesn't the blond bombshell need every minute of the ninety minutes to prim herself for all those adoring boys falling at your feet?" She looked suspiciously at him, knowing he intended to interrupt her conversation with Connor. She shot right back, "No worse than having to avoid all of the snapping elastic bands flying from all of those braces in the girls screaming your name "Hey, what can I say McClosky, I'm loved by young and old."

She shrugged, turned and left for her room. She would wait until they were back in the hotel, sneak over to Connor's room and find out what was up with him. Patrick was turning against Connor for some reason and that was not a good thing. She needed to find out why. Her instincts were igniting inside of her like a live electric wire and she would not stand by while Patrick singled out another one of them as he did with Elizabeth.

****

All of them were back in the room by 7:30 p.m. as instructed, but in truth they all knew the routine and had it down pat right to the last detail. They could get ready for the show blindfolded. Chloë was going with a more formal look for this show, deciding on a full length, body hugging sexy blue dress. Slits on both sides of the dress exposed her shapely legs; she knew when she stepped away from her microphone, the Spanish boys would swoon. Her stylist had left her hair long but added lots of wave, all held together by copious amounts of hairspray. She loved Brittany's look as she entered the room. She was wearing a silver sequined sleeveless blouse resting on top of a black sequined short skirt. Her blonde hair was now almost as long as hers but straighter and laced with strands of color: pinks and blues. Her wrists were covered in bracelets and bands. The two of them loved big rings and tonight they wore them on each of their hands. The boys were a stark contrast in style. Michael, once conservative now carried a bolder look with a sleeveless black t-shirt and shockingly bright sequined red pants. They were tight like spandex and he wore large black pointed dress shoes.

Prominently displayed on his shoulder was his Union Jack tattoo. His hair, long and teased was a far cry from the conservative look he used to wear. A hoodie and jeans was pushing it. Not anymore, but he looked good and the girls would go crazy. Juan, exuding his Latin heartthrob good looks to the hilt, was also sleeveless, wearing a tan colored leather tank top with dark brown tight leather pants. He wore cobra snake cowboy boots to top it off. He would sweat buckets in the leather underneath from the lights, but that was his problem. Connor dressed the most casual she had ever seen him dress. Usually, he was the wildest and most unruly looking of the four boys, but tonight he wore a modest navy t-shirt with a few graphics and tight white jeans with black boots. There were lots of strings and leather bands on his wrists. His hair much longer - all of the boys had grown their hair out - was teased in multiple directions. His enormous good looks still shone through and the girls would faint all over the place when he approached them on the edge of the stage. Patrick was his usual aggressive self with an 'I don't give a shit look' consisting of tight faded blue jeans with no shirt. His muscled upper torso, covered in black hair, was it. He had Reebok wrist bands carrying his custom drum sticks. His long black hair, naturally wavy surrounded his strong muscled face. He was extremely attractive, but his personality washed all that away. Girls could care less how he treated them. After concerts, they lined up like sheep for him. It was sickening.

They were thirty minutes away from show time and the place was crackling like fire with excitement. Avery called all of them to attention as he spoke: "Alright guys it's almost show time. I hope all of you are feeling great tonight and ready to put on an extravaganza. There are over 90,000 fans in the stands, more than another thirty thousand on the floor. and at least that many in the parking lot watching the big screen. Not to mention a worldwide audience of millions, if not billions. Is that enough pressure for you?"

In unison, they all replied, "Nope!"

He continued, "I didn't think so. You've been doing this long enough now I guess. But this is the biggest stage by far, even bigger than the Rose Bowl. Keep it together out there, stay away from the unscripted theatrics will you please. I'm tired of answering to hundreds of reporters how you somehow float in mid-air. I still don't know how you do that, and frankly I don't want to know. Now I'm going to let Jim speak for a few minutes before I come back. He will go over the choreography with you, so listen up." Avery and Bentley walked over to the counter nearby and leaned against it as his stage director went over the timing of the choreographed stunts, the sets and the costume changes. It was turning into a Cirque du Soleil show.. He looked at Bentley, absolutely stunning in her outfit of black leather pants, white knit shawl over her shoulders, bare from her white sequined tank top. She was focused yet watchful for trouble, her instincts for trouble by Best on full alert. She was always in protection mode when it came to the kids in the band, and he loved her for that. Her strength when combined with her beauty was about as sexy a combination as one can imagine. He was so much in love with her he had to pinch himself to snap back to attention as Jim was staring at him, waiting for him to take over. He cleared his throat and stepped forward.

"You know the song lineup, just like you rehearse every single day. You know it in your sleep. The new songs will be introduced by Patrick from his perch behind the drum set as they come up. Your fans, as you know, will tear this place apart if you told them to, so please, don't tell them to. Real Madrid football team will tear you apart if you bring down their house, okay!"

All six of them let out a round of laughter at Avery's playful but half serious crack. They all knew he was right. Their fans would burn the city of Spain to embers if they asked them to. The magnitude of their popularity entered the room as if an elephant had squeezed through the dressing room door. They watched as Bentley stepped towards the door and opened it. Instantly, the room echoed with a cascade of cheers, stomping and clapping from over a hundred thousand people just a few hundred feet away. She closed the door then looked at all of them before saying, "Your popularity has grown a hundred fold since your last tour. It's no longer teenagers begging their parents to pony up hundreds of dollars to come to your live shows. The parents are here too, not to chaperone, but also to watch the greatest band to ever perform. You have all become that celebrated. The world is watching. Everyone has become fans. Spain's King and Queen are in the audience tonight. Queen Infanta is one of your greatest fans and wants to meet all of you after the show. Bring them and the good people of this country your best. Sing from your hearts, and leave it all out on that stage. You are Superstars, each and every one of you, but remember, be full of class on stage; give them what they want, a hell of a show, but keep it contained. Encourage them when they leave here tonight to be respectful of their city and no violence after the concert. Will you guys do that? From here we go to France and we want to continue performing, understand? Monies raised from this tour are going to the relief efforts in India; be mindful of that. That's all I have to say. Thanks everyone, and we are so proud of each and every one of you. Go get em!"

The six of them filed past Bentley and Avery, offering up fist bump's as they left single file. All except Patrick, he didn't even look at the two of them as he filed past. "Just as well," thought Avery. The two stepped in behind Patrick at the end of the line, the roar of the crowd filling the hallway as they closed the dressing room door behind them. Uniformed security lined the concrete walls of the tunnel leading up onto the stage. The same tunnel the famed Real Madrid football team used to enter the field. As they reached the stairs leading to the backstage, Michael stopped and looked back at Avery and after a nod from his manager, climbed the stairs leading onto the back of the stage where the stage director, Jim Holland, waited, headphones on and clipboard tucked under his arm, he waved the kids up on stage. Once everyone was up they gathered in a circle around Jim and listened for last minute instructions. He had them install the wireless remote controls to the back of their pants and then hide them underneath their shirts. The sound of the crowd was deafening. Avery could see the sky was now dark, but the air was still and warm. He could see from his vantage point a stretch of the crowd along the one side and they were growing restless, stomping their feet, shouting and there were lots of banners being held up declaring Spain's love for Vasallus. "It just seemed like a few weeks ago he had met with Best in a Los Angeles pub to discuss the formation of Vasallus," he thought. How far they had come, so fast, too fast he knew, but their growth and popularity was out of his control. They were bred for this or should he say, they were *manufactured* for this. Their success and popularity didn't just happen. This was all by design. Robert Best, an evil entity, created all of this for his purpose, even his and Bentley's roles were all created by him and they were powerless to stop it.

He was suddenly overcome with a great sense of loss and despair. He found himself taking a second to close his eyes and say   a quick prayer to God, asking for His guidance and wisdom and for His protection of the kids of Vasallus who were pawns in His enemy's evil plans. He looked up and could see the kids about to enter the stage. Michael and Juan were doing some last minute adjustments to their guitars, Patrick was twirling his sticks in his hands like a cheerleader in a marching band. Avery looked over to see Chloë smiling back at him, nodding her head as if, it seemed, she had heard his prayer and was telling him that everything was going to be okay.

The P.A. announcer came on and a booming voice in Spanish began to introduce Vasallus. The sudden roar from the crowd was incredible. The city of Madrid and the country of Spain were about to experience the show of a lifetime. All six of the kids burst from behind the giant curtain and entered the stage to a thunderous applause. Immediately the music for the first number began and the kids instantly became performers with Connor stepping up to his microphone stand singing the first number to a delirious crowd of over 100,000. Avery could see the helicopters buzzing overhead, filming the show for future concert video sales, as well as news helicopters beaming back the highlights to TV stations around the world.

He reached over and pulled Bentley in close and held her tight. The two of them wrapped their arms around each other, not wanting to let each other go, the combined thrill of the show and the cold fear of their reality locking them together as one.

****

Chloë was singing a solo ballad about halfway through the show when she first noticed the light at the far end of the stadium, hundreds of feet away. It was at first a dancing light amongst the myriad o of flashing cameras to cigarette lighters turned on as beacons, but this light was different. It was intense and beckoning to her. She needed to investigate.. It was calling out to her, through her subconscious. The audience had quieted almost to complete silence as they soaked in her beautiful ballad, not wanting to miss a single word. The shock when she suddenly shot forward, across the entire distance of the stadium, just above the heads of the screaming fans below her was felt by everyone. In a flash she had travelled hundreds of yards, seemingly floating without the aid of wires or mechanics of any kind. She stunned the crowd into complete silence. This lasted for just a few seconds when the tens of thousands of people finally realized that it was part of the show and they suddenly snapped out of their trance and began to go wild. They screamed, stomped and clapped their approval of the stunt.

Avery and Bentley stood frozen at the back of the stage as they witnessed once again the ability of the kids to fly in mid-air. The stage director, Jim Holland, pulled his headphones off and threw them and his clipboard onto the floor, turned and walked off the stage. The helicopters flying overhead seemed to fly closer to the top of the stadium to let their cameras confirm what their eyes were seeing. Millions of fans around the world would be seeing in full HD video Chloë McClosky floating in air. His head began to ache already in anticipation of the upcoming press conference where he would have to explain what just happened.

Chapter 22

Chloë continued the song as she searched for the source of the brilliant light she saw from the stage. She looked left and then right but could not see it. Confused and disappointed, she sensed something she had not felt when she first saw the light from back on the stage. Suddenly to her left and slightly behind her, standing in one of the exits hallways to the tunnel behind the grandstands was a man, a soldier, large in stature and surrounded by a brilliant and beautiful light. She darted towards him, oblivious to the crowd trying to touch her from below her. She now floated in air directly in front of this man. She stopped singing and barely recognized the band had broken into the next song. She then must have disappeared from view, because they no longer stared up at her. They were now watching the stage and moving to the words being sung by Juan. He had broken into a Latin upbeat song that had the crowd on their feet and dancing wildly. It didn't matter to Chloë. She stood motionless in front of this glowing soldier, unsure what to say or do. It was as if they were suspended in time, separate from everything else.

The soldier reached out his massive hand towards her, curling his fingers in a motion for her to join him in the tunnel. She floated towards him until she was right beside him. She had to look up until the back of her head touched her back to stare into his eyes. The soldier had long locks of wavy dark hair, some strands separated from the rest with beads. He had many scars. She could see some etched from his eyes down his cheeks until they disappeared into his beard. The light that surrounded him felt wonderful and familiar, and she didn't want to leave. She finally cleared her throat and asked, "Who are you?"

When he smiled, the goodness radiated from him and filled her with a sense of comfort and safety she had not felt since…since the mansion. The pounding of the door. *Boom. Boom.* Now she remembered the light from the foyer of the mansion. The light that saved her from the outstretched talons of the Beast! She looked up at the soldier and noticed the huge handle of his sword on his hip, and she wondered if that was the sword that pierced the light. She was about to say something again when the man spoke. His booming voice was clear above the chaos that surrounded them, "Fear not Chloë, for I am forever watching over you. I am Abgar, son of King Tiridates, conqueror of the Beast!"

Her mind stumbled, no understanding coming through when she heard him continue, "You are my direct descendant Chloë, as was your mother Kathleen."

"My mother Kathleen? I never knew her. She died while giving birth to me."

"Your mother was very brave, Chloë. She gave her life to give you life."

She felt her emotions shattering. She knew nothing of her mother and she wished she had. She lifted her head up once again to the glowing apparition and said, "I am born of the Beast. I am the Beast. My mother sealed my fate when she bedded the Anti-Christ. I am the daughter of Satan, don't you see?"

The man continued his voice loud and commanding when he spoke, "Do you feel your heart beating in your chest, Chloë? Do you feel that same heart ache when you think of Father O'Sullivan? When you sing, does it make your heart soar?"

"Yes."

"You are also human, Chloë. That is what makes you feel. Don't ever forget that. The Beast does not feel that. He only feels evilness, blackness and nothingness. You feel the light, goodness and love. Do you not?"

"Yes, but I also feel the blackness and nothingness. Sometimes I find myself in an awful place of total darkness. I cannot feel anything but dread, despair and fear. I am neither heard by Him in that place, nor does He hear the cries of Elizabeth."

"You have been chosen Chloë, because of your lineage to my Father. The Demon is using you and the others for his final plans to destroy humankind. Be strong Chloë; be vigilant. He will not abandon you for you are also His child. Do you understand what I have told you?"

"I think so. Abgar can I ask you a question? Does God love me?"

The massive soldier raised his arm and placed his hand on her shoulder before saying, "He loves you with everything He is. His love for you will set you free, when He is ready. Now I must go, and you must return to the stage. Don't ever close your heart Chloë. My sword is always near. There are dangerous times ahead for all of us. Together and with His love we will conquer the evil that threatens us all. Remember that Chloë."

In an instant the soldier was gone and she was back on stage just as Juan was finishing his number. She received puzzled looks from the others, but when she stole a glance up at Patrick he was truly seething. His eyes glowed an awful menacing red, and she knew he would come after her later. So be it. She was no longer afraid of him or Best. She had received a gift from the soldier tonight, and she would protect that gift with her life. The soldier had given her the gift of hope.

****

Robert Best stood in the expansive but empty living room of the expensive mansion that overlooked the hillside leading up to the soccer stadium where Vasallus was performing. He looked out of the wall-to-wall windows and could see the tens of thousands of fans who were in a frenzy as they watched their idols perform from inside the soccer stadium. His eyes did not require binoculars. He saw all, and he witnessed the appearance of Abgar, son of Tiridates in front of McClosky. His blood was boiling in his veins, and he envisioned his talons shredding the neck of the soldier and watching as his headless corpse fell to the ground. He was losing them he knew, and it wouldn't be much longer until all of them discovered their true lineage. His time was running out, and he needed to move things along much faster. Tonight he would inflict serious chaos and confusion into the minds of the common people, and soon they would turn to him for redemption and salvation as the failures of their leaders would expose their weaknesses and inability to lead them out of the brink of self-destruction. He would be the way out for them. He was the answer. He has always been the answer.

His laughter almost caused the giant windows to shatter into the night.

****

Avery and Bentley frantically combed the crowd with their eyes for Chloë as she disappeared into the crowd. "Where did she go?" they thought. She had miraculously zipped across the heads of the crowd to the far end of the stadium, floated for a few seconds then disappeared. It was frightening and even more so when she disappeared. He turned to Bentley and shouted above the noise of the crowd, "Stay here. I'm going to make my way to the far end of the stadium and see if I can see her. Call me on the radio if you see her first. I'll be right back."

She stepped in front of him blocking his path and replied, "You told me you would never leave me alone when we were on tour. I'm going with you."

He hesitated for a second and agreed, "Come on let's go." They turned and headed for the gangway leading to the tunnel that ran behind the grandstand seats and housed all of the vendors. As they made their way through the tunnel area, they noticed the concessions and vendors were relatively quiet. Everyone was in their seats enjoying the concert. As they made their way towards the last place where they had seen Chloë before she disappeared, they noticed a bright light in one of the exit hallways leading from the seats far ahead. The light was in contrast to the dimly lit tunnel housing the concessions. As they got closer, the intensity of the light grew. There were no people or fans in the area, and they were alone as they approached the hallway leading out into the stands. He felt Bentley's hand tighten around his, as they came around the corner of the tunnel into the hallway. As they did, they were blinded by a light so intense they instantly raised their hands to shield their eyes. He could make out shapes in the light and hear faint sounds coming from within the source of the light, but not much else.

Then a strange thing happened. The light seemed to open up exposing a large figure, a man maybe, silhouetted in the brightness. He was motioning with his hand to come forward. Sensing danger, Avery stood firm and held Bentley's hand tight. Then he heard a voice from within the light boom out, "Do not be afraid. Come into the light. I know who you are, and I have been waiting for you."

Unable to move, he stood, motionless until he was jarred loose from his frozen state when Bentley pulled his arm forwards, urging him to move, "Avery, we must go towards the light. Don't you feel it? Please, come on." His body reacted to her urging and pulling, and he found himself propelling forward to this intense light that beckoned them. Suddenly, they found themselves surrounded by the powerful light, and everything else around them melted away. Bentley clung close to him and he could hear her heavy breathing and wondered if she could hear his. He didn't know what else to do, so he called out to the light that swirled around them and asked, "Who are you? Where is Chloë?"

A powerful voice echoed back, "I am what you think I am. Your lives and the lives of Vasallus are in great danger. All of humankind is exposed to the evil one that has made his return. Be strong and be vigilant. Be firm in faith as the wicked one will come for you. Your faith will protect you. Do you understand?"

It was Bentley who replied, "I believe in Christ. I believe in you." Avery could feel her gaze upon him. He spoke, "I don't know you very well, but I believe in your existence, and I want to know you more." He didn't know where those words came from; he just opened his mouth and out they came. The voice from the light boomed once more, "Anarchy, death and chaos are nearby. Tools the evil one will use against you. Hold firm and stay close to the kids. Protect and watch over them. That is what I am asking of you. Do you understand?"

Avery replied, "How can we protect them? Best has let us live only so we can help facilitate his plans for Vasallus. He will kill us when he no longer needs us, and then he will kill the kids."

"Trust in Me is faith. I say to you again. Secure your faith in the Lord God and His Son, Jesus Christ and do as I say. Now go and keep vigilance over them. Do not fear for I am with you."

Bentley cried out to the quickly fading light, "Don't go, please. We have more questions!" The words were lost in the sudden darkness in the hallway leading out to the grandstands. The loud sounds of Vasallus and the pounding, stomping and cheering of the rabid fans enveloped them once again.

****

The concert was coming to a close. Robert Best stood in the empty living room and stared out, his dark blood seething at the appearance of his enemy within the walls of the stadium. He clearly had seen the light of Him that gathered in the tunnel hallway of the stadium. He could not determine why His presence was there, but it would be for one purpose and that would be to warn someone. Was it Chloë when she flew with her microphone to the far end of the stadium? No even He wouldn't risk that. Was it Johnson or even Paxton? Maybe. But why warn them? They were as good as dead any day and there was nothing He could do to stop that. Someone else, but who? He would contemplate that further after he wreaked some death and destruction first.

He walked out the front door and approached the two men inside the vehicle. He yanked open the door, scaring the two of them as the driver instinctively moved against his partner on the passenger side. "Get the fuck out and launch. Now. Do you understand?" The driver, older than the passenger spoke, "We are to receive a text when it is time. Who the fuck are you, anyway?"

Figuring the older guy would know more than the younger

one, he reached over the driver and grabbed the younger of the two with such speed neither one nor the other could react. He pulled the passenger out of his seat and onto the driveway so hard, his skull split open like a watermelon. Blood and brains spilled down the sloping driveway towards the street. The driver, shocked, leaped from the vehicle, muttering, "I will launch the rockets as you command."

Within a few minutes the garage door opened and the huge Humvee, its engine roaring at the weight of the payload on its back jolted out of the garage and up onto the driveway. Best could only smile as the driver emerged from the front seat and out onto the driveway with an AK-47 pointed at Best, "You fucking cocksucker! Kiss my…" Before he could even squeeze the trigger, Best had torn his throat clean off of his neck, killing the idiot instantly. The mercenary fell onto his back, his shredded throat pumping blood into the air. He knew he should have done this himself anyway so he jumped over the dead corpse and into the front seat. Kicking the truck into reverse and spinning the steering wheel to straighten the Humvee, he felt the front tire lift as it rolled over the head of the dead man with the torn throat. He laughed hysterically at the vision of the man's head exploding like a tomato under the tire. When the truck was lined up to face the stadium, he jumped out and climbed on top. Manipulating the controls to arm the missiles as if he were a trained weapons officer, he then sighted in the target area. The concert had ended and the thousands of fans who were watching the concert from the parking lot were soon joined by thousands more departing the stadium. The place was teeming with tens of thousands of adoring Vasallus fans. Perfect.

The three Sidewinder missiles all left their respective jackets simultaneously, lifting the Humvee onto its front wheels with the force. There was a massive swooshing sound as the missiles ejected from their mounting brackets combined with the glowing light from the rockets flames as they soared up into the dark sky. Then they immediately ducked downwards in a death spiral towards the unsuspecting revelers. The news and security helicopters continued to hover in their positions in what was surely a shocking few seconds of disbelief at what was about to happen. Best laughed like a kid in a toy store, banging his fist in triumph on the Humvee dashboard as he watched the trajectory of the missiles drop from the sky into the crowds below.

The impact of the three missiles forced a huge flame upwards hundreds of feet into the air that swallowed up two helicopters immediately. The chaos that followed was like a sex addict watching porn. It was incredible. Best soaked it in, enjoying the pandemonium that filled his mind as his eyes swept across the destruction. There were endless flames, bodies on fire running blindly, blown-up body parts everywhere. People lay helplessly injured and mangled. It was a beautiful sight.

Suddenly, the cab of the Humvee was filled with a bright light. Excitedly thinking for a second that He was upon him, he realized it was the search light of an army helicopter. It was one hell of a bright light, he laughed as he climbed out of the truck. Within seconds, less than fifty feet in front of him, he could see troops armed with machine guns dropping on ropes to the ground. His physical body had already left the area. His mind stayed a little longer to take in all the fun that followed. He watched in delight as the troops stormed the truck only to find no one. They would have to be satisfied for now on the quick discovery of the source of the terrorist attack.

****

The explosion that rocked the backstage area was tremendous. Avery and Bentley were thrown to the ground from the shock of it, and so was everybody else. After ensuring Bentley was okay, the two of them rose and ran towards the kids. They were making their way herded by security towards their dressing rooms. All of them were shaken but fine. The head of security came bursting into the area and commanded all of them to follow him. There had been a terrorist attack outside the stadium and many people had been killed by a bomb. Strangely, Avery, found he was not afraid. He knew this would likely be the norm from here on. He and Bentley ushered all the kids and stage hands out of the area before they followed close behind into an open area where several army helicopters stood by to whisk them to a safer place.

He and Bentley huddled together with the six members of Vasallus in the helicopter, watching it lift up and into the air before banking sharply away from the chaos below. He closed his eyes and said a prayer. He thanked God for saving their lives and let Him know he was ready for the fight against His enemy.

Chapter 23

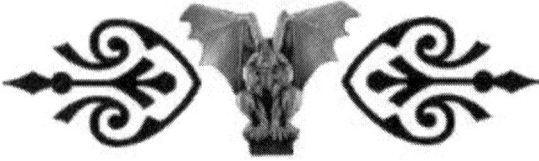

The Los Angeles weather was its usual balmy and sunny comfortable 74 degrees. What L.A. gives in beautiful weather, it takes it away with its horrible traffic. Sam, back at work after an extended leave, sat on Interstate 10 in his L.A.P.D. unmarked Ford Taurus. He contemplated turning on his flashing lights and siren to circumnavigate the traffic using the shoulders or medians, but he decided to stay with the flow. In no hurry to arrive anywhere, he would use the the time to think. Since Ann suddenly left for home, he and Beth had been in the dark. He had not heard from Father O'Sullivan, since the two of them visited the mansion. Avery and Bentley were now in Europe on tour. It was difficult to concentrate on his current caseload of homicides, and his boss, Bitters, was starting to grow impatient with him. He was not his usual self, and maybe Bitters was thinking that he returned too soon and needed more time off. He needed to be back at work; otherwise, he would go crazy with worry and uncertainty. He thought about reaching out to Ann but ultimately decided against it. After all, she had her reasons for returning to London. The woman had endured so much; the cruelty of death and evil had been wrought upon her. The more he thought about Ann, Vasallus and Father O'Sullivan while sitting in the gridlock, the more he knew he needed to do something, anything that would shed light on their predicament.

He flipped his red and blues on, and squawked his siren several times to attract the attention of the cars ahead of him. He then pulled out of the traffic and onto the shoulder, accelerated past the logjam and gunned it for the nearby exit. He decided to head to the mansion. He would snoop around Patrick's room, maybe stumble onto something. He would look to see if Best kept a room or an office in the mansion. He really had no idea what he would be looking for; he just needed to do something. His investigative instincts told him that the mansion was the key; there were answers to be found there. He accelerated even faster down the shoulder spattering gravel back into the gridlock resulting in honks from livid and cursing drivers. Reaching the exit to the Brentwood Heights neighborhood, famous in 1994 for the O.J. Simpson white Bronco police chase, he would wind his way through Brentwood to the coast and take the coastal highway to Malibu. Traffic in the exclusive Brentwood neighborhood was light, and he was able to travel quickly.

Twenty minutes later he pulled into the winding circular driveway of the mansion. He stopped in front and surveyed the situation. There was only one other car parked out front, a BMW 535 coup which was either Avery's assistant, Amber, or another employee. The mansion carried a full time staff of five, he knew, so he was prepared to use his badge to gain entry. He would first however, walk around to the side and enter through the studio and engage the assistant if she was indeed inside. He had his lock picks in his jacket pocket where he always kept them. Now in police work, lock picks were as standard as a flashlight and handcuffs. He made his way around the corner of the mansion towards the studio where he almost gave himself away to the gardener busy working the shears on a bush, expertly trimming it. Immersed in his work, he didn't notice the startled police detective dart into the archway leading into the studio. Not wanting to explain himself to a low level employee before he even made entrance, Sam was grateful to escape without having to explain his reasons for being there. He tried the office door and it of course was locked. He peered through the glass in the door and saw no movement. He leaned over and looked through the window that led down the hallway and again saw no movement. It looked deserted. Amber could be in her office working and would hear him walking through the door, but he could easily explain the door was unlocked and no one answered his knocking. If she didn't come out of her office then he would look around, and if by chance, someone did encounter him then the badge would make an appearance.

In less than a minute he was through the door and into the studio. He quietly made his way down the hallway and peered into each office. He listened for any activity or sounds but heard nothing. Amber could easily just be up in the mansion making herself something to eat in the kitchen. Satisfied that he was alone he entered Avery's office, took a quick look around and then left to find Best's office. The next office was Bentley's; tastefully decorated of course and nothing of interest to him he needed to see. He did take notice of the Holy Bible that was on the corner of her desk. She obviously kept it close, either for quick reference or for comfort. He surmised she kept it close for quiet comfort amongst the evil that surrounded her. He left her office and walked across the hallway to an almost empty office. It appeared to be a spare office with very few decorations and little else besides the usual computer and printer. Sam opened each of the drawers finding them either empty or with a note pad along with pens and other office supplies. It was in the fourth drawer he opened that something caught his eye. There was a large note pad turned upside down. He took it out, flipped it over and was amazed to see an intricately drawn picture in pen of what appeared to be a human, a male, and nude. He looked to be in terrible pain. He seemed to have wings on his back that were broken and twisted, and he appeared to be falling. It was a doodle drawing but of such high quality and detail it was astonishing. It was the eyes that made Sam look twice. The eyes in the drawing exuded many emotions; most of all pain and sorrow. It was a beautiful and terrible drawing all at once. There were other drawings and he flipped the page in the pad to the next one. Again the detail was astounding in its clarity. It was a picture of a place that was dark, far away and empty. There was a young woman in this place. She appeared trapped, in terrible pain and her face was looked eerily familiar.

There was a large hole in her chest, surrounded by blood. The picture was gruesome and it reminded him of someone who was trapped in a terrible place, like Hell maybe. The he recognized the person in the picture. It was Elizabeth Leroux. Someone had drawn a terrible image of her with a gaping hole in her chest and imprisoned in a place where she desperately wanted out. "Who would draw such a grisly image," he thought. Then he knew. These were doodle art images drawn by Best. This was his office that he used when he visited. He quickly flipped through some of the other pictures that he had drawn. There was one of Father O'Sullivan with a large knife or dagger in his chest, his arms pointed upwards as if pleading to God for His intervention but there was a large door drawn into the clouds with the message written across it:, "Closed for good. Try taking the stairs downwards." The images were startling. The depiction of Elizabeth shocked him and conjured up all kinds of terrible thoughts. He closed the notepad and was about to put it back in the drawer when the voice made his pulse race and his chest tighten.

""What are you doing Detective?" It was Amber, the office assistant.

He stuttered for an answer, "Oh hi Amber. My apologies. I knocked on the studio door but there was no answer and the door was unlocked, so I came inside looking for you and ended up in here."

"Did you find anything interesting, Detective?" Her voice dripped in sarcasm. She was coming on a little too strong, so he decided to put her in her place, "Nothing but a notepad of sick drawings. Any idea who the artist is, Amber?"

"No idea, Detective. Shouldn't you have a search warrant or something to come in here snooping around without permission?" He looked at her, realizing she was going to make this difficult, so he decided to humiliate her: "Listen Amber, I would suggest you go back to your office and continue pressing the buttons on that photocopier, or whatever you do. I'm going to finish taking a look around, and then I'll let you know when I'm done. How does that sound to you?"

She seemed to hiss like a snake when she replied, "How about, instead, you take your fucking ass the hell out of here before I place a call into 911 to report an intruder. How does that sound cop?"

He was appalled at her language, but he was done playing with her. He stepped around his desk and grabbed her by the arm, twisted it downwards, her mouth distorted in protest. He slammed her down into the office chair, pulled her arms to the back of the chair and then hand cuffed them together making it impossible to move except for her legs. He would tie those together next if she made any further fuss. Her face seethed hatred towards him, and she spat, "Wait till Avery and Bentley hear about this intrusion or better yet, Mr. Best. He'll kick your Jew ass all over this place."

"I think Avery and Bentley would be interested in knowing what an Anti-Semitic little bitch is working for them. Not too sure how kindly they will take to that. Why don't you sit tight while I have a look around? Oh, I guess you don't have much choice, do you? I won't be long and I'll have you back typing letters in no time." She thrashed about, her legs kicking, but she soon realized she wasn't going anywhere. She shouted, "I'll press charges for assault, unlawful confinement, the works motherfucker."

Sam ignored her and instead went through the rest of Best's things. He reached back into the desk drawer and retrieved the note pad with all the drawings. Placing it on the desk to take with him later he said, "Your boss is quite the little drawer isn't he?" She cursed at him and he continued looking around. A thought came across his mind as he stood in the middle of the almost empty office, "What kind of things would the Anti-Christ have lying around in an office?" The thought almost made him laugh out loud. He continued to look around the office until he approached the only piece of artwork that hung on the wall. A simple, landscape painting, maybe two feet by three feet in size. He pulled it off its hooks and discovered a safe in the wall behind it. It had a combination dial. He instinctively tried the handle but it was locked of course. He turned to Amber who just rolled her eyes and said, "Don't even try, I don't know it. Never even knew it was there. He is hardly ever here, doubt if there's anything in it."

He studied her for a second and noticed something he never noticed before. Something he has seen before in others. Her eyes. They were bright red! That was strange. He turned back to the safe. Another thought occurred to him. Not really a thought, more like a tiny voice. The voice inside his head was telling him three numbers. 6-6-6. The mark of the beast? Why not. It was worth a try. He spun the dial to the right several times and stopped on the number 6. He spun it twice counter clockwise and stopped again on the number 6. He suddenly heard a low growl coming from behind him. "What was that," he thought. He turned the dial clockwise to the right and stopped at the number 6 again. He grabbed the handle and pulled. He was not expecting the safe to open but when it did the cold hard fear gripped him. This was no ordinary safe. It was a safe hiding place for Satan. The door swung open. Inside was a large, leather bound book. His curiosity overcame his fear and he reached into grab it when he was suddenly stopped by a horrible sound from behind him. He turned to see Amber, or what was once Amber, but was now a gruesome looking abomination. Her face had turned a dark black with patches of white from her original skin color still showing through. Her mouth was grotesquely enlarged, exposing freakish looking teeth, stained brown, some broken and others long and sharp. Sam stood frozen, stunned at what he was witnessing. She leaned forward, pulling and contorting her arms over her head, the office chair tipped-over and falling to the floor. With her arms completely twisted backwards she jerked her wrists with incredible force, snapping the handcuffs that bound them. She continued to morph into some hideous creature and her voice deepened, hoarse and guttural, demonic sounding when she roared, "Get away from that safe, Jew. I'll tear you to pieces." As she spoke her last word she launched herself at him with such speed, he never had a chance to react by reaching for his gun. She was on top of him and he was amazed at her strength.

He tried to roll her off, but her grip on him was like steel. She lifted her arm back and delivered a blow to his face that caused all of the light in the room to disappear. Everything went black and he could barely hear the sound of her laughter. The light slowly squeezed itself back into his mind, and he saw the vision of her fist come hurtling down on top of his face again. He moved away at the last second, and the blow glanced off of the side of his head. It was a hard blow, but not nearly as devastating, as if it had hit him flush in the middle of his face. He used all his strength to throw her off him. The momentum of her missing her mark with the last punch put her off balance somewhat, and he was able to cartwheel her to the left and off of him. She rolled against the wall and gathered herself back into a crouching position. Her face had now opened up, deep open wounds spread across it. Her lips stretched to their limit from the over enlarged mouth causing them to split open. Blood, mixed with puss flowed from her wounds. Hell had opened its doors and thrown this creature into the room.

He jumped up, pulled his 9mm Glock from his shoulder holster and pointed it at her head, "Don't fucking move. I'll blow that ugly mass off of your shoulders if you so much as move." Sam, keeping the gun steady in front of him, pointed at her head, moved back around the desk and towards the safe. She braced to launch again at him. "She was protecting the book. Why," he thought. "What was in that book that she wanted to kill him from getting?"

With his back against the wall in front of the safe, he held the gun in front of him, aimed at her head and was prepared to pull the trigger if she moved. He reached back with his free hand and probed for the book. He could not feel it. The safe was empty. That was impossible, and as he turned to take a look there was another voice. He turned his head towards the sound of the voice and was shocked to see the Spanish gardener standing in the doorway of the office holding a gun. He held the gun in a steady hand, like a trained professional and screamed, "Drop it. Drop the gun! Now!" He looked into his eyes and realized he would shoot him at any second if he didn't drop his gun. But what about Amber? He looked down at her, and there was no longer a demonic looking beast transformed from what was once the office assistant. Instead, it was Amber, back to her human state again, her face covered in bruises and she was crying out, over and over, how I had attacked her. Sam looked up at the gardener as he put his gun down on the floor and shouted, "Listen to me. I am a police officer. This woman attacked me. Put down your gun."

Placing the gun on the floor, Sam rose, and Amber launched herself at him. He tried to reach for his gun and would have if a gunshot hadn't rung out. He could hear it first then he felt it. A bullet tore through his stomach sending him flying against the wall. He fell to the floor on his side and could see the gardener frozen in shock at what he had done. Sam began to lose consciousness, knowing he was dying. If the bullet didn't kill him then the demonic beast, Amber, would. His vision blurred, and before the final bit of light left his vision and cloaked him in darkness he could barely make out the shape of Amber attacking the gardener. He could see blood and pieces of flesh being thrown around the room, as she tore him to pieces. He hoped he would die first before she finished with the gardener. He didn't want to see one of his limbs cascading through the air.

****

When he awoke and opened his eyes the light that pierced through his blurred vision stung. His eyes watered and he batted his eyelids to get some clarity. He could see shapes around him in the room. He tried to speak, but his mouth and throat seemed full of sand. He was so dry, he had to force his tongue off of the roof of his mouth. When he got his tongue loose and moved it around inside his mouth to search for moisture, it felt like a dry stick hitting a wooden wall. His teeth were coated with a thick material. But he was alive. He moved his head towards the blurry shapes, and the motion caused him to moan. Suddenly the shapes began to move all at once towards him. He heard voices. They sounded familiar. Then he felt something against his face, warm and wet. Someone was wiping his face. A nurse. He was in a hospital. He remembered now being at the mansion. Amber. Oh God, he began to moan again as the dreadful images came flooding into his awakening brain. The voices became clearer. He heard his wife Bethany. Then another woman's voice he recognized but could not place. A straw was placed between his lips, and he instinctively sucked the water into his parched mouth. The relief that came with it was unbelievable. Now moistened, his tongue moved around delivering moisture to all parts of his mouth and throat. He opened his mouth to speak, but nothing came out. He put his lips to the straw again and sucked more water. He then looked towards the blurry image of his wife whose face was inches away from his and spoke in a dry and raspy voice, "Where am I?"

Beth continued to wipe his face with the warm cloth, as she replied, "Sweetheart, you're in Los Robles Hospital. You've been under for three days. You've been seriously wounded."

He remembered the gunshot. He asked, "What happened?"

"You were shot in the stomach and left for dead by an unknown assailant. The gardener was killed. Listen, honey, we don't need to talk about this now. We'll talk more later after you get some more rest. The nurse went to get the doctor. He'll be in any second. I love you so much, Sam. I was so scared when I got the call. Thank God you are going to be okay. So please, get some rest. I'll be right here. Seb is right here too, honey."

"Wait a minute. Amber, the secretary at the mansion. Where is she?"

"She just left a few minutes before you woke up. She saved your life, Sam. She found you and the gardener. She administered first-aid to you while waiting for the paramedics to arrive. She applied a pressured dressing to your bullet hole in your stomach that the doctors said likely saved your life. She'll be back later to check on you and say hello. She is a hero, Sam."

As the exhaustion pushed him into a sleep, he could hear his wife converse with the nurses and doctors, but all he could think of was the last thing Bethany had said to him. Amber was a hero and saved his life. As the darkness filled his mind, he knew he had been skirting the edge of Hell for some time. Now he felt fully immersed in it.

Chapter 24

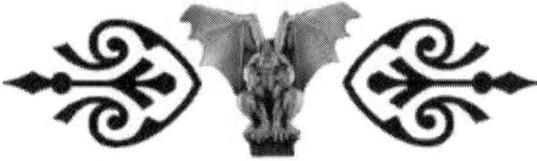

Everyone was devastated by the loss of life in Madrid due to the terrorist attack on the concert crowd of the Vasallus performance at Santiago Bernabéu Stadium. The citizens of Madrid including its Mayor Miguel Pisani saw the attack as the fault of the Spanish government and Prime Minister Eli Lopez. The people blamed their lack of security as the main reason. People took to the streets by the hundreds of thousands in angry protest. The people felt the government knew the security risks in hosting the Vasallus concert, but it had not taken adequate measures to ensure the necessary security. How could a Humvee armed with American made missiles just park in the driveway of a residential home and launch a devastating strike against innocent people only a few kilometers from one of the biggest events Spain has ever hosted since the 82 World Cup? The people marched in protest in front of the Palacio de Zarzuela in Madrid that housed the Royal family urging them to use their powers to oust the government of the Prime Minister. Worldwide support of Vasallus grew after the attack. Youth throughout the world took to social media to spread the word that society was using any means possible to stop Vasallus and its popularity.

Robert Best sat in his comfortable office in New York watching the news channels work the story of the Madrid terrorist attack. This was just the beginning he thought to himself. He planted story after story using the worldwide appeal of Facebook, Twitter and other social media channels to spread the conspiracy that governments throughout the world, fearing the rise of unrest of the world's youth, were trying to censor and silence Vasallus. Now it was time, he knew, to take things to the next level. It was time to target the most powerful man in the world. The world, as he had planned, was beginning to come apart at the seams. God's fury certainly helped his cause with His storms and earthquakes. The world was beginning to feel real panic and fear. Vasallus had subliminally planted the seeds of doubts since its first song, 'Don't Hold Back,' hit the airwaves in what seemed an eternity ago. The world had embraced the music and the message. The world needed real leadership as crisis after crisis began to rack up around the globe.

The world was turning to the United States and its President, Stanley Kipshaw, to lead it back to stability and normalcy. Citizens wanted the United States to flex its muscles and take out the terrorists once and for all along with the countries that supported them. He had Patrick go after the President's daughter to destabilize him in the only way that would, his own child. It was brilliant. The President was fragile right now, and Best would move swiftly to finish him both as a man and as President. He would setup an interview with one of the news networks, likely CNN, to speak out publicly to defend Vasallus and the music and then take the opportunity to speak to the world over the need to come together as one people, one voice in a world seemingly falling apart. He still had some work to do, and he still needed time for Vasallus to continue to spread unrest around the world. He knew, though, once his message, using the wonderful tools of social media, had infected every corner of the world, he would drop the guillotine and chop off the heads of human beings, steal their souls and use the tears of Heaven as his bath water. His laughter at the thought reverberated through his office, down the hallways to the elevators and up onto every floor in the building. The thousands of workers that shared this building rushed to the windows of their offices fearing another impact from an aircraft had struck again. If they only knew, the sheer joy of the most evil force this world has ever known had generated the sound that struck the most fear in their souls.

Best also knew He was mobilizing at great speed. He was turning to the kids of Vasallus, warning them. He revealed Himself to Chloë at the concert in Madrid as well as Avery and Bentley. "So what?" he thought. It was too late for Him. The world was doomed and there was nothing He could do about it. As He was intent on inflicting storms and cataclysmic disasters on His people, he would swoop in and steal what was most precious to Him, their souls. He was intent on wiping out earth as we know it today and replacing it with His son, Christ, and the souls of people who truly believed. The believers would be gone. Forever. His scorched earth would be empty of humankind. Christ would come home to an empty house.

The souls of human beings would forever be locked away in his house. The knowledge that his presence would be surrounded by the cries of tortured souls for all eternity was staggering to him. The swords of the seven sons of that bastard King Tiridates would not help Him now. It was too late. Far, far too late. He laughed again, sending people to the floor throughout the building to embrace the pending impact that would not come. It made him laugh even harder at the thought.

****

Sam opened his eyes. The memory of the attack at the mansion flooded his clearing consciousness. He looked around, half expecting Amber to pounce on him from the other side of the room. There was no one in the room. He was alone. He thought about Amber. She was no assistant to Avery or Bentley or that was not her purpose. She was a demon, planted by Best to watch over the mansion, while he was not there. But why? Then remembered the safe on the wall in his office. Of course, he thought, the memory of the contents in the safe coming back to him. It was the book inside that safe that made Amber go demonic. "What was in that book?" he thought. It had to have been important for Amber to reveal her true identity and try to kill him. He thought about that for a second. She attacked him, the gardener mistakenly shot him; yet he was still alive. He should be dead. Maybe it was true that he was cloaked in God's protection. "Was that his purpose? Was God's purpose for him to discover that book?" He knew with every fiber in his body that he needed to get back to the mansion and find that book. The book held a key to this saga. He felt it when he reached into the safe to retrieve the book. An incredible sense of danger and evil overwhelmed him, when he put his hand in that safe.

The door to his room opened and a nurse walked in, noticing he was awake, approached his bed and said, "Good morning Detective Showenstein. You look much better, I must say. Rest is doing wonders for you."

He stared at her intently as he asked, "How long have I been in the hospital?" She wrote down numbers of his vital signs from the machine beside his bed as she replied, "This is the morning of the fourth day. The first two days you were in a medicated induced coma, you woke briefly yesterday and it looks like now you're making a big step."

Four days? Jesus, he needed to get out of here. He asked, "Where is my wife? When can I get out of here?" She stopped writing numbers on her clipboard and turned towards him, looking down at him with a look of incredulity and said, "I know you cops are tough and all that, but I never thought you to be stupid. You're not going anywhere, Detective. You have a hole in your stomach that is still bleeding. Miraculously, and I say that literally, the bullet never damaged any of your internal organs. A few more days of rest and as long as your vitals continue to remain strong you should be out of here. The doctor will come by later and explain all that to you."

He asked, "When you say a few days, it sounds like far more than two. Tell me the truth, when am I getting out of here? There is much I must do." She shook her head in a mild form of disgust that he would be considering when to get out of here in his condition. She replied, "Maybe a week, likely longer Detective. That decision is up to the doctors and you can have that argument with them later when they come by." She finished up and left the room a few minutes later, while he sat in silence and thought about lying in this bed for another week. He needed to get out. Now.

****

To the complete shock of the world, France chose not to cancel or delay the Vasallus concert three days after the events in Madrid. Avery and Bentley believed the government of France feared more the unrest that would follow from fans, if they did not allow the group to perform. As they stared out the side windows of their limo, the two of them marveled at the readiness of the city. They had finally been allowed to depart Madrid this morning for Paris where the kids would be performing tonight. Escorted by limo service from the Vasallus private jet at Paris Le Bourget Airport, they made their way through the La Defense district of downtown and its tall skyscrapers to their hotel, where the kids would rest before they made their way to the Stade de France. The massive football stadium was already prepped for the biggest music concert ever held in France. Bentley squealed at something outside her window, "Avery, look. Unbelievable!"

He leaned across his seat and out her window to see what she was so excited about, and he saw it, and all he could say was, "Wow!" The skyscraper, Tour First, was completely wrapped in an image of the six kids of Vasallus. The picture was as tall as the building itself. It was at least seven hundred feet. It was breathtaking and splashed across the center of the image were the words "Paris Accueille Vasallus!" (Paris Welcomes Vasallus) in giant letters. He looked up at Bentley from leaning across her lap and said, "We should have driven with the kids in their limo. I would have loved to have seen the look on their faces when they saw that building!"

Soon they had the kids assigned to their rooms in the luxurious Sofitel Paris Hotel, and they could themselves take a few moments to rest and relax from the torrid pace they were on. They had about six hours before they needed to accompany the kids to the stadium. The two of them stripped off their clothes and climbed into bed, fighting the exhaustion that shook their bodies to embrace each other and share some intimate time that was a rare event in their lives lately. They allowed their hunger for each other to take precedence over intimacy. Their lovemaking was passionate but quick, and both of their bodies unable to fight the exhaustion, they were soon asleep.

Avery quickly found himself immersed in a place surrounded by danger. He was in a night club in Los Angeles, alone, and he was searching for Bentley in the sea of gyrating and dancing bodies. The music was loud, pulsing with beat, women and men oblivious to their surroundings. He approached a long haired brunette wearing a low cut dress in the back that went all the way down to the crack in her ass. It was Bentley. He placed his hand on her shoulder to get her attention, and when she spun around he was horrified to see it wasn't Bentley but a beautiful woman with a hideous and demonic face, her eyes glowed a menacing red. Shaken by his encounter he backed away, and the woman turned away from him and kept dancing. He looked around the jammed dance floor and spotted a woman on the second level, beautiful, staring at him, her body moving to the music. Her breasts inside her loose fitting dress seemed to move back and forth independently. He was about to look away when she opened her mouth, and her tongue, like a serpent, slithered out and snapped at the air about three feet in front of her. He looked away, knowing he must be having a nightmare. He looked around the dance floor again, watching as beautiful women walked past him, smiling and at the last second before they passed by, their faces would change into a demonic and blank rage. He needed to either wake up or get out of this place. He needed to find Bentley and get her out of here. He pushed his way through the middle of the dance floor; the people pushing him in every direction as he tried to maneuver his way through. The dance floor was growing more and more crowded, People were getting angrier and angrier at him, their evil faces flashing hatred, threatening him with their evil stares. He was trapped. The music became louder as the people around him closed in. He pushed into the crowd with all his strength, and he could not make any progress. He became frantic as he scanned the demonic faces surrounding him to find Bentley. He called out, screamed above the beat of the music, but no one could hear him.

Then he saw her.

She was on the second tier against the railing, staring down at him. There was a very handsome man beside her, his arm wrapped around hers. He leaned down and began to kiss then lick her neck. She briefly closed her eyes and tilted her head back with passion. The son-of-a-bitch would get a beating if he could get through these people. He watched and was horrified to see Bentley was enjoying the passionate kissing and licking by the stranger immensely. The man then stood up and stared directly at him. His eyes were burning a deep red and the recognition froze him. It was Best. Then he tilted his head back and laughed. His laugh was so loud, it could be heard above the drone of the music. He watched as Bentley leaned down and began to kiss and lick Best's neck. He cried out to her to stop, but she either couldn't hear him or didn't care. He tried to push his way through the suffocating crowd around him, but he could not move. Evil and demonic faces darted in and out in front of him. They closed in, and as they did he could see the claws at the ends of their arms snapping like shears. He would be torn to pieces, as he stood helpless watching Best fondle the woman he loved. He felt the first set of claws punch their way into his rib cage, and he screamed.

****

"Avery, wake-up. Wake-up. Sweetheart, you're having a nightmare!" She shook him furiously, and he finally began to snap out of it, lifting himself up onto his elbows, sweat quickly mixed with the cool air conditioning of the room, chilling him instantly. He looked up at Bentley, not fully awake yet and looked around the room for Best. He heard her say, "Honey, wow, you really had a doozie of a dream. Come on, you need to get a move on. We need to be out of here in forty five minutes."

She was completely dressed and ready for the concert. He looked around the room for a second then asked, "Jesus, what time is it?" She replied, smiling, "It's just after 4:00 p.m. I got out of bed and you were snoring like a truck driver, so I let you sleep a little longer and went and got ready. I checked on the kids and they were all up, excited and ready to perform. They have amazing energy. I'm worried about them though. I'm scared how this is all going to end for them, Avery. Best is using them as his pawns, and they don't even know it. There must be something we can do, other than just babysit them."

"I know sweetheart, I feel the same way. Useless to be precise. I, or should I say we, have to have trust that Father O'Sullivan will come through and lead these kids to safety." He reached up with his hand and pulled back her long dark hair that had fallen over her face and moved it back behind her ear and said, "I love you Bentley. I will not let anything happen to you or those kids. I promise." He watched as she reached down and kissed him on the cheek, and he felt her vibe through her kiss. It was a vibe that said nothing could protect her or the kids from what was coming their way. She was right. He could not protect them from the evil that surrounded them. He would, however, die trying. He was not afraid and that, he contemplated, was even scarier.

****

Ninety-three thousand Vasallus fans packed inside the stadium. The government prohibited all outdoor screens from being placed to broadcast the concert outside in the parking lots. Security was incredible, as the French government was taking no chances and would not tolerate violence of any kind. This was the first concert in many by Vasallus that was not overshadowed by violence, death and destruction. The kids performed all the hits off of the first three albums and the entire fourth record, yet to be released. The fans screamed for the members of Vasallus to do the floating in the air trick they had done at every concert in the past, but the kids stuck to the music this time. The fans got over the fact they wouldn't be entertained by imagery and tricks and settled in to soak up the historic concert. The kids; performances were through the roof, and their talents seemed to be increasing even more. The roars from the 90,000 plus crowd inside the stadium could be heard throughout most of Paris.

****

Europe and the rest of the world were going out of their minds for Vasallus and there seemed to be no end in sight. Social unrest in the United Sates had fully set in and the administration of President Stanley Kipshaw scrambled to control it. Europe was out of control with the nation's youth taking to the streets by the hundreds of thousands in defiance of society's rules. The world was teetering on the brink of anarchy, and it would be just a matter of time before a rogue nation bit back with disastrous results. In recent history when chaotic events happened around the world, countries turned to the United States to provide leadership in times of crisis. The United States was most affected by the social upheaval taking over the world, and it was on the verge of busting at the seams as the public school systems had collapsed, widespread rioting in the nation's cities were the norm, and murder and suicide rate were off the charts.

The President sat on the corner of his daughter's bed along with the First Lady and fought hard to keep the tears at bay, to be strong in front of his wife, but it was proving more and more difficult. The world was falling apart around him, nations everywhere were turning to the United States and his administration for leadership, and he was powerless to provide it. The evil that had wrapped its claws around humankind was residing in his daughter. Alexis had become Satan's vestibule. She had lost so much weight she looked worse than a stricken anorexic in her final days. Her hair had mostly fallen out; her face was covered in open sores, cuts and bruises. The world was left wondering what had happened to the most powerful man in the world. He had not been seen in public for weeks. He was right here beside his daughter, watching over her, and praying for her. Alexis was slowly being killed by the Demon, he knew. There wasn't anything he could do for her. There was nothing a hospital could do for her either, so they brought her home to keep a close vigil on her. Her bedroom mirrored her hospital room. Monitoring equipment filled the room and the constant beeps from the hooked up machines became the normal sounds of her room. His Chief of Staff, Adam Rinker, and the family's personal physician were the only ones besides his wife allowed in his daughter's bedroom. He had somehow been able to keep the rest of his staff away, but their growing concern over his absence in the face of the worldwide chaos was creating turmoil in his inner circle over his competency to lead the country.

He held his wife's hand tight with one hand and wiped his daughter's forehead with a cold cloth with his other. A voice called out to him inside his head. The voice said two words and when he registered the two words and what it meant, he looked down at his daughter and then to his wife and said, "Honey, I'll be right back." He quickly stood up off the bed and exited the bedroom, leaving his wife, Leah, to call out after him in bewilderment. He stepped out into the hallway of his daughter's bedroom in the White House and asked the agent standing guard, "Where's Adam?" Before he could respond, he heard the voice of his Chief of Staff coming from the hallway behind him say, "I'm right here Mr. President. What's up?" Stanley turned towards him, and in a voice tinged with panic as he watched Adam approach, concern stitched into his face, "Make arrangements to get Air Force One ready. We're leaving for Rome tonight."

Shocked, Rinker replied, "Rome, Mr. President? Why would the President of the United States, who hasn't been seen or heard from in weeks, suddenly show up in Rome?"

"Then we'll take a private jet. I don't care how we get there, Adam. I need to get to Rome. Tonight."

"Jesus, Stanley. You can't take a private jet tonight. Think of the security issues. That is impossible."

"Then you get the President's plane ready to fly in thirty minutes or I'll drive myself to Dulles and take the next Delta flight. Do you hear me?"

Stunned, Linker asked, "It's the priest. You want to meet

with him."

Stanley stared at his Chief of Staff and his friend and said, "Father O'Sullivan. I must see him in the Vatican. Alexis is dying Adam. He is the only one that can help her now. We will be there only long enough for me to convince him to get on the plane and come back here with us. Notify the Italian government we are landing in Rome, but do not tell them why. They cannot know it's because we are going to the Vatican. It must be kept secret. Tell them it's only for refueling and I will not be getting off the plane. Use our CIA field office in Rome to make arrangements to secretly get me off the plane and to the Vatican. Do not alert anyone at the Vatican of my planned visit. I will place a call to Father O'Sullivan once I am outside the walls of the Vatican. Father O'Sullivan is not known there, only by a few, so it's likely we will be entering through an obscure entrance. Do you understand Adam?"

Chapter 25

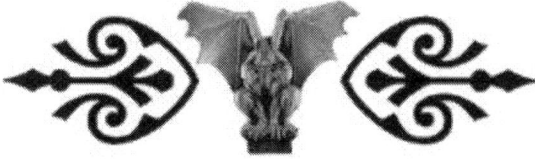

Houston, Texas, was home to the two largest Christian Churches in the United States. The Glory To God Fellowship Center with a seating capacity of over 17,000 boasted attendance numbers of close to 50,000 worshipers per week. The congregation was led by the enigmatic, Pastor Humphrey Jolens, who electrified his followers every week with sermons filled with stories of the advancement of evil in our society and how our children are drowning in the waters of social media. In Pastor Jolens words, "There is a poison in what our children are drinking that is killing them. Our children are swallowing every venomous word being sung and spoken by the plague that is being spread by Vasallus." His sermons were dominated by the need for the people of Glory To God to rail against the music our youth are embracing. He continued, "Cities across the world are burning to the ground by followers of the Satan inspired rock band Vasallus. As Christians, we have a responsibility to stand up against such wickedness. Our governments will not stop the word of the Devil, but we as a Church, will not stand any longer for the poison that is infecting our youth."

Jolens would not limit his rants from his Sunday pulpit. He went first from local television to preach his message to censor and shutdown Vasallus completely to national television stations. His message was now reaching a national audience, and the attention it was generating was not going unnoticed. Robert Best had seen and heard enough. It was time to put this pompous asshole out of his misery. He could easily shred him to pieces and be done with him, but it might inspire another egomaniac to pick up the mantel Jolens was carrying, and it could pick-up even more steam. He had a better plan to shut this preacher up once and for all.

He let the producers of CNN know through indirect sources that he would be interested in having a debate on national television with Jolens to defend the music and lyrics of Vasallus. He would use the opportunity to stamp out the irritating movement of the Christian Church to denounce Vasallus as evil and irresponsible. CNN seized the opportunity to put the man who created the biggest rock band in history on the hot seat against one of the most influential Christian leaders in the United States. Jolens thought God had made an intervention with this opportunity. He would fry this Best in front of a television audience of millions. He would not stop with the Christian community in the United States. He would use his Church's money and influence to reach out to the entire Christian community around the world to tune into the debate, and voice its word to end the reign of Vasallus after Best is left burning in ashes from his blasphemous vitriol. He cited the fact Europe was in complete chaos as Vasallus rolled over their youth with their music that promoted hate, fear and social disorder.

The producers of CNN, giddy with the huge interest building in the televised debate around the globe, fanned the flames of controversy by hosting non-stop segments with Christian leaders from throughout the world as well as supporters of Vasallus that included celebrities, powerful business people and influential government officials. It was taking on a life of its own that was shaping up to be a flashpoint of the ageless debate of the moral Christian beliefs versus the desire of today's youth to believe and live how they want, be damned of what society, government or Church has to say about it. Surprisingly, leaders of other religions around the world joined forces with Christian leaders on the debate turning the event into epic proportions. Best couldn't have scripted it any better, as he watched the debate swell in interest and popularity putting the mega popular Vasallus in the spotlight for completely different reasons. It was still a spotlight, the biggest one so far, and he would take full advantage. He would use the opportunity to thrust a dagger into the heart of God's word, turning Christianity, already a rapidly declining belief into an afterthought in the annals of human history. He would shake the foundation of their beliefs to the core, and the days that followed the debate would see unprecedented social change. He could feel the swell of laughter building within him, threatening to explode outwardly for the world to see how truly happy Satan, the Anti-Christ, Lucifer could be if that was possible.

****

After the Paris extravaganza, Vasallus had a few days off before they were moving on to the two most anticipated stops on the tour, Dublin and London. Anticipation had been building for weeks as the cherished and beloved Chloë McClosky and Michael Lockwood would be returning to their homelands performing with Vasallus. The press was having a field day with the upcoming concerts, and the Vasallus fever that gripped the two nations the day the band was formed was now threatening to turn each of the two countries upside down. Video surfaced of the duet of Chloë and Michael when they were only twelve years old performing at an Irish school academy. Stories were running in the papers of the sad and tragic deaths of Michael's father, Dalton Lockwood and Chloë's birth parents. Michael's mother, Ann Lockwood, had surfaced recently after years out of the public spotlight to support the British churches that had been rallying support for the upcoming CNN debate between Best and Jolens. She had a rich history in the British spotlight many years earlier with her philanthropic efforts as the daughter of the very rich and powerful Sherman Oakley. She appeared recently on Channel 4 News in an exclusive interview outlining her support for the Church against the music of Vasallus of which her own son was a member,

The highly acclaimed news channel in Britain and its star journalist, Megan Hawthorn, got immediately to the point in her twenty minute segment by asking, "Ann, please share with our television audience, the people of Britain, why you are speaking out against the music of your own son, Michael."

Ann, looking beautiful and dignified, knew millions of people would be watching the live interview, answered, "I love Michael more than any mother can love her own son. He is an incredibly talented young man, and I am very proud of who he is and what he has done. I agreed to this interview, not to defend my son's music but to bring awareness to the British people on the evil that the founder of Vasallus, Robert Best, represents."

Hawthorn replied, "The world is about to witness the debate of the ages, Ann. Tell me more about the man, Robert Best."

"Robert Best is the embodiment of evil. He recruited the mega talented kids of Vasallus, manipulated them for his purpose, and that was to spread evil and mayhem around the world. My son is a good person, and so are the other kids of Vasallus. Best has poisoned their minds and brainwashed them to spread his message to the youth around the world."

She clearly did not expect the interview to have gone in this direction, Megan continued, "Ann, those are powerful accusations. Are you not concerned with retribution actions by Mr. Best to denounce your claims?"

Ann was not fazed and added, "Whether people are Christians or of any other religion, even atheists for that matter, they need to be afraid of Robert Best."

"How so, Ann?"

Ann leaned forward slightly in her chair to emphasize her next words, "I have met Best personally many times over the years, and I will tell you this. He is the Anti-Christ in human form. He is extremely dangerous, and he is using this debate to spread his message of hate and fear to the entire world. He needs to be stopped. I will fight against him till my last breath. I will free my son from his evil clutches if it kills me."

The respected journalist's sharp reply was un-editable in the live interview, "Jesus Christ!"

****

Robert Best, in his Los Angeles condominium, shook with a rage so severe it threatened to vibrate the building off of its foundation. He had just watched the interview with the Channel 4 reporter and Ann Lockwood. That fucking bitch! How dare she talk about him like that! He wanted to kill her so bad it consumed his mighty rage like nothing he'd experienced in centuries. He knew he needed to focus on the debate later that night, but the image of Ann Lockwood attacking him on British television devoured him. He concentrated intensely to simmer his rage. He closed his human eyes and directed his thoughts to finding the whereabouts of Lockwood. He wanted to kill her before he took the stage against Jolens. His mind was a black mist blowing across the landscapes of Britain, searching for her, seeking her scent, her soul. His mind probed and penetrated every inch of that pathetic island and could not even sniff a trace of that bitch! "Where was she?" His mind raced with that thought. She was protected by Him. Of course! He was cloaking her from his probing mind. The rage returned when he thought of Him. "Why did He continue to protect her?"

His scream broke every window in the condo and blew the glass out of his large 72" TV. Her death was imminent, and he had to console his rage with that thought. The death of humankind and the tears that would fall from above was enough to calm him. In fact, he jumped in glee from his chair to prepare for the epic debate in Houston in just a few hours that would strike a crippling blow to the word of God. His smile quickly turned into a laugh at the thought of the vision of the look of horror on the divine heavenly face of Him.

****

"Why would she do that? Why would my own mother go on television and say that about us?"

Chloë quickly spoke, "Michael, do not blame your mother for what she said. She neither attacked you nor Vasallus."

Brittany nodded in agreement, "Chloë's right, Michael. Your mother loves you, and this is her way of protecting you."

The group was relaxing and watching T.V. in the expansive living room of the six bedroom suite at the Claridge Hotel in London, when the Channel 4 News interview came on with Ann. The kids had been secretly moved into the Claridge by Avery and Bentley after the Paris concert for a few days off before the show in Dublin. It was Juan who spoke next, "Your mother has a big mouth, Michael. Maybe you should pick-up the phone and tell her to keep quiet or maybe we can pay her a little visit." He looked over at Patrick as he said the last sentence.

Enraged, Michael turned to rush Juan when Connor stood in his way, "Come on Michael, take it easy. He didn't mean anything by what he said. He's just sticking up for Mr. Best is all. Like all of us should." He looked back at Juan and scolded, "Give us all a break Juan and keep your mouth shut for a while, okay?" Chloë stood up and guided Michael back onto his chair and said, "Hey Michael, it's all going to be okay. Soon we will be rocking it out in front of our home fans! I can't wait to perform in front of my fans. I miss Ireland so; it's going to be so much fun." Michael seemed to relax as he pondered the thought of performing in Wembley Stadium in front of his fans, "It's going to be epic, huh Chloë!"

Juan replied, "You guys get to perform in front of your fans. Do you know what it would mean to my people for Vasallus to perform in Venezuela? It would mean everything to them and to me." He sank deeper in the big cushions of his chair, knowing Vasallus would never perform in the tiny country.

Patrick interjected, "Grow up you pussy. Who the fuck cares about Venezuela but you anyway? If the Master thought it was important for us to perform there then we would but we're not, so fucking drop it."

Juan, for the first time Chloë could remember, showed real contempt for Patrick. "You're an asshole sometimes, Patrick. Tell me, why do you call him the Master anyway?"

Patrick looked at Juan, his eyes clearly reflecting danger, and spat, "Careful Jimenez. Don't want to have to stand in front of all your precious reporters hiding your bruises with sunglasses, do you?"

****

The showdown between Robert Best and the music of Vasallus against the powerful and influential Pastor Humphrey Jolens would be held in the CNN studios in Jolen's city of Houston. Best could care less if they held it in Jerusalem. He would verbally and mentally destroy Jolens. The pompous prick would eat his words. He couldn't wait.

It was being promoted by the pundits as a debate, but in reality it was the CNN host, Ron Truman, sitting on one chair, Best and Jolens sitting on two other chairs. They were minutes away from live T.V. as the stage assistants worked on the remaining details. Each of them had a cup of coffee in front of them, and Jolens surprised both Best and Truman by placing a copy of the Bible on the table in front of him. Best seethed when he thought of the audacity of Jolens and just minutes before the cameras were to roll, he said to Truman, "Please ask Humpty boy to get rid of the book." Jolens chuckled at the remark and retorted, "Makes you uncomfortable does it Best?"

Best did not even look at Jolens or acknowledge his comment and flashed a stare at Truman that clearly unnerved him, "He gets rid of that comic book or I walk, and there will be no debate."

Truman ordered Jolens, "Get rid of the Bible, Pastor." He motioned for a producer to come and get the book. Jolens refused, "It is obvious to me and it will also soon become obvious to the viewers that Mr. Best is intimidated by the word of God. I will not allow this man to bully me into removing His word. It is the very reason we are here today. To debate what the word of God has to say against the profane excuses of a man bent on spreading words of hate and fear mongering. The book is my strength, my beloved. So, Mr. Best, we are about to begin. I suggest you begin to focus on what is ahead of you over the next hour."

The sudden rage by Best shocked Truman and Jolens as well as the surrounding producer, assistants and cameraman. He stood up, grabbed the book and threw it across the studio with such ferocity it embedded in the drywall. An explosion of shattering pieces hit the floor accompanied by studio wall picture frames falling from the violent impact of the heavy book.

In a calm and quiet voice, Best looked at both Truman and Jolens and stated, "Can we begin?"

****

"That was Jenn back in Los Angeles. She asked if we knew about the episode on CNN coming up in a few minutes. Apparently, Robert Best is squaring off with Pastor Humphrey Jolens of Houston on the immorality Vasallus's music is having on the youth of the world."

Bentley looked at Avery and replied, "Does she know we work twenty hours a day and are so cut off from the rest of the world it's not even funny. Why is Best jostling with a heavy weight like Jolens on national TV?"

Avery sat up on the overstuffed couch in their suite at the Claridge, and motioned for Bentley to join him on the couch as he flipped the channels searching for CNN. "Apparently, according to Jenn, Jolens is the spokesperson for a group of the largest Christian churches in America who have rallied together to speak out against the music of Vasallus. Their word is apparently being heard for CNN to give them airtime with everything else going on around the world." He finally found the 24 hr. news channel just as the host, Ron Truman, was introducing his guests, the Pastor and Best. Bentley remarked, "Best is so impeccably dressed and manicured he looks almost plastic." Avery chuckled and added, "He probably had the producers spray him down with lacquer. He looks pathetic." He turned up the volume as Truman began.

"Robert, you know why we're here today. Before we let Pastor Jolens ask you questions, please explain to our television audience around the world the worldwide success of Vasallus. Where did the members of the group come from, how did you find them, and how do you explain their phenomenal success?"

He focused on the camera as he replied, the confidence oozing from him like oil, "I would be happy to, Ron; however, I have explained this question many times, which makes me wonder why such a respected TV personality like yourself would ask such an over-explained question."

"An attempt to set the proper perspective right up front, Mr. Best. If you may, please explain."

Best explained, "It was simply a matter of seizing an opportunity that presented itself, Ron. These kids, young and mega-talented and successful in their own right come along once in a lifetime. But to come around, all at the same time and different parts of the world was a miracle. The next step was to determine if they were interested in forming Vasallus. Once they agreed, the hardest part was making these many superstars from different cultures come together in a close knit group or family. Not only did they become close, Ron, but also they became brothers and sisters. I give most of the credit for this to my partner and the driving force behind Vasallus, Avery Johnson."

Truman countered, "Obviously they could not have been that close, Robert, as one of the members, Elizabeth Leroux, left the band soon after the North American tour."

The mention of Elizabeth clearly bothered Best, but kept his cool and replied, "I thought we were meeting here today to allow Pastor Jolens the opportunity to speak directly to me regarding Vasallus. Pastor Jolens, I take offense to your accusations that Vasallus are unethical, immoral and purveyors of hate."

Avery knew Best had just cleverly reflected the conversation away from the suspicious disappearance of Elizabeth Leroux. He watched as Jolens took the opportunity presented by Best to go on the offensive.

"You left one adjective out, Mr. Best. Fear mongering. The lyrics of Vasallus's music has clearly been written to elicit a negative social response to authority and those in a position of influence. They have left no one out Mr. Best, attacking school teachers, government officials, police, the Church of all faiths to name just a few Mr. Best.

"If I may interrupt for one second, Pastor. Every one of

these examples you mentioned are public institutions; therefore, they are open to criticism which is exactly what Vasallus's music is trying to convey. The youth of this world and everyone for that matter are being forced to learn from books that are lies, government officials creating laws that protect them but do nothing to advance society. The same government officials both in the United States and all over the world that is corrupt and bent on self-indulgence and self-promotion. They continue to strip the individual rights of its people from all societies for their own gain. Church officials like yourself Pastor are hypocritical and bigots. The biggest pyramid scheme in the world is the Church. You brainwash millions to listen to your hyperbole only to hide your real intent to fleece them of their money for your own selfish gains. You should change your name Pastor to Robin Hoodwink. You steal from the poor to feed the greed of the rich. I've seen your cathedrals, the house you live in and the cars you drive. The opulence you and others like you surround yourself with is from the pockets of the people who fill your stadiums disguised as a church. You molest our children and pay off corrupt police officials to get away with it. I find it all pathetic and offensive." Both Jolens and Truman had tried to interject during Best's rant, but he expertly and smoothly pushed them to the side. The TV cameras picked up their feeble attempts to gain control.

Bentley and Avery sat on the couch, stunned at what they had just heard. They knew that Best with his incredible self-confident attitude and sincerity would have hit a major nerve with millions of people world-wide... They willed Jolens to take back control from Best. They were wrong.

"Nice speech, Mr. Best. You just described the acts of a few in an attempt to paint entire institutions with the same brush. Deflecting responsibility away from your creation, Vasallus, is abhorrent and the time to account for their reprehensible behavior is not only the responsibility of the Church, but also Government. Laws are being broken by the spread of their hate, fear and lawlessness. You and your sidekick, Johnson, will be held responsible."

Truman stepped in, "I would like to welcome…" Best cut him off and attacked Jolens remarks, "Vasallus's music is the truth and a reason for their massive success. You are a hypocrite Jolens. Tell the audience what kind of car you drive?"

Avery could see Jolens squirm with that question. He looked every bit the wealthy preacher, dressed in an expensive suit and tie and an expensive watch peeking out from the cuff of his shirt. "I don't think the kind of car I drive is of relevance. Let me…" Best cut him off, "Answer the question Pastor. What does the pastor of a church drive these days? To reflect the people that crams your services every weekend, I'm sure it's a modest Buick or Ford sedan?"

The pastor fumbled with his words. In any other place or situation he would command the conversation and direct it any way he wanted, but up against Best he never stood a chance, "I drive a decent car. Gets me from Point A to Point B."

"Is that right Pastor? Point A to Point B in a church paid for Mercedes S600. One of six luxury cars at your disposal. You're a pompous ass Jolens and a phony, and I would hope the TV audience can see that. The kids of Vasallus work their tails off to bring the great music that carries a message of truth to people everywhere."

Now Truman did interject, "Robert, it is true President Kipshaw's administration is looking into censorship laws to curb the acidic tone of Vasallus. Will you fight the censorship?"

"I challenge President Kipshaw to censor Vasallus. You know why Ronnie? Because the people around the world, and not just in the United States, will not stand for it. People want the truth, and they're sick and tired of the lies. I know I am."

Jolens feebly added, "The people want the truth to come from the word of God. Your truth is the biggest lie, Best."

Best shot Jolens a look that would not have been picked up by the cameras, but Avery bet Best's eyes reflected the hatred he was feeling, "It's time for you to be quiet Jolens. No one is listening to you. No one is listening to President Kipshaw either. In fact when was the last time the public heard from their leader, Ronnie? What this country and the rest of the world needs is true leadership. Someone who has the ability, skill and courage to speak the truth."

Truman replied, "Sounds like a campaign speech?"

Best turned and looked directly at the camera when he replied, "Maybe it is, Ronnie. Maybe it is."

****

The interview ended shortly after with Best effectively minimalizing Pastor Jolens concerns to nothing more than petty whining. The Church's efforts to take out Vasallus backfired miserably. The reaction to the CNN segment was through the roof and replayed over and over on websites such as YouTube. Everyone it seemed weighed in on the debate of Freedom of Speech to the responsibility of government to limit that right. One thing became clear in the days following the interview, music mogul Robert Best had emerged as a powerful voice for the people everywhere.

Chapter 26

It was still a few days before Vasallus would slip out of London to Dublin for its performance to the tens of thousands of highly anticipated Irish fans. Avery and Bentley could clearly see how overjoyed Chloë was as the day approached. It was wonderful to see her excitement bubble over, and it had spread to the other members. Everyone was in a great mood and anxious to depart for the secret flight out of London, and so it was a shock when the two of them opened the door to their suite to see Chloë standing in the hallway, tears flowing down her cheeks, upset and shouting, "Michael has disappeared. He never came out of his room this morning when breakfast was delivered. I'm afraid for his safety. I don't know what to do."

Bentley reached out for Chloë, pulling her in close to comfort her, wiped her cheeks with the sleeve of her housecoat and said, "It's okay, Chloë. He just likely needed some air from being cooped up in the room for a few days. He'll be back soon."

Avery stepped out in the hallway, always cautious now, looked in both directions and then said, "Come inside and tell us everything Chloë."

Bentley guided her, sobbing with emotion, to a nearby sofa. She sat beside her and held Chloë tight. Looking at the two of them for a brief second, Avery was reminded of his sister when she was that age and her dream boyfriend in high school dumped her. His mother cradled his sister much the same way as Bentley was now comforting Chloë. He pushed those memories away and asked Chloë, "Sweetheart, did something happen in the room between Michael and the others? Was he upset?"

"He and Juan went at it over some things Juan said about his mother, but it was quickly resolved and nothing more became of it."

Bentley swung her hips around so she could look Chloë straight on, then asked her, "What did Juan say about his mother?"

She watched as Chloë used her sleeve to wipe her tears before she replied, "We were all watching T.V. when Channel 4 news interviewed Mrs. Lockwood. She said some bad things about the Master, I mean, Mr. Best. Juan didn't like it and told Michael his mother should keep her mouth shut. That kinda set him off."

Avery asked, "What happened then?"

Chloë continued, "Connor intervened and told them both to cool their jets. Juan then made the comment about why Vasallus wasn't performing in Venezuela and how unfair that was. Patrick fired back that no one cares about that country. It got pretty heated for awhile, but it soon blew over and everybody was back to hanging out again. I'm worried about Michael, Bentley. Do you think he went to find his mother?"

****

Michael climbed out of the taxi, paid the driver and stood in front of the huge mansion he grew up in. He could not understand why he has not seen his mother for so long. Why did she not visit him in the United States or when they were on tour? Why didn't any of the other parents visit? He never paid it any thought before, but standing here now, he couldn't stop thinking about it. Where had Father O'Sullivan, Chloë's caregiver, gone? It was all kind of surreal for him. He pushed that away from his mind for now. He was here to see his mother. He has missed her terribly. He pondered that thought for a second, as he approached the entrance. He hasn't missed his mother at all. Never even thought about her for a very long time until yesterday when he saw her on television "Why was that," he thought.

****

When Bentley returned to the room after escorting Chloë back to her own suite, assuring her that we would find Michael, he said to her, "He's gone to see his mother. We leave this afternoon for

Dublin. We have to find him, Bentley. He's not safe away from the others. I remember Ann mentioning something about the fact she could not visit or see her son. It was unsafe. Come on let's go. We'll start at the residence."

"Which one? She has several here in London and in the country."

A thought occurred to him that frightened him as he replied, "You know, she might not even be in the country. If Michael doesn't find her here, he might leave the country to search for her."

****

There was no doorbell, he remembered, at the front entrance, just a large metal hook in the middle of the heavy wooden doors. He almost never entered the home through the main entrance. He and his mother would always drive into or get driven into the underground parking garage of the condo estate and would enter the home through the garage. He picked up the heavy metal clanger and banged it several times against the thick wood. He thought about who might answer the door. A butler or maid, maybe? An assistant? It has been so long since he'd been here, he wasn't sure who his mother had on staff anymore. A few minutes passed so he rapped on the door once again. The home was so big, and if there were no staff on shift there was a chance no one could hear him if mother was on the second floor in her bedroom. He began to worry, contemplated other places his mother might be at. He checked the time on his watch. It was still mid-morning. She should be home. He didn't have a cell phone. Never needed one. He used only his iPad to communicate with his legions of fans through Twitter and Facebook. He wished he had one now; he could just call her. Then he thought twice about that. He didn't even have her cell number. He tried the huge brass handle on the doors to see if, by chance, they might be open. They were locked of course. He was about to turn and make his way to the garage side door to see if it might be open when he heard a sound. The sound of a heavy wooden door opening.

****

Quick showers and they were out of the Claridge and into a taxi within thirty minutes after taking Chloë back to her room. Avery gave the driver the address to Ann's downtown condo estate and squeezed into the backseat beside Bentley and held her close. Bentley looked terrific despite having barely any time to get ready and with the weather in London cool and its typically gloomy overcast she decided to wear a sweater underneath her long black leather jacket. With black leather gloves and black boots and her hair pulled back in a ponytail, he couldn't help himself as he smiled. That prompted a response from her, "What are you smiling about? Did I say something funny? What am I missing?" He reached out and took her gloved hand in his and said, "I was admiring how beautiful you are and thinking how together with our black leather we could pass for a couple of British agents. Then I thought maybe we are a couple of secret agents, heading off to intercede between a son and his mother."

"I'm afraid how Best will react when he finds out Michael has disappeared. We need to find him and get him back to the hotel before he finds out," she worried.

"Best will not find out Michael is on his own unless someone tells him. Oh shit!" They both looked at each other at the same time, thinking the same thing, *Patrick!*

****

For all the hype and press coverage of the CNN interview with that moron, Jolens, it was over in minutes, and the rest of the hour was a feeble attempt by Jolens to save face in front of his Christian followers. Even Truman desperately tried to turn things in Jolens' favor to try and salvage the show, but it was a waste of time. Best walked out of the CNN studio the second the interview ended, but before he did he made sure Jolens felt his wrath one more time, "Nice job Pastor, or maybe you should be called Patsy Jolens. Tell the other crony leaders of your useless faith to prepare and get ready." He watched as Jolens looked at him as if he were staring at a complete lunatic. Maybe he was, he laughed to himself. Jolens replied, "Ready for what, Best? Another album release by your pets. More hatred and fear to spew onto the good people of this country and around the world?"

"People are sick by the likes of people like you, Patsy. Nobody's listening to you, especially after millions just watched you puke all over yourself in front of the cameras with your pathetic attempts to sound relevant. Go home to your fancy cars and mansions, because your days are numbered." He watched the pastor's face grow red with anger as he replied, "Are you threatening me, Best?" Before turning and leaving the red faced preacher to fume, he gave him one last ominous warning, "Yes. The time is near. The paradise promised to you in the good book wedged in that wall over there is all a lie. I will see you soon, Patsy Jolens."

He turned away from the red faced pastor, leaving him shaking with rage and let out a hearty laugh that was heard by everyone on the studio floor. He was surprised to hear Jolens, a man of God, shout out behind him, "Asshole!"

A few minutes later he was out on the sidewalk, the acrid air and humidity of Houston hitting him like a slap in the face. Then suddenly something else hit him like a slap. A sense of danger overwhelmed him. It could be only one thing. The kids. There was trouble. He needed to be alone, so he could close his human eyes and search the realms of this earth for the source of trouble. He walked briskly towards the end of the CNN building and turned the corner, searching for a back lane or an unoccupied building entrance. He spotted a lane across the street in the adjacent building. He could see the large blue garbage bins behind the building and bordering the back lane. He ran across the street, dodging oncoming traffic and entered the lane. There was no one in the vicinity just cars at the opposite end of the back lane racing by. He made his way between the two large bins and knelt down against one of them, shutting his eyes and searched his mind for the source of trouble. It didn't take him long to see it. It was Michael. Alone and standing in front of a large house somewhere in London. What was he doing, and why was he alone? He was rapping a metal knuckle on a large wooden door. No one was opening the door so he turned to leave, then tried the door handle but found it locked. What was he up to? Then he suddenly turned back towards the door. The door was opening. Somebody inside the large house was opening the door to Michael.

When his mind crystallized the face of the person who had opened the door, he actually sucked in a breath of air with surprise. He sprang off of the ground from his kneeling position and prepared to enter another realm. His son had opened a window he never thought was possible. He had not been able to see Ann Lockwood for a very long time, ever since his adversary decided to place her under His protection. The presence of Michael removed the cloak.

It was time to move.

****

When the heavy doors opened, the two of them stood just stood and stared at each other. Tears spilled from Ann's eyes as she cried, "Michael. Oh Michael." She stepped out of the doorway to embrace him, the two of them silent for a moment as they held each other tight. Finally, Ann stepped back and looked at her son, wiping the tears from her eyes when she said, "Michael, I can't believe it's you. What are you doing here, son?"

"It has been so long since I've seen you. I just needed to see you Mom."

Reality of the situation hit her, knowing his visit here was dangerous for both of them and she reached out and grabbed his hand, ushering him inside the house, "Come inside my son. We have lots to talk about. You're right. It has been far too long." She guided him into the living room and the two of them sat across from each other, not saying anything when she asked, "What brings you here, Michael. I thought you were in Dublin?"

"We are, Mom. We're supposed to be flying out later today. No one knows we're in the city, certainly not the press. We're just chillin for a few days after the show in Paris and the fiasco in Madrid." He smiled, and Ann could see how much he has grown in the months since she had last seen him. At seventeen he looked far older, his hair long, dark and styled. He was extremely handsome, and it was no wonder the British press followed the group non-stop. The city would be in chaos, if they knew their beloved

Michael Lockwood from Vasallus was in town. She smiled warmly and asked, "Does Avery and Bentley know you are here?"

He looked down towards the floor when he replied, "No one knows I came here. I watched your interview with Channel 4 News, and it made me upset that you would say those things about Mr. Best. I wanted to come and see you and tell you that Mr. Best is not an evil person, Mom. He really isn't, and he treats all of us like we were his kids."

She stared at her son for a second, trying to think of the words to say to him without upsetting him. He had come here, not to see his mom because he missed her, but to scold her for talking publicly about Best. She was about to respond when a voice from behind her sent a bolt of fear down her spine. It was a voice that she has heard in this house before.

"You should listen to him. That's good advice he's giving you. How have you been, Ann?"

She tried to move, but fear had frozen her in place. She could barely breathe, as she tried to move her head towards the demonic voice of the evil monster that has brought nothing but death and destruction to her life. She could see Michael was surprised at his appearance, but he was not scared. She watched as Best moved into the living room in front of her. He stared at her intensely, not saying a word, his eyes on fire when he suddenly turned and barked at Michael, "What are you doing here? Why aren't you at the hotel?"

Michael instantly became defensive, unsure what to say, and before he replied, Ann hissed, "Leave him alone. He came here to talk to me, to defend you. You can't keep these kids locked lo up like slaves, Best. This is my son and he needs to see his mother."

Michael glared at his mother, "Mom, that's enough. It's okay, Mr. Best, I will leave." He stood up to leave when Best shouted, "Sit down." He then looked back at her and spat, "I could never find you, He has made you invincible from me. It was only through Michael coming here could I see you. It is time for you to die, Ann. Your charades have gone on long enough." Michael, stunned at what he was hearing, shouted, "Master, what are you saying? This is my mother! I know she shouldn't have spoken that way about you on television, but you can't harm her."

The speed for which Best slugged Michael was a blur. The blow to his face sent him flying over the couch and onto the floor. He groaned as he struggled to get up. Ann screamed, "Leave him alone, you monster!" She never saw the punch and only felt its impact after she had hit the wall ten feet away. She slumped to the floor and struggled to maintain consciousness. She squinted at the blurry images in front of her, barely making out the transformation of Best into his demonic beast form. "This was it," she thought. She was going to die here in her own home, just like her husband was almost eighteen years ago, except now, she would be torn apart in front of her own son. She could only watch in horror as Best screamed like a wild animal, tearing his shirt off his body as if it were tissue paper. He transformed into his demonic persona that she has seen several times before. She was not terrified for herself, but she was mortified to watch her son having to witness Hell opening up in front of their eyes. She watched as Best's arms bulged and his legs grew like tree trunks. His skin was purplish grey, slimy and his face was difficult to look at. It was misshapen, large and with long cuts opening up that oozed a yellowish slimy puss. His teeth became elongated, uneven and stained. He went from this immaculate looking man to a hideous looking monster in just a few minutes. She looked back at Michael, and he had fallen to the ground on his knees, horrified at what he was seeing. She shouted at him, "Michael. Michael, come over here. Listen to me. Come over here now." There was only a few seconds before he was fully engulfed in his demonic shell. She hoped he would not kill Michael, and maybe if he stayed close to her, it might give them some more time to think about what to do. "What could she do?" She thought. This was insane. She had no problem dying, but she would do so protecting her son.

Michael stood up, staring at the Beast in front of him. He looked over at her and slowly made his way towards her. The stench that was emanating from Best was choking the air coming into her lungs. "Is this what Hell smells like? She would find out soon enough," she thought.

The Beast was about to make a move on Michael when there was a pounding on the front door. She watched in horror as the creature floated in fluid motion towards the front door ready to annihilate whoever came through it. The pounding continued, and then she recognized the voice shouting. It was Avery. She closed her eyes, willing him to leave, knowing what would happen to him if he walked through the door. Michael sat down beside her on the floor and asked, "Mom, are you okay? You're hurt. I am so sorry. I should have protected you from him." She brushed his cheek with her hand before replying, "I'm okay son. This isn't your fault this is happening. There is nothing you can do. Wait a minute, there is something you can do."

She looked into his eyes as he watched her, waiting for her instructions. She raised her voice loud enough that the Beast could hear her from the other side of the room, "Pray Michael. Pray to God for His love to save you from the Hell that is in this home. Pray!"

Just then the front door burst open, and Avery along with Bentley rushed into the room and straight into Hell. Bentley gasped, "Oh my God! What is happening! Ann. Michael. Sweet Jesus!" The two of them took a step back as the Beast screamed at her and Michael. "How dare you use those words in front of my son! I will shred you to pieces, bitch!" Ann shot right back, "How dare you call Michael your son. He is not your son. He is born of my blood, the blood given to him by the Lord God Almighty! You are a liar, a coward, a monster who could never have been a part of creating something as wonderful as my son."

The creature was on top of her, sending Michael sprawling against the wall in the process. His blood red eyes glowered at her, hatred coming off of them like sparks from a welding torch. "You ungrateful whore. I gave life to him, made him who he is, his talent. You've been lucky to be alive this long. Tonight you will die in front of your son. Just like you watched your husband die in front of your eyes. Your son, my son, will watch his mother die." He cocked his bulbous head backwards, staring up at the ceiling as if to mock the heavens and laughed a sound that came straight from Hell. He reached down and clamped his claws around her throat with such force, she instantly felt her lungs completely shut off from any oxygen. She flung her arms around him, trying to get her fingers at his face and into his eyes. She could see the blackness reach the corner of her eyes, slowly moving towards the middle of her vision. She would be dead in the next few seconds. The Beast screamed in delight above her. His scream was suddenly muted when he was walloped over the side of his head by a marble statuette, swung with devastating force by Avery, sending Best flying off her. She immediately rolled onto her side, desperately trying to get air into her lungs. She heard Avery's voice over top of her, shouting at her if she was okay. The room was spinning out of control as the air slowly made its way into her lungs. She blinked several times as she tried to clear her vision. She could see Michael, crying, crawling towards her on the floor. Then she heard Bentley scream, "Avery, watch out!"

The claw of the Beast slashed out at Avery, tearing away flesh from his bicep and sending him crashing to the floor. He had avoided total severing of his arm by turning at the last second. Ann could see him clutch his bleeding arm, Bentley at his side. She rolled back on to her back and looked up at the beast moving towards her once again. The rage in his eyes was pure death. He was going to kill her now. There would be no more choking the life out of her but an instant stab to her heart from his dagger-like claws. She rolled her head towards her son and mouthed the words to him, "I love you, Michael." Everything was happening it seemed in slow motion. She rolled her head back towards the Beast as he lowered himself onto her, ready to crush the life from her and send her soul straight to Hell. She closed her eyes, her mind registering the screams from Bentley and the shouts from Avery. It was too late, she was going to die in the next instant. She took that instant to silently pray to God for His forgiveness that she was unable to protect Michael. She asked Him to shield Michael's eyes from the death blow that was headed her way.

The blow did not come. Instead her eyes were forced open by a light so intense and bright she had to lift her hand to shield her eyes so she could see. The light filled the room, engulfing it in brightness. The Beast was on its knees in front her, his head bent to the side from the intensity of the light. It began to scream as the origin of the light became apparent. Through the light came a huge and gleaming steel blade, then a large hand of a man gripping the handle of the sword. The hand was followed through the light by a powerful arm and the complete outline of a man, a soldier, at least eight feet in size, his hair long and stringy. The intense light that paved his entrance, now disappeared behind the soldier. The warrior stepped towards the Beast and declared, "I am Davit, son of King Tiridates, soldier of God. Leave this room at once creature or feel the wrath and the power of the Lord upon you!"

The Beast cart wheeled away from the soldier and off Ann. He rolled about ten feet on the floor then sprang to his feet and screamed, "Your command means nothing to me soldier. I could cut through your armor as if it were fabric and tear your heart out of your chest." The soldier, his muscled arms gripping the sword, swung the huge blade in an arcing motion towards the Beast and replied, "Then I suggest you make haste, creature. Before you depart, feel the power of God in your bones." Ann watched in amazement as the soldier moved his sword swiftly towards the Beast, followed by a powerful beam of light bouncing off the tip of the blade, across the room and into the chest of the creature. The soldier named Davit, commanded, "The Lord God Almighty, commands you leave at once. He will not tell you again. My sword will cut your head off and then throw it into the flames from where you came, evil one."

The laughter that escaped from the Beast's throat was ear splitting. Ann covered her ears and then watched in horror as the Beast used his power to direct every object in the large living room towards the soldier. She watched as Bentley and Avery barely ducked in time as a silver platter sliced the air above their heads. Hundreds of objects, from the surrounding walls, and off the floor, launched themselves at the soldier. The soldier knelt to the ground and lifted his sword high in the air, then arced it down and in a circular motion that created a bright force field around him. Objects fell to the ground in front of the soldier, unable to penetrate his shield. After the Beast stopped launching objects at the soldier, he stretched his claw-like hands towards the floor in front of the soldier, exploding it. The floor collapsed around the soldier. They all watched as the soldier struggled to maintain an upright posture. The Beast moved towards him, laughing and then screaming, He then shouted to be heard above all the sounds of carnage around them, in a voice that was not English, but the same Latin that Ann had heard before from the creature, "Tempus enim prope est Dei annuntiare. Et bene sit eis mors. Et non est, qui liberasti illos. Rex tibi, et fratribus tuis, et revertar. Et dabo ultionem meam. Dic regi, et Deus tuus qui ("Tell your God the time is near. The death of His beloved man is upon them. There is no saving them. I will return for you and your brothers and your King. I will have my revenge. Tell your King and your God that."

The booming sounds of the Beast, the carnage of the objects flying through the air and the floor exploding around them suddenly ended. The room became eerily quiet and still. Ann looked around her. The Beast was gone. He had left. The soldier of God had saved them. She struggled to stand up then was offered a hand by Avery. Michael was gone. The Beast would not leave him here after this. He had come to kill her and was almost successful. They all turned to see the soldier step towards them. The light returned, and its intensity and brightness caused them all to wince momentarily. The departing soldier called out to them, "I am Davit, Ann, and you and your son are my direct descendants, and I will protect you under the commandment of our heavenly Father. Do not fear the road ahead of you for it will become less troubled. The Beast will not harm Michael, not yet. Your son will be safe for now. I have been waging war with His enemy for centuries, but soon it will be over and for that, like you, I am grateful. Now I must leave. Be strong, all of you, for there are many battles to be fought ahead. Glory be to God!" They all watched in wonder as the soldier, his body filling the room, walked slowly backwards into the light, his eyes reflecting the love of God he fought for, his body becoming smaller as the light swallowed him further. Like the first thing that had pierced the light, the tip of his sword was the last to slip into the beacon of brightness.

The three of them, witness to the miracles of God, watched the fading light leave the room.

Chapter 27

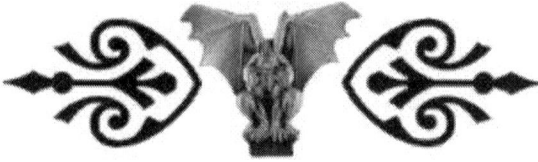

They began their descent into Fiumicino Airport in Rome. Flying commercial was a twelve hour flight over the Atlantic, but the mid-size executive Challenger 300 jet had them touching down in just over ten hours. His Chief of Staff, Adam Rinker had somehow managed to locate the private jet keeping Air Force One and all of its security issues and questions that would need to be answered back in Washington. He pulled in some favors from a rich benefactor of the President, and the jet was fueled and its pilots ready to take off within thirty minutes of his phone call. The risk of the trip was not lost on Rinker who scolded his boss one more time, "You know how many fires I will be extinguishing, because of this little junket? We easily could have sent this jet with some agents to pick-up the priest and bring him back to Washington. A phone call from your office to the Vatican police would have been sufficient to round up O'Sullivan and have him transported back, co-operative or not."

"Jesus, Adam, we've gone over this, how many times? Father O'Sullivan's identity and presence in the Vatican is known only to a few. I can't risk alerting the police, which would force the priest to go into hiding to protect his anomininity. He heads up a secret committee I'm sure is fiercely protected from discovery from the outside world and even within the church. He came to the White House to warn me. He will meet with me if he's here. But it has to be quiet. Okay?"

He watched his good friend shake his head before replying, "This is your party, Mr. President. How do you plan to locate this priest, quietly, when we arrive there?"

Stanley suppressed his smile before answering, "I have connections. After all, I am the President of the United States!" In reality, he had the protocol to reach the priest before the wheels lifted off the runway at Dulles. He had earlier instructed the head of the FBI to send agents from the Irish Garda to the priest's church in Balbriggan, outside of Dublin. A co-operative church administrator by the name of Mrs. Beckeridge was more than willing to give up the whereabouts of O'Sullivan in Rome."

Rinker looked him suspiciously, "What did they do to her to give up his contact information?"

"Relax Adam. A little story was concocted."

"A story?"

"We told her, their beloved Chloë refused to perform until she met with Father O'Sullivan immediately. The agents were desperately trying to find O'Sullivan in time."

Rinker shook his head again, "The upcoming concert in Dublin! The one the whole country would implode if it was cancelled. Quite brilliant, I must say, Mr. President, but what if Mrs. Beckeridge contacted O'Sullivan and let him in on your little ruse?"

"To late for that. I've already spoken with the priest, confessed how I obtained his contact information and asked for the Lord's forgiveness."

"I doubt that and the Lord knows, I'm sure, that being the most powerful man in the world, you have exceeded your allotment of allowable sin. O'Sullivan is still willing to meet with you?"

Returning to a more serious tone, Stan replied, "Yes of course. I did not ask him to come to the United States tonight. I didn't have to. He already knew why I was coming to see him. He knows about Alexis' condition."

Rinker shook his head for the third time. "Then why did we go to all this trouble to get here? Why didn't you put him on the next plane to Washington? How would he know about Alexis' condition? Come to think of it, forget I asked."

"There is someone else he wants me to meet at the Vatican. If I agreed to come to Rome and meet with this person, then he would accompany me back to the United States. He felt the arrangement was justified considering the ploy I used on his assistant back in Ireland."

"Okay. I hope this works, Stan. For Alexis sake. We will, however, play it by the book on security. Our field office will provide escort to the Vatican. Non- negotiable."

The President slapped his Chief of Staff on the shoulder, followed by the reply, "Agreed!"

Minutes later, the jet taxied to a quiet corner of the airport, far from the terminal. Three large black sedans were waiting.

****

The three sedans gathered in a darkened lane along the southeast building of the Vatican, near the entrance to the Holy Palace. A large wall, covered in shadow, hidden from the nearby courtyard stood before them. The cars were hidden from security patrol, but it still made Rinker nervous.

"Where is O'Sullivan? It's just a matter of time before the Vatican police show up. How do I explain the President of the United States is on a stakeout outside the Vatican?" Stan looked over the seat to the other side of the limo, then said, "Will you relax Adam? The police are not coming, I can assure you. Father O'Sullivan will be out soon."

"From where? We're wedged into this corner with no doors or windows. Is he going to pop up from behind one of those bushes over there? This is ridiculous. I feel stupid. Wait a minute! Look, over there!" Stan followed his gaze to the end of the wall and could see a faint light and movement. A door was open in a wall that had no doors. A man was walking towards them. As he came nearer they could see he was a priest. Not Father O'Sullivan, but a much older, grey haired and overweight cleric. As he approached the limo in front of theirs, two agents stepped out and engaged the cleric in conversation. The old priest turned his head towards their car, back to the agents, spoke some more than began walking over to their limo. As the priest came closer, he lowered his window and the priest quietly called out, "Mr. President, I am Father Ricci. I have been asked by Father O'Sullivan to escort you into his office."

He was about to answer when Adam leaned over and replied, "I will be accompanying the President, Father." The old man leaned his face into the frame of the opened window and looked at the two of them before replying, "I was told to expect that. Please gentlemen, follow me, quickly if you will, before the patrol makes its way back past this point." Stan looked over at Adam and said, "Let's go."

Rinker spoke with the security detail and then joined the priest and the President on their way into the secret doorway leading into the Vatican, "We're breaking so many protocols here tonight, Mr. President, I cannot count that high." Stan could not argue with that statement and could only offer, "I know this is crazy, Adam. You also know I will do anything to save my daughter." The two of them fell into silence as they followed the old priest across the grass towards the opened doorway. When they reached the doorway, Father Ricci turned to them and said, "I will not accompany you inside, while you meet with Father O'Sullivan. Please enter and follow the hallway until you reach the end. It will be dark, but do not stop until you reach the door at the end of this hallway. The door will be locked. Knock on the door, and Father O'Sullivan will open it." At this, the priest motioned with his arm for them to enter. They did so, not sure what else to do, and once the two of them were inside the dark hallway Father Ricci wished them good luck and closed the door. Any light from the outside was now gone and they were engulfed in complete darkness. It was Adam who spoke first, "What's with the cloak and dagger? I can't see a thing. How the hell are we supposed to find this door?"

"I hope you're not panicking because you have Lygophobia. He said the door is straight down the hallway." He could hear Adam scoff as he replied, "I don't even know what that word means. I'm sure the light from my iPhone will be enough. Let's go." Stan smiled in the darkness as he listened to his friend fuss. He could only hope from this point that Father O'Sullivan could help his daughter. Within a few minutes they were at the end of a long tunnel and literally bumped into each other as Adam walked into the wooden door. "Jesus, we're like a couple of amateur versions of Indiana Jones." He reached up in the darkness and put his hand on his friend's shoulder before replying, "Remember where we are, Adam. Do not use the Lord's name in vain, especially considering we are in one of the holiest places on earth."

He could imagine the glare staring at him through the darkness. Finally he instructed, "Adam, knock on the door." They waited for what seemed an eternity after Adam knocked, but in reality it was less than a minute. The door opened into a cave- like room, dimly lit with lanterns mounted on the wall. The figure of Father O'Sullivan stood inside the room, "Mr. President. Mr. Rinker. Welcome to the Vatican. Please come in." Entering the room, they both embraced the extended hand of the priest. He was dressed completely in black including the formal long robe of a cassock. If there was any apprehension of the entire journey, it melted away being in Father O'Sullivan's presence. Stan could feel the holiness and the love of God emanate from the priest. He didn't waste anytime with further formalities, "Father O'Sullivan, if you may, I have come here under unusual circumstances to say the least. I need your help. There was someone you wanted me to meet. If you don't mind, I would like to meet this person right away so we may be on our way back to the United States." Before he could say anything further, he was cut-off by the priest, "Alexis is in no immediate danger, Mr. President. I will explain, but first, follow me into my office. I have tea waiting for us. There is a lot to discuss."

It was Adam who spoke next. "Father, we have a long flight to Washington in a very comfortable jet. We will have lots of time to talk, while we're in the air." The two of them watched the priest smile and then reply, "I only sleep on airplanes, young man. The softest mattress for sleeping are the clouds holding up the aircraft.

Don't you agree, Mr. Rinker?" The two of them looked at each other as the priest turned and began walking out of the room. As they followed, Adam whispered, "Did he just call me 'young man'? I'm older than he is for Pete's sakes."

A short walk down a hallway led into a small and cramped office. The space appeared as if carved out of a Vatican storage room. Either the building had run out of office space completely, or a need for secrecy was required. Stan knew the answer as he asked, "I feel, if you don't mind the expression, like you're sharing space with the maintenance crew who keep this big structure running. Will we be interrupted by men carrying tool boxes and wearing coveralls, Father?"

The priest chuckled at his comment and replied, "No worries of that happening. We are quite safe from any interruptions, I can assure you. I use this space for several reasons, Mr. President. Firstly, outside of Father Ricci, His Eminence, no one knows I am here. Secondly, I have quick and quiet access to and from the Vatican as you just experienced. And finally, this room is adjacent to a very important room, a room like no other I can assure you. It is a room you have been summoned to, Mr. President, by someone who will change your life forever. Now before you enter that room let us discuss further what we discussed in my visit to the White House."

Stan broke in, "Father O'Sullivan, with all due respect, my daughter is dying and we must leave at once. The plane is ready to take us. You said earlier that Alexis is not in immediate danger. You have not seen the condition she is in. Her body is inhabited by a demon, Father. I need you to intervene on her behalf with the demon that is terrorizing her. I don't know how much longer she can hang on. Her physical state has deteriorated badly. There was an incident in the hospital...with Father Nicholson...He died...I, I think Alexis or whatever is controlling her, had something to do with the priest's death." The memory came flooding back and he struggled with emotion. He continued, "Excuse me, Father. It was terrible. The First Lady is beside herself, herself heavily medicated at home. I have to help my daughter, now Father. Whoever the hell you want me to meet, then let's get on with it."

Father O'Sullivan was quiet, not saying a word, just staring at him. Then after a long silence, he stood up from behind his crowded desk and said, "Yes, I agree. It is time for you to meet that someone. Please, follow me."

The two of them stood also and followed the priest. A strange feeling crept into his stomach as he followed the priest. He anticipated the priest was taking him to meet with the Pope. He had met the Pontiff in his first term as President, so they had that familiarity. Stan found him to be a warm and gentle person, but he had eyes that reflected a steely resolve. He had enjoyed his brief company very much during his papal visit to the United States. They had not walked very far when the priest stopped in front of a door. Surely, His Holiness did not keep his office in the cramped space that occupied this area of the Vatican? Father O'Sullivan did not say a word, just looked at them, his effervescent blue eyes sparkling in the poorly lit hallway. He finally spoke. "Mr. President, I will leave you alone in this room, for who you will meet will appear shortly. Mr. Rinker, if you may, please accompany me back to my office." He was about to protest, but the strange sensation that had begun when they were back in the office was now coursing through his body. He nodded at Adam in an unspoken gesture that it was okay, that he was okay. He watched the two of them disappear down the hallway before he turned to the wooden door. This meeting the Pope under such strange circumstances added to the feeling of gale force winds blowing through his stomach. He reached down and pressed on the heavy latch of the wooden door. He had to lean on the door with his shoulder to push it inwards. It was a very old and thick door that opened up into a room, empty except for a small confessional booth at the center. "Where was the Pope," he thought he would be meeting? Kind of creepy. The room was dimly lit, and the walls were empty of any paintings, pictures or ornaments. There was a large crucifix on the wall facing the confessional booth.

Stan stood in the middle of the room, not quite knowing what to do. He stood next to the booth facing the door and waited for the Pontiff or whoever he was supposed to meet. After a few minutes, impatient, he contemplated walking back to O'Sullivan's office and telling him to get his ass in the limo. The silence was eerie, and he looked over at the confessional booth. The weird sensation he felt amped in his stomach as he stared at the booth. He was Catholic, but he had never been to confession. He felt compelled to sit in the booth. He did not know why, but he felt an invisible hand guiding him towards it. He had nothing to confess, so why would he need to sit in confession? Why was he even in this room? This was stupid. He turned towards the door to leave, then stopped. A voice inside of his head spoke to him. It was clear in its instructions. A voice as clear as water spoke to him, "Sit down, Stanley, and hear Thy word." Stan obeyed the voice in his head and climbed inside of the tiny cubicle and sat down. The sensation in his stomach was threatening to move upwards. He struggled to keep the nausea at bay. Then it happened, and he knew his life would never be the same.

The room exploded in a brilliant light. The epicenter of the light was directly in front of him where the crucifix had hung on the wall. He tried to shield his eyes from the powerful light that enveloped him, but it was useless. He slowly moved his hand away from his eyes, and he was astonished that he could see in the light and its brilliance did not hurt his eyes. In fact, he found it inviting and warming. Then he was amazed beyond anything he had experienced in his life up to this point. A voice boomed through the light. The same voice he heard in his head. The voice was deep and as loud as the light was bright; yet, it did not hurt his ears. The voice was beautiful somehow. It called out to him, "Your daughter, Alexis, is in the clutches of Thy enemy. You have asked for Father O'Sullivan's help; yet, you do not pray. Do you believe in Thy Savior Jesus Christ?"

He was overwhelmed at the magnitude of the situation,

and he found himself speechless and frozen for words, when suddenly his mouth opened and he spoke, "I don't know what to believe, Lord. I do not pray because I believe in the here and the now. I'm trying to save my daughter. I was hoping Father O'Sullivan would help me." He instantly felt foolish after speaking those words. The voice boomed once again through the light, "You are unsure of what to believe, and yet you ask My church for help." He tried to offer up an explanation, but the magnificent voice echoed like thunder, "Listen to my words, Stanley Kipshaw. You live in extraordinary times. You are the leader of the free world. My enemy, Lucifer, is making his move on humankind after hundreds of years of silence. He will come after you and your family. You must be ready and vigilant. Do you understand?"

"Yes. but what must I do to protect my family and lead the people?"

"Have faith, Mr. President. Set the example for your family, your people, and the entire world."

He was bewildered by these words, and he pressed for answers, "Tell me what I must do, Lord. The Beast has already come for my daughter, how can I help her?"

The voice coming from the light began to fade as it spoke, "Believe in Thy word. My word commands all. Hear My word through prayer. Wait for My word for I am near."

Stan tried to ask another question, but the voice went silent and the light vanished. The room was cloaked in the weak light of the candles. He struggled with the emotions that coursed through his soul. He could not control the tears that came to the surface then overflowed down his cheeks like a current. He began to sob, his shoulders bobbed up and down from the spasms. He has not cried like this, he recalled, since he was a boy. A miracle was bestowed upon him tonight. He could see now. The vision was beautiful.

He stood and stepped out of the cubicle. He felt something he has never truly felt in his life before. When he opened the door to the hallway and watched as his friend and advisor, Adam Rinker and Father O'Sullivan approached, he broke out in a smile that he knew stretched across his entire face. His daughter would be alright. He no longer felt despair or fear.

He only felt hope, and it was wonderful.

****

Adam watched his friend emerge from the room as he and the priest approached. There was something completely different about him, in the way his body moved, and in how his eyes were alive, and even in the poor light of the hallway he could see the President had been witness to something extraordinary. There was a streak of white down the side of his hair that was not there before.

What happened in that room?

Chapter 28

All of Ireland vibrated in anticipation of the Vasallus performance. The city of Dublin, fully aware of the enormous popularity of Chloë McClosky and her triumphant return to her homeland for the first time took no chances on security. The Irish Garda buttoned down Croke Park Stadium and the surrounding area with the same level of security provided to the Pope's address the previous year to the country's Catholic. The group had flown into Dublin Airport earlier in the day under secrecy, but it did not matter. A crowd, numbering in the tens of thousands started gathering in anticipation of their arrival. They rimmed the perimeter fence along the runway where the Vasallus private jet, the ultra-luxurious Gulfstream V taxied and come to a quick landing. The cheers and screams enveloped the jet as the members of Vasallus stepped out of the plane, down the stairs and onto the tarmac, but it was the appearance of Chloë as the last member out of the plane that drew the biggest cheers. The Irish loved her, and they cheered wildly for her. Chloë and the others stood and waved for a few minutes before climbing into the limos.

Demonstrations had begun days earlier on the streets of Dublin, surrounding cities and the Protestant cities in the north including huge anti-government protests in Belfast. The police had barely contained the violence as the Irish youth embraced the message hidden in the music of Vasallus like gospel. Just hours before the concert there was a surprise appearance by Patrick Benning of Vasallus on the streets of Belfast, gripping a Megaphone and whipping the protesters into a frenzy. He screamed out to the thousands of demonstrators to stand up against government control, and to take back control of their lives by saying no to those in authority. His five minute speech was cut short as the Police Service had heard enough and moved in with tear gas, batons and meanness bent on putting an end to the uprising. Police waded into the crowds swinging their batons with their orders to break the will of the thousands gathered through a show of brutal force. Hundreds lay on the streets bleeding profusely, dozens dying from their injuries. The overwhelming show of force backfired on the government as the amateur video taken on the scene by dozens of protesters with their cell phones went viral, eliciting worldwide condemnation against the Police Service of Northern Ireland.

Denial by Vasallus on the involvement of Patrick Benning in the riots in Belfast solidified the Dublin Garda on their decision to arrest Patrick and shut down the concert. Video clearly showed Patrick standing on a platform in the middle of the crowds screaming into a Megaphone. However, another video quickly surfaced that showed Patrick and the creator of Vasallus, Robert Best, at the renowned Our Lady Hospital for Sick Children in Dublin, signing pictures, posters and concert t-shirts for the kids. Confirmation from a hospital spokesman confirmed the video and the hospital was shocked that the authorities would taint the wonderful act of kindness shown by the young Benning by linking his presence to the terrible riots in Belfast. Arresting Benning, while they figured out how he could have been at two places at once, presented no option for the authorities and the concert but to proceed. The Garda did erect a security zone by placing barriers in a perimeter stretching four blocks in every direction of the stadium to keep rioters and demonstrators at bay. The country was coming apart and the ignition switch, they knew, was Vasallus. They weighed the better of two evil scenarios: One shut down the concert and deal with the aftermath of massive protests; two, allow the concert to proceed and deal with the riots that would occur after the show. They decided on the latter, as this would provide extra time to prepare by moving more police into the area of Croke Park.

****

The afternoon before the show, Avery and Bentley, in an attempt to deflect the terrible events in London, decided to distance Michael and the rest of Vasallus away from the pressing crush of the media and fans. They loaded them with the exception of Patrick, who was nowhere to be found in the hotel, into a van with black tinted windows and secretly slipped out of The Clarence Hotel and headed to the countryside. Michael acted like nothing had happened at his mother's home. The two of them were not surprised by Michael's behavior; in fact, they expected it. They had planned a trip for Chloë, a surprise and one that Bentley had talked about for weeks when they knew they were coming to Ireland. They asked the other kids if they wanted to be part of the surprise, and they were all for it. They were anxious to get away from the gathered press at The Clarence. Avery drove them partly by GPS and partly by memory of their previous trip to Balbriggan. He knew it would just be a matter of time before Chloë figured out where they were going, and then the GPS could be switched off as she would happily guide him the rest of the way. Bentley wanted to take her to surprise Mrs. Beckeridge at Father O' Sullivan's parish in Balbriggan before heading back to prepare for the show. As they slipped through the city and north on the M1, Avery and Bentley smiled at each other as they listened to the sounds of Chloë's beautifully sounding Irish lilt and her excitement as she explained to her band mates the splendor of Dublin.

Bentley looked over at him and spoke loud enough to be heard from all the shouting and laughs coming from behind them, "Honey, I honestly don't know how you can navigate this traffic and this van driving on the opposite lane and the steering wheel on that side. I'm weirded out being a passenger on the side where I should be a driver!" He smiled back as he replied, "It is weird, trust me, but it's not as difficult as you would think. It's all these damn roundabouts that have me confused." She reached over and squeezed his hand, leaned over the seat, gave him a peck on the

300

cheek and said, "Thanks for doing this, sweetheart. She's going to be so excited!" He looked back at her. "Wait till you see the other surprise I have for her!"

****

They could have driven all the way to London and Chloë likely wouldn't have noticed, as she was enjoying talking up a storm. It was Michael who caught on to Avery's stares in the rear view mirror. He shouted out to Chloë, "Hey, what's up with the Irish. Why would they call a town, Swords?" Chloë stared at him for a second before saying, "Swords? It's not the name of a town, silly; it's the name of the surrounding county. What do you care Michael? Why would you ask that anyway?" Confused, she whipped her head around and stared out the front window of the van, then the side windows, realization hitting her and she screamed, "Avery, we're going north aren't we? Are you and Bentley taking me to Balbriggan?"

Their smiles confirmed it, and she squealed with delight. "I'm so happy! Thank you so much! Hey, everybody, you get to see my birthplace! I can't wait to see Father O' Sullivan and Mrs. Beckeridge!"

Soon Chloë was leaning over between the two of them in the front seat, guiding them to the small parish that carried so many fond memories for her. Then suddenly she changed her mind, giving them different directions, "I want to go by my mother's house first. Can we do that please, Bentley."

Bentley looked at Avery, read his "I guess so" look and replied, "I think we can do that Chloë. You'll have to tell us how to get there." Chloë looked back at her, concern etched across her face as she replied, "I don't know, actually. I've never been there before. Take the next left, Avery." Her sudden commands felt like she was pulling the directions out of the clouds when she quickly gave another direction, "Take the first right out of the round-a-bout and then the first left." Avery did as he was told, wondering where this was going. He took the first left out of the round-a-bout when Chloë shouted, "Slow down Avery, we're almost there. Okay, stop. Stop! This is it! This is the house where my mother lived!" They all sat in silence for a few minutes, while Chloë stared out the side window at the non-descript narrow two storey townhouse, squished between two others exactly like it, just painted a different color. They watched her move to open the passenger door and climb out. Avery whispered to Bentley, "It's okay, let her go."

Chloë climbed out of the van in complete silence, and her long blond hair instantly caught and was tossed by the wind as she walked out on the street in front of her house. She made it as far as the sidewalk in front and stood, staring, not moving for several minutes. Bentley climbed out of the van and joined her, putting her arm around her shoulders, "Do you remember this place, Chloë?" She glanced up at her before replying, "I've never been here before in my life, but it feels like home. My mother lived with other family members here. It was a home full of love. I can feel it." Bentley hesitated, recollecting what she remembered reading about Chloë's past, then replied, "It was your mother and father's home, sweetheart. It was also your grandparents' home." She looked back up at her confused, but she remained silent. After a few long minutes she declared, "My mother was a very brave and beautiful person. I wish I could have known her." She dropped her head onto Bentley's shoulder for another minute, lifted it then said, "Can we go see Father O' Sullivan now?"

****

The arrival at St. Colmcille's Parish was bittersweet for Chloë. The disappointment in learning of the news of Father O' Sullivan's absence was only slightly tempered with Mrs. Beckeridge's squeals and hugs. After a heartfelt visit for half an hour, they boarded the van again. All felt Chloë's disappointment at not being able to see Father O' Sullivan when Avery announced, "We have one more surprise. Are any of you in a rush to get back to Dublin?" There were a chorus of no's throughout the van when Bentley added, " Chloë, we know how disappointed you were that you never got to see Father O' Sullivan. We hope that where we're going next will make you feel better!" The mood in the van immediately picked up, especially that of Chloë's. With the help of the GPS, he pulled the van into the hangar area of the private jet service that Bentley had pre-arranged with the charter company. As they all climbed inside the sleek and luxurious executive jet, Juan asked, "Where are we going Avery?" Brittany jumped in by shouting, "Please tell me you're taking us to the private mansion of Bono!" When the jet took off into the sky, it was Connor who broke the surprise to Chloë when he disclosed, "I'd love to see where Chloë grew up before Vasallus!"

Forty five minutes later, they touched down at the small commercial airport in County Mayo, home of St. Patrick's Academy where Chloë had lived since she was twelve before joining Vasallus. She was almost in shock as the academy van was waiting for them on the tarmac to take them to the school. When Bentley had called the academy to set this up, she had expected a complete rejection to her request to bring Vasallus and Chloë McClosky for a special visit because of the group's controversial music and the violence associated to the band. She was met with the complete opposite, the school would be thrilled and honored to have their beloved Chloë pay them a special visit. When they arrived a few minutes later at the academy, Father Joseph McKracken, head of St. Patrick's was waiting for them in front of the school along with the entire staff and the school body.

They watched in delight as Chloë waded into the sea of kids, signing autographs on notebooks, backpacks and whatever else they asked of her. Soon she was joined by the remaining members of Vasallus, all caught up in the innocence of the moment, the spotlight of the press and fans in Dublin far away from this distant place. It was Father McKracken who called out to everyone, "Children if you will please take Chloë and the rest of Vasallus into the auditorium where we have something special planned for all of you." The squeals of excitement from the kids filled the hallways, as everyone made their way into the school auditorium.

When Chloë entered the auditorium and saw who was on the small stage, she was flabbergasted, looking back and forth between Bentley and the stage, fighting back tears as she cried out, "Thank you so much Bentley!" On stage was Chloë's very special friends, The Celtic Woman, the group she toured with when she was fifteen in the United States. The ladies beckoned Chloë up on stage, all taking turns to hug her, then handed her a flute. Soon everyone was seated and the Celtic Woman along with Chloë broke into traditional Irish ballads that had everyone in the auditorium mesmerized. They handed her a microphone and instructed her to sing her favorite Irish song, "The Ballad of Athlone." She giggled as she took the microphone and stepped to the front of the tiny stage and began to sing. Both Avery and Bentley were physically moved at the powerful melody that only Chloë could elicit. Bentley struggled with tears as Chloë, looking beautiful and radiant, allowed her perfect tone to soar showing everyone in the school that she was truly special. To see her so happy, Bentley closed her eyes and thanked God for this moment, for bringing joy to Chloë, who has seen nothing but fear and chaos for so long. Soon the girls from Celtic Woman joined her in the chorus, and the song was electric, touching everyone. Even the other members of Vasallus were moved. Bentley motioned with her face to Avery and then over at Conner. They both could see the tears flowing down his face. It was just a very special moment for all of them, something they needed for a long time.

****

Later that night, they all gathered in the dressing room for final instructions from the stage manager before they took the stage to close to 95,000 wild Irish fans at Croke Park Stadium, the largest stadium in Ireland. Not even the presence of Patrick could dim the mood of the rest of Vasallus, certainly not Chloë. She was rejuvenated, glowing with happiness, anxious to hit the stage. They all were. Hair and make-up artists were busy putting the finishing touches on Chloë and Brittany's hair. The two of them looked absolutely stunning. Chloë, in her sparkling green sequined tight body dress would leave the Irish boys salivating for days afterwards. Brittany, at seventeen, was a beautiful young woman whose life has been filled with tragedy; yet, she continued to perform like a professional. Bentley had released a full expose story on Brittany in *Music Talks* magazine, her employer that showed the strength and courage of such a young, beautiful and mega-talented star. She put the band ahead of herself and her personal feelings, always. They all did. The tragic suicide of her mother did not slow her down, and she continued to perform on the tour at an unwaveringly high level.

What the article in *Music Talks* did not mention was the evil control Robert Best has over young Brittany and her band mates. Like the band Watermark, also under Best's control that she interviewed so many years ago, each one had little or no say in Vasallus. Patrick wrote the songs and all were expected to perform them. There was nothing she or Avery could do to change that. They were on a crash course for catastrophe, and the train that was taking them there was unstoppable. She and Avery, Bentley knew, were unlikely to survive this, but both of them were committed to the end, death waiting for them. They would protect and stand over these kids until the end. It was these rare moments of joy and happiness, like this afternoon had been, which gave both her and Avery hope that maybe somehow God and his angels would defeat the evil that flowed through their veins.

****

They hit the stage to a wave of cheers that thundered down on them like a coming storm. The lineup of songs arranged by Avery would have them sing three straight up tempo numbers followed by a solo ballad by Chloë. When the stage lights dimmed and a green spotlight came down on Chloë, the crowd went nuts. The giant video screen that covered the entire back wall of the stage came alive with images of Ireland and its beautifully landscaped countryside. When she began to sing, the crowd instantly went quiet, soaking in every word of her beautiful voice. Standing together at the back of the stage, it was one of Avery and Bentley's favorite moments to hear Chloë sing one of her signature ballads. Bentley snuggled close to Avery as she said, "Her voice is so beautiful that it still takes my breath away. To see her so happy, singing in front of her country with these beautiful images in the background, it's so hard to imagine the furor these lyrics create and the violence that follows." Their conversation was suddenly halted when there was a sudden rush of noise coming from the crowd. A second later they could see why. Chloë began floating straight up in the air, at least twenty feet in the air, still singing her heart out. The scene was incredible as her body meshed as one with the giant images behind her on the video screen. The helicopters buzzing far ahead suddenly dropped from the sky to get a closer look with their cameras. No one would believe she actually was floating, but think instead that she had wires unseen lifting her up making the stunt spectacular, but both of them knew better. This was no stunt. Chloë could do this floating trick at will. They all could. They hadn't experienced it for a few shows now so it was a shock to see it, but expected at some point. As the ballad reached the final chorus, Chloë floated out towards the middle of the audience. She stood thirty feet in the air, her arms stretched towards the open roof of the massive stadium, her voice soaring. She rotated in a circle as she sang the final bars of the song, the crowd stunned by what they were seeing. She sparkled like an emerald in the lights high above the crowd. It was a sight; the Irish would talk about for years if not generations.

When Chloë returned to the stage she was joined by the others for a few more group numbers, and then in a major surprise joining onstage were Ireland's music icons, U2's Bono and Edge. Juan shared a lengthy guitar solo with Edge that brought the crowd to their feet in a roar with delight. Bono and Michael delivered a raucous rendition of U2's hit, "The Streets Have No Name". After a few more shared numbers with the U2 boys, they left the stage to deafening cheers and replaced when Connor took center stage to deliver his major hit before Vasallus, "Follow Me Follow You". It took a few seconds for the crowd to clear the after-image of the spectacle of Chloë's performance and then the appearance of Bono and Edge, but it didn't take long before Connor's incredible voice and handsome looks had the girls crying, screaming or fainting.

Behind the stage Avery quipped to Bentley, "Look at how Connor can move a crowd. He is a special performer. I never get tired of his voice. He's amazing."

"He is special isn't he? I just want to make sure you two never forget that." The sound of Best's voice stunned them both. Avery swirled around to see Best standing directly behind them. His sudden arrival was a shock, but his physical appearance was bizarre. He could hear the air in Bentley's lungs draw inward. He looked like a mannequin, his skin air brushed to a gloss that made him look plastic. When he spoke only his lips moved, and his other facial features remained frozen in place. He knew Best was changing, and that his earthly appearance became more and more difficult to maintain. That meant time was running out for them. The time was near. He could feel it.

Chapter 29

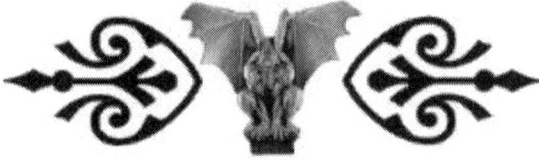

The flight from Rome to Dulles Airport in Washington was filled with quiet conversation between Adam and himself, bouts of snoozing, thoughts of Alexis, but mostly thoughts about the miracle he had just experienced in the Vatican. Adam pressed him for details but he deflected on what he had experienced with a story by Father O' Sullivan to pray and ask for God's help. If he only knew how true that story really was. His Presidency and his leadership of the free world was under attack. Not by a terrorist group or an invading army but by something far more dangerous.

Father O'Sullivan was sound asleep within minutes of take-off, and his snores never quieted during the entire flight over. He didn't know what to expect when the priest met with his daughter other than he carried the power of God within him, and he would keep his daughter safe. He looked at his reflection in the window of the aircraft and could see the streak of white now prominent in his hair. How would he explain that to the press? New look? Hardly. He didn't care anyway, because there were far more pressing matters ahead for him.

One of them was the increasing situation along the western border of Iran with Iraq. Intelligence reports for weeks indicated heightened activity in an area outside the city of Khorramabad, capital city of Lorestan Province. The fear by the United States that the activities were masking the positioning of the Shahab – 3, the new and deadly medium range ballistic missile that could easily deliver devastating damage to Israel's biggest city, Tel-Aviv. Pressure was mounting by Israel for the U.S. to use military force to take out these missile bases. Adam informed him a few minutes previous that the Joint Chiefs was calling for an emergency meeting, "Stan, you have to meet with them. You cannot delay them any longer. They believe you're ignoring their concerns. I know you're not, but we have to make some decisions on the Iranians and soon before they are fully dug in with those bloody Shahab's. Once they are within range, they might as well fire off a nuclear bomb, the effect will be the same."

He dropped his head, deep in thought, then after a minute looked up at his Chief of Staff and stated, "Convene an emergency meeting with the Joint Chiefs for 9:00 a.m. Notify Vice President Rancour to return from holidays. Have the chopper pluck him off the golf course in the morning and get him there by 9:00. When we land, I want agents Myers and Booker waiting to take me and the priest to the White House. No one else." Adam stared at him for a second, "Why Myers and Booker?" The quick reply did not mix words, "I trust them to keep their mouths shut. It could get ugly with Alexis tonight. They were there in her bedroom during the incident and in the hospital. Give me the evening with the priest, Adam. You've been through enough. I need you rested and clear headed for tomorrow morning."

****

Father O' Sullivan had asked for a few minutes alone in his bedroom for prayer. Stan took the few minutes to meet with Leah alone in their bedroom. She was frantic, standing vigil over Alexis all day, while she waited for him to return with the priest.

Choking back tears, her emotional state raw, she sniffed, "It's horrible, Stan. The temperature in that bedroom is freezing. The heat is on full blast in there; yet, I can see my breath. It refuses to have any blankets placed on her. Oh Stan, I'm scared to death we'll lose her. I don't know how Dr. Simmonds is holding together through all of this but he is a saint. He has been punched, puked on and sworn at more than once. He is worried for her though and wants her returned to the hospital. There is only so much he can do here. Her vital signs are up and down. When it breaks into a rage, her vital signs soar and that is dangerous. We have to do something."

"You keep referring to her as 'it'. Has it been that bad?"

She took a tissue from the nightstand, blew her nose, then replied, "Yes. That is not our daughter in that bedroom, Stan. I don't know where Alexis is, but she's not in there. Can Father O' Sullivan get her back?"

****

Thomas stood at the foot of Alexis's bed, the cold in the room caused his breath to steam up into a cloud as he spoke, "I know who you are, and I know why you are here with Alexis."

The emaciated and beaten body of Alexis Kipshaw, dressed only in a sleeveless nightie in the hard coldness of the bedroom, kicked her head back in the pillow and laughed, more like a grow, that became more and more animated. Her eyes were black as coal that radiated into a dark red color when she became agitated. They were that color now, "Fuck you priest. You don't know shit. You travelled all the way from Rome just because the bitch's Dad is the President of the United States. You're pathetic O' Sullivan. Leave us alone."

Thomas was dressed only in black. He was wearing only his long sleeve shirt, black pants but no jacket and the cold reached deep into his bones. Before stepping out of the room to retrieve the coat from his bag, he replied, "Why are you here?" The beast in Alexis barked a demonic laugh that echoed loud in the bedroom before repeating, "Fuck off." Thomas tipped the bottle of Holy Water onto his fingertips of his right hand, drenching them, then leaned in close to Alexis, marked her forehead with the sign of the cross before continuing, "Prayer to St. Michael the Archangel. In the Name of the Father, and of the Son, and of the Holy Ghost. Amen." The prayer, as expected, elicited another round of guttural laughter from the spirit in Alexis. Thomas stepped away from the bed and exited the bedroom, closing the door to the obscenities hurled his way.

The warmth of the hallway instantly washed through his body. His body suddenly let out a shiver that caused his shoulders to shake. The two Secret Service agents, Booker and Myers, stationed in the hallway stepped aside as the President and the First Lady approached. Thomas took Leah's hand in his and took a second to stare into her eyes, letting His unspoken words of encouragement register into her tired and worn eyes. He looked up at the President and then back to Leah before stating, "Can we sit down for a minute?" The President led them into a study down the hallway, where he and the First Lady sat close together holding hands, listening intently when he spoke, "First off I want to tell you that your daughter, Alexis, is a very brave and strong young lady. She is very ill, but she will survive. Dr. Simmonds must not enter the room alone with her. It is too dangerous, but he must hold vigil until she recovers. It is important she is monitored closely."

Leah cut in, "Father, Dr. Simmonds, has been in to see her every thirty minutes. There is nothing he can do to cure her from this demon. Please tell me you can help her?" She was on the edge, close to a meltdown. He reassured her with words, "Mrs. Kipshaw, I am not going to understate what is happening to your daughter. The demon has found a home in her soul, why he has chosen Alexis does not matter, but he resides in her all the same." The audible groan from the First Lady was filled with anguish as she dropped her head onto the President's shoulder, "Please God, please God." Thomas continued, "Like a terrorist that drops a suspicious bag in a train terminal, Satan is an expert in creating fear. He wants your husband scared, terrorized, distracted to the point he drops his guard in his role as the most powerful man on earth. He is coming after humankind, God's most treasured possession, in a final strike to destroy them. He needs the people of this world to believe that your husband is a coward and incapable of leading them through the turbulent times ahead. Terrorizing your daughter is to distract your husband, not to hurt the child. If he intended to kill her, he would have done so, but he needs her to use her condition to weaken your husband's abilities. Do you understand what I am saying, Mrs.

Kipshaw?"

She lifted her head, used a balled up tissue in her hand to wipe her tears, then replied, "I cannot comprehend what you're saying Father, but I trust you. I feel the hand of God is on your shoulder, always, and that brings me comfort. Please do what you can for her, Father. She does not deserve this; she is only fourteen and is a great kid. Don't let her die, please." Thomas looked at them both. "Your daughter will not die, I promise."

****

He entered the bedroom, complete with a warm sweater, to discover Alexis, sitting in the corner of the bedroom, her legs crossed, trying her best to stifle a laugh. It was then that Thomas noticed the two dead agents on the bed. The agents Booker and Myers had been brutally murdered. Both of their heads had been completely spun around and they were arranged on the bed, sitting cross legged, one at the foot of the bed and the other at the headboard. They were sitting facing out with their backs and faces almost touching. It was a gruesome sight. Alexis sat in the corner, the Beast inside of her bellowed with demonic laughter as the shock of the two dead agents registered.

****

Thomas re-entered the bedroom after Alexis had been restrained. Medics took the bodies of the two agents away, and after he had attempted to reassure the First Lady that it was not Alexis who had killed the agents, but the demonic beast that lay host to her soul. Killing the agents was extreme, and he was certain that the spirit in Alexis was either Satan himself or one of the children, most likely the Benning kid. This was something he would enjoy. He had made a call overseas to Avery, waking him at 4:00 a.m. in the morning to check on the kids. After a few minutes he called back to state all of them, with the exception of Patrick, were together watching T.V. Bentley knocked on his door, but there was no response. She did say that he was definitely in his room because she could hear laughing. He thanked them, reassured them that everything was fine and that he hoped to see them soon. He hung up the phone, the dread of knowing what the two of them were going through watching over the kids with the threat of Best at every turn, weighed heavy on his soul.

Alexis was back on the bed, on top of the sheets again, quiet but staring at him intently, waiting for him to make his move. He could sense real fear, not from Alexis but from Patrick inside of her. This was something he did not expect. He walked around the bed never taking his eyes off of her. Her eyes followed him, fear etched across them. He stopped beside the bed, leaned down and once again made the sign of the cross with his thumb on her forehead. She instantly reacted; her body arched, in pain, a groan slow to escape as if the pain was coming from a long way away. He followed it up with another prayer from Ephesians, "Most glorious Prince of the Heavenly Armies, Saint Michael the Archangel, defend us in our battle against principalities and powers, against the rulers of this world of darkness, against the spirits of wickedness in high places." He then reached over to the bed posts and re-attached the restraints to her wrists.

He watched as Alexis bolted upright in bed, the straps stopping her from going any further, her face contorting in rage, her eyes turning black as she glared at him, and then it screamed, "Fuck you priest and your prayers. Are you trying to be cute? Do you really think you can prayer me the fuck out of her?" Thomas looked into the black eyes as he replied, "Yes I do, Patrick. Quite easily actually but before I do, I have some questions for you." The reaction at the mention of Patrick startled him. Alexis's body reacted as if it had been punched. It growled, "Who are you, priest?"

Thomas went on the attack, "You don't know who I am, Patrick? You have seen me many times. You don't see me now because you have chosen to embrace the dark spirit that haunts you. He will destroy you Patrick when he no longer needs you."

Patrick went berserk, and the body of Alexis shook ferociously, trying to free himself from the restraints. He boomed, "I will kill you priest. Untie me, you cocksucker!"

Thomas continued, "You proclaim him to be your Master in the hope he will keep a place for you at his side. It is all a lie, Patrick. He will kill you and banish your soul into the fires of Hell for all eternity."

Patrick looked at him, the rage coursing through him like a tidal wave, "Who are you? You're not just any priest. How did you know who I am?"

Thomas reached over and placed his hand on Alexis head, then said, "I am the truth, I am life. I am hope for those who have none. I am the light for those in the dark. I am the good in all that is bad." The reality of who He was shocked Patrick. His dark eyes opened wide; Alexis's mouth opened wide in surprise, and then he spoke, "It is You. How can that be? You are nothing but a priest!"

Thomas allowed his eyes to settle on Patrick's for a minute longer before he continued, "My love is strong enough for you, Patrick. Remember that. For all that you have done, My love welcomes you. Accept My Son, Jesus Christ, as your Saviour and all of your sins will be forgiven." These words, Thomas knew, would cut deep into the tortured soul of him. He did not expect, however, what followed.

****

Patrick's soul, the half born of man, stared into the incredibly blue eyes of the priest. Those eyes sparkled of life! A life he has never known, a life he knew he could never have. Yet the windows of heaven had opened for him at this very moment, and all he had to do was accept the invitation and enter. He wanted to mouth those words so badly, but the dark side of his soul fought those urges, beat them back, forcing him into an eternal battle between the dark forces and the light that occupied his soul. He was finding himself falling toward the priest's eyes that shone blue like the skies of Heaven. He inched closer, the dark side of his soul slowly losing its grip on him. He opened his mouth, his emotions sliced into the dark spirit, courage building from a place he barely recognized, words reaching his tongue, coated in a goodness that felt like silk as they made their way towards the blue windows. "I...I...accept...the. The words were right there, on the verge of falling out of his mouth, and through the windows of Heaven and a promise of a life he never imagined how desperately he wanted. He fought hard against the dark spirit that was fiercely trying to stop him from speaking the words that would forever banish it. The incredible power of God flowing from the hand of the priest was like nothing he had ever experienced. He found himself free of his restraints, no longer binding him to the bed. He reached up with both hands and placed them on the hand of the priest that was atop of his head. The power of the Lord pulsed through his body like an electric current. He suddenly felt free, his soul breaking free from the chains that bound him.

The blow from his Masters fist slammed into his emerging soul like a freight train sending the hope and love that was so close just a second ago, further away than ever. The bedroom erupted in exploding chaos. The priests hand fell away from his head, and he watched as he stood and stepped away from him to face his Master. He felt the horrible pain of loneliness, helplessness, misery and despair return to his relieved dark soul. The Master had come for him, and he was angry. Unthinkable rage. Patrick's soul shook with fear with the knowledge of what would happen to him as a result of allowing God inside. He would die horribly, he knew, and would quickly join Elizabeth in eternal damnation. He could barely hear the shouts of the priest. It didn't matter anymore. He was as good as dead. Maybe he had never lived..

****

Thomas fell into the leather cushions of the couch in the President's study. The look on his face as he exited the girl's bedroom was enough for the President not to say a word and leave him be. Patrick was dead, and it was his fault. He took a chance to save his soul and he failed. The boy never had a chance and he could only watch in horror as his human eyes witnessed the spiritual death of a tortured soul. Satan snatched young Patrick from him at the last possible second. He was two words away from accepting Christ as his Savior. He let his guard down, and it cost Patrick his life. He closed his eyes and prayed to God that Patrick's soul would someday have the chance to experience His love that he so desperately wanted.

****

Stan and Leah were rushed to the Bethesda Naval Hospital by the Secret Service, minutes behind their daughter whose life was clinging by the balance. He would never forget the look on Father O' Sullivan's face as he emerged from Alexis's bedroom. He looked like he had seen a ghost, a hundred ghosts. The cries of his daughter stopped him from asking any questions but it was likely the priest wouldn't answer any of them at the moment anyway. Stan knew in his gut what really happened in his daughter's bedroom. The priest had not been spooked by a hundred ghosts.

He had just fought the Anti-Christ in a spiritual battle for his daughter's soul. He squeezed Leah's hand as he dropped his head to his chest, closed his eyes and prayed. Little did he know his night was just beginning.

Chapter 30

Sam was all alone in his hospital room as he awoke from what seemed an endless pattern of sleep, periods of wakefulness surrounded by doctors, nurses and sometimes his wife and son. The doctors were always in panic mode, ordering the nurses for more of this or that, start this or that. He hated it all, and just wanted to rest for a few more days, so he could get the hell out of there. He needed to get back to the mansion. His discovery of that book meant something. It certainly had meant something to that evil bitch, Amber, enough for her to want to kill him. Sam closed his eyes, envisioning that book. When he cracked open the safe door and stared at the large, leather bound book, he remembered, it reeked of evilness. The book, he knew, was a key to all of this. What that might be, he had no idea. The only way he would find out was to return to the mansion and find the book. Would it still be in the safe? He doubted it; likely it had been moved someplace never to be discovered. Another gut instinct inside of him whispered it would still be there.

He looked around the room to get his bearings. His room had been full of flowers and he wondered what had happened to them all. Beth must have had them moved to the house. That was good, he thought. It meant that he would soon be released and allowed to go home. Why else would she move the flowers? He tried to sit up but the pain in his stomach reminded him why he was still in the hospital. The shards of white hot heat reached his brain causing him to fall back on the pillow and catch his breath. "Damn, that bullet did a number," he thought. After a minute the pain subsided, and he tried to sit up again. The pain was excruciating, his forehead broke out in beads of sweat, but he somehow was able to sit up. He held on tight to the side rails and looked over at the chair beside his bed. A blue plastic recycling bag was on the chair, and it looked like his clothes were balled up inside of the bag. Then he realized that the nurses had thrown his stuff in the bag in anticipation of Beth coming to pick him up today. He needed to get up and out of here before she arrived. She would never take him to the mansion, instead locking him into his bedroom with someone from the department stationed outside his door to ensure he stayed there until was fully healed. She was a doctor after all, he thought. Well, his wife would be pissed when she arrived at the hospital only to discover he had slipped out. She would just have to understand that he was also a cop, and this cop knew they were running out of time. The evil forces mobilizing on earth certainly weren't waiting for him to heal. He needed to get to the mansion.

He lowered the rail on the side of the bed and slowly swung his feet to the side so they hung over just above the cold tiled floor. The pain soared up to the base of his neck. He was dizzy and it was a reminder to go slow. After a minute his head cleared, and he pulled himself closer to the edge of the bed until his feet made contact with the floor. The cold floor made the bottom of his feet tickle. Clutching the side of the bed, he lowered himself onto the floor and then up into a standing position. He was weak, but determined. He took a step, didn't fall or stumble so he took another, then another and still remained standing. The pain was unbearable, but he could handle the agony. He paused, and then made his way to the chair and his clothes in the plastic bag. As he dressed in the bathroom, he silently thanked his wife for packing loose fitting clothes for his trip home from the hospital. Blue jeans would have been out of the question, the swelling in his abdomen making it impossible.

He stepped out into the hallway and was surprised to see no one coming down the hall. There was no activity anywhere. Strange he thought for a major hospital. Maybe the staffs in this ward were gathering somewhere for a pre-shift meeting or something. He made a beeline down the hall for the elevator, before the nurses discovered he was not in his room. He wasn't worried about staff on the main floor seeing him, as they would have no idea who he was. It was only the staff on his floor who knew that he had not been discharged. The elevator doors to the main floor opened up, and unlike the floor he departed there was activity everywhere, people coming and going. No one even paid him any mind, as he slowly shuffled through the front doors and out of the hospital. He quickly hailed a taxi, climbed inside and gave the driver the address to the mansion in Malibu.

****

Bentley awoke from a terrible dream. In it, she dreamt about Patrick sneaking into their bedroom intent on killing them both. Avery engaged him to protect her, eventually succumbing to the evil forces that fuelled Patrick. She looked over at the hotel bedside lamp to check on the time. It was just after 6:00 a.m. She slid slowly out of the bed in order not to awake Avery, until she noticed that he wasn't in bed. She felt a slight twinge in her stomach, an early warning system of danger that she had come to rely upon. She walked into the living room of the hotel suite to discover Avery sitting in the dark and talking on the phone. He glanced up at her, and she saw the look of pain on his face. She listened to him say, "When will this nightmare end, Father?" The call ended and she watched as Avery stood up, still in his boxers, his white hair ruffled in a sleepy mess, and in a voice tinged with sadness, "It's Patrick. Something has happened. We need to get into his room." Panicked she listened in horror as Avery replayed the events told him by Father O'Sullivan. "This is a nightmare that has no ending, Avery. Come on! Let's go check on him. Maybe Father O' Sullivan is wrong." The look on Avery's face showed he didn't believe her. He stated, "We'll have to get hotel security to open his room. We would need a battery ram to get in there." She thought for a second and said,

"We booked the rooms remember, and we picked up and distributed the room keys to the kids. They will give us another one to his room. Before we get security involved, we need to see what is behind that door."

The two of them walked down the hallway to Patrick's room on their way to the elevator and down to the front desk, Avery stopped and leaned in close to the door and listened for any sounds but did not hear anything. He tried the door knowing it wouldn't open without a card, but instinct made him try anyway. The two of them were stunned to find it opened and not fully latched. They entered his room, and the harsh cold bit into them. They reached for each other partly for warmth, but mostly because they knew that death was in this room and seeking each other's comfort was a natural reaction.

****

The taxi pulled in front of the mansion. Sam looked out his window and surveyed the huge house and the surrounding grounds. All was quiet. Just like the last time. This time he would be more prepared and would not be surprised again despite his condition. It is then he realized he had no gun and no wallet even to pay the driver. He gazed into the front seat and made eye contact with the driver through his reflection in the rear view mirror. Sam was about to state that he did not have a wallet when the driver cut in and said, "Detective Showenstein, no need to worry about my fare. It was taken care of. Have a nice day." He was stunned by what he just heard and asked, "How did you know my name? Who took care of the fare?" The driver took his eyes from the rear view mirror and turned in his seat to face him, replying, "Please hurry detective. There is someone inside who anxiously awaits your arrival." Dumbfounded, he opened the door and climbed out. He watched the driver wheel the taxi around the circular driveway and back past him. The driver stared at him through the windshield. His eyes glowed a bright red!

His mind raced, "What was happening?" He wished he had a gun as he approached the house. He thought about going in through the front door but his instincts told him to go back in again through the side door and directly into the offices of Avery and Best. He needed to retrieve that book as quickly as possible. Danger was all over this place. Danger and evil. He made his way around the side of the house. The pain in his abdomen from the gunshot wound reminded him again of the danger in this place. He found his way to the door to the offices and the studio of Vasallus. He glanced through the window and saw no one.

He opened the door, unlocked, and walked straight into Hell.

****

Avery and Bentley approached Patrick's bed. The cold air was overwhelming, their breath rose out of their mouths in misty plumes. The terrible stench of death and the cold was unbearable. As they came closer to his bed, they could see a body on the bed, naked, black and blue from a smattering of terrible bruises. Then he heard Bentley gasp, "Oh my God, Avery. Look at his face!" He looked up into the face of Patrick. His mouth was stretched open in a death gasp as if someone had pried open his jaws in a sick over stretched-pose. It was a gruesome sight. He barely resembled Patrick. His body was not the muscular, hairy chested and physically built young man that he was but instead a destroyed, skinny wisp of a man. His genitals lay to the side. What he had gone through was unimaginable, thought Avery. He reached over and moved his right leg so he could see his thigh area. Confirmation of Patrick's birthmark of the three backwards sixes, or musical notes was faint but there. The two of them stood up, in shock and stepped back. For a minute the two of them said nothing, the gravity of what they were seeing was staggering. Bentley wrapped her arms around his waist and began to sob, "He didn't deserve to die. The terrible things he did were not his fault. I hate Best for what he has done to these children. I want to kill him, Avery." He was about to reply when there was a commotion behind them.

****

"Hello Sam! You sure have a hard-on for this place. Your guts are still drying on this floor and you're already back." Robert Best or the Beast, stood in the hallway leading into the offices. He was in a semi-demonic state, Sam could see. He still had the shape and form of a human, but his face had deteriorated and had the look of cracked clay. His eyes burned red and his teeth were no longer perfectly even and white but instead yellow and had early stages of rotting. He smelled terrible. Like death would smell.

"The book. I want that book, Best. I know it's here, and I also know you don't want anyone to have it. Why is that? What does that book reveal?"

Best took a small step towards him, his face catching more of the light coming through the windows. He had stepped from the pit of Hell and into this room. He was not afraid of him. He had looked forward to this moment for a long time. He has terrorized his family, killed his brother and made Patrick do terrible things, all for his pleasure. No longer. He would kill this thing, somehow, right here. He needed to get that book; it was the key to all of this, he was certain. He would play this game of back and forth with Best until he could pinpoint the whereabouts of the book, and then he would kill him.

"Would you like to see this book you want so badly, Sam? Why would you be so interested in a book you know nothing about?" Sam felt a shard of pain jolt his stomach. He looked down to see his grey sweatshirt soaked red with blood. He had opened up his wound on his way over here. He needed to get back to the hospital, but not before he got his hands on that book and killed this monster. Best continued, "Would it surprise you if it was just a Bible? Oh, wait a minute, you're Jewish; you wouldn't know the difference between a Bible and a comic book, would you Sam?" With that he laughed and when his face moved, pieces of the clay fell to the floor. Sam pressed, "Then let me see it and I'll tell you."

****

Avery and Bentley wheeled around to see an emerging light take shape against the wall. The light was especially bright, forcing them to shield their eyes. Avery reached over to Bentley and pulled her close. The light quickly broadened, enveloping the entire wall of the large hotel room. Soon a man began to take shape in the light, a soldier of immense size, just like they had witnessed at the stadium in Paris and at Ann's mansion. Seconds later a man, over seven feet in size towered over them. A large sword inside a golden scabbard swung on his hip. He was different than the man that emerged from the light at Ann's. The man looked mean, angry and Avery was not sure he was friend or foe until he spoke, and his voice surprised the two of them. It was soft spoken, kind and unlike his physical appearance. His voice, though quiet resonated through the room, "I am Babbken, son of King Tiridates of Armenia and a soldier of God. I know who you are. Do not be afraid of me. I am here to claim the body of Patrick. He was my direct descendant and I was to protect him, but as you can see I have failed him."

Bentley stepped towards him, "We met someone like you in Paris a few days ago, a soldier of God named Abgar. He told us to be strong, to watch over and protect the kids. Patrick would not allow us to get close to him. I feel terrible! I...I...we should have done more!" Bentley began to sob again. Avery held her close as the soldier continued, "This is not you or Avery's fault, my dear. Unfortunately, Patrick took this path until it was too late. My role was more to protect others from him, as best as I could, but there is a powerful force behind him, and I wasn't always successful."

He stared at the giant of a man and asked, "What do we do from here, Babbken? How can we really protect these kids? We can't protect them isn't that right?" The soldier stepped towards them both, the light swirled around him like a mist, his eyes were cast in a blue light that promised hope and declared, "You may not be able to swing a big sword like my brother Abgar and I, but you can give them something they need very much. Give them something that will sustain them through this." The two of them replied in unison, "What?" Bentley continued, "We love these children. We both will die protecting them." The angel named Babbken placed his massive hands on the two of them and replied, "You just said it! Love them. Show them someone cares about them through all this. Take away their fear through your love and compassion for their well-being. They have no one but each other. Let them know they have the two of you and you are there for them no matter what."

Avery looked over at Bentley and declared, "We will Babbken, we will."

The big soldier took his hands off of their shoulders and smiled a big and beautiful smile and announced, "That is wonderful. You already have been there for them, and they know you care for them. Just let them know as often as you can. Now I must ask you both to leave me be if you will. It is time for me to take Patrick's body home."

****

"Go ahead, Sam. It's exactly where you saw it last. Be my guest."

Sam found it difficult to move. His injury was taking its toll on him. He now realized he never should have left the hospital. It was tToo late for that now. He slowly began to make his way past Best and into his office. His body felt weird. Heavy and lethargic. He finally made it into Best's office and then stared at the safe on the other side of the room. It looked a mile away, but it was only twenty feet. His feet felt like they were fifty pounds each. He looked down at his stomach and recoiled at what he seen. Blood was no longer seeping from his stomach, but gushing. It was if the doctors forgot to sew him up after surgery. He was bleeding to death, and he didn't have much time. He made what seemed the long trek across the room to the safe. He could hear Best laughing uncontrollably behind him, as he watched him sludge his way to his safe. What seemed like an eternity he finally arrived at the wall and the safe. Now he needed to remember the combination. "What was it again," he thought as he tried to remember. His fingers felt thick and unresponsive as he tried to manipulate the dial. It wasn't working. He suddenly felt all the strength in his legs give out, and he grabbed onto the door handle of the safe to stay upright, but his arms had even less strength than his legs. He fell to the floor with a thud. He was dying and he had failed. No one knew about the book in that safe. The secret was about to die with him. He lay on his back on the floor, waiting for death to come, Best's laughter somewhere in the distance when he thought, "Why had be bled out so fast, when he was about to be released from the hospital? Where was Beth? What happened to all the flowers in his room? So many questions. He felt sleepy. Where were all the nurses and doctors on his floor in the hospital? How did the taxi driver know his name? So tired and sleepy. His eyes felt heavy. He wanted to close them. The taxi driver's eyes burned red like that of the Beast.

Then he knew. His eyes opened wide for a brief second, before they closed for the final time. Best's laughter echoed in his mind as his life slipped away. He had already died. In the hospital. He was already dead. His faith as a Jew did not include the Devil or Hell, but how many Jews had met Satan face to face like he had. His dying words were a whisper, a prayer. "Hear O Israel, the Lord thy God, the Lord, is one."

Chapter 31

The sun broke through the clouds as the fleet of black Secret Service SUV's whisked the President from Bethesda to the White House. Operating on a few hours of poor quality sleep on the plane over from Rome a few nights earlier, Stan could feel the heaviness of fatigue weighing him down. He leaned his forehead to the cool glass of the truck, as it bounced along Wisconsin Avenue. The past forty- eight hours had been exhausting but after several anxious hours in the hospital at his daughter's bedside he could finally take a deep breath. Alexis would make it. The Demon that almost claimed her life was gone, banished by Father O' Sullivan. The priest was a miracle from God, of that, he was certain. He thought he carried the weight of the world on his shoulders; it paled in comparison to what rested on Father O' Sullivan's. The survival of humankind. He thought about what O' Sullivan said to him as they said their goodbyes at the hospital, before his agents escorted the priest to Dulles for a commercial flight back to Rome. "Stay alive, Mr. President. Be alert for danger that will come your way. Best will now zero in on you and your administration. Be ready. God Bless, Stanley. I hope you don't mind the disregard of your title, but I feel Stanley is more appropriate, considering all that we have been through," smiled Thomas. "If it makes you feel any better and to make it completely fair, you can call me Thomas!"

****

Adam addressed the gathered men and women that included the Joint Chiefs, National Security Advisor Vic Turk, the Vice President, CIA Director Nancy Turcotte, Secretary of Defense William Templeton and Secretary of State Bob Buckett. The room was buzzing with news of the events in the White House with the President's daughter swirling throughout the room.

"Alexis is out of danger and is resting comfortably in Bethesda. The First Lady is with her and I ask all of you to keep Alexis in your prayers. Now..." He was interrupted by the entrance of the President as he made his way to the head of the table. Everyone stood as the President spoke, "Please, sit down. Thank you, Adam for those kind words for Alexis. She is doing very well and should be back on the school basketball court in no time." The wear on the President's face was not lost on everyone and it was CIA Director, Turcotte, who spoke, her voice carrying a tinge of suspicion, "We are glad to hear Alexis is doing better, Mr. President. May we ask of her condition?"

Stan looked at his CIA Director, one of the toughest women ever to grace Washington with a quick reply, "No you may not, but thank you for your concerns. Now we have more important matters to discuss. Vic, will you bring all of us up to speed on the movements in Khorramabad." The tone in the room quickly became serious as Turk stood and approached the front of the room, picked up the remote control and brought the giant video screen to life, so that the latest satellite images of the area suspected of hiding the Shahab – 3 came up. Turk, a barrel chested and lifetime military man with an illustrious career in intelligence liked the President immensely and was usually the first to come to the President's aid when he was under attack by his colleagues. "You can see our friends in the sand have been busy. These shots were taken less than two hours ago. These images clearly show missile batteries are now being mobilized."

Stan asked, "Do we have confirmation they are the Shahab – 3?"

Army General Peter Shuster, answered, "We do not have confirmation as of yet, Mr. President. Intelligence is pouring over these latest images as we speak, we should have confirmation any minute."

"I want confirmation before the next satellite pass. The next set of photos could very well be the plume of the rockets as they head for Tel-Aviv. Is that clear?"

"We're clear, Mr. President."

Stan focused his attention on his CIA Director, "Nancy, what's the latest on the ground ? Are these fanatics ballsy enough to fire on Israel?"

Turcotte, an aging career intelligence hack, one of the few who actually made it all the way to Director and even though at an age where most people would be long retired, piped her reply, "Not only are they ballsy, Mr. President, but anxious to fire their prized rockets. They've waited decades for this moment and President Rakhsha has the blessing of the Ayatollah. Once they have them dialed in for a direct hit, they will push the button, Mr. President."

Secretary of State Buckett added, "All diplomatic channels are, as you requested sir, aware of our imminent attack. We will notify the United Nations Security Council once the attack is underway."

He stood, stepped back against the wall, focused his thoughts and then asked, "There will be severe blowback from the Chinese and Russians. General Stricker, how quickly can we hit these installations once I give the word?"

The Navy Four Star General Dale Stricker, his shock of white hair, forever tussled, without any hesitation replied, "The Fifth Fleet is in position in the Strait of Hormuz and is battle ready, sir. A carrier strike group would smash these positions to dust within the hour of your word, Mr. President."

"Very good. I am giving you the word, General, to strike. Do it now."

The room went quiet for one second, then exploded into action, everyone jumping up and exiting to prepare their departments for what would follow the air strikes. All of the branches of the military would be mobilized to counter what surely would be swift retaliation by Iran and its allies. Stan took a seat and watched the chaos unfold around him. The past seventy- two hours had been a complete blur. He had watched helplessly as his daughter fought valiantly against the Demon that invaded her soul, he had taken an unauthorized flight to the Vatican to retrieve a priest to help Alexis only to be ushered into a room to have a conversation with the Lord. Now he had just authorized military force against an enemy that could very well lead this world into a nuclear war that no one would survive. He closed his eyes, prayed to God for forgiveness for what he had just done and hoped His grace included patience as he tried to straighten a world that was terribly crooked at the moment.

****

Seargent Hossein Pakvar of the feared 23rd Special Division Force of the Islamic Republic of Iran Army had the honor of being the first soldier to launch the much feared Shahab – 3. He wasn't of course the first soldier to fire the rocket, just the first to fire the rocket launcher at an enemy target, rather than aim at a test target miles out on the Iranian desert floor. When he learned of his orders just minutes ago, his first reaction was total disbelief. His country was actually going to fire a deadly weapon into Israel. He was stunned. His second reaction was a sense of overwhelming pride, that his expertise would be the one utilized to bring down the Zionists he hated so badly. His final reaction was fear. He knew the retaliation by the Jews and their allies, especially the United States, would be brutal and deadly.

****

Captain James Anderson, CO of the aircraft carrier, USS George Washington, walked into the command center to address his F-18 Hornet pilots and service personnel. Tension in the room was heightened as the pilots knew they were about to be given orders for a mission. Not knowing what the mission would be is what had them on edge. The George Washington carried forty-eight F-18 Hornets plus another eight support aircraft and six helicopters. Thirty-six of the Hornets were about to be deployed. "CO on deck," barked the squadron leader, veteran navy pilot Barry Stone.

Anderson didn't waste any time, "Orders had come down from Navy Command. Satellite images confirmed Iranian troop movement had moved into strike position, the Shahab - 3 missile batteries along the Iraqi border outside of Khorramabad. These missiles were within range of Tel Aviv and intelligence reports confirmed a missile strike was imminent. We fly immediately to launch a rain of hell on these desert monkeys. Captain Stone, you're up. Brief your boys on the target package. Wings up in thirty minutes. Suit up boys, it's show time."

****

Seargent Pakvar waited for his orders. He was ready. The Korean made Shahab - 3 was programmed to strike in the heart of Tel Aviv, carrying a medium range ballistic missile warhead of twelve hundred kilograms of devastating firepower. He looked down the tree- line to his left and could barely see the outline of the next horizontal positioned launcher. There were thirty mobile launch pads hidden in this mountain terrain. How many of these missiles would actually fly today was unknown to him. Most likely all of them, because the ones that didn't would surely get obliterated by the American fighter planes. He glanced at his battery mate, and he looked more nervous than he was. They all knew what was about to happen. They were all scared.

****

Thirty-six F/A-18 Hornets screamed across the Persian Gulf, each carrying two 2,000 pound bombs. As expected anti-aircraft fire filled the skies within minutes of launching off the flight deck of the George Washington as they crossed into Iran. Stone gave the orders to climb to 26,000 ft. to minimize the anti-aircraft fire from the ground. The short trip to the target area would consume all of their fuel quickly, as they pushed the aircraft to its maximum power in order to account for their heavy payload. Minutes after entering Iran airspace, Stone ordered his squadron to lock-in targets and release. Up to seventy- two bombs dropped from the sky on a trajectory course for the hilly terrain of the Iranian and Iraqi border. As each plane dropped its payload then immediately banked, climbed to 32,000 ft and bee-lined it back to the carrier, a fleet of unmanned drones made its way into the kill zone to document and photograph the damage inflicted by the airstrike that would be dissected immediately by commanders.

****

Pakvar and the rest of the soldiers gathered heard the subsonic sounds of the retreating aircraft high above them. There were so many of them and how could they have been discovered? They were completely invisible from the sky and from passing satellites. Then they heard the explosions coming from a great distance and they now knew what was happening. Diversionary targets were sacrificed in order to give them the opportunity to launch their missiles. He now knew orders would come at any second to launch. He barely had time to absorb the thought when his radio squawked. His commander screamed their orders, " راه اندازی می ک ـ ند، راه اندازی می ک ـ ند،

راه اندازی می ک ـ ند! حالا،حالا، حالا! الله ب زرگ ا ست! الله ب زرگ

ا ست!" (Launch, launch, Launch! Now, now, Now! Allah is great! Allah is great!")

He raced to his launch position at the base of the missile. He was sweating profusely. Everything was happening so fast, it was a blur. He never imagined how he would feel when the time came to execute the orders to fire the Shahab. His years of training kicked in and he furiously pounded out the codes in the computer keyboard. The roar of the massive missile lifting out of its steel cradle was deafening. He stepped back for a second and watched the launch pad lift towards the sky. When he heard the final snap of metal locking in place, it was time to enter the final code. He reached over, hesitated for one split second, gave thanks to Allah and punched in the four digit code. The sudden rush of air around him was incredible as the rocket fuel burned then suddenly ignition kicked in and the ground around him shook as the missile broke away from its metal straps and lifted towards the sky. Seconds after, he heard the sound of a second explosion a hundred yards to his left as the next Shahab became airborne. For the next few minutes, he watched in awe as a series of explosions along the tree line triggered the huge missiles to lift into the sky and then even out as they made their way to Israel. It was then his shoulders fell, his body relaxed and he turned to his comrade; the two of them embracing the joy, knowing they successfully carried out the most important mission ever given to the Army by their beloved Supreme Commander, the Ayatollah.

****

The F/A-18 Hornets dropped from the sky one by one onto the tiny flight deck of the George Washington, each of them snagged by the arresting wire and then immediately steered into its resting place along the flight deck. The aviators climbed out, shouted whoops as they pulled their helmets off of their heads and climbed down onto the deck. Their jubilation of a successful, large scale attack was quickly muted with the news of the massive launch of the unknown Shahab - 3's. The knowledge they had been duped by the Iranian military into launching a full- scale attack on diversionary targets in order to mask the launch of the real Shahab's was devastating. They waded into the command center to begin hearing the news that Israel had been hit because of their failure.

****

The men and women sitting around the table went from controlled chaos to complete silence as President Kipshaw entered the room. The failure of intelligence on the ruse orchestrated by the Iranians was catastrophic. CIA Director Turcotte was on the hot seat and Stan did not waste any time going after her, "What the fuck happened, Nancy?" Everyone listened as Turcotte tried to explain the failure by her agents in Iran. She finished her feeble attempts to defend her agency by taking a shot at the Joint Chiefs: "Navy and Army Intelligence did not know the scope of the Iranian capabilities?" The room was about to get out of hand and Stan interceded, "Alright, now is not the time to point fingers. Nancy, your agents screwed up. Let's move on from that but don't make that mistake again. Now, give me the latest on the damage inflicted by the Shahab's on Tel Aviv."

Buckett cut in, "Mr. President, thirty Shahab 3's were launched and twenty-seven successfully made it into Tel Aviv. Israeli Tamir Interceptor missile defenses were only able to shoot down three

Shahabs. One- third of the city has been wiped out with casualties estimated to be around eighty- thousand. Loss of life was severe because the Iranians specifically targeted the heavily populated south district. The Shahab's can be dialed in with devastating accuracy."

Stan looked over at his friend, Adam, and asked, "What is the political fallout with the Chinese and Russians?"

He watched as Adam exhaled before replying, "Both the Chinese and the Russians have recalled their diplomats from Washington. They are incensed that they were not consulted before the attack." Stan answered, "Too damn bad. Like they would consult with us. Okay, everyone. Listen up. Thankfully the Iranians did not target the Israeli Parliament. They were in full session at the time. The entire government could have been taken out. Why they didn't and targeted only civilian population, we need to find out. I have spoken with Prime Minister Ben-Shahar, and after some tense discussions he has confirmed his retaliatory strike is underway, and if the United States does not launch a military strike within the next twenty four hours, his next move will be a full scale nuclear attack on Tehran. The threat his country has lived under from Iran ends. He assured me that either the Ayatollah drops to his knees at his feet in forgiveness, or he will reduce the entire city of Tehran to dust."

It was the subdued Turcotte that gasped, "My God!"

****

Robert Best sat at his desk in the Malibu mansion. Lying back in his office chair, his feet propped on the desk, he let his mind drift as he surveyed the damage to the Jewish city of Tel Aviv. What would Kipshaw do to make up for the blunder his war planes caused? The Iranians were in full blame mode of the flawed American decision to attack their missile sites. They claimed the missile launchers were necessary considering the aggressive buildup of the Israeli military in recent months. By no means did they ever consider firing on Israel. However, the attack by the Americans on their missile sites and in conjunction with the Israeli buildup left them no choice. Best laughed at the logic, but it served his purpose agreeably.

His thoughts turned to the death of Patrick. Unfortunate, but necessary. He was going to die soon enough along with all the rest of Vasallus anyway. One more performance from Vasallus is all he needed. The biggest show they had performed to date would be the upcoming show in Wembley Stadium in London. He would ensure it sends the youth not only of London over the edge, but also the entire world. The death of Vasallus, for all the world to see, would cause a brutal chain reaction of violence against authority, everywhere. Why? He'd make sure their spectacular deaths were a result of police and government over reaction to Vasallus's role in citing the extreme violence associated with their music.

His body began to shake with rage just thinking of the little prick's audacity to even consider O'Sullivan's offer of Christ's love. Accepting Christ brings death. Not just death but an eternity in a miserable cauldron of despair, fear and terrible loneliness. At least he'd have company with the bitch, Leroux.

Robert looked down at the floor at the bled out Detective Showenstein. Did Showenstein tell anyone of the book? Did he tell his wife? He doubted it, because he would have no idea what the book was or what importance it carried. But he returned to the mansion to look for it. He had sensed the importance of it when he saw it in the safe. It was his brother Jacob, the Rabbi, who came oh so close to figuring out the importance of the book, before he gloriously dropped a wooden stake through his chest in his own synagogue. What was it with these Jewish brothers, one a Rabbi, the other a police detective who brought them so close to the truth behind his true relationship with God. Biblical scholars over the centuries had always hinted at another version of the Revelations existed but never found. The book was his curse. If found, it would surely be the end of his existence. It was the ball and chain that bound him when he was cast from Heaven. The book could not be destroyed, could not be buried or taken from this world. It must be present on earth at all times, forever exiling his existence in this world, always in plain sight to Him. The release from Him and the final destruction of the book only came with the destruction of humankind. Keeping the book hidden from humankind was easy. No one knew of its existence so no one looked for it. Then how did Showenstein see it? How did he think of the combination to open the safe with the threat bearing down on him. The end of times was near. It was He who was opening the eyes of human beings to their fate and their salvation.

He was running out of time.

Chapter 32

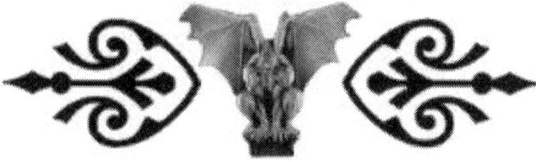

The angel of God had left with the body of Patrick in his arms, but not with his soul. The soul of the troubled Patrick Benning was firmly in the grips of Satan. The departure of Babbken left a void, an empty space that was undeniable. Bentley, overwhelmed with sadness, sought refuge in the blankets of her hotel room. Avery tried his best to console and reassure her that they would get through this, but it wasn't working.

"He is going to kill the rest of them, Avery. He will kill us! All of us will die."

"Honey, we have stayed alive this long, because He has a plan for us. Don't you see?"

She turned her head, so she could stare directly in his eyes when she replied, "What plan is that? Elizabeth is dead and Patrick is now dead. How much longer do you think he needs these kids to perform? He already has the world turned upside down with their music and performances. There is nothing more for them to do. When I saw Patrick's death face. it chilled me to the bone, Avery. I cannot help but think of the others like that, discovering them in their beds: their souls ripped away and cast into a place so frightful their early bodies are left with that look of horror etched on their face, a permanent acknowledgement of the horrible place they have been sent. That look will haunt me for the rest of my life. We should have been able to help him. I can't imagine how alone and scared Patrick must have been at that time." He watched, as she buried her face among the blankets and sobbed. She was blaming herself and him for Patrick's demise and it was killing her. He hated himself for not being able to take away that pain. She was right; they should have been there for Patrick, somehow. They tried to stay clear of him; he was as evil as Best. He was also human and just a kid, he reminded himself, and that thought sent a shiver of pain into his heart. He climbed on top of the bed, under the covers and cradled Bentley before whispering into her ear, "I'm sorry sweetheart. I will not make the same mistake with the rest of the kids.

She protested against his claims of guilt, but he never heard her. The rage building inside of him against Best was palpable. He needed to plan -- a plan to protect Bentley and the kids from the Hell that was coming their way. Eventually the two of them became lost in their own silence as they struggled with the pain of losing Patrick. Soon they dozed into a deep sleep. A banging on their hotel room door snapped them from slumber like a pail of cold water.

****

They never checked out of their rooms at the Claridge in London; instead, they chartered out of Dublin after the concert and secretly slipped back into the hotel in the heart of London to prepare for the huge show in Wembley Stadium in a few days. When Avery opened the door to his room to find Ann Lockwood standing there, he shouldn't have been surprised; after all, she only lived minutes from the Claridge. He was, regardless, still surprised to see her here, especially since they knew how dangerous it was for her to be anywhere near her son. Taking a second to gather himself, he asked, "Ann, I am surprised to see you here, especially after what happened at your mansion."

Ann accepted the hugs from both him and Bentley before replying, "I know Avery, but I took precautions. I suggest we move into your room and out of this hallway before Michael steps out of this room and sees me." They quickly moved into the room and took seats in the living room of the large suite. Bentley poured them all a fresh cup of coffee before taking a seat beside him on the couch. Ann continued, "How is your arm, Avery?" He quickly shrugged it off, "Just a scratch, Ann.

I'm fine thank you."

Ann drew in a breath before continuing, "I am afraid I have some very bad news, but first, have you watched the news this morning?" The two of them looked at each other and both replied, "No." Avery reached over and clicked on the T.V. and didn't have to surf very long as it was on almost every channel. Ann was silent as she let the shocking news of the attack on Israel sink in. Powerful rockets, launched from the Iranian border along Iraq, exploded in the heart of Israel's biggest city of Tel Aviv with devastating results. Tens of thousands of Jewish citizens were suspected killed in the attack. Israeli warplanes had already been dispatched, launching air strikes against civilian targets in Tehran. There were reports of Israel considering a nuclear attack on Iran. The United States and the rest of the UN Security Council were holding emergency meetings in New York and had released a statement urging both sides to accept an immediate ceasefire until a resolution could be tabled. U.S. President Stanley Kipshaw, a close ally of Israel, strongly urged Israeli Prime Minister Ben-Shahar to immediately cease the attacks on civilian targets, or face severe counter measures.

Bentley shuddered, "Dear God! What is happening? The world is falling apart." She fell back into the cushions of the couch before resting against Avery. He was about to say something when the television journalist launched into another breaking story, "We are now going live to New York. Outspoken music executive, the founder of Vasallus, Robert Best, is holding a press conference on the sidewalk in front of the United Nations. Susan, what can you tell us about the press conference with Robert Best?" The news channel switched to a reporter on scene in front of the United Nations Building in New York City, "Thanks Mark, we are about to go live to hear Mr. Best speak. As you know. he is the creator of the highly influential rock band, Vasallus, that has caused millions of our youth around the world to rail against authority. We suspect Best will come out and speak to those youth in Israel and Iran directly. For what purpose we are about to find out, Mark."

The cameras quickly switched to Robert Best stepping up to a wall of microphone stands. They watched in horror as the demonic Beast disguised as a leader to the youth of the world began to speak. His face was gleaned to a glossy shine, the sun reflecting on his skin like a mirror. He did not call out to the youth of the world to rally. Instead he spoke directly to President Kipshaw, "Ladies and gentlemen, in light of what has happened in the last few hours in Tel Aviv and now in Tehran, it is clear the world has moved into extremely dangerous territory. We are, for the first time since the Cuban missile crisis, faced with the very real threat of a nuclear attack that will not only kill millions of innocent people in these two countries but will surely prompt retaliatory attacks from neighboring countries and the worlds superpowers. The world needs leadership, real leadership right now in order to avoid the inevitable destruction of our planet. The leaders of the free world are meeting behind me in this building as we speak. I guarantee you each of these countries are first and foremost, out to avoid the fate of their own countries first and be damned with anyone else. The President of the United States will only accelerate the tensions that will escalate quickly into a full-scale nuclear exchange between the superpowers. He is incapable of leading not only the United States safely through this crisis, but as a leader to the entire world. I am that leader. I am capable of diffusing the tensions that are growing by the minute."

A flurry of questions from the reporters in front of him came the second Best paused in his speech, "How can you possibly diffuse these tensions, Robert?" Best cut him off by replying, "I am not going to stand here to answer questions or explain myself. I simply called this press conference to declare my intentions." Another reporter blurted, "What are your intentions, Mr. Best?"

"This will be my last statement and there will be no more questions. By the end of today, I will have personally ended this sudden threat of mass annihilation between Israel and Iran. I will speak to the leaders of each of these two countries and end this threat, while you're supposed leaders cower in fear in the closed doors behind me. It is what real leadership is and supposed to do. Thank you for your time and twenty four hours from now, I will stand once again in front of this podium to answer all of your questions. Thank you." Best immediately turned and began walking down the sidewalk, while a media crush surrounded him. He eventually made his way to a limo where his handlers cleared a path; he slipped inside, the door closed and the car pulled away from the curb and disappeared. The live broadcast then cut back to the reporter, Susan Armitrage, holding a microphone only feet from where Best's limo exited. "A bizarre press conference to say the least, Mark, and one, that this reporter found difficult to cover, knowing the real danger and threat to innocent people in that part of the world. It was daring too for the Vasallus creator to declare a preposterous proposal to broker a peace deal between these two countries that just hours ago declared war by attacking each other's countries."

****

Avery let out a gasp of air in a swoosh, "Holy shit! He's crazier than a loon. Nothing he does will diffuse this conflict in twenty-four hours. He's going to look like a moron after this, and any credibility he thought he had will be gone."

Ann placed her coffee cup back on the table, and as she sat back she replied, "What if he is capable, and what if he does indeed broker a peace deal in the next day between Israel and Iran?" He looked at her like she was crazy, but he knew she wasn't, far from it, "What are you saying, Ann, that he could pull this off?"

"That is exactly what I'm saying. Why else would he call that conference if he wasn't able to pull it off." Bentley added, "We all know he is capable of this. He is the Anti-Christ. Why would he though, is my question?"

It was Ann who replied, "Bentley, that is exactly it. He is the Anti-Christ and what is his objective? What has always been his objective with Vasallus? To influence the world to his authority. What better way to expand his authority on a global scale than by showing an outrageous act of leadership by being the hero to broker peace in the most dangerous conflict this world has experienced since World War ll. It ratifies the message sung by Vasallus to the youth of the world through their music that has rallied them against the current leadership and authority. It is brilliant. It takes him one step closer to completing his ultimate objective."

Spoken barely above a whisper, Bentley asked, "What objective is that?" He looked at the two of them, confirming what all of them were now thinking, "The destruction of humankind by destroying their souls."

****

Avery and Bentley, still dressed in their robes, poured fresh coffees, offered Ann room service breakfast, and she declined. Bentley asked, "Ann, when you first sat down you mentioned you had terrible news to share with us. Was it the news of the attack on Israel or is there something else?" Watching her body language since she arrived, Bentley knew that something terrible has happened. Was she aware of the death of Patrick? She listened as Ann spoke.

She watched as Ann struggled with the news that brought her here. Her lower lip quivered, prompting her to cup her mouth for a brief second, before she stated, "It's Sam. He's dead." It was Avery who groaned, "Oh my God, no. Please tell me that's not true. Oh God." The jolt of this news hit both of them hard. She asked her, "How did he die, Ann?"

She stood up from the couch and paced the room before she finally came to a stop in front of the large windows overlooking downtown London, "He was shot by a gardener at the mansion in Malibu two days ago. He succumbed to his injuries hours after arriving at the hospital." Avery shot out off of the couch, almost shouting when he asked, "He was shot at the mansion by a gardener? What the hell happened? How did you find this out?" Ann looked back at him, "I'm sorry Avery. I received a call from Bethany yesterday. She said that he went to the mansion to investigate something, and I guess he must have surprised the gardener who thought he was an intruder.

Amber heroically intervened and applied life saving CPR that allowed him to live long enough to get to a hospital. He just lost too much blood, and he died hours later. The gardener has not been seen since, and the police are looking for him."

Bentley cried, "This is terrible. Poor Beth and Sebastian, oh my God. We're next, aren't we? It wasn't the gardener that killed Sam. It was Best. I can promise you."

Ann replied, "I thought the same thing, Bentley. There is a full honor guard funeral by the LAPD tomorrow. Will you come with me? I will take us in my private jet and we will leave this afternoon and land in Los Angeles tonight. We will return immediately after the funeral."

"Avery, you go with her, please. I'm not leaving these kids alone. I don't trust anyone else to watch over them. Ann, I'm afraid we have terrible news of our own to share with you."

They started at the beginning when they received the phone call from Father O'Sullivan and the discovery of Patrick's body in his room and the appearance of the angel, Babbken, who came to take the body of Patrick away. This news hit Ann hard, another member of Vasallus now dead, further clarifying how all of them were in grave danger, including her son. She fell back onto the couch and muttered, "This nightmare will never end. We don't have much time. Best is moving fast now."

They sat and planned what they would do next. When it was clear Bentley wouldn't have it any other way, Avery reluctantly agreed to leave her behind, but only after Ann insisted she would deploy her own security team to stand guard outside Bentley's room and the rooms of the kids. She tried to lighten the mood by cheerfully declaring, "Hey, maybe we can have a pajama party in our room and keep the kids in here the whole time and play some board games or something." Avery held her in his arms, responded with a kiss then said, "That's not a bad idea, actually. Be easier to guard, and you will know where the kids are, that's for sure. Let's do that, but I don't think you should say anything about Patrick. Not yet."

"These kids will know something is up. They have a sense for each other. They will want to know where he is at the very least."

Ann agreed, "I agree with Avery, Bentley. Keep it light and fun for them. You can say that Patrick accompanied Avery on a charity appearance. Keep the television turned off so they're not exposed to the news channels. They have enough on their plates without having to worry about the events in the Middle East. The concert at Wembley is in two nights. We will be back well before that."

Bentley asked, "Do you really think they will go forward with the concert with the threat of a nuclear war imminent?" Avery responded, "If Best is successful negotiating a ceasefire, and I have to think he will, then he will certainly want the concert to move forward as a sign everything is back to normal. He will use the concert at Wembley to shine the spotlight further on himself."

After a few more minutes of discussion, Ann gave them hugs goodbye and informed Avery that she would have her men here within a few hours, and a car would be sent to take him to the airport and to the Lockwood private hangar, where her jet would be fuelled and ready to go.

****

The funeral for Detective Samuel Showenstein was full pomp and pageantry by the LAPD. It had been almost six years since an officer had been killed in the line of duty. The tragic story of the death of his former partner, Steven Benning, eighteen years earlier was added to the headlines in the papers and television crews covering the funeral. With everything that was happening in the world, this funeral was but a speck in the media landscape. In the law enforcement community the funeral was a very big deal.

Beth was happy to see them as they arrived at the gravesite, reserved for close family and friends and members of the LAPD. The Jewish cemetery was overwhelmed with a sea of police officers in full uniform. Jewish family and friends gathered, the men respecting tradition with all of them showing a tear on the left side of their suit jackets, above the heart. She hugged them both close, choking back tears, "Thank you for coming. Where is Bentley?" Avery was about to respond, when Sebastian walked up when he noticed them approach his mother. "Sebastian, how are you doing? Your Dad was a great man, and I will miss him very much." There was nothing more he could really say in these circumstances. After some muted small talk between all of them, Seb excused himself and returned to family relatives. The dignitaries from the LAPD were in place, and the service was about to resume. Everyone was now waiting for Beth. She looked at the two of them and asked, "Will you stay after the service? Come to the house and we will talk. There is something I want to share with you."

****

Avery and Ann arrived at the Showenstein home after the service to find it already full of people including members of the LAPD and many from the Jewish community who knew Sam. The Jewish tradition of passing around eggs to commerate the cycle of life was offered to them, and they both accepted with thanks. Soon, Beth came out of the kitchen and despite the pain of just burying her husband, she smiled radiantly at them: "I'm glad you were able to make it over. Please, let's take a few minutes alone. We'll go into Sam's office." Her strength was amazing and Avery couldn't imagine how she was coping. As they stepped into Sam's office, closed the door and were seated, Avery declared, "Beth, I am so sorry about Sam. He was truly a great man. He was very brave and a very good policeman." Beth wiped her nose with tissue then replied, "Thank you Avery, thank you both."

Avery continued, "There is something I must tell you, Beth." He watched as she braced for more terrible news, "Patrick is dead. Father O'Sullivan notified us to check on him in his hotel room in London where we were staying. He was dead in his bed." The news hit Beth like a hard punch in the stomach, Patrick was like a son to her and Sam for many years until his recent descent into his evil ways. "Oh my God, that is horrible, just horrible, Sam." She began to sob and he watched helplessly as Ann stood up, grabbed another tissue off of the shelf and handed it to Beth, and then placed her arm around her. "I'm sorry to have to tell you this today, Beth, but you would have heard of it soon enough and we both wanted to be the ones to tell you and not from a T.V."

She stifled her cries, wiped her eyes dry and then declared, "We're all going to die, aren't we?" Ann pivoted in front of her and replied, "No we will not. Beth, there is a something bigger than all of us happening on earth right now that none of us can truly understand, but I believe that God has kept all of us alive this long for a reason. Protect Sebastian, Beth. Stay close to him. If there is anything I can do, please let me help." She looked up at her, then said, "We will be fine, Ann, but thank you. The department, until the investigation of Sam's murder is completed will be giving us full protection. Honestly, when Best wants to strike, no amount of police protection will help us anyway. I am at peace with that. It is Seb I am worried about, not myself."

Ann looked at him before replying, "Beth, would you like us to take Seb with us. I have the very best security men watching the kids of Vasallus. Seb could join them." Beth shook her head as she responded, "Thank you Ann, but he will be safer here, if that's even possible. The police will have this place sewn up tight like Ft. Knox." She reached out and held each of their hands in hers and stared at them intently, her tears brimming the bottom of her eyes, threatening to spill over when she said, "Before Sam died in the hospital, he told me to tell you both and Father O'Sullivan something." Avery asked, "What did Sam say, Beth?"

She could no longer control the tears, as she continued, "He said it was Amber. She turned into the beast and attacked him. She made it look like Sam was attacking her when the gardener came into the office with a gun. He shot Sam and then he watched as she attacked the gardener, tearing him to pieces."

Avery asked, "Why did Sam go to the mansion?"

Wiping her tears again, she replied, "He was there

searching for clues on Best, when he discovered an ancient book hidden in a wall safe in Best's office. He never had a chance to look at it before Amber went crazy. He said he felt it in every fibre of his being that the book held a secret. A secret that holds a clue to Best. He said for you to find that book. No matter what. Find the book."

Chapter 33

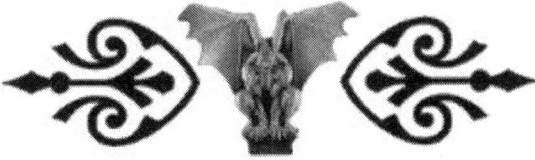

"Who in the hell is that?" An incredulous looking Russian diplomat asked the other permanent members of the United Nations Security Council. The French representative looked at the television one more time before stating, "Is this some sort of joke? This man should be arrested!"

U.S. Ambassador to the United Nations, the bright orange haired Geoff Plouffe, the young and talented up - and - comer in Washington promoted to the plum position at the U.N. by the President was aghast at what he was watching unfold on the multiple television screens in the meeting room of the United Nations. Robert Best, music mogul and founder of Vasallus was conducting a press conference outside this very building stating he could guarantee a peaceful resolution and ceasefire between Iran and Israel. The Israeli's would go completely mad and likely punch in the codes to arm their warheads instantly. He asked for everyone's attention, "Ladies and gentlemen, due to the circumstances unfolding before us, I must excuse myself and convene with my government's administration. I suggest we reconvene later today, after everyone has had a chance to update your governments."

The Chinese Ambassador angrily asked Plouffe, "This idiot will accelerate the tension even more than it already is, Ambassador Plouffe. May I suggest the Secretary-General make an immediate statement to the press to denounce this fool?" Plouffe looked at the other members gathered around the table and suggested, "I agree with Ambassador Jintao. Sir, what do you think?"

Secretary-General Olaf Alm, a Norwegian, calmly replied, "I also agree with the Chinese Ambassador, but I will wait to make that announcement until after we reconvene and I know more about this Robert Best. We will reconvene at 4:00 p.m. this afternoon. Ambassador Plouffe, present a full report on this Robert Best to the council when we reconvene. Thank you." The Secretary-General stood, motioned for everyone else to rise, then turned to one of the assistants standing against the wall and gave her directions to notify the press that he would give a press conference at the end of the day.

****

President Kipshaw excused himself from the meeting with the Joint Chiefs and asked his Chief of Staff, Adam Rinker, to join him in the Oval Office. Once the two of them were alone in his office, Adam asked, "What the hell is Best doing? Does he realize that those preposterous statements will only exacerbate the situation and put diplomacy at risk? Jesus Adam, this is ludicrous. That man is out of his mind."

Stan stood silent for a minute and contemplated what Best was doing. He looked at Adam and knew he could be trusted with what he was about to reveal. He was not only his Chief of Staff but had become his closest friend over the years in office. He was in the hospital room when Alexis attacked and killed the priest. He was with him at the Vatican. He turned away from the window and looked at Adam intently before speaking, "Adam, do you remember our visit to the Vatican?" Adam responded immediately, "Of course I do, I was a co-conspirator to a breach of protocol that could have landed my ass in a military prison cell for the good part of my adult life. Why do you ask?"

"Do you remember when Father O'Sullivan brought me into that special room?" He watched as Adam nodded his head. He continued, "What happened in that room, Adam, was nothing short of a miracle. What I am about to reveal to you, I have told no one, not even Leah." Sensing the President was about to reveal something incredible, Adam crossed his arms, took a step closer towards him and asked, "What happened in that room, Stan?"

Stan hesitated, looked at Adam and wondered if his friend would think he had lost his marbles, "I spoke with the spirit of the Lord, Adam. Just like Moses did at the burning bush on Mount Horeb. He warned me that Robert Best was the Devil, that he was Satan and that he would come after me, discredit me and my administration. He would take me out in his quest to become the New World Order Supreme Leader. He instructed me to prepare and to fight against his lies and deceit. I have now heard the first salvo of lies from Best. Just like the Lord had said in His warning."

Adam stood, stunned, disbelief etched across his face. He knew that something had happened in that room but nothing like this. He didn't know what to say so he just blurted, "That is incredible. I am beyond words, Stan. Are you sure?" He knew better than to question his friend but it was just an unbelievable story. He thought of Father O' Sullivan's visit to the White House weeks earlier and how much the President was enraptured with the priest when he first met him. Then he thought back to the bedroom of Alexis Kipshaw and her transformation into some sort of beast, possessed by something not of this world and then the incident at the hospital. He thought of the dead priest lying on the floor, his head twisted completely around, Alexis Kipshaw laughing at his reaction to the brutality. He wanted to kill her right then and there. The trip to the Vatican, the bizarre cloak and dagger and the secret doorway at the isolated side wall of the Vatican building that housed Father O' Sullivan. The secret room now claimed by the President was the meeting room of the Creator. He didn't know what to think, so he continued: "I believe you, of course, but do you really think Best is capable of stifling the conflict between Israel and Iran? Why would he do that?"

Stan walked close enough to Adam to put his hand on his shoulder. "By ending the horrifying threat of the first nuclear exchange between two countries he will be seen by the world as a man who is the ultimate hero and leader. It will not only severely undermine the credibility of my Presidency but will propel him forward to what he is ultimately seeking." Adam asked, "What is he ultimately seeking?"

Stan dropped his hand from his shoulder, inhaled, and then replied, "The leadership of the entire free world!"

****

Ambassador Plouffe entered the Oval Office of the President, wondering why the Secret Service had ushered him to the White House to meet with the President. He didn't have to wait long to find out. Chief of Staff, Adam Rinker and the President were waiting for him. After handshakes were exchanged, President Kipshaw asked him to have a seat and got right to the point.

"Ambassador Plouffe, I understand the Security Council are meeting this afternoon in regards to the press conference held by music executive, Robert Best." He was surprised information from a meeting by the Security Council of the United Nations, if not delivered by himself, would make it to the President's office so quickly. "Yes that is correct, Mr. President. I must say, Mr. President, that I am curious as to how this information would have made it to your office so quickly considering it is my duty to inform you of such meetings? I literally walked out of the U.N. meeting, when I was asked to come to Washington immediately." The President looked at him and smiled, "Don't sweat it, Geoff. You will be back in New York in plenty of time to brief the Secretary-General. I felt it important, we have a discussion in regards to this Robert Best before your briefing to the U.N. Adam, if you will."

Rinker took the cue and stood, paced in front of the Ambassador and continued, "We would like you to talk the Secretary-General into releasing the following statement in regards to this Robert Best."

****

Geoff was still in disbelief after his meeting with the President and his Chief of Staff as he was whisked back to New York in one of the President's helicopters. They wanted the U.N. to discredit Robert Best in a statement by dismissing his press conference as nothing more than an attempt to undermine the President of the

United States by using the crisis in the Middle East as a way to respond to the President for his attempts to censor his superstar rock band, Vasallus. It was all nothing but a media ploy by Best to take credit for diplomatic progress currently taking place between the U.S. Administration and the governments of Iran and Israel. What shocked him was the admission by Rinker and the President that Best would indeed be successful in diffusing the tension between Iran and Israel within the twenty- four time frame he claimed. Shockingly, if he was successful in diffusing the crisis and did indeed take full credit it would put the United States and the rest of the world at an even greater risk than existed currently between Iran and Israel.

He let the reality resonate through his brain, as he climbed into the diplomatic car of the U.N. waiting for him on the tarmac of JFK airport to take him back to the U.N. The President was intending to take the credit for Robert Best's successful peaceful ending to the crisis in Israel!

****

He sat in the backseat of the all black Cadillac XTS and watched the cars fly by as the driver expertly manoeuvred through the mid-afternoon New York traffic. He stared at the back of the driver's head for a brief second, as he thought he looked familiar. Not the familiar of having him as a driver in the past, but something else. Then the driver slightly turned towards the backseat and asked, "It is a beautiful New York City day, don't you think Ambassador?" Even the driver's voice was familiar. He must have had him as a driver before. It was not as though that was unusual, as the motor pool for the U.N. was not so extensive as not to acquire the same driver more than once. Yet he was more than familiar. He knew him somehow, but how? Then he spoke again, "How was your meeting with the President, Ambassador?" How would the driver have known he had just met with the President? The white skin of his freckled hands began to turn a slight red as they always did when he sensed trouble. He leaned forward in his seat, focusing hard to identify the recognition, "I didn't realize the diplomatic car pool of the U.N. was privy to the private meeting details of its occupants?"

The driver looked back towards the backseat once again and Geoff could see his profile much better this time. The driver's face was polished to a glossy shine. His jaw- line was rigid, but it looked as if it were made of plastic. When he spoke his perfectly straight teeth gleamed a ridiculous white, and the recognition began to materialize in his mind. His eyes narrowed as he stared in stunned disbelief as the identity of the driver hit him full force. It was Robert Best. He was driving the diplomatic car. How could that be possible?

"How the fuck did you get this car? How did you know where I would be, and how did you get clearance to enter the diplomatic security zone at JFK?" To many questions, he knew, as he struggled with the enormity of Best's actions. Instead of answering his questions, Best only laughed. The uproarious laughter filled the small space of the Cadillac with a demonic cackle. Who the fuck was this guy?

Geoff shouted at Best, "Pull this car over now, you fucking maniac. I don't know how you pulled this off, but your ass will be rotting in a jail cell for diplomatic kidnapping. Guess that will thwart any chance for you to save the world, huh?"

What happened next was beyond words and sent him collapsing backwards into his seat, unable to tear his eyes off of what he was witnessing. Best had turned his head in a complete 360 turn until his chin rested on the backrest. His hands continued to steer the car at a wild clip through traffic. The waxy and glossy face stared at him with menace; then his mouth opened and let escape a demonic bellow of laughter that forced Geoff to lean further back into the upholstery in fear. He had to be in a nightmare. This was impossible. Then Best spoke, "Hang tight Ambassador. We might as well have a face to face chat while we drive. What do you think?" A large piece of the wax-like material on Best's left cheek dislodged and fell to the floor of the backseat. A large black hole in his face opened up, exposing a cracked, grey-like skin underneath. His eyes bulged and as he continued laughing, he shouted, "Oops! Would you mind picking up that piece at your feet and placing it back on my cheek?"

Geoff somehow found the words to shout, "Who the fuck are you? What are you? Stop this car, you monster!" He suddenly thought of his cell phone in his pocket and reached for the clip on his belt, unsnapping the Blackberry and bringing it up to dial 9-1-1. The creature in front of him began to laugh hysterically again, "Go ahead, Ambassador, call the police! Tell them we are driving a black diplomatic Cadillac, and the driver is driving the car, while staring through the back window!" The laughter was deafening. He needed to get away and tried the handle of the door and cursed as it just flopped loose. Whatever was driving the car took a sharp turn between traffic and entered a residential side street, accelerating the powerful car down the narrow street. The hideous looking face of Robert Best smiled at him from above the backrest and then said, "So what exactly did the President ask you to tell the Secretary-General?"

He put everything he had into the punch. His military training taught him to angle his knuckled hand, so the blow to Best's decaying face would make a second strike unnecessary. He grabbed onto the door handle as the car careened out of control down the narrow street lined with cars on both sides. The blow to Best's face caused another chunk of his face to fall off, exposing more death flesh underneath. The car plowed into the parked cars on the right as Best's faceless body struggled to maintain control. Geoff was thrown to the right side of the car, his head cracking against the passenger window. The momentum tossed the car violently to the left, once again smashing it into a row of parked cars. His body lurched to the left, and he now realized he did not have his seatbelt on. He was being tossed around like a rag doll. He glimpsed the destroyed face of Best bouncing on top of the backrest, his eyes shifting to the left and to the right, enjoying every second of the carnage. He laughed like a kid on a wild carnival ride, "Yippee! This is great fun! What do you think Ambassador?"

He cocked his fist to deliver a final blow to whatever the hell was driving the car, knowing he would die regardless, when suddenly, the car came to a screeching halt that sent him flying almost completely into the front seat. He lifted his bloodied face and struggled to get back into the backseat when Best drove a powerful blow with his elbow into the side of his head that was like a charge of thousand volts of electricity blasted into his brain. White shards of pain fell like rain inside of his head. He could barely hear Best scream, "Did that hurt Ambassador? It didn't? Okay, then how about this!" The fist hurtling towards him was just a blur as it smashed directly into his nose, exploding it in a shower of blood. His mind was erupting in a hail of white light that turned to black instantly. He was dying, and as the last seconds of his life ebbed away he realized he never had the chance to think about why this was happening to him in the first place. He was just a loyal and hardworking public servant who had just been targeted and killed by a monster. He wasn't exactly sure why but it didn't matter. He was dead.

****

Best climbed out of the wreckage of the Cadillac, stepped off of the street and onto the grassy boulevard. He heard the sirens screaming towards the scene. He looked back into the crumpled car and laughed out loud at how much fun that just was. He didn't expect it to go down that way; he never did, but boy that was great fun. He turned to walk towards the next cross street and away from the descending police and emergency vehicles when he saw the kid. A boy, black, approximately ten years old maybe, stood twenty feet away staring directly at him, as if he had seen a ghost. He then realized half of his face was lying on the floor mats of the backseat. He smiled at the boy, knowing his hideous features would leave a scar on the boy's brain that he would carry the rest of his life, and as he turned to walk away he called out, "Hey kid. You're looking at me like you've seen a ghost. I'm no ghost kid, I'm the Devil. Remember that kid when you talk to the police. You saw the Devil!"

The boy stood, frozen in place as the stranger disappeared down the street. He could feel the hands of the firemen on his shoulders, as they picked him up and carried him away from the wreckage that threatened to explode in a ball of flames.

He knew the Devil when he saw one. He had watched many movies with his older brothers, and he knew he had just talked with the Devil. His older brothers wouldn't believe him, he knew. They would just make fun of the fact that he had peed his pants when the firemen brought him home.

Chapter 34

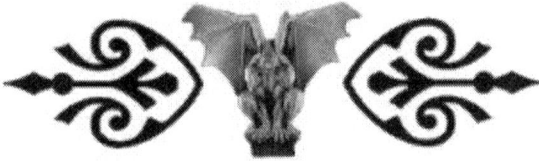

The bizarre press conference by Robert Best on the steps of the United Nations Headquarters in New York City was played over and over by all of the world's news channels, but by no more than the granddaddy of all news channels, CNN. The coverage had even overshadowed the conflict itself between the two Middle Eastern countries. Experts from around the globe weighed in on the debate of whether or not Best would even be given an audience with either of the two countries leaders and none of them gave him any chance of ending the crisis. Reporters camped outside the Claridge Hotel in London in the hope of catching Vasallus co-founder and manager, Avery Johnson for his comments on his partner's outlandish claims were unsuccessful. Johnson and his girlfriend, *Music Talks* journalist Bentley Paxton were nowhere to be seen. There was talk that the upcoming mega Vasallus concert at Wembley Stadium might be cancelled due to the overwhelming security risk. There were already pockets of demonstrations by the British youth rising up against British authority. Leading up to a Vasallus concert, the same dilemma faced British authorities that other countries have confronted. Cancel and surely be met with a backlash of ferocity by the millions of youth in retaliation, or allow the concert to proceed and brace for the violence that would precede and the anarchy to follow.

"What is Best doing?"

Avery stood in front of the mirror in the bathroom of their suite at the Claridge and put the finishing touches to his expertly cut, but very white hair. He looked over at Bentley who was doing the same albeit with a curling iron and replied, "This is very much by design. He truly believes he can pull this off and it's likely he will. Can you imagine his popularity in front of the world if he does?"

Bentley placed the hot iron on the counter, then turned towards Avery and asked, "Why, Avery? Why would he want to get involved in this conflict? Best is not capable of an act of humanitarian kindness. What are we missing?"

"You're right. This is completely out of character for him. He is bent on destroying the world, not saving it. I guess we'll just see how this plays out. Come on, sweetheart; we're going to be late for the press conference, if we don't get out of here."

The press conference for tomorrow night's performance at Wembley was in thirty minutes. The press conference was right in the facilities at Wembley. They had prepared for a full house of two hundred media plus making it by far the largest to date on this European tour. The buzz regarding Vasallus and the return of Michael Lockwood dominated the media in the U.K. on every social media platform. Government officials asked local radio and T.V. stations to turn down the coverage of Vasallus in the hope to avoid full scale rioting. They were unsuccessful as radio stations pumped out Vasallus songs around the clock. Television stations ran stories on the kids of Vasallus non-stop, and Twitter was on the verge of crashing as Michael Lockwood filled the Twitter world with Tweets of his excitement to perform in front of his home city.

The two of them scrambled to get ready when Bentley headed for the door, calling out, "I'm going to round-up the kids and bring them in here. We're still in agreement to downplay Patrick's no-show until after the press conference?" Avery came out of the bathroom carrying his suit jacket and replied, "I still believe that's best. I'm sure they are aware something bad has happened and they may have questions. but I think the excitement of the day and the upcoming show tomorrow will buy us some time before they lean hard on us for Patrick's whereabouts. Let's just get through this conference, get back to the hotel and sit them all down." Avery was cut-off by the ring of the hotel room phone. Before picking it up, he looked at Bentley and said, "Must be one of the kids wondering when we're heading out of here." Picking up the phone he answered, "Avery Johnson." Bentley watched him listen, and his face become animated before she heard him bark out orders, "Cancel the press conference altogether. I'm not putting the kids through that. Tell them they will have to make due with the post-concert press conference." He hung up the phone and stated, "Change of plans. The press conference has been cancelled. Apparently the media throng camped downstairs, on the sidewalk and surrounding side streets is out of control. Everyone wants a statement from us in regards to the actions of Robert Best. I've decided we're going to stay put right here and wait this Best sideshow out."

Bentley turned towards the door again and replied, "Good. That means we can spend the day with the kids and talk to them about Patrick. I'm going over to their room and let them know there is no press conference and to come to our suite for the afternoon."

"Good idea."

****

Israeli Prime Minister Ben-Shahar was livid. He shouted at his military commanders that enough time has been wasted talking about the American businessman, Robert Best. It was time to respond to the attack by the Iranians. The twenty-four hour period he had promised the American President had passed and he was tired of waiting to respond. Tens of thousands of his countries citizens had perished at the cruelty of the Iranian regime. He would make them pay dearly. He turned towards the head of the Israel Defense Forces, his Chief of General Staff, Yitzhak Zion and commanded, "It is time to expel the darkness of our enemy. I want Tehran reduced to dust before the end of the day."

Zion immediately protested, "Forgive me, Mr. President, but you must consider a non nuclear response. We can inflict just as substantial a loss without the use of nuclear weapons. The message to the West and the rest of the world is if that we use nuclear weapons to respond to Iran, it will only isolate this country and the Jewish people around the world. It will put us back to pre-World War 11 levels."

Ben-Shahar seethed at his General, "That is exactly my point, General. The world must be shown that the Jewish people and their country will no longer tolerate a target at their backs. A nuclear response is the only way to take away the fear my people have carried for centuries. Our enemies will no longer spit at our feet; instead, they will cower in fear for the targets that are at their backs. This is the defining moment in our people and our country's history, General, and I plan to ensure that it is done. Do I make myself clear? Good, now carry out your orders. You have forty-five minutes to set the launch codes on my desk. Now move!"

Five minutes after his General left the Prime Minister's office in silent protest; there was a loud knock on the Prime Minister's door. He had distinctly told his assistant he was not to be disturbed over the next forty-five minutes. The only person he would see was the General. He ignored the knock until another volley of bangs echoed through his large office. "Who is it?" He yelled into the door. There was no response. He punched in his assistant's extension in the phone and it rang through with no one picking it up. The anger swelled within him, threatening to explode like the bomb that would soon be screaming towards Iran. He walked around his desk and to his office door. He opened it and was thinking of busting his General's nose with his fist, as the weak military man had returned to try and talk him out of the attack. The man standing outside his door when he opened it was the last man on earth he ever expected to see: The American businessman, Robert Best.

****

Ten minutes after Bentley left the room, and she returned with the five members of Vasallus right behind her. Avery observed that all of them had been ready for the press conference. He couldn't help but marvel how beautiful, if that was possible, Chloë and Brittany were becoming every day. He couldn't believe they were still only seventeen years old. Their beauty was stunning to see even after all of the time he and Bentley had spent with them. Watching Bentley and how beautiful she was herself interact with the girls and how close they had become took his breath away. Sometimes he just had to pinch himself at how lucky he was. Connor, Juan and Michael, their hair coiffed, all plopped down on the large couch. It was Michael who asked, "What's up, Avery? Bentley said we aren't going to the press conference? My fans have been looking forward to seeing us speak. I wanted to take the opportunity to give a shout out to my city, know what I'm saying?"

Avery was about to respond, when he was interrupted by Juan, "It's about Patrick. He's gone missing and that's why you've cancelled the press conference."

Now Avery was able to respond, "No that is not true, Juan. Hey, everybody, let's not sweat the press conference, okay? I know you wanted to take that opportunity with your fans Michael. I get that, but really, we're here to perform and that is exactly what all of you will achieve tomorrow night in the biggest show of your careers."

Connor asked, "Then why did you cancel the press conference?"

Brittany threw her hands up in the air in a mock gesture and rolled her eyes before she spoke, "Come on guys! Who cares? It's only a press conference. It's not such a big deal that we spaz out on Avery."

Juan repeated, "Where is Patrick, Bentley?"

Bentley glanced nervously at Avery before replying, "We need to talk to all of you about Patrick." She paused to gather herself, unsure exactly how to tell them when Juan cut in, "He's dead, isn't he?" Connor looked at Juan and shouted, "Stop it, Juan. You're talking out of your ass right now. Let Bentley and Avery tell us what's going on."

It was Avery who delivered the news that sliced through the room like a razor sharp Ginsu knife, "I'm afraid Juan is right.

Patrick is dead. I'm so sorry."

Chloë and Brittany simultaneously gasped, and Connor blurted "Jesus!

Juan exploded, "What happened, Avery? Tell me what the fuck happened to him!" He leapt from the couch and jumped on him so fast he had no chance to react. His strength was surprising, and he could feel the anger well up inside of Juan as he screamed, "You're lying! Patrick is not dead! He can't be. Please tell me you're lying!" He was finally able to get Juan under control with the help of Bentley and Connor. His heart was breaking as he watched Juan break down. He sobbed uncontrollably, burying his head in his arms, rocked back and forth. Bentley and Chloë surrounded him, consoling him when Michael shouted out, "Grow up Juan. Who the hell cares about Patrick, anyway? No one here liked him. We hated him, including you. He was an evil bastard who did terrible things. We're better off without him. This world's better off without him."

Juan came unglued. He picked his head up out of his arms and glared at Michael, his voice seething when he hissed, "Patrick was my brother. He was your brother, you asshole. He was all of ours brother." Avery quickly scrambled out of his chair and joined Connor in front of Juan to block him from launching himself at Michael. Michael continued to shout at Juan, "He was not my brother, not ever. We may have carried the same mark, but I'll never admit to being a brother from the blood we shared."

The confrontation was interrupted by the cries of Brittany as her wails filled the room with a pain that everyone felt. "What is happening to us? We're all going to die. Don't you see! First it was Elizabeth, and now Patrick. We're marked, because we're going to die." Avery watched as Brittany fell to her side, sobbing uncontrollably. Bentley rushed over to her, "No baby, that's not true. You're not going to die, I promise you. It's going to be okay." It was Connor who added, "Bentley, she's right. The Master is using us for his plan. He is using us to poison kids' minds all over the world. I know this; yet, I can't stop myself from performing and singing those horrible lyrics. None of us can. He is controlling us, and when he doesn't need us anymore he will kill the rest of us."

Chloë shouted so forcefully it surprised everyone, and the room became silent. Then barely above a whisper, she declared, "You're right Connor, and so are you Brittany. We've all been to that dark place where Elizabeth is at. We know what happened to her and what is happening to her soul." She looked at Avery and then Bentley before continuing, "There is no hope for us now. We were born of his blood, marked by him, and our birth mothers were murdered by him to isolate and control us." To hear Chloë talk so abruptly of their demise shocked him, and he looked over at Bentley before saying, "Chloë, all of you, listen to me. I know you feel alone and scared, but I promise that you are not alone. Bentley and I will never leave you, never abandon you. We will find a way out of this." Chloë cut in, "I know you and Bentley mean well, Avery, and we are thankful to you for that. I know that my singing is a vessel carrying a message of death and destruction. I will not do it anymore, and if that means the Master kills me now then so be it. I can't do this anymore. All hope is lost." Everyone in the room sat frozen in silence, as Chloë 's words cut deep into their souls.

Everyone jumped, when there was a loud pounding on the door. The interruption temporarily suspended the tension that was on the verge of exploding in the room. Bentley quickly lept up from beside Brittany, softly stroked the side of her face, then made her way to the door just as the pounding began again. Chloë cried out to Bentley, just as she was about to open the door, "Please, it's for me. I will answer it." Confused at Chloë's reaction, Bentley stepped back and watched as she slowly made her way to the door. When Chloë finally opened the door, the shock of their visitor almost made her lose her balance. It was Father O' Sullivan.

****

Iranian President Mohammad Saidi prepared for his meeting with the Supreme Leader, the Ayatollah. The attack on Israel, ordered by the Supreme Leader and based upon intelligence reports gathered by field agents was hugely successful. The diversion created to draw an attack by the United States was brilliant. Their inability to stop an attack on Israel was not going over well with the Israeli people. The Supreme Leader would want to gloat in front of him on how the operation not only killed many Jews, but also how it brought humiliation to the United States. He was entitled to brag; the operation couldn't have worked out any better. He was curious as to how he would handle the American Robert Best's claim to forge a ceasefire with Israel. American people are such idiots, he thought. If they only knew what would soon be in store for them.

He was quickly ushered into the office of His Eminence. He was accompanied by the Vice President of Security, personally requested by the Supreme Leader. As they walked into the office and the door closed behind them, Saidi was stunned to see the American, Robert Best standing beside the Supreme Leader. He was speechless, the words unable to escape the tip of his tongue. His astonishment at the appearance of Best inside His Eminence's office quickly turned to anger. He took a step toward Best, raised his fist and shouted, "What are you doing in here? You will be shot at once you fool. Get away from him, or I'll kill you myself with my own hands." He quickly turned to the Vice President and commanded, "Get security at once. Now."

"Stop, you idiot. Sit down. Both of you."

Saidi was shocked and protested, "But your Excellence! This American brings you shame with his presence. How did he get in here? I don't understand!" Saidi glared at his Vice President of Security, as if the breach of security was his fault.

He was aghast as he watched Best walk behind the Ayatollah, stop then give him a slap on the shoulder like some cowboy in those American movies. "Thank you gentlemen for meeting me today. Congratulations on the success of your attack. Just wish you would have killed a few more of those

Jew bastards. Anyway, we have some business to discuss and your Grand Pooba here was nice enough to arrange this little meeting." Best was interrupted by the raging Vice President who had heard enough, "Excuse me your Excellence, Mr. President, but I will not stand in a room with an arrogant American bastard only to listen him disrespect the Supreme Leader. I don't know how you got in here or who you think you are, but your little charade has come to an end."

Best had his back to the Vice President, admiring a beautiful wall rack made of gold that housed a least a dozen ceremonial swords, while the Vice President raged. When the Vice President was finished he replied, "Nice speech. At least someone in this room has some balls." The outraged Vice President never even saw it coming. Best had removed one of the gleaming swords and in one motion with a speed undetected as anything but movement, sliced the large blade across the Vice President's throat, decapitating his head instantaneously. The Ayatollah recoiled in his chair at the sight of the headless corpse hitting the floor; it's opened neck spewing blood all over the immaculate room. President Saidi gasped, and his throat filled with terror as he cried out, "Who are you?"

****

The murder of Ambassador Plouffe on the streets of New York City was creating all kinds of rumours in the media. Leading the way was the story that it was a hit orchestrated by the Israeli government in their anger over the debacle of the bungled attack on the Iranian missile sites. The stories combined with the overwhelming police presence in the city had put its citizens in a state of fear. CNN was running the story that only a miracle by American businessman, Robert Best, in his bid to diffuse what would soon be the world's first nuclear attack since the Second World War, as the only thing that could stop the inevitable. That miracle was only a few minutes away, as word came down that a joint press conference between Israeli Prime Minister Ben-Shahar and Iranian President Saidi was about to begin in a hastily called press conference in Cairo, Egypt.

President Kipshaw and his top aides gathered around the large screen TV in the Situation Room and sat in stunned silence as they watched the unfolding events. When the news channel picked up the feed from Cairo, Stan dropped his chin to his chest and prayed. In the centre of the screen and flanked by both Ben-Shahar and Saidi was the despicable, Robert Best. He could neither watch nor listen. The men and women around the table were buzzing like bees as the unbelievable story unfolded. Best had somehow brokered a deal between these two warring countries and saved the world from the brink of an all-out nuclear war. Everyone was shocked that Best had somehow managed to pull off the unthinkable. He exchanged a look with his Chief of Staff, Adam Rinker. He looked as if he might vomit his breakfast all over the meeting table.

The Anti-Christ, disguised as Robert Best to the world had made his first move. It was a big one.

Chapter 35

"Father O'Sullivan. It is you. I cannot believe it's really you," Chloë whispered as she stood in the doorway, staring at Father O'Sullivan.

Bentley stood to the side, unable to move as she watched the two of them in the doorway to the room. She was joined by Avery and the two of them continued to be silent as Chloë came to grips in seeing Father O'Sullivan for the first time in a long time.

Words started to spout out of her, mixed with tears of joy, as she ecstatically declared, "Father, it's really you! I have been praying to see you. God has answered my prayers, because here you are!" She wrapped her arms around him and hugged him tightly not wanting to let him go. The two of them watched as Father O'Sullivan lifted Chloë's chin and smiled as he looked into her eyes and said, "You have become such a beautiful young woman, my dear. You have the eyes of your mother. Your mother was beautiful like you, Chloë." They could see her expression change as she asked, "I wished I could have known my mother, Father. I bet she was very brave." He gave her another big hug before replying, "She was a very brave woman. I see her in you Chloë; the same courage is in you."

Bentley stepped beside Chloë, putting her arm around her shoulders and whispered, "Let's show Father O'Sullivan to a chair. What do you say? I'm sure he has come a long way and must be exhausted."

Giggling she gave Father O' Sullivan another hug and turned and walked back into the living room of the suite. Avery and Bentley took a minute to speak with Thomas as Avery exclaimed,

"I can't believe you're here Father! We just told the kids about Patrick's death, before you knocked. They are very distraught, and hope is a word they feel does not include them."

Thomas looked at the two of them briefly, his blue eyes sparkling, before replying, "I know. That is why I'm here."

****

Robert Best took refuge once again at the Malibu mansion. The mansion was now his place of last stand. It is here where he would execute the final steps of his plan that he had waited centuries to inflict on humankind. He stood and took account of the space he had built below the offices and studio of Vasallus. It was a like a bunker, only because it was below ground. The contractors had secured the walls with reinforced steel to protect it from the waters. This close to the ocean, one did not have to dig very deep to hit the water line. He would no longer stop by his New York or L.A. offices; however, he would keep them open for appearance purposes only.

His physical body would not last much longer. It was already breaking down fast, and he required copious amounts of makeup to keep up his appearance. He would be making a lot of appearances over the next several months, and as the world inched closer to its own annihilation by their own hands before the final event preceding the Rapture. Time was no longer an ally but his worst enemy, next to God. His enemy would soon wipe the earth clean of His treasured humankind, only to start anew with His begotten Son as King over those who were saved during the Rapture. The Tribulation would be a disaster for Him and His Son. There would be precious few left on this earth for the Son to rule.

The space was required to maintain his earthly persona of Robert Best, but what he really needed was a place to keep the book close and out of sight. The book was the curse given to him by God so long ago when he cast him from his flock. The book was the blueprint for man to destroy him. The book must remain on earth and could never be destroyed by him; otherwise, it would break the Covenant with God. The book must also be near. He was allowed an existence independent of God, only if the book remained on earth. For centuries his spirit was kept hidden deep within the bowels of earth, undetectable by man, the book always with him. Only occasionally would he allow his spirit to venture through the souls of mankind, feed the world its share of misery and despair, tragedy and hopelessness before returning to his hiding space. Only now, to enact his plan, he must expose the book to discovery. The chance that the book would be exposed and used to destroy him by His beloved man was his curse. It was shocking to learn that Showenstein had discovered the book in the safe. He would not make that same mistake again. No one would find it down here, before it was too late.

The Covenant. He hated Him. His body shook with a hellish rage, and he fought to control it. There was no time to waste on rage. He would get his revenge for what God has done to him. Take away the souls of His believers. Leave Him with nothing. When He discovered the depth of His loss, maybe then He would be willing to negotiate.

Destroy the Covenant in return for His precious mankind. His rage quickly turned to overwhelming joy.

****

"We are cursed Father. We carry the mark of the Beast. We are of his blood. Two of us have already died, and soon the rest of us will follow. Millions of people around the world are destroying their cities and defying authority, because of the influence of our music. People are dying because of us. I can't do this anymore. Now that Patrick is gone, I feel liberated almost. A burden has been lifted."

Juan added, "I agree with Connor, Father. We were always under the thumb and watchful eye of Best through Patrick. I could feel it, and so could the others. I do not want to perform tomorrow night. I will not perform. I will no longer be a part of his plan to destroy."

Avery responded, "Listen, everyone. We must perform. It is too dangerous if we do not. Best will know immediately if we don't perform and will act swiftly to hurt one or all of you. We cannot take that chance. Until we have a plan to remove you from this we stay the course."

"What do you think we should do, Father?" Bentley asked.

Father O'Sullivan stood and paced the room, deep in thought, taking his time before he replied. It was the first time since he appeared that Avery noticed he looked considerably older than the last time they saw him. Nowhere near how old he looked before his transformation, but he had aged. "Could the youthfulness instilled into him by God be wearing off," he thought?

"I agree with Avery. You must perform. It is too dangerous for you, if you do not. Best will not tolerate the betrayal, and his evilness has no boundaries. Have faith in the Lord, children, for He will not abandon you."

Michael reacted swiftly to Father O'Sullivan's request to have faith, "Father, how can you really expect us to have faith in a God that has clearly abandoned us. Two of us are dead, and the rest of us are on the verge of the same fate. As much as I want to perform in front of my fans, I agree with the others. It's just too much to bear; especially this concert at Wembley and what our lyrics will do and the millions on pay-for-view watchin.."

Connor added, "The youth around the world are in full denial of social order. This concert could send them over the edge completely. The ensuing damage could be irreversible."

Avery looked at Bentley, astounded at the depth of the kid's concerns over their music's effects on others. This is the first time they had ever spoken about it so fervently. A glimmer of hope began to seep into his soul. Father O'Sullivan was about to speak when he was interjected by Chloë.

"Father O'Sullivan and Avery are right. We should perform. We will be safe, temporarily at least, if we do." She looked up at Father O'Sullivan and then to the others when she spoke next, "We will perform. We will be ready."

****

The collective sigh of relief was felt around the world by

everyone as the newscast of Robert Best flanked by the President of Iran and the Prime Minister of Israel signed not only a ceasefire but a stunning peace accord that would see Israel give up the Gaza Strip to the Palestinian Authority for a new Palestine state. People everywhere celebrated the incredible news and the miraculous feat accomplished by American businessman Robert Best. Even Jewish people around the world showed signs of thankfulness that the decades old war with Palestine would finally end. It was a shocking twenty- four hours that left heads of state around the world wondering just how Best managed to pull off the impossible. How the coup was executed by Best was never explained, but theories began to circulate on how he managed to bring peace to the Middle East on a scale never thought possible.

The theory that Best received the biggest laugh as he watched the endless coverage on his favorite news channel, CNN, was the one from a woman in Britain who declared Best was an angel of God. She went on to say the peace accord could only have come from a miracle by God. In-depth stories also began to appear on who this man was; the businessman Robert Best. There was talk of his career as a musical genius, record producer, manager and the creator and founder along with Avery Johnson of Vasallus. Attempts to locate Avery Johnson for a statement on his partner's amazing feat were unsuccessful. Best watched as a reporter stood outside the Claridge Hotel in London where Johnson and Vasallus were holed up before the big concert in London the next night in the hope of catching a statement. He thought about the concert at Wembley. Biggest of the tour to date. The pay-per-view around the world for this show would be astronomical, especially with Best's new found popularity. People will want to demonstrate their appreciation, by showing their support through Vasallus. He planned it this way and was counting on it. The concert would open up Vasallus to a segment it have only brushed up against: The parents of the youth already obsessed with Vasallus, the general population and the curious. The eyes of the world would be on Wembley tomorrow night. The world would not know what hit them.

Best leaned forward in his chair when the news channel cut to another reporter from Washington, stationed outside of the White House. Reporters were waiting for President Kipshaw to make a statement on the events. The reporter was running with the story that Kipshaw would have to answer to the questions as to how a music executive from Los Angeles could broker one of the biggest peace deals in history, while the President and other world leaders could not. CNN anchors pointed to the theory that if Best was to run for President in the next election he would win in a landslide.

The plan was unfolding spectacularly. Best smiled from ear to ear as he leaned back in his chair in the bunker. He was smiling so hard he had to be careful he didn't dislodge all of the makeup to keep his face intact. He needed to learn how to not to smile so broadly. He would be doing a lot of interviews in the weeks ahead and the last thing he needed was a chunk of his face to fall off while he was talking to a live television camera.

He couldn't control himself as he broke into laughter, and as he did he felt pieces of his face begin to loosen and dislodge, falling onto his arms and then onto the floor. Who cares, he thought. He'd just go into the bathroom and slap some more of the fill material into the holes.

****

The kids returned to their suite to hang out and they agreed to get together again in a few hours and order room service. Avery and Bentley, along with Father O'Sullivan sat down over a pot of tea. Thomas asked, "While we are waiting for Ann, tell me, how are the two of you holding up?"

Avery squeezed Bentley close, then replied, "We're doing the best we can, Father. Losing Patrick was a shock, and the appearances of the angels has been a little overwhelming. It's the five kids in that room down the hall that give us the strength to carry on. Their courage is beyond words, Father, and quite frankly, if they can be as brave and courageous as they are, then so can we." Bentley added, "Tell us, Father, about Patrick. Is he in a good place right now?"

They watched as he dropped his chin. Her question brought back memories that were not pleasant. He looked at them with those incredible eyes, but this time they were filled with an overwhelming sadness, "Patrick, despite the terrible things he has done, was just a boy, controlled by an evilness that used him for his own devices. In the end, Patrick defied this evil, followed his heart and accepted Christ as his Savior. It cost him his life, and he knew it, but he accepted Him willingly. He was an exceptionally brave young man."

Bentley couldn't stop the tears that were streaking down her cheeks as she thought of Patrick, his death imminent, accepting Christ. She wiped her eyes with her sleeve before saying, "That is so sad, Father. I just wish we could have done more for him, maybe showed him more that we cared." Father O'Sullivan quickly responded, "Please, my dear, do not feel any burden for Patrick's death. It is not yours to bear. It is mine. I failed Patrick. I did not save him in time. The Beast is one step ahead of us, but I have a plan. It is one of the reasons I am here."

"A plan, Father? A plan to do what?" Avery asked.

"Before Patrick died, he held my hand as I invited his soul to accept Jesus Christ as his Savior. The Beast was all around us, in a blinding rage as to what Patrick was doing and before he swooped in and killed Patrick he gave me this." Thomas produced a small USB drive and handed it to Avery. It was in his hand when he was clutching mine. Before he died, he whispered the words, "Give this to Avery. Make sure Vasallus get this."

Bentley, her eyes wide with wonder, asked, "What is on the drive?"

"His last words were, "They are my songs to make-up for all the damage my music has caused. Get this to Avery." Those were his last words. He was taken, brutally, right in front of me by the Demon."

Bentley drew in a sharp breath, "That is awful. I can't imagine what that must have been like for you, Father."

"I was unable to save him. I will live with that for the rest of my life."

Avery asked, "Let's take a look at what Patrick wanted for us." He accepted the USB from Father O'Sullivan and leaned forward to his laptop that was sitting on the coffee table. He quickly woke up the computer, plugged in the USB, waited for it to come up, and then saw the one lone file folder on the USB drive. The file was aptly named 'Songs for Survival'. Avery opened the file, and a list of over 100 compositions filled the screen. None of the compositions were named, listed by number only. He double clicked on the first song and it immediately launched into Avery's composer software. He quickly scanned the musical score and accompanying lyrics. Father O'Sullivan and Bentley leaned in close on each side of him when the priest commented, "Look at the complexity of this music. I have no clue what I'm looking at but all of those notes up and down along that line are amazing. Is the song useable, Avery?"

Avery fell back into the big cushions of the couch, his mind racing. He was silent as his mind took in what he was seeing on the screen. He heard Bentley somewhere in the background ask him if he was alright, when he finally spoke, "Brilliant. I don't know what to say." He quickly moved back to the computer and opened another song, titled number two. Again Avery studied the song for a few minutes, and then opened another one. Then another one. This went on for about twenty minutes, until he had opened up about thirty songs. He was speechless and turned to the others and declared, "You are witness to a collection of music that could instantly be called a treasure of masterpieces. It is incredible, what he has written. It is by far the best music Patrick has ever created, and as you know he has written a lot of incredible music. These songs, at first glance, would survive to be enjoyed by future generations. They are invaluable." Avery found himself shaking, as he continued to stare at the screen.

Father O'Sullivan asked, "The lyrics, Avery, seem odd or worse, uninspiring. Is that because I don't understand music?"

Avery stood up and began to pace the room as he continued, "Patrick has written these songs as if he were writing poetry. Like the songs he has written for Vasallus to date, those collections of songs, and the ones they performed and recorded that had incited so much violence around the world included subliminal messages, hidden truths that the youth figured out quickly and combined with the power of social media. These songs became their anthems, their wake-up call to take control of their lives away from their parents, guardians, teachers and authority figures. These 'Songs for Survival' will have the complete opposite effect. These songs are quite simply, Father, poetry. They are so beautifully written, I can't wait for the kids to get back home to the studio and begin to perform these. This collection, without looking at another one, will change the world for the better."

Bentley, her voice filled with hope, almost shouted, "This is unbelievable! The kids will be thrilled. When can we show them these?"

Avery thought for a second longer and then replied, "We will begin rehearsing them immediately upon return to the mansion when the tour is complete and Best is no longer focused on Vasallus. Let's wait before we say anything to the kids. We need to think more about these songs. We need to protect them." He was interrupted in his thoughts by Father O'Sullivan.

"Avery, don't you see? The answer is right in front of you."

They both looked at Father O'Sullivan when Avery replied, "See what, Father? That quite likely, the greatest collection of music ever written is sitting on my computer, and we are the first to have laid eyes on it?"

Father O'Sullivan's next words shocked the two of them.

"Vasallus must perform these songs tomorrow night. It might very well be the last chance they ever got to sing them."

Chapter 36

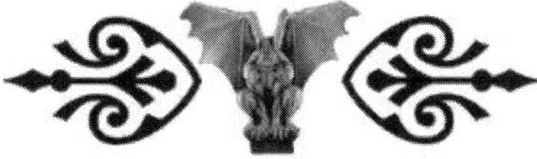

Satan bathed in the darkness of his realm. It restored him and was the one place he was completely in control. God could not see or sense him in this place. It is why he often spent his time here. The dark energy vibrated through the blackness, enveloped him and gave him his purpose. It is here, all the despair, misery and sadness of the world met as one. It is in death that the souls of humankind came to him. His cauldron of souls was full over the course of time, but it was not full enough. The last push to ensure Hell spilled over was near. He wanted to check on his two very special inhabitants. Of the millions that have come to him here, these two were his most special.

He was their father.

He swam through the darkness, the way a swimmer breaststrokes in a pool. Millions upon millions of damned souls called out to him as he sought out Elizabeth and Patrick. If he was lucky, he would find them together with their blood drawing them close. Doubtful, he chuckled, considering Patrick brutally killed her. The combination of groaning, moaning and cries of pain from millions of lost souls filled the abyss, surrounding him, filling him with a melancholy of purpose. This was home. Earth was not his home. Here he was the King, and it was here he bowed to no one. The Lord would never come here; even He was vulnerable in this existence.

Where were they?

It was not possible to hide from him. Yet he could not feel their presence. It baffled him. His anger began to swell as his mind swept through the vastness, searching, the damned souls of his children nowhere to be found. He came across a sight that temporarily distracted him. He watched the beautiful sight of the quivering souls of Marie Jimenez and Nancy Campbell, attempt to recoil further back into the blackness, away from him. Their suicides brought them directly to him. His anger caused him to linger with them for a little longer. He filled their tortured souls with images of what would happen to their children when he was done with them. Their children's souls would soon be trapped in an eternal damnation of pain and suffering. The cry of pain from them both was sweet sounding. He moved on from them like a rolling thunder.

The thought of Elizabeth's and Patrick's escape from here touched his senses. Impossible! Where were they? Then he realized that Patrick had been saved by the priest. It was the only reason he was not here. How could that be? He had felt the soul of his son drop right through him to here. He must have been snatched right back by Him. The tortured souls surrounding him in the blackness pushed away like a school of fish in the ocean, when they sensed danger. His roar pulsed through the chasm like a powerful tremor.

Where was Elizabeth? Was it possible, He somehow stole her soul from him? She was nowhere to be found. If He could take her, what would stop him from taking all of them?

His fury boomed through this existence. The Master of Hell, Satan, was angry. His hatred for Him consumed him, and he would wreak havoc to His precious humankind. He entered his realm, stole the souls of his own children, and for that He will pay with the lives of millions.

An epic event of unprecedented destruction and death was in store for Him. His anger grew, as he thought of the betrayal.

He returned to his bunker to prepare.

****

The next morning, the day of the concert, Bentley and Avery lay restlessly in bed of the hotel suite. It was a sleepless night for both of them. They said goodnight to both Ann and Father

O'Sullivan well past midnight. Ann had insisted that Father O'Sullivan stay at her estate, at least until after tonight's concert. It was too late in the evening for the priest to put up much of an argument, thought Bentley, as she snuggled in closer to Avery.

"Did you notice any changes in Father O'Sullivan?"

Avery rolled onto his side, their noses almost touching as he replied, "I did. He is getting older. He looks tired. I can't imagine the stress he is under with the weight of the world on him."

"The secret Vatican committee, SOSL, that has been his life's work and Best, the kids. I'm thinking that the miracle that made him young, the Lord's miracle, was to give him the energy to lead this fight, but is now wearing off. His mission is either ending, or he is running out of time. Let's pray for him, Avery." The two of them held hands under the blankets, as Bentley whispered: "Dear Lord, hear our prayer. Whatever role you have for Father O'Sullivan in the days and weeks ahead, please continue to give him the strength and the wisdom to carry out your plans. Give Avery the strength and courage to protect the kids and the vision to see the danger that comes our way. Amen."

****

Chloë heard a knock on the bedroom door and called out, "Come in." She giggled as Michael's long hair appeared around the door before his face. "Come on in Michael. Jeepers, your hair is almost longer than mine."

Michael, still dressed in his clothes from the night before, entered the room. "Hey, Chloë. Got a minute?" She patted the spot on the bed beside her, "Of course, just beginning the ritual of getting ready." He smiled at her and teased, "You're kidding right? It's 8:00 a.m. and we don't leave the hotel for another seven hours at least." She laughed right back at him, "You see how long this hair is, right? It takes me almost two hours to blow-dry and style it. Then I have to do my makeup. Have I mentioned my clothes?"

Michael was getting a kick out of this, she could tell, and he asked her, "Why bother? You spend another two hours in hair and makeup before the concert at the venue anyway?" She slapped him playfully across the shoulder as she replied, "That's beside the point. Never mind, it's a girl thing, okay. You think I'm bad; you should put a timer on Brittany. Now she needs mega prep time!" The two of them laughed, a rare moment for the two of them in a very long time.

Michael suddenly became solemn, his voice lowered as he spoke next, "I know it's likely we're not going to be alive much longer, but whatever happens to us Chloë, I just want you to know that I'm proud of you. I'm proud to call you my sister. No matter how terrible we came onto this earth, at least the Master cannot take that away from us. I..I love you, Chloë."

Tears surfaced and then spilled over as Chloë reacted to what he had just said, "Oh, Michael. I love you to!" The two of them held each other for a minute, thoughts of being brother and sister, always known but never spoken of, bonded them even closer. Finally, Chloë spoke, "Listen, Michael, we cannot give up hope that we will find a way out of this. He has a control over us, I cannot deny that, but we also have the blood of the Lord flowing through our veins. That is what keeps me strong, Michael. Focus on that, it will be enough, I promise."

Brittany's blood curdling scream froze them both.

****

"You're aging Father, aren't you?"

Father O'Sullivan accepted the morning tea from Ann and sat back down on the chair across from hers, "Is it that obvious?"

"Not obvious, Father, just noticeable. What is happening to you, Father? Please tell me."

He was quiet as he replied, and she barely made out his reply, "The Lord works in mysterious ways, my dear."

"You never slept last night, did you Father? I heard you downstairs in the kitchen. The burden you carry, Father, must be enormous. Why has the Lord chosen you for this burden? Why has He chosen me to give birth to Satan's child? Why Vasallus? What is Michael's and the other kids' roles to play in all of this. Please tell me there is something greater for Michael and the others, that it's not just to poison the minds of the world to prep them for Satan's final plans. Please tell me there is a greater purpose for my son." She placed the tea on the plate on her lap and held her hand up to her face, as she fought back the tears.

Thomas took the teacup from her lap before it fell to the floor, took her hand in his and allowed the flow of Christ's love reach deep inside of her before he replied, "I have been chosen by Him to lead His fight on earth against the demon, Lucifer. You have many questions, Ann. I understand that and my heart aches for what the Demon has done to you and your family. The Lord also understands your pain but like me, you have also been chosen by Him. He needs you to continue to be strong for your son and for Him. These are very dangerous times, Ann. He will call upon your sacrifice soon, Ann. Will you be ready?"

She studied him for a long moment, His love flowing through her until she realized what he had just asked her. Now she understood her purpose. It was clear. It did not frighten her, it made her stronger. She also knew that she had always known this, somehow, and now the Lord was speaking to her directly.

She gripped Father O'Sullivan's hand firmly before replying, "I understand, Father. I will be ready."

****

Connor was suspended high in the air with Best's hand wrapped around his throat. He was squeezing so hard, Connor's face was turning purple. He was desperately gasping for air.

Chloë screamed, "Stop it! You're killing him!"

Best turned towards her, his face contorted in rage, his demonic voice grated, "Tell me where she is! Tell me or I'll kill him!"

Brittany, Michael and Juan stood beside Chloë, all of them

frozen in fear. Chloë responded, "Who are you talking about, Master! Please Master, don't kill him!"

Best roared like a wild beast, his rage out of control. They all watched in horror as he drove Connor straight back into the wall, pieces of the broken wall falling to the floor. Connor screamed in pain. Chloë had never seen him rage against them like this. They only had seconds before Connor would be dead, "Who are you looking for Master? Bentley? Mrs. Lockwood?" She and the others watched in horror as Best suddenly dropped Connor to the floor then turned towards them. Chloë could see the changes in his earthly body. He was coming apart; his face was cracking all over, and pieces threatened to fall off. What is happening, she thought? Connor writhed on the floor, as his lungs fought to let air in. The demonic eyes of Best were fiery red as he moved towards her. When he was so close to her they almost touched. He stormed down onto her, "Where is Elizabeth? Who took her? Who saved her? Tell me or I'll kill all of you!"

Then she knew. He had lost her. She was missing from Hell and that meant only one thing. She had been saved. The realization that God had entered the realm of Satan's Hell and saved Elizabeth shook her to the core of her very soul. The sudden joy she felt for Elizabeth, her sister, caused her to teeter back on her heels, almost falling backwards. It was a joy she had not felt since they were saved at the mansion by the angel with the sword. She was so overjoyed, she never even felt Best's vise-grip hands wrapped around her throat.

There was hope for all of them. She felt it in every fiber in her body. Then a voice brought her back to the now.

"Take your hands off of her Best!"

He loosened his grip on her throat as he wheeled around at the sound of Avery's voice, "You!"

Chloë could see Avery and Bentley were now standing ten feet away. Both of them were still in their lounge clothes, Avery's white hair was still tussled. He commanded Best again, "Move away from her, Best, or I swear I'll kill you with my bare hands!" The command from Avery was almost comical to Best, and his rage seemed to have been replaced by amusement. "You're kidding me, right? Look at the two of you. Did you come over here to start a pillow fight?" Laughter escaped Best's throat like a hellish cackle. His out of control rage had now been replaced by a calm demeanor as he listened to Avery shout, "Did you forget what tonight Best is? Killing these kids would have spoiled your biggest night, your biggest stage. Remember the world is watching you. You're their hero now, remember? You saved humankind from a sure thing apocalyptic fireball. I'm sure the youth of London are tearing apart the city in their allegiance to you right now. Do you want to mess with that by killing the kids and ruining the big stage?"

Chloë and the others watched the standoff between Avery and Best with amazement. Best could have shredded Avery in a split second but he didn't. Best realized he was right and he threw his head back in a hearty and demonic laugh when he spat, "How could I have been so absent minded? Avery and Bentley, please accept my most humble apologies. Please carry on with your day and your pre-concert preparations." He turned to the four of them and then to Connor and stated, "Make this concert tonight your best ever. I'll be watching!"

They watched as Best turned and headed for the door, stopped in front of the defiant Avery, leaned in close and said, "You're lucky this time, Johnson. Now get them ready!" He looked over at Bentley and sneered, "I must say, Ms. Paxton, I now know why Johnson is so smitten with you. To look like you do first thing in the morning, well let's just say, he's a lucky guy!"

Avery was about to say something, when Bentley hissed, "Go to Hell, Best!"

Best chuckled as he made his way to the hotel room door, opened it, then turned before he stepped out, "I think I'll do that, Bentley!"

****

The two of them were back in their room after they had spent some time with the kids. They were now joined by Ann

381

and Father O'Sullivan. The morning's events were explained, leaving the two of them shocked. Thomas looked at Avery and said, "I could say that was very foolish to approach Best in that state, but it turned out to be the right thing to do and very brave. You saved those kids lives, Avery.

Bentley added, "The kids are more determined than ever to perform. She looked over at Avery, then back at Thomas and Ann. "I think we should wait to tell the kids about these songs. Tonight is too dangerous. Best is completely out of control. You heard him in that room, Avery, he said he'll be there tonight. If these kids sing these songs, we are as good as killing them ourselves. He will go ballistic. He was that close to killing Connor and Chloë in their room. We just can't risk it."

Avery leaned forward, took Bentley's hand in his to try and reassure her, "I think you might be right, sweetheart. It is too dangerous. Father, do you agree?"

They watched as Father O'Sullivan rose from his seat and walked towards the window, deep in thought. He closed his eyes and said a prayer, in silence but yet obvious to the others that he was praying. They waited in the awkward silence until he finally opened his eyes and spoke, still facing out the window, "We have precious little time, I'm afraid. The Lord's patience is coming to an end. We must begin final preparations."

Avery and Bentley were well aware of the beliefs of SOSL and the decades of long work Father O'Sullivan has dedicated to the Vatican's theory. Avery looked into Father O'Sulivan's mesmerizing eyes, causing him to briefly hesitate before asking, "Father, with all due respect, but we must protect these kids. If they perform those songs tonight, they are as good as dead. I will not allow that to happen. There will be another show in a few weeks in Tokyo they can perform those songs, just not now, not after what happened this morning. Best is coming apart, I could see it in his eyes and hear it in his voice. He will be there tonight."

Thomas turned away from the window and took a few steps towards them, "We don't have a few weeks, Avery. The world doesn't have a few weeks. The demise of life as we know it is upon us." Bentley whispered, "I don't understand, Father. What do you mean?"

"What I mean Bentley is, very soon, God will unleash his fury on human beings, ending all life as we know. There will be a reset on earth, Bentley. It has been written and cannot be prevented. It is God's word."

She was in disbelief, her eyes tearing, turned towards Avery, then at Ann and replied, "Please don't tell me, God, that after all we have done to stop Best and protect those kids, it was all for naught? God will kill us all anyway? I'm sorry Father, but I don't see a benevolent God in any of this. What happened to His mercy? His love?" Ann immediately came to her side and took both of her hands in hers and whispered to her, "It will be okay, Bentley. We will survive in a much better place. It is impossible to understand, but your faith is now being challenged by the Demon in Best. The strong and the faithful can and will survive what lies ahead. That includes you and Avery. Our job is to protect the kids of Vasallus from the clutches of the Beast, when that time arrives for us to be with Him."

Father O'Sullivan stepped in front of the three of them and said, "I have a plan. The kids will defy the Beast tonight and sing their hearts out for the Lord. They will sing for the salvation of humankind. Now we have lots to do before the concert so we need to get busy. The kids will not know about the songs until right before the performance. They do not need to prep or rehearse these songs. Is that correct Avery?"

Avery thought about it for half of a second before replying, "No they do not. They can play anything we put in front of them, especially these songs. What is the plan, Father?"

The two of them sat in stunned silence over the next hour as they listened to Father O'Sullivan and Ann lay out the plans for the greatest and most dangerous night of Vasallus's lives and theirs.

Chapter 37

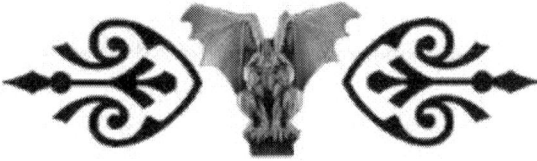

The Metropolitan Police Service in London was about as ready as a police force could be for what was in store the day of the Vasallus concert: full scale violence, rioting and mayhem. They were bolstered by regiments from the U.K. Armed Forces giving them an overwhelming presence in and around the city. Every borough in the city had a police barricade setup. Command posts were placed in strategic locations throughout the city that would coordinate the movement of personnel into other areas when violence broke out. Like the other cities on this tour, London was no different and opted not to cancel the concert. Backlash was more feared than pre-concert violence. The city was well schooled when it came to large scale security planning. They have been targets of major terrorist attacks, soccer riots and home to the most protected Royal Family in the world.

Pockets of violence related to the legions of Vasallus followers broke out earlier in the week and none bigger than the school shooting in the affluent neighborhood of Kensington. It was here that a high school student opened fire killing thirteen students, two teachers and two administrative staff before killing himself. He left behind a manifesto of sorts, naming students in the school as unworthy of Vasallus's loyalty due to their unwavering support of their school and teachers. A killing spree of this magnitude would have shocked the world months earlier, but it was happening with such regularity around the world that citizens everywhere had begun to accept this type of behavior as normal.

The youth were hitting the streets the afternoon before the concert and looking for trouble in a show of defiance to please the ones they worshiped, Vasallus. The dark and very angry spirit of

Satan blew through the swelling crowds beginning to gather in neighborhoods throughout the city. They marched on the streets with intentions of mayhem and violence, but the mist that flowed over and through their bodies ensured they only thought of murder and extreme violence. The Demon, still angered over the loss of Elizabeth and Patrick, would ensure London felt his wrath. Soon police barricades became outmatched and overwhelmed as massive mobs descended upon them. Police officers were being beaten by the angry mobs, and it did not take long for orders from above that they should begin using lethal force, if necessary. Police started with tear gas, then water cannons to move the crowds back, but they were unsuccessful in fracturing the mobs and dispersing them. Instead, it only angered them more and caused them to fight back even more violently. Everything changed when a youth slipped through the crowds of a large mob fighting with their fists against the sticks of the police on Baker Street in the Marylebone neighborhood. He came close enough to stick a snub nose .38 revolver into the face of young policeman, involved in his very first riot control assignment, and he proceeded to blow a hole in the middle of the officer's face. The gunshot shocked everyone around the fallen officer including the rioters. The police reacted with overwhelming force. Tactical squads of the Metropolitan police moved in with armored cars and opened fire on the crowds, killing dozens with high caliber ammunition usually reserved for the battlefield. The streets of London had now become a battlefield.

Satan moved like the wind, quickly and with direction to the other riots breaking out all over the city, filling the darkened souls of the young rioters with the false sense they were in an actual war. Soon the whole city was under siege.

The Prime Minister and the Mayor of London conferred and of course were completely unaware of the dark spirit that had swirled in their offices, tricking them into thinking everything was under control. So they decided to allow the

Vasallus concert to continue. The Metropolitan Police Commissioner had assured the politicians the riots would be under control within a few hours. After all they were just a bunch of kids acting like it was Halloween night, he told them. The Commissioner increased the security zone around Wembley and ordered another regiment from the armed forces to further strengthen the zone.

****

It was time to leave the Claridge for Wembley and Bentley left the room to round up the kids, while Avery phoned their head of security to bring the limousine to the loading zone in the basement of the famed hotel. The Claridge frequently hosted VIP's and knew how to ensure their privacy and security was never compromised. He instructed security that the seven of them would be travelling together in one limo. The city was under attack from within, and he did not want to risk any of them being separated. Bentley returned a few minutes later.

"They will be over in twenty minutes. Brittany is on her fifth outfit and counting. Chloë assured me she will have her dressed and over here in twenty. Those girls are so cute sometimes." She smiled as she thought of Brittany undecided on what to wear. The uncertainity of the evening and the fear that accompanied it stepped aside in her mind as she giggled to herself, envisioning Chloë prodding Brittany to hurry.

Avery was about to respond when his cell phone rang. Answering it, he turned to Bentley and silently mouthed, "Ann." After a few minutes he hung up the phone and immediately called his security, "James. Cancel the limo. We're going to Wembley in Ann Lockwood's car. All of us. Have the team up here in the room to escort us through the lobby to her car. When she arrives out front, I will let you know to send them up. Have your cars out front to escort the Lockwood limo to Wembley. Thanks."

Avery looked at Bentley after he hung up and stated, "Ann thought it would be a good idea for all of us to be together. Father O'Sullivan is still with her and insisted. He needs to speak with us, while the kids are getting ready at the stadium."

****

The shock of the sudden appearance of the Vasallus entourage being hustled through the lobby of the Claridge and out onto the street and into a waiting limousine happened so fast, the stunned paparazzi and media assembled in the hotel, poured out onto the sidewalk to shoot some lucrative photos. They never had a chance. A few of the paparazzi took off in front of the cars to follow, but they were quickly swallowed up in the heavy downtown London traffic. The stretch limo had two sections with large opposing benches in each section. The five members of Vasallus easily fit in the one section, while Ann, Father O'Sullivan, Avery and Bentley took up the second section. Ann's head of security rode up front along with her driver. Bentley sat across from Ann and admired how beautiful she looked in her shimmering gold sparkling dress, "Ann, you look incredible." She smiled back and replied, "I clean up pretty good, don't I. I can say the same about you, Bentley, and you don't even get ready for a few hours yet."

They made small talk for the rest of the short drive to the stadium, and upon arrival the driver knew the exact VIP entrance into Wembley. Thomas shook his head at the number of police and army soldiers ringing the perimeter around the massive stadium, "Is it like this at all of the performances, Avery?" Avery turned away from the glass windows and answered, "Maybe not to this exact extent but pretty close, Father. I can't imagine what's going to happen when they perform their song list tonight. The 90,000 plus fans could tear the place down in protest." Thomas paused before asking, "Do they know yet if they will be performing these songs?"

"Not yet, but they will soon enough. Do you think Best will make an appearance tonight?"

Thomas hesitated then replied, "No. He will not risk a confrontation with Him now. He will have that time, just not tonight."

As they pulled into the underground parkade in an obscure part of the stadium, Avery thought of what the priest had just said, referring to Him. Was he referring to himself? Heavy stuff, he thought as he helped Ann and then Bentley out of the limo.

****

It was an hour before Vasallus would take the stage and the place was already jammed to capacity. Vasallus never had a warm-up band perform prior to their entrance. No one in the stadium wanted to hear anyone else and a warm-up band would likely be stormed and beaten. The thunderous clapping and foot stomping in the stands had already begun in anticipation of the start of the concert. It was pandemonium. Thousands of police and armed forces around the city were barely keeping control, and inside the stadium it was like a large pot of water slowly coming to a boil.

Avery sent word to the assistants to gather the kids into the lounge. It was time. He gave Bentley a reassuring hug, looked her in the eyes and whispered, "You look gorgeous as usual tonight. I can't wait for the time where everything will be normal, and we can do something as simple as pushing a grocery cart around a market, dressed in sweat pants, a hoodie and you in tight, skimpy jogging shorts." She leaned in close, kissed him deeply and staring into his eyes, replied, "So simple but yet it seems so far away." Then she smiled, gave him a playful punch to his ribs and continued, "How come I have to wear the skimpy shorts? You look pretty good in a pair of tight shorts yourself." He winked, then answered, "I could wear those Speedos' I've been saving for the right occasion!"

"Why don't we come back in a few minutes?"

The two of them turned to see Father O'Sullivan and Ann standing in the entranceway to the lounge. Giggling, Bentley called out, "Busted for too much cheese. Come on in. The kids will be right in."

A second later the door burst open and the five of them filed into the room. Michael led the way, and everyone could see his excitement right away. Ann instantly made her way to him and gave him a big hug and then said, "You are so darned handsome my son. How you keep a straight face on that stage with all of those girls throwing themselves at you!" Connor cut in and quipped, "Excuse me, Mrs. Lockwood. They are throwing themselves at me, not your son. Sorry Michael!" The two of them laughed and high fived.

Brittany and Chloë laughed and joined in, "This is Michael's house, Connor. Tonight the girls are here to see their favorite Brit. Cheesy tattoo included!" The two girls high fived when Juan kept it going, "Trust me Brittany and Chloë when I say, the British girls will not be able to resist the Latino abs!" He followed it up by flashing his trademark defined abs. The antics even had Thomas breaking out in laughter. It was a great moment for all of them, but Avery had to move things forward when he cut in and called for everyone's attention.

"Okay everyone, I need your attention. It's almost show time so listen up. Tonight is a very special night in your history as a band for many reasons. It doesn't get any bigger than right here in London. You are loved and adored here probably more than any other city. Like Chloë in Dublin, this is Michael's night. It is also the first show without Patrick. There is a drummer up to speed that will take his place, but expect it to be looser than what you are used to with Patrick. The kid on the drum kit will be doing his best; he is very talented, but he is not Patrick. Now I didn't intend to throw a wet blanket over the high spirits in this room, but we have a very special surprise for you tonight. I am going to have Bentley take it from here."

Surprised, Bentley stepped forward, smiling at Avery as he brushed past her and took her seat. "All of you know how gifted Patrick was as a songwriter. Tonight we have a gift for you from him. In the last few seconds before Patrick passed, he asked Father O'Sullivan to get this collection of songs to Avery so you could perform them tonight." The room had fallen completely quiet, the roar of the distant crowd barely audible over everyone's focus on Bentley. She continued, her emotions wavering as she spoke, "He called them his 'Songs for Survival'. They are an incredible and beautifully written collection of songs that are not just major hit material like everything he has written for you, but these have been written to inspire hope, to end the violence and mayhem that his previous songs you have performed have caused around the world. He wants Vasallus to change the world, but this time he wants you to save the world. So Avery?"

Avery stood up, kissed Bentley on the cheek as he took over from her, "Patrick did some very evil things, and we all know that. These songs are his way of saying he is sorry for what he has done and for what he has written. In front of your Master, he defied him and gave his life to the Lord. That is the most courageous thing he could have done, but before he died he found the strength and courage to pass these songs onto Father O'Sullivan. I ask you. Will you forego what you have ever known and perform these songs tonight? It is up to you. It will be very dangerous so the decision to perform them in front of this crowd and worldwide television audience is completely up to you. I don't know what Best will do, but he will come after you, after all of us. Are you prepared for that? Bentley, Ann, myself and Father O'Sullivan will be here right alongside you for whatever comes our way. We will face it together." He stood back and was silent while the kids sat stunned, quiet. Chloë broke the silence when she stood up; her eyes filled with tears and declared, "I would be honored to sing these songs. I have waited so long for this." Brittany spoke up as she stood next to Chloë and added, "I have dreamed of singing these kinds of songs since we became a band. Let's do it." Connor and then Juan added, "Let's do this for Patrick. Let's sing these 'Songs for Survival'. I don't care if it puts me in danger."

The kids then began to gather together, their excitement uncontainable. Avery handed out the song sheets for the song lineup. What would take months of rehearsal to perform these songs together as a group, would take Vasallus ten minutes. The first time they would ever play these songs would be live on stage in less than an hour in front of over 90,000 people and millions more on pay-per-view television.

Ann focused her gaze on Father O'Sullivan. Getting the kids out of this stadium alive after their performance and out of reach from the raging Demon had both of them searching their souls if they were doing the right thing.

****

Vasallus took the stage with a thunderous applause that threatened to collapse Wembley. The fans were going out of their minds as their heroes hit the stage. When Michael finally came on stage after the other four, it was pure pandemonium. Giant monitor screens on both sides of the stage flashed video backdrops of the Union Jack flag then collapsed onto the Union Jack tattoo on Michael's arm, drawing deafening cheers and applause. Michael started the show off by standing front and center with his lead guitar at the microphone and launched the first song off of the 'Songs for Survival' collection that subdued the huge crowd momentarily as they struggled to register the song in their minds. That quickly changed as they realized Vasallus were starting the show off with new material from a new album not yet released which electrified them even more. The song was a U2 type anthem song, but instead of a shout out to defy, the lyrics screamed compliance and cooperation. Michael's guitar hooks were so catchy; they instantly brought thousands out of their seats. All five stepped towards their microphones and shouted the lyrics with the giant screens behind them serving as video backdrops that reinforced the song's message of hope and redemption. When the song ended, the applause was mixed as it was clear to Avery and Bentley that the unexpected introduction to the show had not resonated with everyone.

The band continued with two more songs led by Connor and Juan that seemed to be garnering more support from the crowd. The songs were incredible, but the fans were here to have their defiant beliefs reinforced by Vasallus and instead were being told by these new songs to embrace and comply, to build and strengthen society. Fans were confused but obviously loved the new sound. The defining moment came when the stage quieted and darkened, then a spotlight fell upon Michael, alone, sitting on a stool at the front of the stage, an acoustic guitar on his lap. Before he sang he spoke to the crowd in a muted but controlled voice.

"Thank you London for embracing Vasallus and allowing us to debut our new songs. I love this city, I love this country. It is where I was born." A thunderous roar erupted throughout the stadium as Michael recognized his roots. "The world is on the brink of war. Our city surrounding this stadium is teeming with violence. Youth everywhere have had enough and are fighting back against authority and society's rules." Once again, deafening applause cascaded down from every rafter and section of the stadium. Michael continued, "Vasallus has, through our music, helped fuel this message of defiance. The five of us are the faces of this movement."

The dark stage lit up another stool. Chloë sat with a microphone, the lights bouncing off of the sequins of her silver skirt and spoke, "Vasallus will no longer sing songs of hopelessness, defiance, or oppression by our governments." The huge crowd had become as quiet as a school classroom being scolded by the principal. A third spotlight silhouetted Juan to the right of Michael who picked up from Chloë, "In order for this world to survive and to flourish we must have our youth leading the way. We are the future, and it is up to us to support the good things our governments are doing to better this world, not tear them down." The next spotlight shone down on top of Brittany, the giant screens behind her flashing her face as she held up the microphone and spoke, "We ask that you embrace our new music and the message we are trying to project. It will take a tremendous amount of hard work to change the world for the better, but it begins right here, tonight." The first chords of Michael's acoustic guitar began to play through their words as the spotlight lit up Connor at the opposite side of the stage from Brittany, beside Juan. "We ask our fans around the world to do something good today, tomorrow and every day from here on in. If we don't, then this world will not survive. Our Lord has blessed all of us with a gift to love. Join Vasallus to help us spread the message of love."

That was it. The words spoken by Connor ignited something in the crowd. It was like they have been waiting forever for Vasallus to speak and sing to them in this way. A wave of applause and cheers like nothing they have ever heard before spread around the stadium. In unison, 90,000 plus fans stomped their feet, hollered and cheered their support. It was an incredible sight as the stage lit up and all five members of Vasallus stepped forward to a microphone stand with Michael speaking once again, the crowd quieting instantly, "Our friend and brother, Patrick Benning gave us these gifts of incredible songs of survival before he sadly passed away. To his memory and to the memory of our sister, Elizabeth Leroux, we dedicate the rest of this show." The five of them began singing a beautiful ballad of redemption and hope, the message clear and undeniable. Their voices harmonized exquisitely, each of their voices falling into each other's like a seductive whisper. The ballad continued, delighting the huge crowd with the beautiful lyrics and graceful voices. The realization that Patrick had passed and the recognition of the long forgotten Elizabeth seemed to strengthen their love for Vasallus further.

Unknown to everyone, a mist filled with hope and love blew into the stadium and swirled around the thousands like a silk blanket. The tension, anger and feelings of frustration had been lifted and carried out of the building by a set of invisible hands and replaced with a sense of hope and a willingness to make positive change. People throughout the stadium simultaneously put their arms around each other and moved to the beat of Vasallus. It was an incredible sight.

Avery and Bentley, joined by Father O'Sullivan and Ann, stood marveling at what they were witnessing. The speech at the front of the stage by the kids had not been planned. They did it on their own as if they had been planning it for weeks. They spoke from their hearts, and it showed. They were all witnessing the miracle of God's love shining down on Vasallus and the thousands of fans in the stadium, and it left them so moved they never wanted it to stop.

Father O'Sullivan braced his soul for what was coming

their way. As the others swayed to the beat of the music, he closed his eyes in prayer. He prayed for the strength to stand up to the evil that was on its way this very minute.

Chapter 38

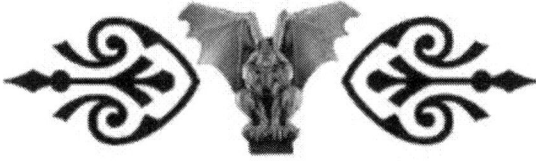

President Kipshaw, along with the First Lady and his daughter, sat in the comfort of the living room in the White House. They were sipping hot cider when a knock on the door down the hallway grabbed their attention. Alexis jumped up, "I'll get it. It will be for Dad anyway, but I'm going to tell whoever it is that it's family night. Not to be disturbed!" They watched her bound towards the hallway without waiting for their response. Stanley marveled at how well and how fast she was recovering from her demonic possession. His wife, Leah, and he barely spoke about it anymore, the terrible memories serving no purpose to continually dredge up. Their daughter was healthy and had no memory of that time so they let those terrifying times remain in the past. The world was close to an all-out war, and the fact the three of them were able to sit together as a family was a miracle in itself. The knock on the door would likely end that and pull him back into the latest crisis.

The two of them reacted to the giggles coming from their daughter down the hallway. Must be his Chief of Staff, Adam Rinker. He was the only one who could elicit laughs from Alexis. When the two of them came around the corner and into the living room, Stan just shook his head, "I guess enjoying some time with my family was too much to ask for a father. What's up now, Adam?"

It was his daughter that answered, "Dad we have to turn on the TV. Vasallus are performing live in London. Something is going on!" He turned towards Adam, annoyed that he would get his daughter excited about that band. "Sweetheart, I have already told you. You are not allowed to watch or listen to their music. It is forbidden. Adam, you know this, why would you bring this up?"

Adam, his face etched in excitement, replied, "Mr. President, turn on the TV. You have to see this. It is a miracle. All of you need to see this." Reluctantly he picked up the TV remote but before he did, he spoke to his daughter, "I'm sorry honey but I have to ask you to go to your room. I will not allow you to see this." His daughter instantly protested, but she was cut off by her mother, "Stan, please. Adam would not expose Alexis to anything if it wasn't important."

He studied her for a few seconds and realized she would not back down, so he pushed the button on the remote and turned it to the channel Adam had instructed. The concert at Wembley was packed to the rafters with fans but was as quiet as a hospital ward. Very strange. The five kids of Vasallus were all sitting on stools in front of the stage and talking. He caught words from the five members that astonished him. They were preaching about hope, acceptance and embracing their governments and authority. It was a complete 360 degree turn from anything they had spoken or sung about in the past. He looked down at his daughter and could see she was completely transfixed on their words. It was an unbelievable scene. Then he heard words that floored him. The good looking blond boy at the end of the stage, Connor Asker, he remembered, spoke the words of God's love. He was asking the youth of the world to do something good. To spread God's love. He then watched as they launched into a ballad singing the praises of love and acceptance. Sitting in his chair, watching and listening to this from the other side of the world with his daughter who had been exposed to so much evil was unbelievable. The four of them sat, transfixed on the screen of their TV. It was Alexis who broke their silence, "It is so beautiful!" Then she said something that shocked him, his wife and Adam, "Praise Jesus! Praise the Lord!"

****

Wembley Stadium had turned into a revival of sorts, the

inconceivably great music of Vasallus with its positive and moving message had the crowd dancing in the aisles, their arms raised to the sky in jubilation. It was like the tens of thousands of fans had been given some happy drug and they couldn't get enough. The songs and the lyrics were cutting a direct path to their hearts, filling their souls with hope. A growl from behind them that drowned out the music from the stage made them turn in fear. What all of them knew would be inevitable, yet had been lost in the moment of what was occurring on the stage had arrived in the form of a raging earthly persona of Robert Best. They watched as Best's body tried to handle the rage that was coursing through its veins. The Beast and all of his rage was about to explode.

"How dare you defy me with this treason music!"

Father O'Sullivan acted swiftly, moving towards the Demon, his hand clutching a crucifix and declared, "In the name of the Father, the Son and the Holy Ghost, I command you off of this stage and far away from this place." Best, his face threatening to fall apart, laughed, then shouted, "Shut up, O'Sullivan." He turned and slugged Father O'Sullivan hard with a closed fist in the jaw, sending him crashing to the floor. Avery reacted in horror, "Leave him alone, you coward. Can't you see what is happening here, Best. The kids are defying you. Can you hear them? You're losing them, Best."

Best attacked Avery, his fist quickly finding the middle of his face, exploding it in a splash of blood that buckled him over. Then he followed it with a devastating knee to his head, sending him sprawling to the floor of the stage. Dazed and hurt, he could hear Bentley scream, "Leave him alone! She shocked everyone when she slapped Best hard across his face, causing a large piece of his cheek bone to come dislodged, leaving his face partially missing. Then a ghoulish looking Best spat, "Nice try, bitch." He backhanded Bentley across the side of the face, sending her flying backwards. Seeing her smacked hard, Avery roared to life and launched himself at Best, the two of them crashing into a set of stacked sound equipment. Avery rolled hard as they fell against the equipment and found himself on top of Best. His mind clicked into a blind rage, and he furiously pounded Best's partially missing face with his fists. With every blow, he could hear Bests facial bones snap and more pieces of his flesh fly away. He couldn't stop. Not until Best was dead. His anger over all of the pain and suffering Best has caused fuelled his rage and he continued to hammer away at his face. The laughter coming from the pulverized Best made him sick and he wailed again and again. Then he heard a voice power through his racing mind. It was Father O'Sullivan.

"Avery that is enough. No more. You cannot kill him with your fists." His fists were covered in Best's blood and he was about to pummel Best again when Father O'Sullivan held his arm and repeated, "No more, Avery." With surprising strength he pulled him off of Best then looked him square in the eyes and said, "We must let him go. There will be another time, Avery. Now is not that time. We must get the kids out of here and to safety. He is here for them, not us. Come, the kids are finishing up. Ann is waiting with a helicopter to take all of us out of here and away from Best."

Avery looked down at Best and was not surprised to see he had disappeared. He looked at Bentley, her tears streaming down her cheeks. He reached out and pulled her close, wiping the tears from her face as he did. Then he heard Father O'Sullivan once more. "Both of you, come at once." Avery did not acknowledge the priest. He just held onto Bentley, unwilling to let her go. He was tired. He was tired of living in constant fear and worry with the burden of Vasallus keeping them alive and together just so their music could further poison people's minds. He only wanted to be back in Los Angeles, alone with Bentley, away from all of this. Just the two of them. Starting a family of their own. Then he felt Bentley's soft touch on his cheek, then her voice, "Sweetheart, look! It is a miracle from God!"

He looked down into her eyes, could see them filled with hope and turned towards the sound of Father O'Sullivan's voice. Bentley was right, it was a miracle. He couldn't believe what he was seeing. Vasallus were just finishing up the performance to the disappointment of the fans who screamed for more. He knew there would be no encore performance tonight. Best was coming for them, and their death would be unavoidable if they did not get them to safety. Waiting for them at the back of the stage, cast in a brilliant light were seven large and magnificent soldiers, angels, their swords at their sides. They were here to escort the kids to safety!

****

He should have killed Johnson, but he had a much more ambitious demise planned for him. He needed to get to Vasallus and end the treacherous garbage they were extoling on the stage. Tens of thousands of Vasallus fans and millions more around the world would watch live on TV their brutal death. Somehow they had turned to Him. It was that pathetic priest and the slut Lockwood. Killing them along with the kids was long overdue. He should have killed the priest years ago. Letting him live only strengthened Him in him. He underestimated the priest's role in His plan. Another mistake. Again. He could no longer afford any more mistakes. He felt the presence of God all around him. His mist blew through the stadium, instilling His goodness in everyone. The music had opened their hearts to Him. The thoughts of what Vasallus had done was making him crazy with fury. It was over. He had taken it as far as he could. He could not afford for this message of hope and acceptance to get out. He had to contain it. Their death on stage would accomplish this. He was perched like a crouching gargoyle on top of the scaffolding holding the array of lights directly above the stage.

What he saw next made him scream in rage. The back of the stage was cast in a bright light, lined with His angels.

****

What happened next was like a dream playing out. Father O'Sullivan, with the precision of an experienced stage manager, quickly ushered the kids off of the back of the stage, past the gauntlet of angels and out to the waiting executive helicopter. Avery and Bentley waited for Michael, the last of the kids to make his way off of the stage and followed quickly behind. They reached the helicopter and were greeted by Ann with a warm hug as she helped the kids get quickly into the chopper.

"We don't have much time. The chopper will take us to Biggin Hill Airport and from there we will take my jet to Rome." Avery turned to help Father O'Sullivan assist Bentley to her seat. He was quickly followed by Ann and the two of them found their seats. Avery looked around the inside of the helicopter. It was luxurious beyond compare and had seating for sixteen. The kids were strapped in, their faces etched in worry and the unknown. One minute they were on a stage in front of over 90,000 screaming fans and the next minute they were scrambling for their lives. He felt his hand being squeezed by Bentley who followed it up with a gasp, "Look!"

All of them stared out the windows in wonder as the bright soldiers of God surrounded the helicopter as its engines roared to life. The soldiers gripped their massive swords with both hands as they scanned the distance between the stadium and the heli-pad. A scream from Brittany pierced through the chopper's engines, "Look. It's the Master. He's coming for us! What are we going to do!"

They all followed her outstretched hand towards the top rung of the upper level of the stadium and could see Best perched, ready to launch himself at the helicopter. There was no resemblance of a human in him. He was completely morphed into a ghastly looking beast. Then he stood up on the edge of the stadium, at least seventy five feet in the air. They all watched in horror as Best stretched himself upwards to the sky, screamed in a rage then dropped off the edge and fell the distance to the ground below. He hit the ground with a thud and then quickly stood up and began to walk towards the chopper. Chloë and Brittany screamed and clutched each other as everyone watched Best advance towards them through the small windows. The soldiers braced for the attack by crouching into a defensive posture, their swords defiantly out in front of them.

Ann broke through the escalating chaos when she turned to the pilots at the front of the chopper and yelled, "Get us out of here! Now!"

****

The chopper raced across the London skyline towards Biggin Hill when Chloë shouted, "Father O'Sullivan! Where is Father O'Sullivan!" Panicking she began to take her seat belt off thinking there was a secret compartment that he would be hiding in. Ann took her belt off and knelt in front of Chloë, took her hands in hers and spoke loud enough to be heard over the hum of the chopper's engines, "Sweetheart, Father O'Sullivan had to stay." Chloë looked at her, staring into her eyes before she replied, "He will be killed. Best will kill him. We must go back, Ann. We must!"

Ann continued, "Father O'Sullivan will be okay, I promise. He had to stay, Chloë, to help the Lord's angels repel Best, and to ensure we got to safety. We will see him soon enough. In Rome. You will see him there." Ann reached up and embraced Chloë; the two of them hugged each other tightly, both of them understanding it was unlikely they would ever see Father O'Sullivan alive again."

****

The Lockwood private jet touched down in Rome three hours after they lifted off from Wembley Stadium. The kids had sat in silence the entire flight to Rome. They had to have been exhausted the three of them observed on the flight over. Ann had explained to both him and Bentley that Father O'Sullivan had arranged for a car to take them directly to the Vatican upon their arrival. The plane came to a stop at a secluded spot in the executive hangars of Fiumicino Airport. There were two long and black Vatican limousines waiting for them. The drivers looked like Secret Service agents Bentley mentioned to Ann as they were all filing off of the plane when Ann replied, "You're close, Bentley. They are part of the Vatican secret police. Their job is to protect the Pope and any VIP's such as Heads of State that visit. I guess we qualify as a head of state!" It was a light moment, and it helped ratchet down the tension hanging over them all like a blanket. Bentley smiled and replied, "Where will they take us?"

The kids climbed into one of the cars, and the three of them stepped into the second limo. Once inside the car, Ann looked at them and stated, "We are going to the Vatican where we will be escorted to the offices of SOSL, the secret department that Father O'Sullivan was a part of in the Vatican that I'm sure has been explained to you. It is here we will wait until, hopefully, Father O'Sullivan returns. We will be safe in the Vatican. Best cannot reach the kids there."

They were interrupted by Avery's cell phone ringing in his pocket. Startled by the sudden call, Avery looked at the caller I.D. and seeing it was the office number of his record company, Alive Records he decided to answer it. He whispered to Bentley and Ann that it was the office in Los Angeles. He answered it and the tortured voice on the other end sent a bolt of fear right through him.

The terrifying cries of his longtime assistant and now the president of Alive Records, Jenn Steinert echoed through the phone. "Avery. Avery, please help me. Dear God, please help me. He..he is doing terrible things." Avery listened in shock as Jenn's voice faded into the background and then replaced by the guttural and demonic voice of Best, "Avery, my man. Off to the big house, are you? You think you and your bitch girlfriend are safe from me there?" Avery cut him off, cutting into his words with a reply that screamed of his hatred, "You fucking touch her Best and I'll rip your head and stuff it up your ass. Leave her alone you pathetic coward."

"Whoa, big boy. You really need to control your anger, Avery. Listen, hold on for one second please. Your partner wants to speak with you. By the way, I'm a little annoyed with you, Avery. I thought you and I were partners. I find out that this slut is your partner. Not much longer, I'm afraid. Anyway, enough yapping. Here she is. Oops, I didn't mean to break your arm, Ms. Steinert. Excuse me for my enthusiasm. Here is your partner. Tell him that I am his partner and not you."

Avery's body shook with rage as he looked at Bentley and Ann's shocked faces. He helplessly listened to the cries of pain from Jenn as Best tortured her. She cried out over the phone, in terrible pain, her voice clipped as her body struggled with the heinous things Best was doing to her. Ave..A....Oh please God. Let me die." Avery shouted into the phone, "Jenn, I'm sorry. I'm so sorry." He had never felt so helpless. To hear the tortured cries of Jenn on the other end, knowing what Best was likely doing to her made him sick to his stomach. He shouted, "Leave her alone Best. Leave her alone! Please, I'll do whatever you want me to. I'll come back to Los Angeles. Please don't kill her."

There was a silence on the other end as Avery listened for a reply to his pleading. There was nothing, then suddenly a horrible scream filled the earpiece of his cell phone. Jenn was dying. Then Best's voice came back on the line, "Hear that Avery. Now I'm your only partner again. Do you hear me! She's in Hell, Avery. Don't worry partner, because you'll see her soon enough." A hideous roar of laughter erupted through the phone. Before Avery could tell Best that he would be waiting for him in Hell, the phone went dead. The phone dropped out of his hand and onto the floor of the car. He found himself losing complete control. He fell towards the outstretched arms of Bentley. His body no longer shook with rage. It was replaced by sobs of sorrow. Months of dealing with fear and the unknown combined with the tragic death of Jenn took him down. He barely heard Bentley's encouraging words to let it out. That is exactly what he did. He even remembered exactly the last time he cried. It was grade six. A long time ago.

He heard himself asking God when it would stop. When would the death stop?

Chapter 39

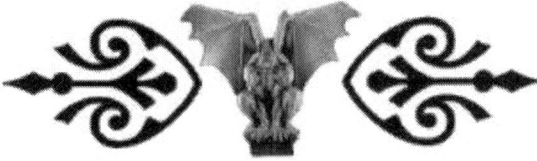

The shock wave from the London performance by Vasallus spread like a tsunami around the world. The result was a state of confusion by the world's youth. They didn't know if they should take a step back and reconsider their feelings about society and embrace what Vasallus preached from the stage through their new music or push back even harder. The media outlets were all over the story. Twitter was experiencing record activity as youth let it be known their displeasure at Vasallus's abandonment of their fans, while others supported their new found message of hope as long overdue. Facebook, for the first time in its history, crashed. Youth were taking to social media by the tens of millions making their opinions known.

Robert Best sat in his bunker, resting and thinking. He had spent the entire night spreading death, despair and misery all over the world. The events at Wembley Stadium and the treason of Vasallus had left him badly troubled. He knew the youth of the world would quickly jump on the new music. It would spread the message of hope like a fire in a rain starved forest. That can never happen. He had to work quickly. Johnson would make sure the new music got out to the world from wherever the prick was holed out. Killing the Steinert bitch and destroying his record company has him riled up a bit. He laughed thinking about the guilt Johnson would carry on his shoulders as he blamed himself for his partner's death. Didn't matter; he would be dead soon anyway.

He needed to do something huge to distract people's attention away from Vasallus. He could no longer wait for God to swing gigantic club down on top of man's head. He was way too slow with this End of Times thing. Best knew exactly what he would do. He was going to do it anyway, but now it would be sooner than later. He would still track down the treacherous Vasallus and kill the group for its disloyalty to him. They left him no choice. Hell, he thought, he was going to do that also.

****

"Her death is my fault. I should have protected her. I should have warned her," a solemn Avery mused.

"You can't protect everyone, Avery. What happened to Jenn was unavoidable," replied Ann.

"I should have had her here with us. She would have been safe."

Bentley reached for Avery's hand, squeezed it tight, then added, "Honey, she would never have gone along with that. She would never have come. If Best wants to kill someone, he will and he can. That includes all of us. He has kept us alive to ensure Vasallus performed. That's over now, so he'll be coming for us and the kids." The last sentence came out as an ominous whisper. The reality of their predicament now clear.

"You will be safe here. He cannot find you, if he cannot see you in his mind." The voice of Father O'Sullivan made them all turn in shock.

No one was happier to see Father O'Sullivan than Bentley. She rushed towards him and gave him a big hug, "It is so great to see you, Father. I thought I would never see you again."

Avery was astonished at Father O'Sullivan's changed appearance from when they saw him hours earlier. He had aged. The encounter with the Beast had taken its toll. He shook his hand and was relieved to feel his trademark powerful handshake did not diminish. "Father, it's good to see you back here safe. How are you feeling?"

He could see the exhaustion in him, the burden he must carry, but his magnificent blue eyes shone even brighter. His spirit was also bright as he replied, "I feel like I just went fifteen rounds with Muhammad Ali. In his prime!" The humor worked, and it lifted a weight off of everyone's shoulders. "We have lots to talk about. Time is running out. Come with me, all of you. There is someone I want you to meet."

****

Avery was still trying to figure out the accommodations and facilities they were in as they followed Father O'Sullivan down the hallway to what was likely another meeting room. Ann had told the two of them on the flight over from London that she has been to the Vatican on several occasions at the request of Father O'Sullivan. The area of the enormous Vatican they were in was all part of the SOSL project, built in secret over the years. It included small and comfortable dormitory style rooms, at least a dozen that he could count. The kids were occupying five of the rooms. There was a small kitchen, a lounge area and a meeting room that sat twenty around a large oval boardroom table. It is here that he turned and asked, "Please take a seat. There is something I want to discuss, before I introduce you to a very special someone." Avery glanced at Bentley who gave him a "what's this all about look". They watched Ann take a seat as though she has been through this before. The moment had quickly become surreal for Avery. He thought about how close they were to being sucked into the abyss of Hell at any moment; yet, here they were, in a secret boardroom of one of the holiest places on earth, the Vatican. It boggled his mind as he listened to Father O'Sullivan begin.

"It was not that long ago, Avery and Bentley, when you thought this old priest from Ireland that showed up at your hotel in Denver was out of his mind. Yet months later, here we are. You have been through so much, the two of you, as all of us have. Events have happened so fast I don't know where to begin, but these events have put the two of you and the kids of Vasallus in grave danger. I have brought all of you here to Rome, to this place, to protect you. It is here you will remain until it is safe. I hope you understand."

Alarmed, Avery asked, "Father, you cannot expect us to remain here in the Vatican indefinitely like prisoners. I just lost a very dear friend today. I will not sit back and wait for someone else to die."

He was positive he glimpsed the priest's brilliant blue eyes diminish slightly before he responded, "I am sorry to hear about your loss, Avery. Ms. Steinert was a very brave woman." Avery was about to question how he could have possibly known Jenn had just died when Father O'Sullivan continued, "The Beast is enraged from the events at Wembley and the betrayal of Vasallus. He killed her, Avery, to hurt you. He wanted you to feel that horrible loss, to feel what he felt when Vasallus sang those songs and to weaken and make you vulnerable."

Bentley stated, "None of us are safe, Father. The world is not safe. Will we ever be again?"

Father O'Sullivan emphatically replied, "Yes, Bentley. The Lord has not abandoned his people, but there is a reckoning coming that all of us will be held accountable to Him. It is time for you both to know the Truth." Bentley interjected, "The truth, Father? A reckoning? What do you mean?"

"Before the Truth is revealed to you, let me explain the origins of this place, the secret offices of SOSL. It all began almost forty years ago in the tiny Irish village of Bandon when, as a young man of twenty nine years, I had just accepted my vows as a priest and was promptly called to Rome to discover my calling. The Lord had chosen me to prepare His people for what was coming."

Avery caught himself staring into the mesmerizing blueness of the priest's incredible eyes again; a pool of questions lay beyond them, inviting him in deeper to discover the secrets. His mouth moved, words came out that he did not knowingly project; yet they were his words, "Father, your calling was not SOSL, was it? You were chosen forty years ago to lead the fight against the Anti-Christ. SOSL was never His purpose for you. SOSL was created by man, by the Church, to lead you to Him."

He watched as the shimmering eyes cast their gaze towards Ann, who to this point had been quiet, but now spoke,

"Avery, the Truth is being revealed to you. What do you see?"

He stood, an unknown force lifting him up off of the chair where he stood facing Father O'Sullivan. The eyes were windows to the blue sky and beyond. The Truth was coming into focus, visions and words filled his mind. Recognition to His purpose sharpened into a clear message.

Ann's words kept coming, "Avery, as I, He also chose you, long ago, before you were even born. You were chosen, Avery, to protect my son, and the rest of Vasallus, the descendants of His beloved King Tiridates, from the Anti-Christ. Do you see that now, Avery?" He did see as she described. He did not hear Bentley's gasp; he only heard the words of Him, projected silently, yet loudly and clearly through Father O'Sullivan. Emotions he has never experienced in his life rushed to the surface of his mind, sending shivers up and down his spine. He found himself reaching out for Bentley's hand, then the feeling of her hand finding his. He squeezed it as the tears came to the surface, rimmed and then filled the space between his eye and eyelid. No longer able to contain them, the tears spilled over and down his cheeks. He stood in front of Father O'Sullivan, in front of God, the Truth cut into him, causing him to stagger slightly. He felt Bentley move in close beside him, her soft cries reaching his ears, the Truth also revealed to her.

The Lord, the Creator was Father O'Sullivan.

****

Father O'Sullivan waited for Avery and Bentley to recover from what had just been revealed. He knew they would have many questions, but now was not that time. They must move quickly.

"The Demon will wreak havoc on mankind over the days ahead. He must be stopped and I need all of your help. I will confront the Beast in his lair at the Malibu mansion. I need you to accompany me, Avery."

Bentley turned towards Father O'Sullivan, "Father, you are talking about confronting Satan for a final showdown. It will be too dangerous for Avery. He…He is…"

"He is mortal. I understand your fear. I'm sorry, Bentley."

Avery held Bentley, could feel her fear, her body shaking and he whispered, "It will be okay, sweetheart. I am in good company. Father O'Sullivan is right. Best must be stopped now. All of us are in grave danger until he is stopped. I will be back, I promise."

She fought back her tears as she put her hand to the side of his face, "You better, mister. I don't know if I could go on without you, Avery."

"You and Ann keep watch over the kids. Keep them safe."

Father O'Sullivan then spoke to both Ann and Bentley, "Get the new music out on the radio all over the world. Use your contacts in the industry, Bentley, as well as Avery's. Spread the message of hope. The world is ready for this. They will embrace the new music, but it will make Best go mad with rage. You will be safe here as he cannot touch you if you remain inside. No one else in the Vatican knows about this place, so do not go onto the grounds; otherwise security will discover you."

Avery added, "Honey, have the kids Tweet and post on Facebook relentlessly about their new music. Upload YouTube videos of them talking and sharing their message of hope." Father O'Sullivan commented, "Good idea, Avery. The more we can put out there, the faster their message will spread."

Ann replied back, "We can do that. We will be fine. Now you must go. End this."

Another voice called out. It was Chloë. She stood defiantly in the doorway, dressed casually in sweats and a sweater, her long blond hair hanging messily down her shoulder. She wore no makeup. She had been crying. Stepping towards Father O'Sullivan, she asked cautiously, "Father, where are you going?"

Thomas took a step towards her and placed his hand on her shoulder, "I must leave, child. I will be back very soon, I promise."

Her eyes reflected the fear she was feeling, "You're leaving for America, aren't you, Father? You're going to confront him? You must not do that, I beg you. He will kill you Father. I could not bear that.

Thomas reached out and held Chloë in his arms. He looked her in the eyes and smiled, "I will be safe, my dear. Avery will be accompanying me. Best would be making a big mistake underestimating him."

She fought back her tears, "Please Father, I know what is happening here. You're not going to confront a school yard bully. You must not confront him, please. He will kill both of you. This is my entire fault. I should not have accepted his invitation to join Vasallus. You would not be here if I hadn't Father, and you would be safely blessing the lives of the people you love in Balbriggan, instead of here battling him." She fell in his arms, sobbing. After a minute of cries, she suddenly stopped and stood in front of him, her eyes determined when she asked, "Father, you're going to destroy the book, aren't you? Please tell me that is not what you're doing?"

Thomas was shocked. How could she have possibly known about the Covenant? "Chloë, how do you know about the book?"

She hesitated, and then replied, "I have always known about it. I just didn't know the importance of it until recently."

Thomas quickly asked, "What do you mean, Chloë? Please, I need to know everything you know about this book?" She took a few steps back and then slowly walked around the room, deep in thought before turning back towards Father O'Sullivan, "I used to spy on him at the mansion, when he would go into his office at the studio. I would sneak into his office before he arrived and hide in the closet, while the others would head to their rooms or to watch TV. He no doubt thought all us were busy in our rooms or together hanging out."

Thomas was astonished, "You put yourself in grave danger, Chloë. I can't believe you did that?"

"I wanted to know more about him, to try and understand his control over me, over us. I had many terrible dreams, Father, about a dark, dark place. It is here I would see Elizabeth. Actually I could not see her, only hear her. Her desperate cries for help haunted me always. I could not help her. I wanted to know if they were just nightmares or real. I prayed they were real, Father, so I could help her. Give her peace."

"He heard your prayers, Chloë. She is safe and in a very wonderful place. I promise you that."

She broke into a smile that seemed to brighten the darkening atmosphere of the room, "Thank the Lord, Father." He smiled back, and together the two of them brought warmth to the room that everyone felt.

Avery was fascinated at what Chloë was saying. This must have been the book that Beth Showenstein told them about at Sam's funeral. Sam was adamant that we find and destroy the book. He interjected, "Chloë, tell us more about the book. It is important."

She looked at him, as though she had not noticed anyone else in the room besides Father O'Sullivan. "Umm, sure, well, I know he would chant gibberish over and over as he stared at the open book. Then he would turn a page and chant some more. It was very weird, as if he were participating in some sort of ritual." She hesitated, her mind trying to remember something, and then she said, "The room would go dark, then cold, very cold. Then he would change. It terrified me so."

Avery asked, "How would he change, Chloë?"

"You've seen him before, Avery. Both you and Bentley have seen him. When he attacked you in our room when both of you tried to protect us. It's when your hair went white."

He silently cursed himself for asking a question he knew the answer, but he needed to understand Best's ties to this book. He poised to ask another question when Father O'Sullivan stepped in and said, "I think we have discussed this enough. I will share more about this book, Avery, on our flight over the Atlantic. It is time. We must go.

Chloë cried out, "Wait! There is something else. I don't know for sure as I'm just guessing, but I think Best has a secret hideout in the mansion. I used to watch him from my hideout in the closet. I would remove the book from the safe on his office wall then sit down at his desk and read it. I think; however, he stopped using the safe to keep the book hidden after the detective almost discovered it. A couple of times after that I would watch him enter the studio, but he would never come out. One time I came into the studio just a minute after he entered pretending to get something, but he was nowhere to be found. There is only one door in and out of the studio." Thomas glanced at Avery, both of them acknowledging the importance of what she had just revealed. Her voice was tinged in sadness, and the tears in her eyes returned. She struggled with her composure, "Please Father, do not leave us. I am afraid of him. He will come for me, for all of us here, if you leave."

They watched as Father O'Sullivan stepped towards Chloë, took both of her hands in his, brought them up to his face and kissed them softly. She studied him curiously for a second, still desperate to make him stay when her facial expressions began to change and recognition began to set in. It was disbelief at first, that it was impossible but quickly changed to jubilation. She had just learned the Truth like the rest of them that set off a torrent of tears in her eyes as she held fast onto His hands, not wanting to let them go. She cried tears of joy before she let go of His hands and fell into His arms, sobs wracking her slender shoulders.

Chapter 40

Minister of Defense Xing Chang Win of the People's Republic of China sat stunned in front of the Prime Minister. He could not speak, the magnitude of his orders freezing him in a state of shock. He did not hear his boss screaming orders and instructions. He was in disbelief about what he had just been asked to carry out.

A full nuclear attack on Japan. Immediately. Wipe Tokyo off the face of the earth. Prepare the defenses for a nuclear retaliatory attack by Japan, NATO and the United States. Second launch command target: Paris, France. Flatten it. The casualties would number in the tens of millions. The casualties to his countrymen, as many, if not more.

A stinging slap across his face by the Prime Minister's Chief of Staff brought him back to reality. The Prime Minister was enraged, screaming orders at his military commanders. Three people had the launch codes for China's nuclear weapons. Unfortunately, he was one of them. The other two were the Prime Minister and the Supreme Military Commander, Xoa Wang. He looked over at Wang, and he looked as if he had seen a ghost. He was close to fainting. He noticed the other man for the first time. He was an American standing behind the Prime Minister, but far enough away that he never noticed him. He looked familiar to him somehow, but could not put a finger on it. "What was he doing here?" he thought to himself. "Who was he?" He dared not ask. The Prime Minister was out of his mind. Wang made the mistake of asking.

"Who is this man that stands behind you, Prime Minister? He is an American. I demand to know who he is. Is he CIA?" That would be the last word Wang would ever ask. The Chief of Staff stepped up behind him, put a pistol to his head and blew a hole through it, obliterating the Commander's face. Wang fell dead onto the floor with a sickening thud. His blood quickly spread across the white carpet. No one seemed to mind, especially the Prime Minister. He screamed at his Chief of Staff to cut the hands off of the dead Commander. The launch keys were on a chain around his neck, just like his were. They were required to wear the chain at all times. The keys, combined with their finger and palm prints would be enough to launch their nuclear arsenal. The Prime Minister had gone completely mad. He felt a rush in his stomach, and he knew he was going to be sick. His body reacted, forcing him to bend over in his chair and wretch. He emptied his stomach, lifted his head only to find the American standing over him. "What the hell is up with his eyes," he thought. They were blood red in color, glowing; he had never seen anything like it. He was about to protest his presence so close to him, when the stranger bellowed, "You weak fool. Maybe I should pump a bullet in your brain."

He looked at this lunatic asshole and then back at the Prime Minister. The American had somehow made the Prime Minister agree to the biggest act of terrorism in history. He could not be a part of this. He glanced down at the dead Commander and then nervously looked around the expansive office of the Prime Minister, looking for an escape. The American sensed it and brought his fist down onto his face like a sledgehammer. The pain sliced through his brain like an electric charge. Two broken teeth fell with a mouthful of blood onto the expensive carpet, joining the coagulating pool of blood and pieces of brain matter from the Commander. They would have to kill him, because he would never give them his key and prints voluntarily. He suddenly thought of his wife and son. He knew he would never see them again. He also knew the retaliatory strikes from the United States and the rest of the world would turn them into dust. An hour ago he walked into his boss's office to discuss the upcoming visit by the Malaysian

Prime Minister. What happened? He looked up at the American, the blood gushing down his chin, then over at the Prime Minister and seethed, "Go to hell you coward! What did you do to make yourself a puppet of this American asshole! I'll die before I ever put a finger on that case!"

The American roared like a crazed animal, "You fuckin people are dumber than I could imagine. No wonder you restrict your breeding. The country is dumb enough, so why make it anymore stupid with more of you dumb shits." His fist shot out so fast Win never had a chance to duck. The blow instantly paralyzed his windpipe and before he could even lift his hands to stop the next blow, the American's hands were around his throat, squeezing with astonishing force. His eyes expanded in their sockets and felt like they would pop out of his skull. He would be dead in seconds. His tongue involuntarily stuck out of his mouth, and he could see it thrash around in front of his face desperate to direct precious air back into his lungs. His right eye burned slightly then popped from his face. He did not see it land on the floor, but he could hear it. His remaining eye caught a glimpse of the Prime Minister cowering in the corner behind his desk. Before he died he managed to spread his lips apart in a smile at the thought of the brutal death that would come swiftly to the Prime Minister soon after his death.

The man squeezing the life out of him was no American. In fact he was not even human. The light of the room slowly then quickly disappeared, replaced with a blackness that always preceded death. A death brought to him by a Demon from Hell.

****

Bentley stood in front of the tiny mirror that adorned the wall in their cramped dormitory- type room in the secret section of the Vatican controlled by Father O'Sullivan. She looked at the lines around her eyes highlighted by the redness from the lack of sleep over the past few days. She knew sleep has evaded her for weeks. The dangerous ride she and Avery partook was taking its toll. She allowed her thoughts to drift to a place where it would just be her and Avery, alone, but together in their own home. She closed her eyes and allowed the dream to grow, letting it take her to that special place. She kissed Avery goodbye as he left for work and watched him wave one last time before he climbed in and drove away. She would go up the stairs and check on their baby. Her thoughts were quickly brought back to the now when she felt movement behind her and then the familiar smell and touch of Avery as he leaned in close behind her followed by soft kisses to her neck. She closed her eyes once again, hoping to will his touches into her dream. She drifted back to their bedroom watching him get dressed for work when he approached her and began to touch and kiss her all over. Her thoughts were once again interrupted when Avery's voice pierced her dream, "Honey, Father O'Sullivan wants to leave immediately. I must go." She turned around and faced him, then wrapped her arms around his waist before protesting, "I don't think it is safe for you to go with Him, Avery. I know who He is, but this is a fight that is beyond you or me, or anyone. I'm scared Best will target you specifically. Father O'Sullivan does not need you in this fight. You have fought enough, it's their fight now."

He looked hard into her eyes and could see the fear resonating in them. He reached up and lifted her chin towards his mouth and kissed her. He finished by kissing her forehead and then replied, "I understand your fear Bentley, I do, but I don't feel any fear when I am with Him. This must end, and He would not ask me to join Him in this showdown with Best or whoever he is if I wasn't needed in some way. You and I and those five kids will not survive this if Best is not stopped, you know that. When he is ready, he will come for us and there will be nothing we can do to stop him."

"We are safe here. He cannot touch us here. Please, Avery, I love you. Stay with me."

He reached out and pulled her close. They held each other for less than a minute, but to him it felt like hours. He released her, then held her face in his hands, kissed her softly on the lips and whispered, "I love you so much. I will be fine. I will be back very soon, I promise. Stay close to the kids. They will be incredibly scared. They will sense the danger through their unconscious connections to Best. They know they have betrayed him, and some of them could have second thoughts. Keep them busy on their social media sites. They must continue to send their message to the youth of the world. The message of hope and love for one another will set them free." He kissed her once again, then turned and left the room and out into the hallway where Father O'Sullivan was sitting in the small kitchen with Ann. Father O'Sullivan immediately rose from his chair, "We must leave at once, Avery. There is a car waiting outside for us." Walking up to Bentley, he took both of her hands in his and squeezed them slightly as he focused his eyes on hers before speaking, "Our Lord has called Avery to the battlefield, my dear. The bravery and courage of the human soul is needed now more than ever. Our enemy has always misunderstood the soul of man. It has been his weakness and will be his ultimate downfall. Avery will come back to you, Bentley. I promise."

****

"Mr. President, you are required at once in the situation room."

Stanley was pouring over the reports on the dismal economic news of another drop in the stock markets. Too many days in a row the stocks had continued to drop. In a matter of days, not weeks the country would fall back into another serious recession. He was beginning to get the sense that he was truly losing control, powerless to stop what was happening to his country and the rest of the world.

He followed Adam out of his Oval Office and down the hallways to the elevator that would take him to the basement of the West Wing and into the massive conference center. "What dreadful news would be waiting for him now?" he thought. Robert Best was unleashing his Hell on earth at a remarkable speed. He was coming for him, he knew, and there was nothing he could do to stop him. He knew one thing for sure; he would not go down without a fight. If Best wanted the keys to the most powerful office in the world, he would have to kill him to get them. As he entered the room on the heels of his Chief of Staff, he couldn't help but think of what a silly thought he just had. The Demon could and would kill him with the snap of his fingers.

He looked around the room as his Joint Chiefs and Security Council scrambled to their assigned seats around the conference table, waiting for the President to take his seat so they could deliver the latest blow orchestrated by Best. They, of course, had no knowledge of what was *really* behind the events wreaking havoc throughout the world.

****

"They left for Los Angeles and the mansion? That is complete suicide, Bentley. I didn't think they would leave so quickly. It is too soon. We have to stop them!" Chloë was becoming upset as Bentley and Ann were explaining to the gathered kids in the small and cramped kitchen. She continued, "Father O'Sullivan is still an old man, and is not some young, sword swinging soldier. He is the voice of God, His eyes on earth, not a soldier. He will die. I will never see him again!" Erupting in tears, she quickly stood and bolted from the kitchen to her room.

Brittany stood to go after her but was interrupted by Bentley. "Let me speak with her sweetheart. The thought of losing Father O'Sullivan is just too much for her. Ann, do you mind finishing up here?"

"Certainly, go Bentley. I will take it from here."

There were no locks on the dormitory room doors, so Bentley knocked once then opened the door to find Chloë sprawled on her stomach on her tiny bed. Her long blond hair had spilled over the side where it gathered like a silk sweater on the floor. Bentley felt the tinges of sorrow as she sat down on the small bit of space available on the bed beside Chloë's sprawled legs. This mega talented young superstar should be enjoying her incredible career, the attention of countless boys only a beautiful seventeen year old girl could do, not having her life torn apart by the demonic intentions of Satan. She reached out and stroked Chloë's hair, the tears stinging her eyes. She was like a daughter to her. She loved her and the others so much. Then she thought of how much pain Ann was in as she watched what was happening to her son and how powerless they both were. Avery was right. It had to end. They had to take the fight to the Demon and end this before he came for them. Many lives would be lost if he wasn't stopped. She quickly whispered a prayer for God to keep them safe. Then another strange thought came to her mind. She had just prayed to God for His protection; yet, she was sure that is exactly who was accompanying Avery to America at this very moment.

****

The National Security Advisor, Vic Turk, his aged face reflecting the burden of the chaos from around the world, addressed the President, "Mr. President. The Prime Minister of China, Pin Shen has been assassinated. He was found dead in his office a few hours ago along with his Supreme Military Commander, Xoa Wang and his Minister of Defense, Xing Chang Win. Outside of his office another dozen support staff dead." Turk sat down after delivering the news, still visibly shaken.

Stan stared incredulously at the men and woman surrounding his table, then asked, "What happened?"

The CIA Director, Nancy Turcotte answered next, "They were murdered, Mr. President. Wang was shot point blank in the back of the head, the bullet taking his right eye with it. Win had his throat torn completely from his neck almost severing his head from his shoulders. Shen's murder was the most heinous."

Stan, shocked at the brutality, asked, "Tell me."

"The body was so completely mutilated, the Chinese government were reluctant at first to divulge the details but after a little pressure from our Ambassador in Shanghai, we were given the details of his murder. Mr. President, Prime Minister Shen's arms and legs were severed and so was his head. His torso was placed on his office chair in front of his desk. His naked legs, the shoes and socks still on them were placed in the middle of the floor facing the door. His head was placed on top of the legs sir. It would be the first image whoever discovered the bodies."

"Where were the arms?"

Turcotte hesitated, and then finished up, "The arms were discovered in a heap on the floor behind the desk."

Stan, his body starting to tremble as the truth began to sink in, asked, "Why the carnage?"

"We have a theory, sir. I'm afraid it is very bad news, Mr. President." She was interrupted as Stan shouted, "For Christ's sakes, Nancy, just tell me what happened in that room."

She looked around the room before answering as if to plead to anyone of the other powerful people in the room to take this question instead of her, "Mr. President, Wang, Win and the Prime Minister are the three people in the People's Republic of China capable of launching their nuclear arsenal. Wang and Win's hands were discovered severed from their bodies. The nuclear weapons launch controls were also found in the office."

Stan gasped, "Dear God."

"We theorize that whoever had murdered the three people necessary to launch their nuclear weapons had tried to force the three of them to place their palms into the launch protocol package and when they refused, they were brutally murdered and their hands or arms in the case of the Prime Minister, severed so the killers could launch the arsenal themselves using the body parts. What the killers forgot to consider is the loss of body heat in the severed hands would not generate the necessary palm prints that would trigger the identification approval to then punch in the launch codes. A careless oversight by the perpetrators, which has all of us and the Chinese mystified."

Stan sunk into his chair as the mental images came pouring into his mind. It was Best. He had attempted to launch a nuclear strike. It was happening much too fast. They had even less time than he had first hoped.

"Mr. President?"

Stan lifted his head to the sound of someone speaking. He had become lost in his thoughts. It was the CIA Director Turcotte. She was waiting for a response from him on the news. They all were. He cleared his thoughts and asked, "Was there a target package loaded into the launch protocol?"

It was Vic Turk who jumped in and replied, "Yes, Mr. President. It was Japan. Tokyo to be more precise. There were enough missiles loaded into the protocol to reduce the largest city in the world to a nuclear waste pile. Dust, Mr. President. There would be enough radiation to kill millions more in the days to follow."

Stan sat speechless, unable to respond. Then the next words spoken confirmed his worst fears.

Secretary of State, Bob Buckett spoke the ominous words, "That is not all, Mr. President. The Chinese are blaming the United States for the murders in a plot to start a nuclear war between Japan and China."

Stan could not believe what he was hearing. His eyes sharpened as he replied, "What in God's name would give them that idea?"

He continued, "There was a survivor. An office support staff in the Prime Minister's office. She is critically injured and likely will die before the end of the day but she was able to give investigators a statement before she slipped into unconsciousness. She stated an American businessman had come from the PM's office and began to kill everyone in the office with his bare hands. He tore people apart as if they were made of tissue paper."

The bolt of lightning hit Stan as if it was thrown from Zeus himself.

Buckett continued, "We are, of course, completely denying any connection or knowledge to this mystery man. The Chinese are convinced we had sent a CIA operator into their government buildings who somehow was able to get into the personal office of the Prime Minister and his inner circle without detection, and then proceeded to brutally kill them all in a bizarre plan to launch their nuclear arsenal into Japan. They believe an attack on Japan by China would give the United States the worldwide sympathy they needed to wipe China off the face of the map."

Stan stunned the powerful men and woman in the room with his next words, "It's not ludicrous, Bob. The Chinese woman who survived long enough to give that statement was not lying. It's the truth. That was an American who did this."

The sound of Buckett's hand dropping to the table followed by the words of shock resonated through the room, "Excuse me!"

He looked around the room, the faces reflecting back in stunned silence, then began, "That man may not be American; in fact, he is from no country. Ladies and gentlemen, get comfortable. We are going to be here awhile. There are some things I am going to tell you that will cause you to deny everything you have ever believed in this world, and others will hear confirmation of something you only heard about in Church from your local pastor preaching about fire and brimstone. Our worst nightmares are upon us, and they are not encased in a layer of steel and are launched from a fighter jet, from the ground or from a submarine. Our constitution, our way of life, is based upon the principles written in our Bible. Well, our way of life, our safety and the safety of everyone in the world is being threatened by the enemy of our Savior, our God and that is Satan. He is real, he is here and he is implementing his final solution. He is after me, he is after all of you, and he is after everyone. Not your money, your fancy houses or your expensive cars. He wants to steal the very souls of humans. He is succeeding as you are now hearing from China. There is a spiritual battle taking place on earth that has now revealed itself to our eyes."

Turcotte interrupted, "Mr. President, please, now is not the time for a Sunday school class. The world is on the brink of a nuclear holocaust. We c...."

Stan cut her off as quickly as she had interrupted him, "Shut-up Nancy. Listen to me everyone. I have met this enemy. He has revealed himself to me. He is the American businessman, Robert

Best."

Cacophony filled the room. Some of them had heard enough and rose as if to leave. Stan's shout pierced the room and all of them turned towards the President only to see the Chief of Staff lead a Catholic priest into the room and were completely shocked to see the famous record producer, Avery Johnson, follow close behind.

Chapter 41

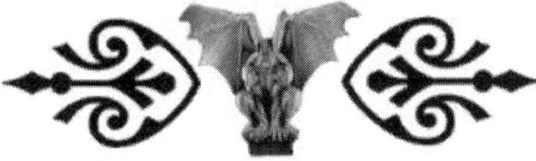

Bentley returned to the small kitchen and joined Ann who was just ending a phone call, "That was the program director for Magic 101.1 in London. The station management has already decided they will air only the latest release songs from Vasallus as soon as they are made available. The request lines have been burning up since the concert with listeners asking for the new music. How soon can the distributors make the music available to radio?"

"Avery uploaded the twenty new songs from the concert the other night to the distribution channels. It will be any minute before every radio station will see the song list available for airplay; as well, iTunes will have them available for download at the same time. We need to reach out to the radio stations around the world faster, to let them know the songs are already available to them."

Ann leaned over her coffee cup towards Bentley; her voice edged in excitement, and declared, "Why don't you conduct a live T.V. special featuring the kids, the London concert and their new music. You can make an announcement during the interview the music is available for worldwide airplay and will be available on iTunes within hours."

Bentley stirred cream into her coffee, quietly thinking about what Ann had just suggested. After a few seconds she stated, "That is a great idea, Ann! Let me run it by my bosses at *Music Talks,* but it shouldn't be a problem. I will get in touch with the NBC affiliate here in Rome and make arrangements for a camera crew on scene." Ann glanced at her with concern, "Bentley, how will you get a camera crew in here. This is a secret office of the

Vatican. We can't do it here. Can we do it off-site somewhere?"

She thought for a minute before answering, "Yes we can. I can instruct the station to have a television crew setup in a hotel suite. It must be done in complete secrecy. They will agree to that. The interview will be huge for NBC. They won't screw it up. We'll have to get the kids out of here however, undetected and over to the hotel. Any ideas?" Ann answered immediately, "Of course. My security team is holed up somewhere close. I can have them over here in an instant to whisk us over to the hotel. Come on, Bentley, get on that phone. Let's make this happen."

****

Robert Best agreed quickly to the producer's request for an interview, almost too quickly he thought. He needed to stay in control, not too eager. He needed to make them feel as if they have scored a major coup with an interview with the biggest newsmaker in the world. The 60 Minutes producer was ecstatic that Best agreed to the interview and informed him that he would send a private jet to pick him up to bring him to their New York studios as rapidly as possible. He quietly turned down the offer for the private jet, informing him that he was quite capable of getting himself to New York. The producer seemed disappointed that he had turned down his offer to have him picked up, fearful he would change his mind when they hung up the phone. At least when they had him in their plane, he would feel more comfortable that CBS would get their interview. The producer let him know that the veteran journalist, James Murphy would conduct the interview. How soon could he get to New York, he asked? He let the excited producer know that he would be in the studio for ten a.m. the next morning. The phone call ended with the sound of the producer's voice shouting in the background as he excitedly announced the news of securing the man who saved the world to an exclusive interview. He knew that CBS would be filling their stations with an onslaught of segments advertising the upcoming interview and for the first time would be shown live. The television news show, 60 Minutes was his favorite, so why not give them the plum interview? The one catch was it had to be a live broadcast. No taping for a future airing. This was not what 60 Minutes does, but the size of the story took precedence. For the first time in its recording history the show would be broadcast live.

****

Bentley finished up her phone call with the news program producer for NBC, and he nearly dropped the phone after learning of the opportunity she had presented for a live interview of Vasallus in a secret location in Rome as quickly as he could put together a camera crew, She was told to have the kids prepared within the hour.

They all scrambled to get ready including Bentley and Ann. The concern, of course, was how fast Chloë and Brittany could get ready. Bentley was a veteran of a fast makeover to cut to a story quickly; this was nothing new to her, but for the two girls to get ready for a worldwide audience in less than an hour was like asking a professional boxer he has forty- five minutes to prepare for a title fight instead of the usual six months. They were not happy, and they let their displeasure be known.

"You're kidding me right? How could I possibly be ready in forty five minutes? It takes me that long just to shower. You're asking us to appear live on television in front of millions of people, and I'm supposed to be ready in less than an hour. Come on, Bentley don't do this to us," chided Brittany. Added Chloë, "Seriously, Bentley, look at my hair! It's a disaster!"

It was Ann who responded when she lightly touched Bentley's arm followed by a wink of her eye to indicate she'd take it from here, "Okay girls, I know you're upset, but we have no choice. Time is everything right now, and the quicker we appear on television and spread your message the more lives will be saved. There is violence happening as we speak around the world, and we need to act quickly to put an end to it. We're sorry to rush you, but it is what it is, okay? So please, you're wasting time complaining. Just do the best you can and let's get moving."

****

Vice President Joe Vandelstaff moved to bring order into the room that was quickly threatening to grow completely out of control, "Mr. President, with all due respect, your story of meeting the maker and your allegations that Robert Best is the Anti-Christ is a bit hard for us to swallow. Your credibility as leader of the free world has come into question, not by the people in this room, but by other countries leaders after the coup pulled off by Best. Do you know how absurd this all sounds to us? Can you imagine what our allies would think?"

Stan quickly responded, "I don't really care what you think, Joe. All I know is Best is pushing all the right buttons, and the one button I am trying to prevent him from pushing is the one that will end civilization. He just came very close to doing that in Shanghai. Now to everyone else in this room. This enemy cannot be fought with fighter jets, or squadrons of army units. This war is spiritual but even more deadly than rockets and bombs. The key for Best in his master plan to end humankind is the office of the President of the United States. Make no mistake people. Robert Best is the most dangerous threat to the safety of the United States and the rest of the world than anything we have ever faced in our history."

Vandelstaff jumped out of his chair, disgust written all over his face, then shouted, "Mr. President, I cannot sit here and listen to this any longer! China is accusing this administration of espionage that almost started a nuclear war with Japan. For God's sakes, Mr. President, we must discuss how we are to satisfy the Chinese that it was not the CIA at the scene in Shanghai."

With a voice draped in calm control but very deliberate, Stan replied, "I suggest Mr. Vice President that you remove yourself from this room if the truth is offensive to you. That includes anyone else. We are about to hear from Father O'Sullivan and Mr. Johnson. I will not tolerate any further interruptions or outbursts. Do I make myself clear?"

Vandelstaff glanced around the room and could see no one

was moving. He looked back at the President, a look of defeat stretching across his face. He slumped back in his chair as he quietly replied, "I'm sorry Mr. President for my outburst. It was out of line. Please proceed."

Stan did not acknowledge the apology and continued, "Father O'Sullivan and Avery Johnson are here at my request. For over forty years, Father O'Sullivan has led a secret office within the Vatican that was unknown to anyone but a few outside of the Pontiff. What he is about to share with you will shock you, whether you consider yourself a religious person or not. Avery has seen the evil of Robert Best up close and personal and has barely survived an attack by the demonic Best. Vasallus has been the key to everything happening around the world as you will soon hear. Gentlemen, thank you for being here. I know how much in danger the two of you are. It is my hope that we can come out of this room with a plan to protect this administration, this government and the safety of not only the people of the United States, but also people all over the world."

Father O'Sullivan cleared his throat and stepped forward. Everyone in the room was instantly drawn to the incredible blue light that shone from the priest's eyes. The eyes projected a holiness no one had ever experienced. They knew this man was very special. They leaned over their tables towards the priest as he began to speak.

****

It was risky to have Ann's security team pick them up at the secret entrance into the Vatican, if they were discerned by the patrolling Vatican police. Fortunately, though, the security team was careful and only approached by car when the last patrol passed giving them a small window to gather everyone into the limo and away from the Vatican before the next patrol made its rounds. NBC was setting up its cameras at the Hotel Alimandi, only minutes away by car from the Vatican. The kids could have walked to the hotel in less than twenty minutes, but they could not risk having them noticed by fans who might cause a scene. The hotel assured the NBC producer complete secrecy and offered them the VIP entrance where the kids would be quickly ushered in and up to the suite unnoticed.

The kids were not as easy. Even the boys complained they needed more time. Getting the girls ready and into a better mood both Ann and Bentley pitched in and helped them with their hair and makeup. Bentley just ran a brush through hers and with the help of lots of hairspray plus a little makeup she was good to go. Working feverishly on Chloë's hair and Ann on Brittany's they made it work and even managed to get the girls laughing at the whole situation. Miraculously, they all made it to the Alimandi within the hour. The kids knew what was at stake and were all in for the interview. The plan was for Bentley to ask them leading questions where the kids could expound on each of their views and why it was important for their fans to leave the old music behind and embrace the new music, which carried with it the message of hope.

****

The most powerful people in the United States sat in complete and utter shock as they listened to Father O'Sullivan lay out the entire history of SOSL and the Catholic Church's belief in the End of Times. The story was certainly compelling, but it was more of the man delivering the grim news. The priest was genuinely believable thought Stan, and he could tell by the expressions of the people around the table they felt the same. The demonic attacks on the seven women around the world that produced the offspring leading to Vasallus and the Demon's plot to use their music to change the youth of the world against authority and society was incredible. As bizarre as the whole story sounded it carried an air of truth, because Father O'Sullivan came across as completely *truthful*. His blue eyes sizzled with sparkle, and everyone in the room had come to believe that the priest was more than just a man, that he was somehow connected to a higher power. They had questions, he knew, and he would give them that opportunity. When Father O'Sullivan finished up, the questions came fast and furious. CIA Director Nancy Turcotte started it off, "Thank you,

Father, for helping us understand this incredible story. I must ask, why did the Demon or Satan, not quite sure what to call him, target these specific woman spread out all over the world? Why not choose seven women in one city? Makes more sense."

Thomas studied the intelligence director and knew she doubted his every word. He answered her question regardless, silently reminding himself these people were some of the most important people in the world, and for the President to not only remain alive but to keep his government together in the coming days and weeks he needed his inner circle to be completely on board and that meant they must believe his every word. "Mrs. Turcotte, if I may, ask everyone in the room for a little more of your patience. To properly answer your question, Director, I must take you back into history. In fact, more than sixteen hundred years ago."

So it began, the incredible story of King Tiridates and his seven sons defeating Satan in the tiny country of Armenia so long ago that would have such a prominent role in the survival of the world in present day. Thomas linked the descendants of the seven sons to the seven women who gave birth to Vasallus, bringing the story full circle.

Avery stood in the corner of the room listening to Father O'Sullivan recount the origins of Vasallus once again. He was enraptured even more than the first time, surrounded by the powerful men and women in the room. He wondered to himself if anyone in the room besides the President had any hint at the magnitude of the priest that spoke before them. It was a surreal moment for him that left him physically weak, and he found himself leaning against the wall with enough force to keep him from toppling forward face first onto the floor.

The heavy set National Security Advisor, Vic Turk, exhaled a loud gasp when Father O'Sullivan finished, "Dear God, Father. I can handle the enormity of a dictator gone nuts or a terrorist killing innocent people, but this is something completely different. I don't know what to think or say. Mr. President, let me ask you. What do you make of this story?"

Stan looked at everyone in the room before answering and then looked at Father O'Sullivan, whose eyes seemed to be speaking directly to him. He then turned to Turk and replied, "Before I do that, Vic, let's hear from Mr. Johnson. His perspective on all of this might bring everything into greater focus for everyone in this room. Avery, if you will."

Avery gathered himself, leaned off of the wall and took a few steps towards the enormous conference table littered with laptop cables and smartphones. He made a gesture to the President that he would take a seat in one of the empty chairs that just happened to be right beside the CIA Director. He fought the feeling her eyes were burrowing into him, looking for the slightest hint of deception to bring their whole story crashing down. He cleared his throat and began, "Thank you, Mr. President. My association with Robert Best began at a lunch diner in Los Angeles more than a year ago. It was here in the diner that Robert Best proposed the idea of Vasallus, that he was the music producer and manager of Connor Asker and Juan Jimenez and was bring them together along with five other super talented kids of the same age to form a superstar band. He wanted me to manage and produce them. At the time, Connor was the most popular pop star in America and Juan was the same in South America. Best's plan to bring together the seven mega talented young stars was fascinating and full of opportunity. I put my own music label, *Alive Records,* into the hands of my assistant to manage, and I took on the project of Vasallus full time. It became very clear, immediately upon landing in a recording studio with the seven kids of Vasallus that they were very special people. Within a few hours of laying their eyes on the sheet music for the very first time, they were performing it together as a group as if they had been playing it for years. It was more than phenomenal; it was downright spooky. In all my years of producing top music stars, I have never encountered anything remotely close to that. It quickly got to the point we were laying down tracks on their first attempt. It was crazy but also extremely exhilarating working with these superstars. Within a few short weeks of these kids laying eyes on each other for the first time, they were touring in stadiums of a hundred thousand people, and in no time they were the biggest act since the Beatles."

The interruption by the Vice President was unexpected and unappreciated by the completely engrossed audience, "Mr. Johnson, please, all of us have kids, some of us grandkids, who make it very clear to their parents who Vasallus is. I think you can skip that part. We get that." The only person in the room that could rebuke the Vice President was the President and he didn't waste any time, "Do all of us a favor in this room, Mr. Vice President, and shut the hell up. One more interruption like that and you will find yourself outside of this room. Do I make myself clear?"

****

Bentley did not need any notes for this interview but did allow herself a small note in the order she wanted to present the questions to Vasallus. The interview room in the expansive hotel suite consisted of stacked chairs in a semi-circle where Vasallus sat facing her. She had started the interview by thanking all of them for agreeing to conduct the interview in front of a live audience. She allowed each of the five members of Vasallus to speak individually on why it was important to have the opportunity to speak to fans. When it was Connor's turn, Bentley envisioned what the millions of teenage girls around the world would be thinking at this moment. Would they embrace his message? Did the about face in their message tarnish his incredible popularity with his fans. He began to speak, and his absurdly good looks did not interfere with his message. He came across as genuine and believable to the camera and the listening audience.

"I have such great respect for my fans. Without them I would be nothing. It is my fans and the fans of Vasallus that make us who we are. It is these same fans who will ultimately decide what is right for them. We can only hope that they embrace our message of hope, respect and love."

She addressed Chloë next, "You had just come off of an incredible return to your home country of Ireland before the performance in London. What was that like for you, Chloë, knowing that you had this message bottled up inside of you that you desperately wanted to get out to your fans. How hard was that for you?" She watched as Chloë struggled with the emotions that quickly rose to the surface. She fought back tears as she replied, "It was incredibly hard; you can't imagine. Knowing the violence that had occurred on the streets of Dublin before the concert then knowing what would happen afterwards when the concert was over was extremely difficult, and the frightening reality that our music was a big part of why it was occurring and that people were being killed and hurt all over my country."

To Brittany she asked, "Vasallus has had so much success and is experiencing a popularity level never seen before in music history. Is this what you expected when you joined Vasallus?" Brittany subconsciously tucked the side of her long blond hair behind her ear as she replied, "Never in my wildest dreams did I expect this. I knew we would be big with the amount of talent that was put together but nothing remotely close to this." Bentley continued with another question, "Do you miss Elizabeth?" Bentley watched as Brittany dropped her head slightly causing her hair to fall back onto her face, she once again tucked it behind the ear as she took a moment to reply, "She was such a good friend. She was my sister. I think of her every day, but I know I will see her very soon and that keeps me together." Bentley never expected the answer so Bentley dug a little deeper, "Explain, Brittany, what you mean when you say you will see her soon."

A tear suddenly escaped the bottom of her eye, taking with it a small amount of mascara as it created a tiny dark path down the front of her cheek. "I feel her spirit beside me always. We all do. I know we will all be together again soon." Bentley decided to leave it at that cryptic message and moved on.

Turning her attention to Juan, she needed to address the white elephant in the room and that is the question of the death of Patrick. She knew it was important for closure on his death, to quiet the multitude of rumors and stories that had circulated throughout the social media world since Vasallus announced his death at the London concert just a few days ago. "Juan, tell your fans what happened to Patrick. I know you were probably the most closest to him. How did he die?"

The sound of the voice that came from her right, just out of her peripheral vision felt like ten thousand volts of electricity had just been transferred to the right side of her rib cage. The room suddenly began to waver and lose focus. She could see the kids' faces contort in terror at the = person entering the set. When her vision cleared, the sight of who had just walked onto the set and sat on a chair beside Juan made her shake in a cold, raw and terrible fear.

"No one is more qualified to answer that question, Ms. Paxton, than me."

The waxy shined and demonic face of Robert Best stared back at her with a look of complete satisfaction.

Chapter 42

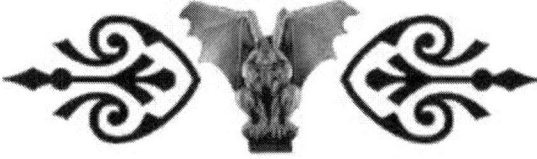

Avery carefully and meticulously went through his and Bentley's incredible journey with Vasallus and the eventual revelation on the true identity of Robert Best through his attack on the two of them at the mansion. He mentioned the first time they discovered the marks each of the kids had on his or her inner right thigh, exposed to them by Chloë in her hotel room in Denver during their first tour. He recounted the seventeenth birthday party for Connor Asker at a Malibu restaurant, when it was discovered that all seven of the kids were also celebrating birthdays on that day. Further investigations by Detective Showenstein revealed that not only were all seven children born on the exact same day but at the exact same time. This reality caused an audible stir among those around the table including a loud gasp from Turcotte.

He detailed the unbelievable music talent each of them displayed including their ability to pick-up a piece of sheet music and without even looking at it, play it perfectly as if they had been performing it for years. The songwriting ability of Patrick Benning was unparalled. He had a cauldron of songs that would keep the group producing hits for decades to come. The boy was more than a musical genius, he was beyond brilliant. Avery stated to them that Best wanted them to be perfect in every way, and in reality they were perfect in every way. The kids had no flaws. Each of them could sing like an angel, play any instrument with ease and were endowed with physical beauty that combined with their musical abilities and brought together in a band that made them a perfect machine to poison the minds of youth everywhere. Avery summed it up by stating, "All of you know how successful the group has been in influencing our youth."

Turcotte no longer spoke with skepticism, "I must ask about the kids floating at their concerts. There were no wires was there?" The question hung in the air for a few seconds as they all remembered the sensational footage. The question remained unanswered as the National Security Advisor spoke.

"As the band's manager, producer and their guardian, why did you allow their music to proliferate?"

Avery was about to answer when Thomas interjected, "Let me answer that question. Best would not be stopped, not by Avery and Bentley, not by myself, not by anyone. The Anti-Christ had a plan and no one would stop him. The heroics of Avery and Bentley kept the kids alive; that was their calling by God. Keep the kids alive so they could fight back. You are now seeing that reaction, starting with their concert in London a few nights ago."

Stan listened intently to them and was astounded at the bravery of Avery Johnson and the journalist, Bentley Paxton. It took incredible courage to stand up to such a foe as Robert Best and risk their lives every day to keep those kids safe. He found himself admiring Johnson and was about to say something when his phone vibrated on the table in front of him. He normally would ignore it when he was in meetings, but he could see it was a text from Leah. He picked up the phone and read her message, "Turn on NBC! Live interview with Vasallus in Rome!"

"Excuse me, Father. The First Lady has just notified me that Vasallus is being interviewed live from Rome on NBC. Bring it up on the screen!"

Avery reacted instantly, "What!"

Within a few seconds the giant screen presented the interview. Avery sat aghast in his chair, stunned at what he was seeing. "What was Bentley thinking?" His thoughts were interrupted by the Vice President, "Father O'Sullivan, I thought you said they were in hiding at a secret location, because their lives were in danger from Best? Live television on a major network doesn't look so secretive to me."

After the childish outburst by the Vice President, the room was quiet as they listened to Bentley speak candidly with the kids. It was captivating as they heard the kids talk about how important their new music was and the message it carried to their fans. They truly did care about the damage their music had done and were sincerely committed to changing that message. The interview was incredibly moving with the questions elicited to allow the kids to speak from their hearts. Now he knew why Bentley had done this dangerous interview. It was brilliant. Get the world to see up front and personal, raw and emotional, the kids speaking the truth. What happened next caused his heart to fall.

Robert Best just walked onto the set and sat down beside Juan to face a visibly shaken Bentley!

****

Bentley struggled with the shock of seeing Best appear out of nowhere. She could see the kids were petrified of him. She made eye contact with Ann off to the side who was frantically giving her the 'cut-it-off' sign to end the interview. The network had agreed to give her one hour, commercial free airtime so the cameras were not going to be shut off. All of this was being captured on live television. She had to make a decision. End the interview and shock the world, wiping out all the good things the kids had just communicated to their fans and the rest of the world or hang in there and continue the interview. She chose to continue.

"Okay, Mr. Best. Tell our audience what happened to Patrick Benning. How did he die?"

The bright lights surrounding the set threatened to melt Best's face right off his skull. It was creepy, and she wondered how the television audience could see it. She braced for his answer when he replied, "The passing of young Patrick was truly tragic and something that will haunt me for the rest of my life. It was discovered that Patrick suffered from a rare form of Leukemia, the fatal NK cell. He fought bravely over the two months it took to take his life. Patrick never told a soul except me, and I kept his promise and never told anyone until now."

She was shocked at the lie and deception from Best. She should not have been surprised as he was after all the biggest deceiver and liar in history. She kept her composure as best she could in front of the cameras and focused on Best, "Tell me Mr. Best about Vasallus's new music and the message of hope, love and redemption. Were you the inspiration behind this complete change in direction for the band?"

The lies spewed out of him like honey, "It was a collaborative decision amongst all of the kids in Vasallus as well as Avery Johnson, the band's manager and producer and myself to change things for the betterment of society. We no longer liked where our message was going, so we wanted to go in a completely different direction. I am thrilled with the reaction from our fans to the new music. Also, Ms. Paxton, call me Robert."

Bentley could feel the thread of doom worm its way through the inside of her stomach all the way up to her throat. She fought down her body's need to throw up as she stiffened to her next line of questioning. She knew that what she was about to do next would likely end in her swift death. What did it really matter? They were all going to die anyway. She stole a glimpse of the kids as they all sat rigid in fear, horrified to what was unfolding. Ann stood behind her son, tears spilling down her cheeks as if she had sensed what she was about to do.

Bentley turned and stared straight into the demonic eyes of Robert Best and defiantly declared, "There have been persistent rumors making their rounds through social media, Mr. Best, claiming you are the Anti-Christ, that you are the devil. What do you have to say about those rumors or are they rumors?"

She could feel the heat of Best's rage reach across the room. His plastic face struggled to stay intact in front of the cameras. The television audience would almost certainly have seen his rage flash for the split second it lasted before he quickly replied, "Sometimes I am forced to make decisions that are unpopular and not everyone agrees with. I am called many names, Ms. Paxton. Sometimes people actually say nice things. Like the people of Iran when I saved their country from nuclear annihilation."

She continued to hammer away, "Some people call you Satan, Prince of Darkness, Lucifer. Are you the Devil, Mr. Best?"

The cameras picked up every word of the rage that vibrated through Best's voice as he replied, "Excuse me? Why are you using such offensive names, Ms. Paxton. I would think you could show me more respect than that considering it was I that gave you the opportunity to join Vasallus on tour and cover them for your magazine full time. Do you remember that, Ms. Paxton?"

"I do remember that, Mr. Best. I also remember that it was I and the magazine I work for that gave Vasallus more exposure through our coverage than you could have ever hoped. Do you recall that, Mr. Best"

"Can we continue with talking about the good things Vasallus is now doing."

"Did you have anything to do with the disappearance of Elizabeth Leroux?"

Something gave in Best, and he could no longer hold back his rage. A large piece of his lower jaw gave way and fell to the floor in a sloppy heap, exposing a gaping hole in the side of his face. The cameraman took the opportunity to zoom the camera in close to show the audience the horrifying images as Best struggled to continue, roaring, "You're out of line, Paxton. I will have my lawyers sue you, NBC and the Lockwood bitch for slander and defamation."

The cameras caught Best as he held his hand to the destroyed side of his face, while he stormed off the set. The producer quickly shouted to break the live telecast to a commercial. Everything turned to pandemonium as NBC personnel rushed everywhere to regain control of the set and get everyone calmed down before they came back from commercial. He finally realized that it was useless. The kids were too shaken to continue, and Bentley continued to sit in stunned silence in her chair. He informed the studio the interview was over and to cut to alternative programming. As he looked out onto the chaos, he knew he had never seen anything close to what he had just witnessed in his thirty plus years in television journalism. The world would be talking about this for days to come.

****

If any of the men and women sitting around the conference table of the Situation Room had any doubt as to the validity of Father O'Sullivan's claims of the identity of Robert Best, they were completely removed after watching the horrifying images of Best disintegrate on live television. The silence was broken by Avery as he shouted, "They are in danger from Best. We must get to them quickly!"

Avery turned to Thomas, but to his dismay was stunned to see the priest was nowhere to be found. He was gone. Vanished. He looked around the room, then over at the President, "Father O'Sullivan. He is gone!"

An exasperated President Kipshaw rose from his chair as his eyes swept around the room confirming with his own eyes what he already knew to be true and what security cameras would not be able to show him.

Father O'Sullivan had simply disappeared from one of the most securest rooms in the world.

****

The producer stepped towards Bentley, still sitting in stunned silence in her chair as chaos swirled around her. Placing his hand on her shoulder, he knelt in front of her, his earphones still dangling around his neck, "Bentley, are you alright? Can I get you anything?"

Bentley lifted her head towards him, whispered, "Save yourselves."

The producer's face twisted slightly in confusion as he replied, "Excuse me? You want us to save ourselves? Damn, that was the craziest thing I have ever seen. Did you see his face? It actually fell to the floor!"

The scream from Bentley froze him in place along with the various assistants in the room, "Did you hear what I just said? Save yourselves! All of you! Get out of here! Go!"

The producer, a ball cap on the top of his head to hide his bald spot, stood up, shocked at Bentley's outburst, lifted his cap off in a nervous reaction then placed it back on before responding, "Bentley, please, calm down. Save ourselves from what?"

The roar that pierced the room sounded as if he were standing beside a lion's cage and had stood too close, "Save yourself from me, fool!"

The producer stood staring at what was once Robert Best. He could not scream, nor could he move. He just stood, terror freezing him solid. The screams from his assistants and the kids from Vasallus sounded secondary, faint and far away. He was about to die a horrible death from a beast creature that looked worse than anything he had ever seen in movies. The thing moved towards him with a swiftness that amazed him. Funny, he thought, that he would be amazed at how fast this monster was about to kill him. The giant beast descended down onto him, its massive, outstretched arm poised to crash down on his head. Before he died, he closed his eyes to say a prayer. He never had time.

****

Ann gasped in horror as the Beast swung its claw like fist over top of the producer's head as if it were a watermelon. It exploded, sending pieces of skull, brain and torrents of blood everywhere. She found herself instantly covered in his flesh. She knew she had no time. She needed to move fast. Get the kids and Bentley back to the Vatican where they would be safe. She now knew they had made a terrible mistake with the interview. They were exposed outside of the Vatican. She saw the kids gathered together in the far corner of the room behind Bentley, a toppled light stand on the floor in front of them illuminating their frightened faces. This was the moment she knew was coming. It was the moment shown to her by Father

O'Sullivan as he held her hands in her mansion not long ago. There was a calling for her in His plan. That calling was now. She caught sight of the Beast, its nostrils flaring hatred as it moved around the room in a killing rage. Death was everywhere. She turned her attention to her son and the rest of Vasallus.

Best moved quickly to one of the fleeing assistants. In just a matter of a few seconds he used his shear- like claws to slice the woman into pieces. The rage poured off of him like a thunderstorm. Ann, now positioned directly behind the Beast, moved quickly over to the kids huddled together like a pack of frightened dogs. She held Bentley by her shoulders and looked her in the eyes. She spoke quickly, "Bentley, you must get the kids across the courtyard and back to the Vatican. The kids will be safe there. I will hold off Best long enough for you to get out of here. Bentley, do you hear me!" She watched as Bentley's mind seemed to click back to the present. She looked up and stared into her eyes as she said, "You cannot stay here, Ann. He will slaughter you. You must come with us, now!"

Ann looked up at Michael, his face etched in terror and shouted above the carnage, "Michael, help Bentley get everyone back to the Vatican. Hurry, there is no time. Connor and Juan, help get the girls to safety. Move!" She quickly reached up and pulled Michael into her arms, hugged him for just a second that she wished could last forever and whispered into his ear, "Go Michael! Remember how much I love you. Don't ever forget that! Now go, and take everyone to safety."

Michael pulled back from her, looked her in the eyes, and recognition of what she was about to do registered in his mind, "No, mom, you can't do this, please! I will stay with you! Please, mom, I can't lose you, please oh please." He helplessly watched as his mom silently mouthed the words, "I love you" then turned and faced the Beast. He could feel his arm being pulled then the shouts of Bentley, "Michael, we have to leave. There is no more time. Let's go!" He felt his body move, willed it to stop but it kept going. He glimpsed the tear- filled eyes of Chloë as she ran beside him, her arm tightly locked around his. He felt like he was floating and did not feel his feet as they pounded on the floor below in unison with the rest of them. He twisted his head backwards to cry out once more for his mother. He could not believe what he was seeing as he strained to stop but there was something else pushing him along that wasn't Chloë, Bentley or anyone else. The huge hands of a soldier, covered in glowing white armor, the angel called Davit he remembered, had clamped his one hand underneath his armpit, his other hand holding an enormous sword thrust outwards.

A second before they burst through the doors and out into the courtyard in front of the hotel, he looked back and caught a final glimpse of his mother, standing defiantly like a warrior on a battlefield, except she did not clutch a sword or a rifle. Her weapon held out in front of her was none of these, but instead her mother's hand clutched something more powerful than a blade. The crucifix of Christ bore down on the Demon like a lightning rod from the Heavens.

Chapter 43

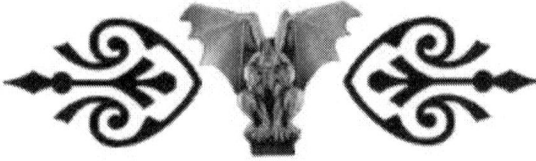

The words flowed from her mouth as easy as if she had written them, but Ann knew better. The Lord was with her as she bore down on the Beast and could feel His love in every fiber of her body. The room stank of death, blood and guts strewn everywhere. She focused in on the lantern- red eyes of Satan as the Beast turned to face her. She could see the surprise in its eyes as he recognized who it was standing defiantly before him.

She continued to pray, "The Lord strengthens me yet weakens the wicked, guides me and misdirects the evil. The Lord is King over all Evil. Stand down…"

The Beast exploded in rage, "How dare you stand before me reciting that garbage while holding that!" The last word came out of the Beast dripping with contempt. He took another step towards her, his beastly body shaking with infuriation. Ann kept pushing with prayer, the crucifix held defiantly in front of her, "Stand down purveyor of all evil, the Lord God commands you. Return to the darkness from where you came. The mightiest of all that is Mighty, He commands you to leave this earth."

Ann braced for the attack that she knew would be coming. She would die in this room, she had no doubt, but she hoped she could keep the Beast distracted long enough for her son to reach the safety of the Vatican. She did not expect, however, what happened next.

The room had suddenly become her bedroom back in London. She was on her back on the floor and she could hear a familiar voice. It could not be, she thought. The voice was her husband, Dalton. This was impossible. A voice whispered to her in her head,

"This is not real. He is deceiving you. Do not listen to his lies." Ann rolled on to her side and tried to get up off of the floor, but an unknown force kept her pinned down. "What was happening?" Then she heard Dalton scream, "Nooo!" The Beast then appeared in the doorway, it's back facing her. It was laughing. A numbness spread through her body, She could feel the dread enter her and the protection of the Lord slip away. She was alone with the Beast just like she was so many years ago. The Beast turned its hideous body around and faced her, its grotesque face expressing pure joy at her plight. Its eyes burned bright as it towered above her, then she watched as the Beast kicked its head back in an uproarious laughter, the sound hurting her eardrums and then it spat, "Did your God abandon you? Left you all alone here to die! So typical of Him. Fills you with hope then snatches it away!" The laughter boomed from its beastly mouth. Its deformed and enlarged tongue, black in color, thrashed in and out as it laughed. Ann fought the nausea threatening to make its way up her throat.

"Why don't we have your husband join you? The two of you can lie there together and get caught up with what you've missed over the last eighteen years!" The Beast swung his left arm around from behind his back, and to her horror he held the head of her dead husband. He dropped Dalton's skull with a sickening thud onto the floor and she watched it roll up against the side of her chest with his face coming to a stop staring directly into her eyes. His death face seemed to be calling out to her subconscious mind. His words were clear, "Why did you do it? Why did you have his son! Why! How could you have done that to me?" Ann closed her eyes and shut them so hard they hurt in the hope it would clear her mind of his voice. It did not work. Her dead husband's anguished voice returned, piercing her subconscious yet again, "He is not my son! Michael is damned. His soul is forever cursed!"

The voice of God broke through the cries of her dead husband, calling out to her from beyond her subconscious, "Fight, Ann. Get up! Strike the wicked one down with my words!" With all her strength she fought against the invisible forces holding her to the floor and managed to get herself onto her elbows then onto her hands and pushed with everything she had to get herself up onto her knees. The room had become dark and cold. She looked up at the Beast and watched as it stared back at her in hatred as she struggled to speak, "The Lord is my salvation. It is He who is the keeper of my soul. Kill me, Demon, and set me free as it will be my gain for I will join the loving God for all eternity."

The Beast boomed, "Silence, you fool!"

"It is you who is the fool, Demon. Your infatuation with me allowed my son and the others to reach safety in the sanctity of the Lord. Your days on this earth are numbered for the Lord's patience is near its end."

The scream from the Beast crushed her ears. Now on her knees, she prayed for the last time, "The Lord is my shepherd; I shall not want. He makes me to lie down in green pastures; He leads me beside the still waters. He restores my soul; He leads me in the paths of righteousness for His name's sake. Yea, though I walk through the valley of the shadow of death, I will fear no evil; for You are with me; Your rod and Your staff, they comfort me. You prepare a table before me in the presence of my enemies; You anoint my head with oil; my cup runs over. Surely goodness and mercy shall follow me All the days of my life; And I will dwell in the house of the Lord Forever."

The Beast, insane with rage, swung its massive arm. Ann shut her eyes as death closed in on her. She whispered one final time, "I love you, Michael. I always have."

The giant claw-like talon of the Beast severed the head of Ann Lockwood, sending her headless torso to fall one way onto the floor and her head the other where it came to rest beside her husband Dalton's. Her death face reflected joy in the knowledge that she would be joining her beloved husband in a beautiful place.

****

Michael was hysterical, determined to go back to the hotel to be with his mother, "Why did you leave her behind to face him? She will die! Please let me go and be with her, please." He bent forwards in his chair, his sobs wracking his body. Chloë knelt beside him trying to comfort him when a familiar voice filled the room.

It was the voice of Father O'Sullivan.

"Michael, come with me. There is something you must see."

Bentley, out of her mind with worry, watched as Michael stood and followed Father O'Sullivan. He stepped towards her before leaving the room, his brilliant blue eyes alive with His wisdom, "You were very brave, Bentley. Do not worry. Everything will be okay. I will be back soon." She stood stunned at the sudden appearance of Father O'Sullivan in the surrounding chaos. "Where was Avery," she thought? She began to feel like she no longer knew what to think, that she was losing her grip on reality completely. Death surrounded her at every turn. She so desperately wanted all of this to go away.

****

Michael found himself in a room devoid of any furniture or pictures with the exception of some sort of confessional booth in the middle of the room that faced a large crucifix on the wall. He turned to ask Father O'Sullivan a question when he realized he was all alone in the room. Where did he go? He was here a second ago? He thought about leaving to find out where he went when he was drawn to a light that suddenly opened up on the wall below the crucifix. The bright light quickly filled the room causing him to look away from its intensity. To his amazement a deep voice spoke from within the brilliant light that drew his gaze once again. This time he stared in complete wonder.

****

Robert Best, still in the suite at the Hotel Alimandi, stood over top of the headless corpse of Ann Lockwood. Her bravery saved the lives of the five kids and Paxton. Stupid bitch. He would just kill them later anyway. They couldn't hide forever in His shadow. They had to be stashed away somewhere in the

Vatican, but where? His dark spirit has visited the inside of the ancient Catholic shrine dozens of times over the years. He never stayed long when he did enter. It was not a good place for his spirit to be in. He took a spiritual beating when he went inside. The Lord considered that place off limits and made sure his spirit felt the full wrath of His goodness, love and hope. It made his spirit sick to be in there. Felt dirty. All he wanted was to terrorize a few highly ranked priests with some memories of sins from their past, but He did not like that. The others must be somewhere inside that he cannot see. A place that only He can see. He would flush them out. Then he would kill them all and cast their spirits in his Hell where he would torture their souls for all eternity. The shock of Lockwood so easily giving her life to save the others was now replaced with the glee of happy thoughts of the screams of agony and hopelessness echoing through the dark chasms of his existence.

He stepped away from the bodies and turned to leave. After all he had a live television interview tomorrow morning halfway across the world. He pulled the collar of his coat close around his face as he exited the suite. He would notify the front desk of the slaughterhouse and then disappear onto the street as a black mist. He needed to create a little spice before the interview with CBS tomorrow morning. Something to really talk about. He knew just what to do, and then he needed to spend some time in his bunker at the mansion to fix up his face. Even he was afraid to look in a mirror. That thought made him laugh even harder as he burst through the exit doors and into the busy lobby.

****

The world woke the next morning to the horrific news of the assassination of South Korean President Ji-hu Kyung and his wife by a team of North Korean government agents. The President and his wife were attending a Euro-Asian Economic Summit in Paris. Security discovered him and his wife in their hotel room brutally murdered. Details of the murder were not being released, but the government of North Korea and the tyrannical leader, Seo-yun Myeong, quickly claimed responsibility for the attack stating it was necessary for the long term stability of North Korea. It went further to state that the South Korean leader was committed to the fall of North Korea and the assassination was necessary. South Korean leaders immediately declared a state of war against Myeong and North Korea and convened a meeting of military leaders to determine an immediate military response.

President Kipshaw found himself summoned into the Situation Room once again alongside his National Security Council. He was starting to wonder if he should just have a living quarters built into this room. He was spending far too much time meeting with his military leaders and top advisors lately. The news of the assassination of Kyung by the insane Seo-yun Myeong was so incredibly ill-timed that he knew it had to be the work of Robert Best. He was continuing his assault on the fragile stability of the world in his bid to undermine his leadership of the West. Topple his Presidency and claim the leadership of a world on the brink of self-destruction would complete what has been written in the Book of Revelations. There was no doubt whatsoever in his mind that the world was in grave danger from this Robert Best, and the predictions written in the Bible and heard over and over again in church since he was a child were actually a reality and that was incredible to him.

****

The Chairman of the Joint Chiefs of Staff, General Townsley Thacker, calmly but deliberately directed an ominous warning to the President, "Mr. President, nothing short of a full military response would be a disaster, both politically and the security of the entire region. If the United States and its allies hesitate now, this Administration will be considered weak and unable to respond to the conflict in Korea. The Chinese government are rudderless with the newly appointed President yet to get his feet wet and would most likely attack Japan within the next seventy two hours." The aging but highly respected veteran of the Vietnam War was unflinching in his delivery that everyone in the room felt. All eyes turned to the President.

Best was on a rampage, Stanley knew. How could he possibly be stopped? If he brought up his name now, his security council would go ape, and the next hour would be spent discussing the validity of Robert Best as the root cause for these events and nothing would get resolved pulling the United States and the rest of the world closer to the next world war. The world needed his leadership, right now. But how, he thought, could he fight this enemy? A military strike against Pyongyang and the headquarters of the Myeong government would most certainly be followed by another barbaric attack by Best somewhere in the world in his bid to take over the leadership of the free world. He looked around the room, staring into the eyes of some of the most powerful people in the world, all waiting for his response to General Thacker when the one person whose eyes he needed to make eye contact with the most, the shimmering blue eyes of wisdom of Father O'Sullivan, were nowhere to be found.

****

Bentley heard the sirens of what must be dozens of police and ambulances racing to the Hotel Alimandi and the carnage of death. She knew in her heart without having to hear it in the news in the coming hours of the death of her friend, Ann Lockwood. She engaged the Demon in a certain suicide fight to save her and the kids of Vasallus. She found herself closing her eyes tightly as she began to pray. She prayed for the soul of Ann, the kids and for Avery. She did not pray for her own safety anymore. Death would come for her soon enough, but before it did she would make sure she got her pound of flesh from that demonic monster. Her hatred for Best burned like a furnace and only his death would cool that hatred. She asked God in her prayer for the chance to swing His mighty sword across the neck of the Beast and end this nightmare once and for all.

****

The assassination of the South Korean leader dominated the news. The live interview with Robert Best, less than an hour away and he needed to make a decision. Stay with the worsening situation in Korea or go forward with the interview. The 60 Minutes producer decided he would stay with the Korean crisis. He was about to shout orders to his director when he felt an uneasy feeling overcome him. It was the weirdest thing, he thought. There was a sense of déjà vu telling him to continue with the interview with Best. A little voice in his head said that if he cancelled the interview something terrible would happen to him. Never had that little voice in the back of his subconscious ever spoken to him so clearly before. He quickly spun his body in a 180 degree turn to confront the person with the annoying voice. There was no one behind him. Of course there wasn't; why would there be? Then something even more unexpected happened. The weird feeling turned into something else. Sinister. No something much worse, he told himself.

Ice cold fear.

His hand acted as though it had a mind of its own, grabbing the telephone receiver and punching in the extension to his director of programming.

"Hey, Hal, we're about to announce the cancellation of the Best interview, what's up."

Hal Rollins quickly replied, "No. We're staying on the Best interview. Go live."

"Hal. Come on, the Koreans are about to go up in smoke. We need to stay with that story. We can't break from the coverage."

"This isn't a request, Phil. Fucking go live to New York, you idiot. Let Murphy know we're on in thirty seconds."

****

"In the twenty seven years I have been broadcasting with this program this will be the first live segment our show has ever done. So in saying that, I would like to thank Mr. Best for choosing this show and our network for this very important interview."

James Murphy played with his glasses, while he crossed his legs, adjusted his pages of notes and settled in for what he knew would be one of the highest watched live news program interviews ever. The NBC interview from Rome yesterday that resulted in the multiple murders of the production team and the terrible death of the beloved Ann Lockwood was all over the news and was holding its own in the headline department with the escalating tension in Korea. Robert Best had barely escaped with his life from the carnage and had heroically and successfully escorted the members of Vasallus and journalist, Bentley Paxton to the safe confines of the nearby Vatican and away from the unknown attackers. Best had suffered a terrible blow to the side of his face from the attackers that resulted in a serious injury. The man was a true hero and just hours after emergency surgery to his face, now covered in bandages, he somehow found the strength to fly halfway across the world to attend this interview. Murphy felt an incredible pull inside to appease this man, knowing he could be doing this interview with a number of competing news teams with other networks, but he chose-- no demanded was a better choice of words-- CBS and specifically himself.

"It is an honor, Jim, to have this opportunity to speak to the people of this great country with you. I have been your biggest fan and I respect your work immensely."

****

The commotion in the Situation Room after learning of the CBS interview with Best and Jim Murphy had everyone scrambling back to their seats, ending their phone calls and emails and focusing on the giant screen on the wall. The sight of the injured Best with Murphy after the jolt from the events in Rome the night before had everyone on edge. All of them were already thinking the same thing even before the President confirmed those same thoughts, "What the hell is Best up to?"

****

Jim took the praise from Best and parked it as he was never a man who got to ahead of himself. These types of interviews, with powerful and important people, required his complete focus. He placed his glasses down on top of his notepad, cleared his throat silently and got the interview rolling, "What happened at the

Alimandi, Robert? Who were these terrorists?"

"I can't say for certain, the attackers all wore masks and identical black clothing. They moved with precision and purpose which tells me they were either soldiers or professionally trained killers."

Murphy asked, "Was Ann Lockwood their target?" Best quickly acquired a look of devastation at the mention of Ann's name, "It is an absolute tragedy the world has lost an incredible person in Mrs. Lockwood. Her contributions to her city and her country will be terribly missed. To answer your question Jim, I believe the kids of Vasallus were the targets. I truly believe there is a faction of nut jobs somewhere out there who are really upset on Vasallus's change in its music views. Fans have been killing each other and innocent people ever since they first took the stage. Of course it's not out of this world to think that there are some people crazy and violent enough to have done this."

"Is Vasallus safe right now?"

"Yes. They are in a very safe place, Jim. No one can reach them to cause them any harm, I can assure you. Not even the devil himself can find them!"

Murphy, using his left hand to emphasize, "I see you suffered a terrible injury in the attack. I think everyone has had a chance to see the video where, literally, a piece of your face came off. What the video did not show is how you received the blow? It appeared that a piece of your face just fell to the floor? What happened, Robert, and will it leave you with permanent scarring?"

Robert took a second to lift his hand to his face in an attempt to show the viewing audience he was indeed in pain then answered the question, "I have been told that a piece of shrapnel from everything that was exploding and flying around the room made impact with my face literally shearing off a piece of flesh. It happened so quickly that the cameras could not pick up the impact of the shrapnel. Will I have a scar? I think that is pretty obvious, but the plastic surgeons informed me I have a 50/50 chance that I might not have any scarring or very minimal. We'll see. Not worried about it, Jim. I'm just glad the kids are safe. "

"Thanks for that explanation. Now let's talk about the merging nightmare in Korea. What is going on in the world? First there was the attack on Israel, now this. You successfully diffused, somehow, the crisis in Israel. What is going to happen in Korea? Will the South attack the North?"

****

The President's National Security Advisor fumed, "Jesus Christ, here we go. Best must be stopped. He is going to unload on this administration. " Looking down the table at the FBI Director, Vic Turk barked, "Richard, make a call to the head of CBS and end this fiasco. Best will have half the country storming the White House in protest, because we're not doing a fucking thing."

The FBI Director's response was interrupted by the President, "There isn't enough time to stop it. Besides we both know, censoring this interview will give Best even more ammunition to discredit this administration. Forget about him and the interview. Turn off the television. Let's focus on the situation in Korea." Stan turned to Nancy Turcotte, the CIA Director, "Who's running the show in South Korea?"

****

Best focused on the camera just behind the right shoulder of Murphy and spoke directly to the television audience, "Of course they will. What else can they do? The dictator Myeong has created this ruse to use his untested nuclear weapons on the South Koreans."

Murphy was stunned at Best's statement, "You're talking about nuclear attack, Robert? This would cause a domino effect in the region that would draw in the Chinese and Japan. This could go global in a matter of hours. Dear God!"

"That is exactly what will happen in the next twenty-four to forty-eight hours. Let's face it Jim, the people of this country and around the world have lost all confidence that President Kipshaw can provide the type of heroic leadership required to lead the world from the brink of a nuclear holocaust."

Murphy had no idea where Best was leading him. He was still in a stupor from the reality of the crisis in Korea, "Is there a leader out there capable of diffusing this pending disaster?"

"Yes I do. The same man who calmed the fears of the world when he negotiated a peace accord between two countries about to start the next World War."

Murphy's glasses slipped from his fingers and onto the floor as he struggled to keep his composure. "Of course. Israel and Iran. You, Robert. It is you who will lead us once again to peace."

****

The television went black and all eyes shifted towards Turcotte, "The Chairman of the Joint Chiefs of Staff, General Kyun has taken command of the country. Intelligence reports stated a full military attack was imminent against the North. Sources were also claiming Myeong was planning a retaliatory nuclear strike if the South attacked. This was likely his plan all along: to incite a war, so he would have a clear excuse to use his weapons of mass destruction."

Stan did not hesitate, "He won't get the chance." Looking at his Chief of Staff, Adam Rinker, he ordered, "Get General Kyun on the Oval Office phone. I will be there in five minutes." He watched as Adam immediately stood up and left the room. Turning his attention to his Secretary of State, Bob Buckett, he ordered, "Inform our allies that our Armed Forces will attack North Korea within the hour." To the Secretary of Defense, Bill Templeton, he ordered, "Prepare our bases in South Korea for a full attack using every military option we have available to us. Commence attack within the hour." Stan continued with Thacker, "Get the Seventh Fleet in position. Bomb every conceivable military installation there is including any building or home associated to Myeong and his cronies. Nancy, I want confirmation of his death before the dinner hour." Stan paused for a brief second then ended with the ominous tone, "Ladies and gentlemen, today we show the world that terrorism and lawlessness by any regime will not be tolerated by this Administration. This is the very reason our military has been in this region for over fifty years. Now let's get to work."

Chapter 44

The early morning five hour flight from Washington to Los Angeles went by in a flash, it seemed, as Avery stood to take his turn in the aisle as the other weary passengers prepared to depart into LAX. He was wound so tight, he could barely keep it together. The tragic death of Ann Lockwood was a terrible blow and knowing she died heroically, sacrificing herself to the Beast, while Bentley and the kids escaped back to the Vatican, did not make her death any easier. He wanted to rush back to Rome and take Bentley away from all of this and hide out in a faraway place where Best would never find them, but he knew that was out of the question. He would always find them and finish them off just like he did to Ann. They both knew that running was out of the question, and in order to survive they had to fight back and with God's love somehow they would find a way to destroy Satan. He was not surprised to hear from Bentley that Father O'Sullivan had appeared at the Vatican and comforted Michael, and as quick as he had come, he was gone again. Avery did not bother to tell her that he was standing with the priest in the White House less than twenty minutes before his appearance at the Vatican. There was no shock anymore in the knowledge Father O'Sullivan's identity. He was a miracle in every sense of the word and he was humankind's only hope for survival.

It was during the flight he watched the unfolding events taking place in Korea after the assassination of the South Korean President and his wife in Paris by the North Koreans. Best was no doubt behind the murders in a bid to create fear and panic around the globe and to further cast a gigantic shadow over the abilities of

President Kipshaw to protect this country and the stability of all countries around the world. Leadership was required to calm people's fears, and Best was making all the moves to ensure he would be in position to lead the world back from the brink.

If people only knew that Best, the Anti-Christ, was in reality setting humankind on a path of no return.

Avery was back in Los Angeles to tear apart the mansion to find the book that Sam had sacrificed his life to discover. It held some sort of key to all of this. When Father O'Sullivan disappeared, Avery informed the President that he was coming here to search for clues. He didn't know what else to do. Something was forcefully telling him that finding the book was his mission and his alone.

****

Citizen's around the world reacted to the televised live interview of Robert Best stating that he and he alone is the only one capable to bring peace between the North and South Koreans and much needed stability to world peace. Everyone was terrified at the very real possibility of a nuclear war breaking out. Supporters of Robert Best hit the streets and airwaves immediately following the telecast. Hollywood celebrities and political foes of President Kipshaw were coming out everywhere in support of naming Best as Special World Ambassador to the United Nations. His success in Israel with the Iranians allowed the movement to gain traction with deafening speed, and soon heads of state in smaller countries were speaking out publically. Social media outlets spread support for Best around the world like a raging out of control forest fire. People everywhere were scared and looked to Best as their savior. A well-known and highly respected Hollywood film director publically named Best as the next Messiah, sent by God to save humankind. Social media went berserk, and it took only minutes before the world was calling on Best to save them and their planet.

The large scale military attack on North Korea by the United States by land, air and sea caught everyone by surprise, especially the allies of the United States. Leaders from Britain, France and

Canada called for an immediate ceasefire to allow for a special envoy that included Robert Best to enter North Korea to negotiate a peaceful resolution. President Kipshaw addressed the nation and laid out his plans to the American people and everyone around the world that he would destroy the military capabilities of North Korea and that the time for peaceful negotiations were over. The United States would not sit idly by, while the threat of a likely nuclear attack by the North was allowed to happen.

A military spokesman for Seo-yun Myeong released a statement to the world press that North Korea was open to the idea of a peaceful negotiation with an envoy from the United Nations as long as it included Robert Best. President Kipshaw did not budge and continued to hammer away at the North with an incredible display of military might. Russia and China were joined by Germany as the first American ally to break away its support for the United States military action. Russian diplomats threatened military action against South Korea, if the United States did not stop immediately.

****

The world was quickly spiraling out of control and Best was jumpy with glee as he waited in a nearby New York hotel, while waiting for word from the United Nations to mobilize. He would wait only so long. and then he would go into North Korea on his own, save the day and seal his position as leader of the entire world. Entering with the United Nations team was preferred as it made him look like the consummate leader, but at the end of the day he needed to stop the lunatic Myeong before he started pushing buttons that would send his plan awry.

The wild card in all of this was the priest. Where was he? He had gone silent. The death of Ann Lockwood likely sent him quivering in a corner of the Vatican where he'd holed up like a scared rabbit. He'd gotten to the priest in the Vatican before, but he was in a place that he could not see; a place He has shielded from his prying eyes. Then he just thought of something that could flush him out. He had a few minutes before he needed to get to Korea.

****

Mrs. Beckeridge, Father O'Sullivan's parish administrator at St. Colmcille's in Swords County, Ireland sat at her desk sorting the morning's mail. She adjusted her reading glasses as the string that kept them around her neck had become entangled in her unruly hair. She no longer tried to style her frazzled mop into anything presentable these days. During service, she would gather her hair with strategically placed clips. This morning her hair just swayed with whatever direction she moved her head. A piece of mail immediately caught her attention. It was a letter from Father O'Sullivan. The parish barely saw him the last several months, his time always in demand in Rome. He rarely used email, as he still preferred the old fashioned handwritten method. It was likely a note to pass along to Rev. Roonan, the church deacon handling mass in his absence. She used the letter opener to expertly slit the envelope open and discovered it was a photo inside a note. She flipped the picture over, and it took a split second before her brain registered what it was. Then she screamed in horror.

It had to be some sick joke from a disgruntled parishioner. The picture had to have been altered with Photoshop or something; she heard that it could be done. She stared at the photo again, a grotesque picture of Father O'Sullivan holding the severed head of Ann Lockwood. He was grinning from ear to ear as he held the head of the poor Lockwood woman up to the cameras in mocking gesture. She knew she would be sick and turned to the garbage can just in time to empty her morning biscuits and tea. She lifted her head slowly as she regained control of her stomach only to suddenly be staring into the eyes of Father O'Sullivan.

"Father, how..how did you get here? I mean, wh..why are you here?" The picture from the envelope stood on the desk. She tried to control the thoughts racing through her mind. She thought about reaching out and turning the picture over when she heard him speak, but it was not the voice of Father O'Sullivan. It was something horrible: guttural, coarse-like, brushed with sandpaper. She looked up into his eyes and knew this wasn't the beloved Father O'Sullivan standing in front of her. The incredible blue eyes of the priest that could light up a room were now two pits of red burning coal. This was no man. It was something from Hell. Her body shook from the fear that pulsed through her veins. Then what happened next made her realize that she would not join her long ago deceased husband in paradise, but instead she would suffer for an eternity in Hell.

Father O'Sullivan leaned towards her over the desk, picked up the photo and held it out in front of him as he roared, "You remember the Lockwood lady, don't you Margaret?" She realized this was the first time in thirty- four years she has worked at this parish for Father O'Sullivan that he had called her by her first name. It was always Mrs. Beckeridge. He continued, "We are very photogenic together, don't you think, Margie?"

Death had come to St. Colmcille's. She closed her eyes and made sure her last words brought her to Heaven, "Our Father in heaven, hallowed be thy name. Your Kingdom come...." The sound of the roar from whatever had come into her office cut her off. She quickly opened her eyes before she continued the Lord's Prayer and wish she hadn't. Father O'Sullivan leaned over the desk towards her and his mouth opened wide, really wide. His face suddenly changed shape, the lower jaw snapping free from the upper jaw until she thought she could look straight down to his stomach. A buzzing sound escaped the massive hole in his face, then it was followed by a buzzing sound, and then she watched in horror as a black cloud of spiders poured out of his mouth as if a pregnant sack had been cut open. They quickly moved across the desk and ran up her bosom, then up her neck. Thousands of spiders poured onto her face that quickly snuffed out her screams. She could feel them pump into the inside of her, filling her lungs and stomach with their biting tentacles. Her eyes went next as they quickly chewed through her eyeballs.

She could no longer speak as she choked on the insects filling the inside of her, but just before they entered her brain through her ears she heard the demonic laughter of the Devil. It would be the last thing she would hear as death finally came.

****

Avery was tempted to direct the taxi past Alive Records before he went to the mansion, but he quickly pushed that thought out of his mind. He needed to get to the mansion and search to find that book. He had no idea where to begin, but he thought Best's office would be a start. It seemed as if he had been away from L.A. forever, but in reality it had been a few months. When he was carving himself a place in this industry, when he was just a kid, it was nothing to be on the road for six months touring as a musician and then managing. He remembered being disappointed when the tour would end. How different things were not so long ago before Vasallus and Robert Best. His record company was thriving and he was falling in love with the most beautiful woman in the world who at this moment was halfway across the world fighting to stay alive.

The taxi eventually pulled into the circular driveway of the Malibu mansion. He paid the driver, and as it sped off he stood in front of the massive house and knew that the house was beyond haunted. It was much more than that. The evilness that spilled off of the place was like toxic waste. It had changed since he was here last. He couldn't put his finger on it as he stood in the driveway staring at it, but he knew deep down that something extremely evil had moved into the place. Something else crept to the surface of his consciousness. A profound sense of doom overcame him that shook his soul to its core. He staggered on his feet as he continued to stand staring at the mansion. He struggled with the understanding of what he was experiencing, but it was very powerful. Then the sense of doom began to formalize in his mind as he began to decipher the message it carried.

It would all end here in the mansion one way or another. Satan would soon be here. He could feel it in every bone in his body. He shook the evil vibes cascading down his spine and began to make his way to the front entrance to the mansion and to the offices and studio of Vasallus. He prayed out loud as he crossed the lawn to the front door, asking for God to give him the strength and the courage he knew he would need over the coming hours.

****

Vice President Joe Vandelstaff pleaded with the President, "Mr. President, we need to pause in our attack, allow U.N. negotiators time to meet with the leaders of the North. We continue bombing the shit out of them they might very well close the window of peaceful negotiations."

Stan was under tremendous pressure from its Allies to stop the military action, Even their friendly neighbors to the north were threatening them with trade sanctions, if they did not stop. Now his own inner circle was closing ranks against his decisions. He would not stop the attack until Myeong was confirmed dead. He knew Myeong was a puppet for Best and he would not allow Best the opportunity to end this conflict on his terms. The result would be catastrophic as Best would almost certainly use the successful ceasefire to convince the United Nations to instill him as some kind of worldwide leader until world peace had been restored. He would do everything in his power as the President of the United States and the largest military at his command to stop the Anti-Christ.

Stan wheeled on Vandelstaff , "Mr. Vice President, you interrupt me one more time, and I swear I will use my executive powers and have you removed from office." Turning to the Chairman of the Joint Chiefs, he commanded, "General Thacker, send in the 8th Army! Now!"

The wily war veteran took a second to sneer at the Vice President before saluting the President, then replying, "Yes sir! Consider it done, Mr. President!"

****

"Bentley, something terrible is about to happen again, I can feel it. How come we have not heard from Father O'Sullivan? We cannot just sit here. I am going crazy with worry."

"Chloë, if there was something I thought that we could do other than you guys continuing to spread your message to your fans that would be more of a help, we would do it. Listen, we're all exhausted and frightened out of our minds. Why don't we make some tea. Come on, Chloë, you and Brittany help me in the kitchen. We'll make some sandwiches for everyone."

Bentley gave Chloë a playful slap on the leg as she rose off of the couch when she was confronted by Juan, who stepped in front of her, "You're not our mother, Bentley. We don't have to listen to you. We can do whatever we want!"

Bentley was shocked at his words and quickly moved to snuff out any type of rebellion, "Listen Juan, you're right, I'm not your mother. But I am your guardian, like it or not. Now, we'll have something to eat, and I'm sure we'll hear from Father O'Sullivan soon enough."

Juan stiffened, "I'm leaving this place. I've got thousands of fans out there including this city that would take me in. I need to get away from all of you. I need to be on my own."

Bentley took a step towards him, "You cannot leave here, it's too dangerous. You do remember, Juan, what just happened a few hours ago when we left this place. This is the only safe place for all of us right now." He glared at her, frightening her before barking, "I'll take my chances."

The voice of Michael spoke next, He had entered the room while everyone was fixated on Juan, "You're not going anywhere Juan, got it? Now get back on your computer like Bentley asked." Juan whirled around on Michael, the anger instantly balling his fists, "How dare you talk to me like that, you British faggot!"

It was Brittany that gasped, "Juan!"

Michael took a step towards Juan, and only a few feet separated the two when he continued, "We stay here, all of us. We stay together and we continue to blog, tweet and post until every one of our fans has accepted our new music and our message. Do I make myself clear?"

Connor called out from the other side of the room, "Hey, come on Juan, chill out, okay? You should see your Twitter feed over here, man, its lights out! Your fans are shout'in out props man! They love the new music!"

No one heard Connor's comments as everyone now focused on Michael and his eyes. What were once hazel in color now shone a brilliant blue, just like Father O'Sullivan's. They were locked onto Juan's dark brown eyes, neither of them blinking, when suddenly Juan relaxed, took a step towards Michael and embraced him before sheepishly calling out, "I'm sorry man, don't know where my head was there for a minute." He then turned towards Bentley and repeated, "I apologize Bentley for talking to you like that. It won't happen again; you have my word. All of you guys, I'm sorry for acting like an idiot." Just as quickly as the tension ramped up, it was diffused with the change in Juan's attitude. The five of them group hugged in the middle of the room, laughing and joking again.

Bentley stood dumbfounded. She knew what those eyes meant. Father O'Sullivan was not here physically but he was *here*. Through Michael, He was watching over them. A weight as heavy as a Buick fell from her shoulders. Tears stung her eyes as she knew, even though they were in one of the holiest places in the world, He had reached out to them to let them know He was here. She prayed and gave thanks and asked that He also watch over Avery.

****

Chloë was back in her cramped room, the single bed small even for her. Leaning back onto the pillow she propped up against the wall, her eyes became heavy and soon she dozed fast asleep. In her sleep she dreamed of Ireland and the Academy where she was the happiest she had ever been. She loved that place and missed it terribly. Her dream returned her there, her caregiver, Sister McGarrigle pleading to tell her more about her travels with Vasallus. "What was it like to perform in front of all those people!" Chloë giggled as she teased her back, "Quite boring Sister. So much so, I was bored to tears!" They both laughed like two friends on a sleepover. Sister McGarrigle's tone suddenly became solemn, her voice draped in sadness, "I'm sorry I let you down. I failed you." Surprised by her sudden change, Chloë quickly replied, "Oh Sister, you never failed me. I love you so much. You have been like a mother to me."

"I couldn't protect you from him. I wanted to but he was to powerful."

Chloë was confused by her statement, asking, "Protect me from who Sister, I don't understand?" Before she could say another word a hellish scream escaped from Sister McGarrigle's throat. An invisible pair of hands seemed to be wrapped around her head twisting it violently in a circle. She could hear the bones in Sister McGarrigle's neck snap as the unknown force continued to spin her head completely around. Chloë cried out, "Stop it! Please stop!"

A familiar voice boomed into the room, "You want me to stop Chloë! This should be your neck I'm breaking for your betrayal to me!" Chloë sobbed uncontrollably, words choking in her throat, "Plea…Please…Master! Stop it!"

She pleaded for the Master to stop killing Sister McGarrigle when she felt her shoulder being pinched and then shaken forcibly. Her thoughts turned to the relentless shaking when her mind began to slow down and then clear. She was waking from a nightmare. She opened her eyes, the light hurting them forcing them closed again. She heard a voice call out to her. She recognized the voice instantly and the joy she suddenly felt overwhelmed her. She opened her eyes again and the bright light this time did not cause her discomfort, only happiness.

****

The shimmering gold armour of the angel Abgar towered over her beside the bed. He dared not sit down in fear of crushing it to pieces. The terror she felt just seconds ago in her nightmare melted away at the sight of the angel of God.

"Abgar, you are back! I was having a terrible nightmare. That means I fell asleep. I can't ever remember being asleep. What is happening to me?"

The long wavy hair of the angel framed a face covered in a bushy beard. His size and ruggedness made him intimidating to look at, but Chloë felt nothing but love and strength emanate from this radiant giant. She asked him, "You have many scars."

Abgar's laughter caused the armoured plates to lift and drop on his huge chest. The sound of steel clanging along with his booming laughter echoed through the room. He replied with great joy, "I have fought many battles, my dear." Suddenly his voice became quiet and serious as he continued, "The time for the great battle between our God and His enemy is upon us. Soon your soul and those of your sister and brothers will be set free, but first He asks of you one more task."

Chloë stared at the mighty angel, her soul filling with hope, replied, "Of course. Please, tell me more!"

Chapter 45

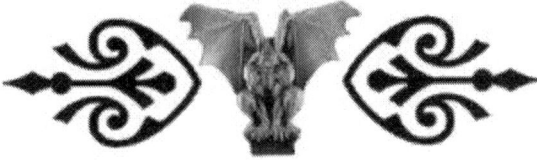

Avery entered the front door of the mansion and instantly felt the evil permeating through it.

That evil force hit him like a slap in the face. He was in a very dangerous place and he could feel the death that lurked around every corner. This was not the place he had left when he was here last. It had changed. *It felt occupied!*

He took a step towards the hallway leading down into the studio; this was when he heard a voice to his right that shook him to the core. It was Detective Showenstein.

"Avery, what brings you to the mansion?"

He turned towards the voice expecting to see a zombie stumbling towards him, but instead a well-dressed Sam stepped from behind the shadows and approached him, "I've got it covered, bud. There isn't anyone getting inside here while I'm at watch."

The shock of seeing Sam was like a punch to the stomach. He didn't know if he was a ghost, a figment of his imagination or if he was actually alive. He sure looked real. He was wearing an expensive suit and tie, beyond what a detective would normally wear on the job. He finally spoke, "Sam, you're the last person I expected to see. I thought you were…" He never finished the sentence, because Sam finished it for him, "Dead, right. You thought I was dead. Sorry to disappoint you."

He hesitated as Sam took another step towards him. He was dead; he was at his funeral. He knew Best was screwing with his mind and he fought hard to keep his sanity, "Oh no, that's great, Sam. I'm glad to see you're okay. You look great, actually."

Sam took another small step towards him as he smiled from ear to ear and replied, "You like the suit, Avery? It's a gift from my new boss. Told me if I'm going to watch over the place, might as well look good. It makes me feel kind of important, you know what I mean, Avery?"

Avery took a small step back before replying, "The look suits you, Sam. Listen, I came by to look for some of my things around the studio. You don't mind if I do that, do you?"

He was almost too quick to reply, "Not at all, bud. You won't mind if I tag along? Have to protect my bosses' interests, you know what I mean."

He stopped and confronted Sam, "Tell me, Sam, who is your boss?"

A sneer formed on the corner of his mouth as he replied, "A very important man, someone who you will kneel to one knee for very soon."

Avery was not afraid of Sam. He knew that Best had placed the very dead Detective Showenstein in the mansion to guard something just like he had done with Amber. She killed Sam to protect something. His adrenaline kicked up a notch. It was true. The book was here, and Sam would kill him before he found it. Confirmation of the book's presence here in the mansion fuelled his resolve and settled his fear. He was more determined than ever, and now he just needed to figure out a way to make Sam stay dead.

"Where is the book, Sam?"

His features darkened with that question and his voice deepened, "I don't know what you're talking about. I think it's time you left, Avery."

"Come on Sam, we both know that book got you killed, and it's also why you're prepared to kill me, aren't you. To protect the book from discovery."

Sam's eyes glowed a deep red, the demonic hatred building inside of him. He watched as he reached into his coat pocket and pulled out his gun, "You stupid piece of shit, Johnson. A bullet to the middle of your face and your pretty little girlfriend won't even recognize you. You never should have come here. I guess it doesn't really matter anyway; you were going to die anyway."

There was no escape, he knew, as he watched Sam lift the gun towards his face. He had to do something or he would die. He needed to get in Sam's head, distract him somehow, but then what? He was about to squeeze the trigger so he blurted, "Is that what Amber told you, Sam, before she pumped a bullet into your stomach? Did she tell you that Bethany would never leave your bedside in the hospital as your life slowly ebbed from you?"

"Shut your mouth, Johnson."

"Your son, Seb, lost all hope of a life with his father when she shot you, Sam. I'm talking to the man who I once called a friend. I know you're inside of this body, somewhere. Fight the dark spirits that control you and help me. Help me so I can protect Beth and Seb.

****

Best could see the Americans were not going to stop attacking. His hatred burned for that useless Kipshaw. He should kill him right now, in front of his cabinet. Tear him to pieces and feed his remains to the Presidential dogs. That would have to wait. He had to act now, and without the United Nations, it was obvious they were dragging their heels. He would put Myeong down on the ground like a dog to beg for the forgiveness of the world for his terrorist acts. The world would be his in a matter of days, and he would lead mankind down a path of no return. He couldn't help himself thinking delicious thoughts of when He was having His way imploding the earth. His hatred slightly subsided when he thought about the return of His son, Christ, after He purged it of non-believers. How disappointed the Son would be to find no one left on earth. They were all at his place! As he disappeared into the mist, his dark spirit reached across the oceans to North Korea, and his booming laughter swept across the Pacific like a raging tsunami.

****

Avery watched as his words seemed to reach into some part of

Sam's brain untouched by death and Best. There was recognition in his eyes, a softening of his dark features and his eyes dimmed. He kept pushing, "Don't leave this world Sam without first taking care of them and ensuring their safety. Seb has his whole life ahead of him. Your spirit will live in him forever Sam, but not like this. His memories of his dad will always be dark and full of fear. Set them free Sam by setting yourself free. Denounce Lucifer and embrace the love of the Lord God. He is your Savior, your passage to His eternal garden, Sam." He was amazed that somehow his words seemed to be finding a place in his subconscious. He watched as Sam dropped to his knees and began to sob, his gun falling with a thud on the floor. Avery quickly joined him on the floor, embracing him in his arms, continuing to talk to him. Then a strange and unexpected thing happened to him. A voice spoke to him in his mind. It was as clear as the afternoon sky. There was no mistake. The voice whispered, "Take his hand, Avery. Invite Sam to accept Me and My invitation to my Kingdom."

He did as the voice commanded and picked up Sam's hand. He barely knew any Christian prayers and certainly knew no Jewish prayers. He trusted the voice that spoke to him and give him the words. He was expecting Sam's hand to be cold and clammy, like death, but there was warmth in his touch. There was life in him, in his soul. He wrapped both of his hands around Sam's and spoke, "Sam, do you take the Lord, our Heavenly Father, as your Savior? Do you reject Satan, father of sin and prince of darkness? Do you renounce your sins and accept the love of His Father, the Lord God?"

Avery held tight onto Sam's hands as he fell over onto his side, his shoulders shaking as the Truth entered his soul. Avery looked into his eyes, they seemed to flicker like a lantern struggling to maintain a flame in the wind and whispered once again, "He has a mansion waiting just for you, Sam, where you can look down and see your family and prepare a place for them someday. He loves you, Sam. Take His love He is offering you. Go in peace, Sam. Go in peace."

Avery could not stop the tears that fell in torrents down his cheeks. He did not know where those words came from. The Lord had spoken to Sam through him. Sam was now free, in a perfect place. He was with Him.

****

The Prince of Darkness was about to channel his spirit into his earthly persona when the vision hit his eyes like a blast of cold air directly from the lips of God. The soul of Sam Showenstein had somehow moved into His Kingdom. It was impossible. What is happening? Then he knew, and his anger swelled like a nuclear explosion. Equally impossible was the fact it was Johnson who facilitated the transfer of the Jew's soul. He had once again miscalculated Him.

Then another vision hit him, and this one hit him like a spear thrown from Heaven. His Truth had just been revealed.

He screamed like a thousand ferocious lions. His screams would not stop for hours. Thousands of years of his careful planning came crashing down like a detonated skyscraper. He had been fooled. Again.

There would be no Tribulation. There would be no End of Times. No Armageddon. The Lord was never going to destroy the non-believers, only love them even more. Then what was He planning? Then suddenly the rest of His Truth was revealed.

His screams reverberated through the Korea's as if the sound barrier had been broken. Millions of people expected they had been hit by an earthquake when they heard the roar spread across the land like a terrible storm.

They could not have known that it was not the roar of a developing earthquake but the cries of Satan, Prince of everything evil, recoiling in the Truth.

The Truth that was revealed to him carried a message.

The Lord was coming for him. To end what He should have finished thousands of years ago. He was coming for the Covenant.

The Americans can have Myeong. His relevance in this universe was at risk.

****

Avery was not shocked when he had left Sam to find a blanket to cover his body and returned only to find his body was gone. He also knew Satan would be here soon. He needed to find that book and destroy it. He wished Father O'Sullivan would get here but he didn't expect him otherwise he would have been here by now. He was on his own. So be it.

He quickly made his way into the studio and began his search in Best's office. The wall safe was wide open with the inside empty. Whatever was in there was now gone. He tore drawers from his desk searching for any clue to the whereabouts of the book. The office was surprisingly sparse. Not even a computer. He tried to remember if Best actually ever spent time in this office. He couldn't and would have to be when he was on tour. He kept very little in his office. There was nothing of any importance, just a few restaurant receipts and another one from a general contractor. The amount made him do a double-take. Robert Best had paid a contractor over eight hundred thousand dollars for some sort of construction. It certainly wasn't anything done at the mansion, because he would have known about it. It is likely something he had done at his L.A. studio, Blackstar. If he didn't turn anything up here at the mansion, he would search the studio next if it still existed. He tucked the receipt from the contractor in his pocket and kept moving. He had a sense he needed to keep moving, and time was not his ally.

He went through all of the offices including Amber's and even his own. Nothing. He went into the recording studio and searched everywhere. Chloë had said Best would come into the studio and disappear. He was Satan, so he could vaporize himself at will, but maybe there was a hidden doorway. He searched the walls looking for anything unusual, a key to a secret passageway maybe? He was reaching, but he was also desperate. He took the receipt out of his pocket and studied it, and then he realized he should just call the contractor. Why didn't he think of that earlier? Frustration was setting in as he pulled out his phone and dialed the number of the contractor. The phone rang and immediately it was picked up by voicemail. The message stated that the company was no longer in business and if their call was for any outstanding jobs or unfinished work for callers to contact the company lawyer. He clicked off and made his way to his office and turned on his computer. Once he had his home screen up he typed into Google the company and pressed enter. The screen came up with all kinds of hits on a Los Angeles construction company wiped out by a fire. He clicked on the link and quickly read the story. Not only was the company's building destroyed by the fire, but fourteen of the company's sixteen employees perished in the inferno. The victims included the company's owner who was also the contractor. The two remaining survivors have since died following the blaze. One died from infection from his burns and the other was the wife of the contractor. She killed herself in her grief over the tragedy. Best. He did this. What could the company have possibly constructed for almost a million dollars?

He decided to take a walk outside; maybe Best had something built on the grounds somewhere. He could feel something inside his stomach begin to churn. He knew the book was here somewhere. He felt it. He felt its evil presence everywhere. He walked around the grounds of the mansion, paying close attention to the expansive lawn for anything out of the ordinary. He had almost completely circled the huge home when he seen it. A discrepancy in the foundation of the south facing wall where the brick ended and the concrete began. The distance between the bottom of the brick and the ground was approximately two feet. A distance of about forty feet had a new concrete surface, an indication of recent construction work in the past few months. There was no basement of course, this close to the ocean, only a slab of concrete. The grass along the wall was also different in appearance than with the rest of the lawn. It had been sodded recently as its color was a lighter shade of green than the surrounding lawn. The area had been trenched, but why? He was determined to find out.

He retrieved a spade from the shed and began to dig along the wall below the brick. The dirt was soft and easy for the spade to dig. In just a few minutes, sweating profusely, Avery had dug out a trench about eight feet long and three feet deep. He took a break by stepping into the shade for a few minutes before continuing when he heard a man's voice behind him. He quickly turned to see a Deputy approach him with his gun drawn, "Stay right where you are mister. Don't move. Let me see some identification."

Avery immediately protested. He didn't have time for this, he needed to find the book before Best showed up and stopped him, "Officer, I live here. I am just doing some yard work. My wallet is in my back pocket. Can I have your permission to reach behind me to retrieve it?"

"No, in fact, turn the fuck around, asshole. Hands up against the wall. You're under arrest."

Avery looked at the cop incredulously, "What? Under arrest for what? You can't just waltz onto someone's private property and start arresting someone for no just cause."

The cop was determined and barked, "Shut up. One more word and I might accidentally shoot you in the back. The owner of this house, the very famous Robert Best, you know asshole, the guy who saved the world from a nuclear holocaust informed our department that an intruder was in his house burglarizing the place. Sure as shit, here you are. Let's go. You're going to jail."

"Listen officer. I live here. I am Avery Johnson, the manager of Vasallus. I'm sure you've heard of them, right? Robert Best is my partner for God's sakes!" An exasperated Avery shouted.

He tried to turn his head towards the cop to continue to protest when he was struck across the side of his head by the cop's baton. The cop was crazy and didn't believe a word he had said. Down on one knee, the blood poured profusely down the side of his head from the blow. He needed to act fast or this cop would kill him. He focused on the shovel leaning against the house just a few feet away.

Avery didn't hesitate and gripped the shovel with all his strength and brought it around the side of his body then raising it over his head in a roundhouse arc before crashing it across the side of the deputy's head, sending him sprawling to the ground in a bloody heap. Avery immediately recognized the telltale signs of Best. The cop was not a real cop, just a soulless thug sent by Best from Hell to stop him. The cop's eyes burned red in rage as he began to pick himself up off the ground. He swung the shovel a second time connecting this time with the side of his face sending him flying to the ground once again. This time Avery did not wait for him to get up. He quickly moved in and brought the tip of the shovel down as hard as he could into the cop's throat. The shovel's blade sliced through his neck, windpipe and jugular, killing him instantly and almost beheading him. Shocked at his actions, he took the shovel and continued digging wondering who would be next to confront him.

He dug about four feet down in the ground; deep enough to clearly see there was much more than a concrete pad under the house. Something had been built underneath the mansion, and he knew Best had something built after Sam had come so close to discovering his secret. The tip of his shovel clanged off the wall and sent a jolt of pain up his arms. Steel. The wall was made of steel. It was impenetrable from out here. He threw down the shovel and dragged the cop into the hole he dug until he spilled over the side and into the cavity, his head flopping like a rag doll missing its stuffing. There had to be a way into the place. The construction company would have needed an entrance in and out of it. He ran back to the rear of the house and entered the studio, frantically searching for some sort of secret entrance. The studio was right above the construction. It only made sense that a door would be built above it. There had to be a secret door. His attention was drawn to a second set of drums in the corner of the studio. Those were new and were not there before. He never even noticed it when he was in here earlier, but he did now. He ran over to the drums and quickly pushed them to the floor, the symbols crashing with a loud bang as Avery worked feverishly. Under the big base was a rubber mat, and when he moved it to the side there was a clear outline of a panel. This was it! He tried to pry the panel out with his fingers but the gap was to narrow. He looked around and his eyes fixed on one of the symbols. He grabbed it and shoved the flat piece of brass into the crack of the panel and the floor and wrenched it back and forth as hard as he could until the panel shook loose and lifted upwards high enough he could get his hands on the edge of it. He pulled upwards as hard as his strength would allow. The wound on his head and his shoulder muscles screamed in pain with the strain but he could feel the panel starting to give. It raised up a few more inches and as he slid onto his back he place his foot under the lip of the panel to hold it from falling back down and used his other foot to kick at the lip of the panel. He brought his leg up and down, pounding away on the edge until it lifted another inch, then another. It was obvious Best had sealed up this entrance after the contractors had completed their work with the intent no one would ever discover it. He needed no doorway.

Finally with one viscous kick the panel exploded into several pieces. Avery stood up and looked down into the hole. It was only about three feet in diameter. It was just big enough for him to squeeze through. It was pitch black inside. "Of course it was," he thought. It was the entranceway to Hell. He ran over to the mixing board and snapped up the rechargeable flashlight from its cradle on the wall and returned to the hole. He shone the flashlight into the hole and was astonished at how *black* it was. The powerful flashlight barely cut through it. He could make out odd shapes around the hole but nothing discernible. He thought for a second how he would get down there, and without a ladder there was only one way and that was to crawl in and drop down. How deep it went he had no idea, and his mind hung onto the vision of dropping down into the hole and falling into a never ending mouth of Hell. There was no stopping now. He hesitated for a second and thought about Bentley and wondered if he would ever see her again. He silently prayed for God to keep her alive and safe. He asked God to somehow make sure she knew how much he loved her.

He dropped into the hole.

****

The panic on Bentley's face and in her voice was obvious, "Dear God, you can't be serious! I won't let you do it, none of you."

The five members of Vasallus gathered in close around Bentley in the cramped living room of their secret hiding place in the Vatican. It was Chloë who spoke next, her voice soft but in control, "We no longer have anything to fear, Bentley. It is He who has commanded us and it will be Him that protects us."

"You will be slaughtered! You know what happened when we left the protection of this room just hours ago. How can you even consider it! Michael, your mother died saving us so we could all return here to be safe!"

Michael gently put his arm around Bentley's shoulders as he spoke, "My mother died to set us free. Don't you see? We must give this final performance. Our message of love, forgiveness and hope for a new beginning, a better future must be heard."

Brittany reached over and took Bentley's hand in hers, "God's angels, our angels, have come for us and to protect us. You will see."

Bentley's chin dropped. She could not control the sobs when they came, her shoulders rising and falling in anguish. She could not lose these precious young people, but now she was certain they would walk right into their own deaths if they left this room. If only Avery were here.

****

The Vatican City Police Inspector General, Camillo Perni, rarely was in the same room with His Holiness. Most of his commands and directives came through his personal assistants. Not today.

He was escorted into the living room of the Pope's Vatican apartment. He expected to be asked to sit while His Eminence entered, forcing him to wait. He did not wait long. He did not even have a chance to sit before the two large doors opened and a beaming Pope quickly entered, embraced him and then spoke, "Inspector Perni. So good to see you! Today is a great day! Do you agree"?

Camillo was shocked to see how His Eminence could be in such a joyous mood considering construction crews were taking over St. Peter's Square.. "Your Holiness, if I may. Outside your window, the Square is being taken over and turned into a stage for a rock concert? I have been ordered to stand down on your orders. These events break every security protocol my office is empowered to enforce. For your security and those of Vatican City, I must put an immediate stop to this."

Still smiling, the Pope replied, "You will do nothing of the sort, Inspector. In fact I would like you to direct your force to put aside its duties for the day and roll up its sleeves and help the crews erect the stage as quickly as possible. This is an historic day in the history of Christianity and know you were a part of it. Today is a great day!"

Camillo struggled to maintain composure, "Your Holiness. I beg you to allow me to secure the Square and put a stop to this insanity! Vasallus and their perverted music performing in St Peter's Square! We cannot allow it!"

The Pope's voice rang with authority when he replied, "You will stand down, Inspector. I suggest you do as you have been commanded. Be grateful that you will have a front row seat to one of God's greatest miracles. Now please leave me be while I prepare for the big show!"

The head of the Vatican's security force turned and exited the Pope's personal apartment, in a state of shock. His Holiness was giddy with glee as he left. *"What was going on,"* he thought.

****

Bentley had witnessed God's intervention first hand over the past months and the miracle she was witnessing now was

479

simply astonishing. St. Peter's Square had been transformed in just a few hours to a massive concert stage. Tens of thousands of people were pouring into the Square. They were coming from every direction. Tourists and locals alike were descending into the area. When she was told by the kids that they were working all of the social network channels promoting a free concert, she was not surprised. Connor and Juan took credit for the logistics of getting the equipment, sound and lights. It was not perfect but it didn't matter.

The seven angels she had come to know stood at attention, their massive swords drawn as they surrounded the area around the Square. Visible only to her and the kids, she watched in wonder as the towering soldiers kept a watchful eye. Their gleaming gold armor sparkled in the afternoon sunshine. Her awe was suddenly interrupted when Chloë and Brittany jumped in front of her, their laughter infectious. Brittany reached over to touch Bentley on the shoulder as she spoke, "You see Bentley! We told you God would protect us! Look at His miracle unfold!"

Chloë screamed with excitement, "Look! The world will see what is happening here! Our message of love, hope and forgiveness will reach people everywhere!" All three watched rows of news trucks being let into the Square by Vatican police. American news giants as well as news agencies from all parts of the world were directed into a large area sectioned off by police. Bentley looked at the two girls and shouted above the building noise, "You better get ready you two. It looks like this will be the biggest concert you have ever performed. I love you both so much. I am so proud of all of you! Show the world how much love you have for them!"

The three of them embraced each other in hugs and tears and were soon joined by Connor, Michael and Juan.

****

A staggering crowd of over 200,000 filled St. Peter's Square and every nook and cranny within miles of the Square. Thousands and thousands more continued to arrive in Rome throughout the late afternoon and into the evening; unable to get anywhere close to St. Peter's but just happy to be in the same vicinity of the historic event.

Vasallus finally took the stage to tremendous applause that rolled through the square like thunder. There were no fancy video screens and special effects to whip up excitement to even higher levels. There was no need. The kids tore into the new music from Patrick's 'Songs of Survival' collection. Their harmonies melted together as one, and the lyrics and its message of hope for a better world electrified the crowds. They danced and stomped their feet. They raised their arms in the air to embrace the love of God that swirled around them.

The magical voice of Chloë resonated though the square in a ballad that touched every heart in the Square with the lyrics of hope and forgiveness. Brittany picked it up with an upbeat number that got the crowds jumping and screaming. Michael, Connor and Juan shared a number that showcased their incredible harmonies. Bentley could see from the back of the stage how happy they were. They were having the time of their lives. Her mouth opened in wonder as she watched what happened next.

The five members of Vasallus floated together high above the stage and the crowds went berserk. The musicians continued to play behind them as the five of them spread out in all directions above the crowds. Floating just a few feet above them, they reached down and high- fived the fans as they moved above them. When they reached the end of the Square, they joined back together and held hands. They waved to the crowds in all directions, when suddenly Chloë moved in front of the others, held her hand in the air, instantly silencing the tens of thousands and shouted, "Do you feel the love of the Lord tonight! It is His hands that lift us above you. It is His miracles that brought us together tonight!" As she floated back to the others, Juan took her place, the crowds silencing once again as he shouted out, "Join us to embrace the message of hope He has given the world." Connor floated beside Juan and lifted his microphone to his face and shouted, "He has given all of us a second chance to make this a better world!" Brittany continued, "Vasallus will make this a better world for everyone, will you"?

Michael pumped his fist in the air, shouting, "A better world! A better world! A better world!" Several hundred thousand people began to pump their fist in the air shouting, "A better world!"

The crowds went out of their minds when powerful spotlights focused on the balcony of St. Peter's Basilica where the Pope was leaning over his balcony, pumping his fist in the air and shouting the words, "A better world!"

Another miracle took place from the stage. Thousands of white doves, seemingly out of nowhere, flew in the air from behind the massive stacks of speakers, high up above the stage. The flutter from the thousands of flapping birds was deafening, but a beautiful sight, reinforcing the message of hope.

News helicopters buzzed overhead, beaming the incredible event around the world. The concert could have gone on for days. It was Michael who first noticed the look of terror etched on Bentley's face at the back of the stage. Soon the others did as well. The crowds knew Vasallus would be back on stage after a few minutes, while they took a break. As the kids reached Bentley at the back of the stage, her words froze all of them in place.

"The angels are gone!"

Chapter 46

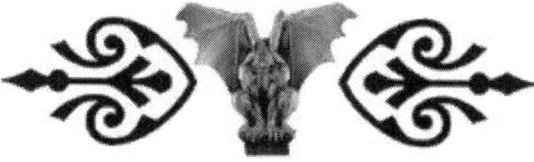

When Avery awoke he looked around in the darkness and could see nothing. He had no idea how long he had been out cold. He instinctively brought his arm to his left side as a blast of pain shot through the left side of his body. His ribs were cracked. He was totally blind in the black tomb. He looked around above him for the opening he fell through. There should have been some light from above that. There was nothing. Complete blackness. He tried in the pain to feel his way around; breathing was difficult as he fumbled with his hands in front of him. Suddenly he felt something bump into his outstretched hand. A rat, maybe. He hated rats, a phobia he has suffered from his whole life. The thought of this black pit full of rats terrified him. As his mind tried to fight back those awful visions he caught a sliver of light on the right side of his peripheral vision. Just a pinhole of light in the abyss. He scrambled through the darkness to the light, stepping on what he knew were more rats. The floor was covered with them. Either there were cracks in this fortress or someone or something had purposefully stocked the chamber with the vermin. He reached the dim source of light and discovered it was the flashlight that had come to rest when he fell through the hole against something solid. When he picked up the flashlight the extra light illuminated a small area around him, just a few feet but enough to show that it was certainly the lair of Satan. Rats, thousands of them crawled over everything and each other in a sea of gnashing rodents desperate for fresh blood. His blood.

Struggling to keep his sanity he looked around in desperation, searching for a way out of this nightmare when his blood suddenly froze in his veins. The deep and throaty laugh that only Satan himself could generate broke the silence, "Searching for something, Avery?"

He turned to see the Demon silhouetted in the darkness, its red eyes burning bright in the blackness like two beacons. Rats flowed over and around him like a river. It was then for the first time he noticed the pungent stench coming off him. He was in Hell and maybe he was already dead. He looked at the creature and could think of nothing else to say, "Am I already dead and is this place Hell?"

In the darkness he could make out pieces of its facial features. He seemed different than the other times he has encountered him but he could also see a piece of Robert Best in those features. He waited for his response and when it did it surprised him, "You're not dead yet, but you will be soon. It may feel like Hell, but it's actually my earthly abode. What do you think? Kind of dark, isn't it, Avery?"

"I see you're helping the county with its rat problem by offering them shelter down here with you."

"You're an amusing man, Avery. The only reason you still have a pulse is because I am allowing it. Let me just say I have a soft spot for you. You mentored me in the music business in an indirect kind of way, and I enjoyed the music business. Vasallus was a fabulous ride I might say. Too bad it all has to end. But end it must. Won't be much of a world left once I'm done with it. Too bad you and that Paxton bitch never had a chance together. You would have made a great couple."

"Cut the bullshit, Best or whatever the hell you are. I want the book that you killed Sam for. Give it to me or kill me. Your choice, but I'm done with the small talk."

He watched as an amused Best reached down through the darkness to a small table where a large object rested. The hundreds of rats that flowed over the book fled as his hand reached for it. He chuckled as he replied, "You mean this? Why all the fuss about this book, anyway? It's just an ancient storybook of my times with the Creator. You'd find it boring, trust me. We have an eternity together in front of us, Avery. Lots of time for bedside stories."

Avery did not hesitate and made a move for the book. He would tear the pages out until the claws of the Demon stopped him. He dove towards the shadowy outline of the book, but with a speed he did not see, the claw of the Demon clamped around his throat. Throwing him against the wall a few feet away, he felt his head slam against the hard wall. He fought to keep conscious, desperately trying to get air into his lungs through the rapidly closing opening in his windpipe. The Demon's face was almost touching his, his eyes less than an inch from his. Staring into the fiery pits he could see a hatred that was indescribable. His breath was so foul, he struggled to keep from vomiting. The Beast roared, "Do that again and you will die instantly. Where are they? Where is Vasallus? Where in the Vatican are they?"

He could not speak; he was seconds away from blacking out. Best was crushing his throat. Realizing he could not speak, Best loosened his grip, dropping Avery to the floor. He desperately sucked precious air into his lungs. The fight to get air caused his cracked ribs to burn in white hot pain. He looked up at Best from his kneeling position and spat, "You're a bigger fool than the good book describes you. I will never tell you where they are. Kill me and get it over with."

Suddenly the bunker filled with a brilliant light, so intense Avery had to shield his eyes. The Beast screamed, then with incredible power bent down and picked him up and the next thing he knew he was flying towards the light like a human frisbee. Instead of crashing into something, he suddenly stopped in mid-air by some unseen force and lowered to the ground. He couldn't believe what he was seeing!

It was Father O'Sullivan. He never would have recognized him if it weren't for his incredible eyes. He was much older, withered almost and hunched over. He was diminutive in stature but he could have been ten feet tall as his face reflected unmatched power, goodness and strength of a warrior king. He was wearing a white robe and held a gleaming steel sword in front of him. His white hair sat un-groomed on top of his weathered face but his eyes were blue orbs of steel. It was He, in Father O'Sullivan, who stood defiantly in front of His enemy. Avery looked up in wonder at the unbelievable sight of the Creator. Holiness poured off of Him in torrents. The roar of the Beast made him look away and as he turned towards the screams of the Beast, he noticed the walls of the bunker for the first time in the light. They were covered in a sea of thousands of human faces, squished together; their mouths open in cries of desperation, their eyes etched in pain and despair. The sound of their cries filled the room. This was no chamber, Avery now realized. This was Hell, and the Lord had come to set them free. The horrible sound of their cries was suddenly muted by the roar from the Beast. Avery remained on the floor, leaning up against a pillar. The rats had pushed back away from the light and sought refuge from the Beast. The Beast screamed so loud, he covered his ears from fear of them exploding, "How dare you enter here! You do not belong here. It is I who commands you! Go before you are destroyed!"

The boom from the light that flew from the end the Lord's sword into the Beast was louder than thunder followed by His command, "You do not command the Lord of the Heavens, the stars, the earth and thy seas. Your reign on humankind is over! There will be no more despair, pain or suffering from your sword, Demon. The stolen souls will return to their rightful place with Me and My Son." The Beast was caught in the grip of the light that had it snared. His rage eventually broke him free from the light and all of a sudden an army of creatures broke free from the surrounding walls and surrounded Father O'Sullivan. They hissed like wild animals and poised to strike Father O'Sullivan down.

A ring of brilliant light abruptly surrounded the creatures who were seconds away from pouncing on Father O'Sullivan. Avery could only watch in wonder as the seven Angels he has come to know, the seven sons of King Tiridates, the seven direct ancestorss of Vasallus thrust their mighty swords towards the creatures. Within seconds their massive and gleaming swords cut down the monstrous creatures like sheep. The Beast sent wave after wave of creatures, all of them swiftly cut down by the mighty swords of the Angel soldiers. The Beast recoiled further into the darkness, but just as fast Father O'Sullivan would cast a bolt of light onto him. Then Avery could see something he never thought he would see. It was a look of utter terror on the face of the Beast. His end was near.

The Beast continued to deny Him, continued to send waves of demonic creatures, all in an attempt to distract the Angels. Then Avery knew why. He was planning an escape and taking the book with him. Father O'Sullivan turned to his right, cast his magnificent eyes on him and then nodded slightly as if He had read his mind. Avery turned towards the book on the table ten feet in front of him. The brilliant light revealed an old and ancient book, its leather bound cover tattered and worn. It was at least two feet in length by a foot wide and five inches thick. He stood and made his move for the book. The three meter run for the book should have taken a few seconds, but it seemed to take forever. The harder he sprinted, the farther away the book seemed. He could not fail Him. He pushed harder but still made up little ground. In his peripheral vision he caught glimpses of the Angels and their mighty swords slicing down the creatures, Father O'Sullivan was thrusting His mighty hand out in front of him, his sword back in his other hand by His side. He could hear nothing, just action all around him. He didn't know why this was happening, but he was not getting any closer to the book. Then he did hear something, but it was a sound coming from inside of his head. It was the voice he heard earlier commanding him to save Sam. The voice had returned and it was once again instructing him. "Do not be afraid, Avery, for I am with you. The Demon has turned your legs to stone because he thinks your soul is weak. Let your love for Me, for My Son, Jesus Christ be known to him. Believe and he will see and when he sees he cannot control your soul. Do as I say and do it now!"

Avery charged ahead towards the book, and as he did so he prayed. He prayed for God's love to wash over him, to cleanse his soul of all his sin. He prayed for Christ to accept him as his personal Savior. He asked God to rebuke the Demon that had control over his soul. His legs felt no different this time; they were still pumping hard, but now he was gaining ground instead of losing and within a few seconds he placed his hands on the book, gripped it tight and turned towards Father O'Sullivan and the Angels. He could hear the terrible cries and screams from the Beast as he ran with the book. Suddenly, he felt a clawing on his left leg and then his right. He looked down and was horrified to see the rats were running up his legs towards his face. There rodent faces bared long sharp fangs. Hundreds of them moved towards him. They were big ones and they all had the same look in the eyes as the Beast. Pure hatred. He quickly swatted them off of him, but they kept coming and then he felt the first sting as one of them bit into open flesh. He cried out and smashed the offending rat with his fist. He was quickly overwhelmed with the rats as they swarmed all over him. They were after the book but he held fast as the bites increased. Avery cried out in agony. He could not hold out much longer. He dropped to one knee as the rats found his face and began to bite his ears, cheeks and nose. He kept his eyes closed tight as he tried in vain to pull them off of him. There were just too many. He prayed out loud, shouting, "Lord, take this book and do what you must. Destroy your enemy and free man from sin." He was dying; he could feel his body weaken. The weight of the rats pushed him further to the ground, now on both knees, but still he hung fast to the book and told himself that the Beast would have to pry it from his dead body. He thought of Bentley and how much he missed her, how much he loved her. He asked God once again to watch over her and keep her safe.

A blast of light hit him square in the chest, shaking his body. The light quickly spread over his entire body. He lifted his head, weak from the attack of the rats and could see Father O'Sullivan, the Lord, a few feet away, his sword pointed at him, the light pouring off of it and onto him. The rats fell off of him, dead from the light of Father O'Sullivan's sword. He watched as He swung His mighty sword in a circular motion, the powerful light destroying the vermin all around them. He noticed for the first time, the Beast was on the floor not far away, weak and struggling to get up. Satan was close to death. He looked back at Him and His voice boomed, "The Covenant gives Satan authority over man on earth, to keep man trapped in sin. It must then be destroyed by man. This is your destiny, Avery. It always has been, since your birth, I have been waiting for you and for this moment. Now do what must be done!"

Avery stood dumbfounded; the revelation by Him on his role left him staggering to comprehend. How could he destroy the book? He was just a man? He looked back at Him for understanding, but He was *gone*! The Angels, soldiers, were gathering and it appeared they too were about to disappear. He stared at the tens of thousands of faces on the walls, their tortured souls crying out for salvation. The Demon now lay still on the floor, his beastly body not moving. He looked again at the book, his mind racing on what to do. Should he tear out the pages? Light it on fire? What if he destroyed the book but didn't break the Covenant? Why didn't Father O'Sullivan tell him what to do? He said the book had to be destroyed by man but did it mean that he had to physically destroy the book? His thoughts were suddenly interrupted by a painful pinch on his ankle. He looked down to the floor and gasped in terror. The rats were amassing once again and thousands of them were heading straight for him. A sound from the other side of the room grabbed his attention. It was the Beast! He was stirring and moving. The faces on the wall began to wail even louder. Their awful cries cut into his soul like a knife. Father O'Sullivan had closed the gates of Hell, but now they were re-opening! Then a vision suddenly entered his brain and then he knew what he had to do. It was clear. He could not physically tear the pages from the book or light it on fire, but the Angels could. He turned once again towards the Angels and screamed the name of the one he met at the concert in Madrid, the one called Abgar.

"Wait! Do not leave! The book must be destroyed!" Avery spun around towards the book, looked down and brought his foot back and kicked a dozen or so of the rats trying to get up his leg. He reached over and picked up the book. This caused the Beast to stand and he hesitated as the Beast regained its strength, snapped its claws and roared so loud he thought his ear drums would explode. He had no more time. The book had to be destroyed now. The Beast roared again and began to come for him, his rage out of control. Avery turned back to the Angels, held the book as high as he could and yelled as loud as he could, "Abgar, do it now!"

He did not know if those were the right words and if the Angels understood what he needed them to do. He didn't even understand, but something inside of him was pushing his every move. He did not hear any voices commanding him what to do, but he did feel *something*! He could see the massive Angel soldiers turn towards him at the same time as a cohesive group. The Demon was now only a few feet away from him, its deadly claws snapping like giant steel sheers. The sound of the Angel's huge swords being pulled from their scabbards filled the room with the sound of clanging metal. He knew he was about to be torn to shreds. He was about to close his eyes in the anticipation of the steel shears of Satan ripping into his rib cage when he witnessed a miracle. The seven Angels, their heavenly bodies surrounded by a brilliant white light, aimed their swords with both of their hands out in front of them towards him. A powerful and bright beam of light leapt off of the tips of each of their magnificent swords that slammed into the book with incredible force. Avery couldn't believe the book didn't go flying from his grasp as he held tight. He could see from his vision out of the corner of his eye the Beast had stopped in his tracks, not daring to come any closer.

Words suddenly entered his mouth, and he found himself turning towards the Beast and commanding, "In the name of the Lord, I command you, Satan, purveyor of all that is evil, forever be bound by a new Covenant. The Covenant drawn by God and delivered by Man, that will keep you chained to the pits of misery and pain of your own doing for all eternity. Humankind will be forever blind to your eyes, the souls of man forever out of your reach. God, the Creator of all life, all that is Good, all that is Love, will forever watch over His Creation. The Son of God, Jesus Christ, will forever keep the chains that bind you from breaking. Hope will always rest in the hearts of Man and will never again be challenged from Evil. This I command, for all humankind, from the Mighty God who rules the Universe because He Created it. In the name of the Father and His only Son, Jesus Christ, I order you back, Lucifer, to the depths from where you crawled from and never return again!" Avery reached back and threw the book high into the air and watched in wonder as the light beams from the swords of the Angels intensified until a cosmic boom filled the room but did not hurt his ears. He watched however, the Beast scream in pain as he held its claw like hands to his ears that were streaming blood. The book disappeared in the light, forever cast away, Avery knew, that would never haunt humankind again.

The Beast was now feeling the full wrath of the Lord's power as the Angels focused their swords with its powerful light towards him. Avery could hear the terrible cries of the tortured souls on the walls disappear. He knew that He had transferred them all to His place. His Kingdom. They were saved.

It was over. He fell to his knees and gave thanks to Him once again. He thought of Bentley and how he missed her, and knew he would be with her soon. He thought about the kids of Vasallus and their incredible bravery, and now they would be set free from the chains of bondage. He thought about Ann, Elizabeth and Patrick, their sacrifice, and knew they were at peace with Him and that He would have a special place for them. He thought of Father O'Sullivan, the courage of a lion and caregiver to Chloë, chosen by God to lead this fight for survival. He hoped he would have a chance to see him again, to thank him, but he knew in his heart that his role in all of this has been fulfilled and he was with Him now. He thought of all the people who had died in this epic struggle for survival and was comforted with the knowledge that they would all be with Him in His Kingdom now, a very beautiful place.

Epilog

The sun shone brightly in the late afternoon with a slight breeze that blew in from the Atlantic carrying with it scents of salt water and decaying fish. The boardwalk along the beach was busy. It was tourist season in southern Florida, after all, but Avery and Bentley hardly noticed. They held each other as they walked, enjoying the moment, stopping occasionally to sit on a bench where they would pull another piece of bread from their bag, tear it into small pieces and throw it out onto the water where the seagulls would swoop down to pluck it up before a fish could snatch it from below.

They had relocated to Ft. Lauderdale into a beautiful seaside mansion almost two years ago. They married in a splendid ceremony right on their private beach, just the seven of them. The kids were nineteen now and were still with them. They wanted to be far away from Los Angeles but loved the ocean, so much so they brought them here to Florida. All of them were enrolled in the University of Miami, leaving music behind for now, but they were together, safe and happy, and Avery and Bentley knew that the five of them would likely never be apart. There was an incredible bond between them that no one could come to understand. They would not stay with them forever; likely they would move on after they graduated from school. They also knew the kids would return to music. It was in their blood, and it is what they loved. They spent free time from their school studies in the studio that Avery had designed in the mansion to play and experiment with a new sound they were working on. They played music now for themselves, and they both knew their incredible talent would once again take them from the studio and back on tour. When they were ready they would electrify the world once again, and they would be there for them to guide and support them.

The world had changed since the events two years ago that almost brought the world to the brink of annihilation. It was a much safer and happier planet. Dictatorships and lawlessness faded away as the will of the people in these countries would not allow lawlessness to rule. President Kipshaw had recently completed his Presidency and retired from politics immediately. He and the former First Lady resided not far from where they lived and would occasionally get together for visits. Their daughter, Alexis, would get together with the kids often and the five of them even had her playing the guitar. The former President never asked him about what had happened to Robert Best or even Father O'Sullivan, content with the knowledge that evil had been defeated and that humans no longer had to fear it.

Out of bread, they moved on down the pier towards a gathering crowd of tourists who had stopped to watch a talented busker sing while he strummed his acoustic guitar. They had both come across this musician many times along the pier, and like always Avery bent down to throw a twenty dollar bill in his case. The musician, who once introduced himself to them as Eric, would wink and nod his head in thanks to them as they kept walking. Soon they were approaching their property on the beach, and they could see the five kids playing volleyball in the sand. They had recruited Alexis to make it three on three. They all waved at the two of them, while they dove for the ball, laughing. Connor called out to Avery to get his attention where he would hold imaginary salt and pepper shakers above his head in a shaking motion to tease him on his hair that had become darker in the months following the events. Avery laughed and waved his hand back in protest.

Bentley stopped; quiet, while she looked out onto the water. Avery turned and looked back, asking, "Come on honey, what do you say we make it a four on four!"

She turned, her face radiant in a beautiful smile and declared, "My doctor said no rigorous exercise for the next six months!"

Avery stood quiet for a few seconds while his brain deciphered what she had said. Then suddenly he got it and he screamed then rushed towards her, picking her up in his arms and twirling her around in a circle, asking, "Is it true? Are you pregnant?" She looked down on him as he held her high, laughing and crying at the same time, then nodded her head and declared, "Yes, my baby, you're going to be a father!" Avery whooped and hollered, all while he carried her in his arms. The kids all stopped their game, cupped their hands to their foreheads to block the sun as they watched the celebration take place down the beach. Brittany shouted, "Hey, what's up with you two?"

They turned towards them and Avery bent down and with his hand placed it on Bentley's belly and looked back, his face beaming. The kids instantly screamed, jumped and hollered and rushed down the beach towards them. Avery turned towards her, tears stinging his eyes as he said, "I love you Bentley Johnson. You have made me the happiest man on earth. I can't believe we're having a baby!"

Bentley cried tears of joy before correcting Avery, "We're not having a baby, honey, we're having babies!"

Avery's dropped and gasped, "What! You're kidding me right!"

She smiled and then laughed, "Nope. We're having twins. A boy and a girl!"

He closed his eyes and held her tight and gave thanks to the Lord for His incredible blessing. As the kids joined their hug, Bentley looked up into his eyes and declared, "I want us to give them the names of Patrick and Elizabeth."

He smiled and hugged her again and almost stumbled as the kids jumped up and down around them, screaming with joy when they discovered Bentley was pregnant with twins.

About the Author

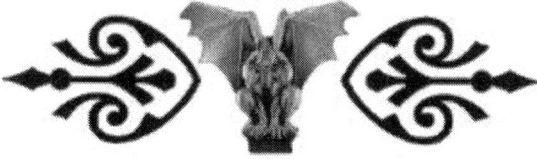

Errol Barr lives in Calgary, Alberta, Canada and has begun work on his next novel, *Under the Sea.*

Feel free to contact Errol at info@errolbarr.com

 @errolbarr

 www.facebook.com/SuperstarsTrilogy
www.facebook.com/ErrolBarrAuthor

Website/Blog: www.errolbarr.com